# PRAISE FOR MEAGAN CHURCH

## *THE GIRLS WE SENT AWAY*

"With beautiful prose and delicate precisi~~on,~~ Ch~~urch~~ ~~inse~~rts readers to the tumultuous Baby ~~                  ~~ ~~creati~~ng a well-crafted and researched ~~                  ~~ ~~ow~~n during this dark period in histo~~ry~~ ~~                  ~~ ~~h~~ of empathy for young Lorraine ~~              ~~ ~~Movin~~g and thought-provoking, *The Girls We Sent Away* is a captivating novel, impossible to put down and one that will be remembered long after you turn the last page."

—Terah Shelton Harris, author of *One Summer in Savannah*

"In this stunning novel, Meagan Church weaves historical research and compelling narrative into an elegant tapestry that brings 1960s North Carolina to life. Lorraine Delford is an endearing and relatable heroine whose indefatigable spirit is sure to win readers' hearts. Even as others try to direct the course of Lorraine's future, she is determined to wrest back what control she can. A memorable portrait of a tumultuous time period, I highly recommend *The Girls We Sent Away* for fans of historical fiction."

—Heather Bell Adams, author of *Maranatha Road* and *The Good Luck Stone*

"Meagan Church's *The Girls We Sent Away* is such an important and vital story. With exquisite writing, Church exposes a murky little pocket of history and a reprehensible practice that surely had a generational impact on families. Through her captivating and thought-provoking scenes, I became wholeheartedly invested in the outcome of her remarkable heroine, Lorraine Delford, cheering for her all the way."

—Donna Everhart, *USA Today*
bestselling author of *The Saints of Swallow Hill*

"Readers will be entranced as author Meagan Church steadily peels away the veneer of the era, revealing the dark underbelly of a secretive and unforgiving society."

—Tracey Enerson Wood, international
bestselling author of *The Engineer's Wife* and *The War Nurse*

"Heartbreaking and heart-stopping, *The Girls We Sent Away* is a beautiful exploration of what it means to be human and how resilient the human spirit is. Meagan Church weaves the absence of choices with the desires of the heart together in another page-turner."

—Leslie Hooton, award-winning author of
*The Secret of Rainy Days* and *After Everyone Else*

"Meagan Church paints a harrowing picture of one woman's experience during the Baby Scoop Era. Timely and emotional, *The Girls We Sent Away* depicts both the devastating loss of faith in those who are supposed to protect us and the ability of the human heart to trust again."

—Laura Barrow, author of *Call the Canaries Home*

# THE LAST CAROLINA GIRL

"*The Last Carolina Girl* is a heart-wrenching and authentically rendered glimpse into the portal of a state's secret dark culture, family ties, and the fierce strength of a young girl's grit and resilience. Church is electric in her delivery of loss, longing, and place. Unforgettable, this a powerful debut to savor."

—Kim Michele Richardson, *New York Times* bestselling author of *The Book Woman of Troublesome Creek*

"Meagan Church has written a compelling and aching debut. *The Last Carolina Girl* is both a story of love and a tale of abuse set in the shadow of the Depression. There, a girl's blind obedience to her circumstances—a kind girl uprooted by her tender daddy's death—comes with a devastating price. Leah's life as an orphan takes her far from the comfort of sand and sea, yet she is armed with tenuous hope and a plan. Gradually, she puts together the puzzle pieces of her fractured life and uncovers truths: family can deceive and betray, but love offers salvation."

—Leah Weiss, bestselling author of *If the Creek Don't Rise* and *All the Little Hopes*

"This spirited, coming-of-age debut whisked me straight to the heart of the Carolinas in the 1930s. I couldn't tear myself away from Leah's journey, from the piney, isolated woods of her childhood to an often bewildering life in the foreign world of the suburbs, where appearances are everything. Church so beautifully interweaves the connections between Leah's deeply sunk roots in the rural South with her search for belonging and her bravery in the face of unspeakable loss. This is a story that will stay with me; I knew little about the eugenics programs that had taken hold in American culture in that time period, and Church's tale left me wanting to research and understand more of this broken, devastating piece of America's history."

—Lisa DeSelm, author of *The Puppetmaster's Apprentice*

"Fans of *Where the Crawdads Sing* and *Before We Were Yours* will find much to love in this evocative and thought-provoking debut. Church reaches into a shameful and little-known pocket of the past to give us a heroine who is plucky, tender, and determined to fight for her autonomy and dignity against insurmountable odds. This book will change the way you feel about the simple question of 'Where is home?'"

—Kim Wright, author of *Last Ride to Graceland*

"*The Last Carolina Girl* is lyrical and atmospheric, a true masterpiece of Southern fiction that will earn its long-standing place among greats on our bookshelves, both for its exploration of a horrific piece of history often overlooked and for its insistence on hope. Church's debut is a must-read."

—Joy Callaway, international bestselling author of *The Grand Design*

"While readers will surely find all of the characters in Meagan Church's debut compelling, the true beating heart of *The Last Carolina Girl* is its fourteen-year-old protagonist: a girl tied deeply to her natural landscape whose abrupt uprooting after the death of her beloved father comes with devastating consequences. Leah

Payne and her indefatigable spirit will break your heart and put it back together again. I tore through this haunting and emotional story."

—Erika Montgomery, author of *A Summer to Remember*

"Leah's story is both humbling and inspiring. Church's ode to the natural world, to the often elusive feeling of home, and to the friends who become family provoke profound reflection. A dark spot in history warps Leah's path, but her resilient and unassailable character prevails. *The Last Carolina Girl* is a breathtaking read and Leah Payne an unforgettable character."

—Lo Patrick, author of *The Floating Girls*

"In this piercing novel, Meagan Church depicts one of the most disgraceful episodes in American medical history: forced sterilization. As a physician, I am deeply ashamed of the real-life actions of the medical community fictionalized so eloquently in this book, but as an author and a reader, I'm grateful for the opportunity to envision it. *The Last Carolina Girl* is a powerful and thought-provoking story."

—Kimmery Martin, author of *Doctors and Friends*

"Set in the mid-1930s in the Carolinas, the book explores lesser-known aspects of American poverty and classism and how the now-discredited ideas of eugenics caused lasting pain… Shines a light on a part of American history that deserves to be better understood."

—*Booklist*

"A dynamic and wrenching tale of family secrets and eugenics. This author is off to a strong start."

—*Publishers Weekly*

"[A] stirring debut...highlighting the true meaning of family."

—Shelf Awareness, Starred Review

*the*
# GIRLS
# WE SENT
# AWAY

*A Novel*

# MEAGAN CHURCH

To Jonas, Kenna, and Adelyn,

May you always know that love has
no conditions. Full stop.

Published by Sourcebooks Landmark, an imprint of Sourcebooks
P.O. Box 4410, Naperville, Illinois 60567-4410
(630) 961-3900
sourcebooks.com

Cataloging-in-Publication Data is on file with the publisher.

Printed and bound in the United States of America.
VP 10 9 8 7 6 5 4 3 2 1

"More and more stars fell as the night deepened. Some of them made clean arcs across the sky, while others disappeared before they had gone halfway. Watching them, I gained the understanding that the planet I was lying on looked like a star from somewhere else in the universe. It too might fall at any moment, taking me along with it."

—Barbara Brown Taylor, *An Altar in the World*

# PROLOGUE

Drowning doesn't look like you think it should. And according to little Barbara Ann Walters, it doesn't *feel* like you think it should either. It's not an obvious splashing and yelling and causing a commotion. The young girl wished it was because then maybe someone would have noticed her. Instead, the Sunnymede pool members went on with their conversations, sunbathing, and lifeguard ogling as the four-year-old bounced from pool bottom to surface and back again.

It was the summer of 1964 in a typical, midcentury suburban neighborhood where a portion of North Carolina's green canopy had been cleared in the name of development. Whether from an aerial perspective or a street view, Sunnymede offered plenty of symmetry, order, comfort. Houses perfectly balanced. Trees precisely pruned. Lawns meticulously manicured. Inhabitants properly prim, for the most part. And a cautionary tale, if not.

On that particular late-summer afternoon, as Barbara Ann struggled in the middle of the pool, the Sunnymede Sisters gossiped in their gaggle. This group of middle-aged women who had spent years bonding over plasticware parties, rummage sales, and ambrosia salad spent weekday afternoons chatting in the shade, careful to steer clear of both the water and the sun. All donned the unspoken uniform of oversized sunglasses, hats, and muu-muus, creating an orderly display of belonging.

On the other side of the pool, the adolescent boys—all in similar swim trunks, all with the same crew cut, all hell-bent on testing boundaries and ignoring the teenage lifeguard—jumped, pushed, and roughhoused into the deep end, too absorbed in their own antics to see anything else.

Including the girl who was about to give up.

Surrounded by a community of people, Barbara Ann sank to the bottom and bobbed back to the water's surface with only enough time to gasp for a small bit of air before sinking again. Her toes pointed like a ballerina's, arched and reaching, before pushing off the pool bottom as soon as they touched it. In the midst of silent panic, she almost looked as graceful as the dancer on her music box. Her arms flapped like wings, fighting to fly her out of her predicament as her eyes pleaded for help in a way her voice had no time to.

As she would rise a few inches above the waterline, the child tried to search for her father. He lounged only a few feet from the water's edge, but her plight prevented her from finding him, focusing on him, calling to him, the man who was supposed to save her.

In truth, the father didn't know what was happening with his daughter. He was too busy watching the bathing suit strap hang off the young lifeguard's shoulder. No one else noticed anything out of the ordinary either. No one noticed her bobbing. Sinking. Struggling. Drowning in plain sight.

# Part One

## NULLIGRAVIDA

# CHAPTER ONE

Lorraine Delford was on the lifeguard stand that day, her skin as bronzed as it would get before the days shortened and the leaves changed colors. Her strap had slipped so that it hung on the curve of her shoulder, exposing a white line across her clavicle where it had once rested. Lorraine ignored the misplaced strap, too distracted by the job at hand and the heat that threatened to turn her sluggish. Thankfully, the breeze offered some reprieve from the oppressive humidity that plagued Charlotte's summers.

At the precise moment that little Barbara Ann needed her, a group of boys held Lorraine's attention as they attempted somersaults from the side. They should have known better, especially that late in the season, when the rules had been well established. But boys being boys, they always did what they wanted.

Lorraine put the whistle to her lips and blew a short but forceful breath. The boys complained and attempted to negotiate, telling her that the other lifeguards let them roughhouse. But, being the only female in a historically male role, Lorraine didn't have the luxury of bending rules. She couldn't risk the appearance of incompetence. So, she blew the whistle again and shook her head at them. With slumped shoulders and mumbled complaints, they exited the pool and plopped themselves down onto lounge chairs that they had formed into a haphazard circle on the far corner of the pool deck, as far from their mothers as possible.

Even after months on the job, Lorraine still felt the need to prove her worth and remind everyone that she belonged. Her father had to give his approval for her to even apply for the job, a requirement that didn't exist for the other lifeguards—all her age, all boys. Though Lorraine hadn't doubted that she would talk him into it. Over her seventeen years of being a daddy's girl, she had come to believe that her father would always make an exception for her. She just didn't know yet that the notion was built more on sand than solid ground.

From high on the lifeguard perch, the breeze whipped strands of her chestnut-brown hair across Lorraine's forehead, where the humidity-induced sweat acted as glue. She moved the loose locks, revealing the thin, pale scar that never seemed to tan like the rest of her sun-soaked skin. She tucked the hair behind her ear and pivoted her gaze across the pool.

That's when she saw the subtle dance of Barbara Ann Walters.

Lorraine had been trained to spot the panic. *But how long had it been happening?* she wondered. *Why hadn't she noticed sooner?* She didn't have time to question herself, not then. Her body responded as it had been taught to. She dove from her high perch and into the pool causing water to splash in all directions and lap over the side. The others sitting around the pool tracked her movement, finally noticing the little drowning girl. The gaggle of women in the corner went silent, and Mr. Walter's brain switched from desire to distress.

In time too short to calculate, Lorraine scooped up little Barbara Ann and placed her on the pool deck as Mr. Walters ran to them. The girl coughed up a stream of water that projected out of her lungs and onto the cement, splashing onto Lorraine's pink toenails as she examined the girl. Barbara Ann shivered, still fighting off the fear that she wouldn't be rescued. She was too confused to cry until her father reached for her. Once in his arms, tears streamed down her freckled cheeks.

"Are you okay?" her father asked her before turning to Lorraine. "Is she okay?" His words came out loud and shaky.

"I believe she's fine, Mr. Walters," Lorraine said, as her heart thumped in her chest from the adrenaline and exertion. "Just got too deep," she said between breaths.

"But she's a strong swimmer," he said, still trying to make sense of what had happened.

Lorraine shrugged. "She must've gotten tired."

Mr. Walters thanked her as he picked up his little girl and walked her to their chairs.

Once back in the stand, Lorraine noticed someone was waving for her attention: her mother. Betty Delford sat in the center of the Sunnymede Sisters, next to Jane Montegue, the leggy chain smoker who lacked a sufficient amount of modesty, according to some in the community. The women always reserved the center spot for Mrs. Delford. Not that she asked them to do that. But she didn't need to. The Delfords' position at the top of the Sunnymede hierarchy had long since been established. It helped that they were one of the first families to move into the neighborhood. Plus, with Mr. Delford's active membership on the homeowners' board and his deaconhood at the church around the corner, they were a family to be admired. Such upstanding citizens. Neighbors you'd be lucky to have. The type who would bring a casserole during a time of need, without even having to be asked.

Mrs. Delford motioned to her daughter, but not with praise for saving a life. Instead, she grabbed ahold of her own swimsuit strap and moved it back and forth while shaking her head from side to side. Reflexively, Lorraine reached for her strap, realizing it had slipped off her shoulder and down her arm once more. She repositioned it and looked away before she could see her mother's scowl.

She knew her mother didn't approve of that suit, the one whose elastic had given up. She knew she should wear her other one, but it hadn't been clean that morning. She also knew what her mother wanted to say to her: "Your reputation shouldn't be soiled because of dirty laundry." Lorraine assumed she'd hear about that at dinner.

A dutiful lifeguard, Lorraine surveyed the pool, checking on each swimmer, happy to see all was well once more. She tried not to think about her mother. She tried to focus on how she had saved the girl. But her mind wouldn't let her be prideful for too long.

A droplet of water trickled down the underside of her arm, creating the sensation of a bug crawling along her skin. Lorraine quickly brushed it away. She couldn't believe how quickly Barbara Ann's play had turned to near tragedy. Mr. Walters was right: the girl was a strong swimmer. If that could happen to her, who else was at risk of drowning?

---

Lorraine was an only child. If she was honest with herself, she got along just fine not having a sibling. While she didn't have a comrade on beach weekends or while ripping into gifts on Christmas morning, being the only child also meant she didn't have to compete for her father's attention. Though with the afternoon she'd had, she wouldn't have minded a sibling who could take her mother's attention away from her that evening at supper. She was thankful that her boyfriend, Clint, was joining them. Maybe with him there, Mrs. Delford wouldn't spend so much time reminding Lorraine of the *important things in life*, like decency, modesty, and reputation.

Like every night in the Delford home, the meal consisted of some sort of hearty offering. Regardless of the season, Eugene Delford required meat and potatoes at every supper, scoffing at the notion of lighter, more convenient fare the few times Lorraine suggested it. During the summer, his wife favored meals that could simmer in the oven while she sat beside the pool: Salisbury steaks, beef stroganoff, shepherd's pie. After spending all day in the sweltering heat, Lorraine didn't feel like eating pot roast or chicken-fried steak. But her mother prepared dinner according to her husband's preferences, not her daughter's.

"Did you hear what happened with the Walters girl this afternoon?" Mrs. Delford asked her husband after he spoke the "amen" and before she picked up a fork to begin eating. Clint and Lorraine remained silent, focusing on finishing their dinners so they could leave the house and spend some time together. Mrs. Delford leaned close to the table, careful to keep her elbows from resting on it. Her hair hung to her shoulders and flipped outward, showing no signs of humidity or of having been weighed down by a sun hat all afternoon. Lorraine, on the other hand, had pulled her hair back into a ponytail, her locks having been tangled from hours spent in the breeze and chlorine.

Betty didn't wait for her husband to stop chewing to respond.

She never did, partly because the news begged to be shared, but also because she knew her husband hungered for the latest gossip as much as she did, though of course they'd never use that word to describe their conversations.

"Mr. Walters was at the pool. I'm not exactly sure why. After all, it was the middle of the day and shouldn't he have been at work? Who knows where Mrs. Walters was. Probably at home as usual or maybe visiting the priest." Mrs. Delford rolled her eyes.

Rumor had it that Mrs. Walters had been spotted at the Catholic church in town, causing quite the controversy amongst her Baptist prayer circle. So desperate to have another child, Mrs. Walters apparently asked the priest for the right combination of Our Fathers and Hail Marys that would open her womb once more. "Voodoo" was how Betty had described it to Eugene.

Mrs. Delford continued. "Jane Montegue was telling me that she heard—"

"I thought something happened to the girl." Mr. Delford had finally finished chewing and swallowing, just in time to try to get his wife's story back on track.

"Yes," she said, "I'm getting there."

"Are you?"

"Yes."

Mr. Delford raised his eyebrows in doubt. If there was anything he devoured more quickly than pot roast, it was a tale dripping with even more juice than a long-marinated cut of meat. Sometimes he needed to help keep his wife on track so the story would come out with fewer diversions and ramblings.

Clint extended his foot beneath the table to tap Lorraine's. They knew better than to interrupt a story. Since the start of summer, Clint had been joining them for the evening meal after he finished bagging groceries at Harris Teeter. He was used to Mrs. Delford's storytelling and Mr. Delford's impatience. He and Lorraine had worked out their own ways of communicating without her parents noticing. With the tap of his foot, she looked at him, his blue eyes wide and watching her, as if encouraging her to eat faster so they could leave sooner.

They had been going steady for two years, but most of the neighborhood assumed them to be a couple long before it was official. Lorraine had needed time to see what everyone else saw. He'd only ever been a friend, a part of all the same social groups—neighborhood, church, school—nearly too familiar to be seen as anything more. But with his persistence over time, she grew to like him.

Mrs. Delford took a drink of her sweet tea before continuing. "Well, little Barbara Ann was in the water by herself today. Mr. Walters was lounging about, not paying any attention when, do you know what happened?" She paused for a moment. When her husband didn't offer a guess, she continued, "She drowned!"

"What?" Mr. Delford's eyes grew wide as a dribble of sauce left his mouth and slid down his chin and through the dark whiskers of his five-o'clock shadow. He wiped it away with his hand before reaching for his napkin.

"Not exactly." Lorraine felt the need to not only correct the story but also stand up for her involvement. "She got too deep and needed rescuing."

"Yes, that's what I was getting at. She got too deep and her father wasn't watching, so Lorraine had to jump in after her. Can you believe that?"

Eugene looked to his daughter, "You jumped in?"

"Yes, sir."

"You pulled her from the water?"

"Yes, sir."

"Well done." He smiled at her. With that bit of praise, her father scooped a second helping of roasted potatoes.

Lorraine played those two words over in her mind, wanting to remember precisely how he had said them. While directives came often, compliments were hard-earned, as if her parents believed that encouragement led to laziness or, worse, pride.

Mrs. Delford interrupted Lorraine's thought. She lowered her voice and kept her eyes on her plate as she said, "Of course, we did have the other incident."

"Another rescue?" Mr. Delford asked.

Lorraine shook her head no, uncertain of what her mother was about to say, though she assumed from her tone and parenting style, flattery would not be part of it.

"No. Nothing like that. Lorraine wore that suit we've discussed. The one with the strap that's too loose."

This time Lorraine's foot tapped Clint's, holding on for support.

"My good one was dirty," Lorraine said, trying to measure her response but also wanting to spit those words across the table at her mother, the frustration at having to repeat her reasoning turning her venomous.

"Then you need to be responsible enough to make sure it's clean. You're lucky your father even let you have that job. Not to mention that we raised you better than to show off so much skin like that."

The room went silent other than the scraping of Mr. Delford's fork across his plate as he scooped up the last bits of his dinner, allowing his wife to handle matters of appearance with their daughter, preferring not to have to involve himself in womanly type things.

As he finished chewing, Mr. Delford broke the silence. "You did well, jumping in like that. Lifeguarding comes with a lot of responsibility."

Looking for an opportunity to change the tone and topic, Lorraine slipped into her best John F. Kennedy impersonation. "I choose to do it, not because it is easy, but because it is hard."

Clint, who had continued to focus on his meal, nearly sucked a pea down his throat. He coughed and took a drink of milk.

"Oh, dear," Mrs. Delford began, "there you go with that space talk again. When are you going to get your head out of the stars?" her mother asked.

"I think the expression is 'clouds,' Betty," Mr. Delford interjected. "'When are you going to get your head out of the clouds?'"

"I know good and well what the expression is." She tightened her grip on her fork and pushed a potato around on her plate, speaking to her food more than to her husband, as if not making eye contact with him meant she wasn't talking back. "I meant what I said. This one, getting caught up in the president's rocketship dreams. Such foolishness."

Lorraine looked at her mother and asked, "What's wrong with dreaming?"

"Nothing," Eugene responded before Betty could.

"Except for getting your hopes up," she said under her breath, still chasing the potato that she had no intention of eating.

"What's that?" her husband asked.

"Nothing, dear." She looked at Mr. Delford and smiled. "How was the roast?"

"As tender as always."

Finally finished with his dinner and hoping for this conversation to end quickly, Clint interjected himself. "She doesn't have her head in the clouds."

"That's right," Mr. Delford agreed. He pushed his plate forward and leaned back in his chair. "You know what you're doing. Senior year, first in your class, you're going to be Mecklenburg High's valedictorian, aren't ya?"

Lorraine smiled and nodded. She was so relieved to be discussing something other than her swimsuit that she could've leapt across the table and kissed Clint in gratitude. She had been working toward that goal since her freshman year. Honestly, she had been first in her class before she knew that rankings even existed, but when she learned that no girl in the history of Mecklenburg High had ever been valedictorian, she had made it her mission to earn that accomplishment. Everyone knew she could. Everyone knew she was well on her way.

"She's going to do it," Clint said. "Then maybe she can join me at college next year."

"So you're okay marrying a college girl?" Mr. Delford winked at Clint, as Mrs. Delford choked on her tea.

"Daddy! I'm only seventeen," Lorraine reminded him. Of course, she planned to get married, but she had two graduations to consider first: high school and college.

"I'm kidding!" Her father was the only one laughing, though Clint let out one forced chuckle for good measure. Then he continued with a fact that, with every passing year, seemed more astonishing. "Not much younger than your mother was when we got married."

Mrs. Delford looked in the direction of her daughter, but instead of seeing Lorraine, her eyes glassed over as if looking into a memory. "We were young. But it was a different time. 'Course you don't need to be like us." She wiped the corners of her mouth with her napkin before folding it in half and draping it across her lap, as she dropped her voice and continued, "You've never been much like me anyways. Why start now?"

Truth be told, Lorraine didn't want to be like her mother. Instead, she had been dreaming of something else, a different path. Her dreams were bigger than getting married before she was twenty, like Mrs. Delford. And, she dreamt even bigger than simply finishing first in her class, like her father wanted. In fact, her deepest ambitions were so big that she often felt too foolish to speak them aloud. But in those quiet moments when she let herself imagine, she would get swept away in Kennedy's dream of the Space Race, of being the first to be among the stars, of stepping foot where no one had before. While her hometown was nice enough, she couldn't help but hope for something more. She had a good family, close friends, grades that could get her into more than secretarial school, a typical path for career-minded girls. But since the moment she had looked through her father's telescope for the first time, she yearned for something bigger, beyond what she knew.

It was all so ridiculous. Too big. Too unrealistic. Yet every time she looked up at the night sky, the longing got stronger, more urgent. She didn't simply want to escape. She wanted to soar free, tumble through unchartered territory, explore new parts of creation, introduce others to a universe wider than they had imagined. She wanted to be an astronaut.

For now, she needed to stay grounded. Focused on becoming valedictorian. Moving through chartered territory. Soon school would start and she could fall back into the rhythm of that world, the one that offered achievement, certainty, a goal that was just within reach. After that, the sky—and beyond—was the limit. Because, surely, the only thing that could stop her was her own volition.

# CHAPTER TWO

Lorraine liked Clint well enough. Of course she did. He had been her steady boyfriend for almost two years now, since he had asked her to the drive-in for milkshakes. She had mistaken his invitation as a group outing, the type they typically did with whoever else in the neighborhood was free to tag along. Then she noticed his red cheeks, his fidgeting fingers, the way he could barely speak above a whisper, and she realized what he proposed was actually a date.

She had to admit that his shyness was sort of cute. Well, except for those times it infuriated her, like when the carhop at the drive-in shortchanged them and Lorraine had to be the one to walk to the window and rectify the situation. Overall, their relationship worked just fine. He was a good guy, well mannered, with a future ahead of him, and her parents wholeheartedly approved. And, in a way, she liked the inevitability of him, like a safety net beneath her feet as she climbed the ladder of possibilities before her.

The two of them had fun together, especially when she could get him to hang out with friends. He preferred the quiet moments they had together, just the two of them. They had shared plenty of one-on-one time over the summer. As much as she liked him, Lorraine found herself counting down to Clint's departure for college, ready for a change. There was nothing wrong with that, she told herself. She was just ready for what life had in store for them next.

Or so she thought.

As the end of summer approached, the afternoon balminess often gave way to cool nights, August dusk not being able to retain the midday heat as the sun dipped low on the horizon. Clint and Lorraine didn't mind the chill in the air that evening after supper. After all, being at the pool got them out from under the watchful eyes of her parents.

The only others in attendance when they arrived were the lifeguard on duty and four junior high girls. Huddled in a cluster on the opposite side, the girls were a second gaggle of Sunnymede Sisters in the making. Each of them sat with legs curled up and arms tucked beneath their towels. That evening, the towels would be used for blankets instead of drying off.

Clint had pulled together two lounge chairs, wanting as little space as possible between him and Lorraine so they could better hold hands. Lorraine noticed that the closer he got to leaving for college, the more affectionate he became, no longer caring if others saw them hold hands or peck each other on the cheek. If she would politely decline, he'd put his arm around her waist and draw her close to him. Thankfully, he had so far refrained from doing that inside the Delfords' home. She knew she would probably miss him and she wanted to spend time with him before he left, but she also sensed in him an urgency, almost a desperation, that grew stronger with each passing day.

Clint interrupted the silence. "You did a great job today. I just wish I would've been there to see it."

"Thanks," Lorraine said, with her focus beyond the pool on

the changing colors of the evening sky. She watched the sun touch the tops of the sweetgum trees and longleaf pines before sliding behind them, as the frogs and crickets sang their evening songs. "I was just doing my job."

"Yeah, but you saved a life!"

Lorraine laughed as she turned to look at Clint. Despite the breeze, his dirty-blond hair remained still, too short to be moved by the wind. Since they were children, splashing in the shallow end, he'd had the same haircut, so short and tight that his hair couldn't hide his scalp, especially in the back and on the sides.

"How's that funny?" he asked, his cheeks rounding, his dimples sinking inward. Her laugh was too infectious to avoid.

"You get so excited sometimes." She noticed his dimples, how they made him look younger, still a little boy, not a college-bound man. "It's just, I don't know, sweet."

"I'm not the only one who gets excited," he said.

"Oh yeah?" Lorraine asked. Clint nodded. His eyes glistened as his dimples grew even deeper. "You're saying I do?"

"Yeah."

"When?"

"When I do this." Clint released her hand and reached for her, burying all ten fingers into her sides and stomach, moving them back and forth across her as she laughed uncontrollably. Through painful bursts of laughter, she pleaded, "Stop!"

"Stop?" he asked. "You want me to stop?"

Tears pooled in her lower eyelids, ready to spill down her cheeks at any moment. "Yes! Stop!"

"Why? You like this," he said, as he continued to tickle her. "Otherwise you wouldn't laugh."

"Please!" She tried not to yell, especially since they weren't the only ones at the pool that night. Finally remembering they weren't alone, Clint stopped. Lorraine wiped the tears from her cheeks as she caught her breath. "You know I hate that."

"But you laugh every time." When Lorraine didn't respond, Clint lowered his voice and said, "You know I love you."

Lorraine still didn't say anything. They sat in silence for a moment, the sounds of her giggles having been replaced with the croaks of toads and the rising and falling vibrations of cicada hums.

Finally, Clint repeated himself and made it clear that he expected her to say something. With her eyes still to the sky, her ears tuned to the calls of nature all around them, she said her typical two words, "I know."

Satisfied with her response, Clint decided to really get her attention by leaning close and whispering in her ear, "I have something planned for tomorrow."

"*You* planned something?"

"Yeah. Figured we'd do something special before I leave for college next week."

"Special?" She wanted to know more. "What is it?"

He inched closer to Lorraine, taking a deep breath and inhaling her unique scent—a combination of baby oil, Coppertone, and chlorine. "Let's just say it'll be an adventure."

Lorraine's eyes widened, a small smile began to form. Those were words Clint had never used before. Intrigued, she asked, "An adventure?"

"Yeah."

Lorraine scooted up in her chair and leaned in closer. "Tell me what it is."

"If I tell you, it won't be a surprise."

"Why does it have to be a surprise?" she asked.

"You're always saying I should be adventurous. So, tomorrow I'm taking you on one." Clint squeezed her hand tightly, enjoying having her undivided attention.

"But what is it?" Excited with possibility, Lorraine wanted details.

"You're just going to have to wait."

If there was anything a girl her age was told to do, it was wait. Even still, she wanted to press him more, ask questions, get to the bottom of this mystery. But before she could ask, she saw Alan Reynolds strolling their way, his shoulders back as his Chuck Taylors scuffed the concrete with each step. He brushed his honey-brown locks out of his eyes, his hair having long outgrown the typical crew cut of boys his age. Their principal always scoffed at his appearance, calling him an unkempt hooligan, but instead of being shamed by the insult, Alan wore the name as a badge of honor.

Seeing him walk toward them, Clint sighed and sat up. He and Alan had never been friends so much as neighborhood acquaintances who tolerated each other. When they had to. Lorraine, on the other hand, enjoyed Alan. She appreciated his humor when others took offense. When most couldn't, she saw beneath the surface, and he rewarded her efforts with fierce friendship.

"Delford!" Alan said, as he made it to the end of Lorraine's chair. "You're the talk of the neighborhood today."

"Oh, yeah?" she asked, trying not to smile too big and risk looking prideful.

"Yeah. Seems you're quite the hero." He kicked off his shoes, the same pair he had worn since he had tried out for the basketball team their freshman year. It took only one practice for him to realize that team sports weren't his idea of a good time.

Lorraine shrugged her shoulders. "It's all in day's work."

"Day's work, huh? I don't think Claiborne here is saving people down at the grocery store." Alan pointed, but didn't look at Clint. Lorraine pulled her feet closer to herself to make room for him as he sat down at the end of her chair. "Stop being humble. What you did was amazing!"

"Well," Lorraine sighed, "not everyone thinks so."

"What's that mean?"

"Instead of telling me I did a good job, Mama told me I wore the wrong swimsuit."

"The wrong suit?"

"The strap was too loose, too revealing." She drew out every syllable of the last word, elongating it as she rolled her eyes. "Guess it wasn't becoming of a lady."

"What the hell's that mean?" The words barely made it out of Alan's mouth before he broke into a laugh that carried across the pool.

"It means she didn't think it was appropriate," Clint said, finally joining the conversation.

As if in a moment just to themselves, Alan and Lorraine raised their eyebrows to each other. She had known Alan as long as she had Clint, all having lived in the neighborhood for nearly the same amount of time. But Alan wasn't like the other kids their ages.

Everyone in Sunnymede knew his story because they knew how to spot differences. He was the boy whose grandparents took him in because, after his mother died, his father left. Ever since, he was tolerated, but not fully accepted. As if paying the penance for his parents' inability to meet an unspoken social standard.

Lorraine continued to look at Alan, trying to carefully choose what to say to Clint, the boy who was defending her mother instead of his girlfriend. Her parents liked Clint, partly because he followed the rules and practiced good manners. For the most part, Lorraine also did those things, especially in the presence of adults. Perhaps she enjoyed Alan's company because she felt more relaxed, more able to be herself because sometimes Clint didn't seem to understand the extra level of scrutiny, the added layers of expectations, pressure, and responsibility that she faced for being a girl. *Did Clint ever worry about the appropriateness of his swim trunks?*

Attempting to muffle her frustration, Lorraine responded in a low voice, "I know what she meant."

In an even lower voice, Clint replied, "She's just watching out for you."

Lorraine's eyes grew wide. *Did he hear what he was saying?*

She let go of his hand. Her muscles tensed. Her breath quickened. "You think she's just watching out for me?"

"Yeah, she—" Clint stuttered, trying to find the right words, the ones Lorraine would hear. "You know this job's a big deal. She didn't want you to mess it up."

"Mess it up?" Now it was Lorraine's voice reverberating across the pool.

"Oh, buddy!" Alan chuckled, causing a staccato rhythm of each syllable.

As Clint attempted to backpedal, pleading for Lorraine to understand that he was only trying to say what Mrs. Delford had meant, Lorraine did what her mother had taught her to: she took deep breaths and counted to ten to keep from erupting.

Alan shook his head and stood from the chair, pulling off his T-shirt and tossing it on the ground in the general direction of his shoes.

"Lorraine, that's not what I meant," Clint pleaded. "I was just saying—"

"Yeah, we both heard what you were saying." Lorraine continued. "I can't believe you would take her side on this."

"No, you're not listening—"

Lorraine's cheeks turned crimson. Her anger wanted to burst from her, but thankfully Alan spoke first.

"Claiborne, do yourself a favor and just stop, man. You've gotten yourself into deep enough water." He tightened the string on his swim trunks and asked Lorraine, "Wanna join me for a dip?"

"Nah. I'm good here," Clint said.

"I was talking to Delford." Alan motioned for Lorraine to follow him before he turned toward the pool, took four giant steps, and dove into the deep end.

Clint saw Lorraine considering the proposal. He leaned close and whispered, "Come on. Just stay here."

Maybe if he had apologized, she would've stayed. Instead she asked, "And what if I want to swim?"

"I want to be where you are."

Lorraine took that as a challenge. She stood up, removed her cover-up, and began walking toward the water.

"Lorraine, come on." Clint's shoulders drooped, his head tilted. She knew that behind the pout was the first spark of anger, but she had already beaten him to that emotion. "Can't we sit here?"

"I worked earlier. You know how many hours I sat in that chair?" She pointed to the lifeguard stand across the pool. Earl had taken over when Lorraine's shift ended a few hours ago. He sat on the post, swinging his whistle in a circle, winding and unwinding it around his index finger. "I'm tired of sitting."

"Lorraine, come on—"

"Sounds like the little lady's mind is made up," Alan called from the water.

"Don't you want to come sit down? It's too cool to get wet." He was right. But even the nearly fall breeze blowing that night didn't stop Lorraine from taking another step toward the pool, especially after Clint had the audacity to defend Mrs. Delford. The cool air hovering over the warm water created a layer of fog that swirled over the top of the pool. As Lorraine dipped her toe into the water, the fog twisted and twirled.

"Lorraine, come on."

Alan laughed and said, "Looks like your girlfriend's braver than you are."

Clint didn't respond with his voice, but he begged with his big, blue eyes. Lorraine knew she had a choice. She could rush back to him and settle into his warm embrace. Or she could defy his desire to keep her all to himself and instead jump into the water. She chose the latter.

Even when Lorraine walked onto the diving board, Clint didn't think she would actually get in. Not even when she began bouncing at the board's edge did he think she'd do it. He sat and watched her jump into the air, curve her body forward, and dive into the depths of the water. With fingers still pointed in front of her, Lorraine dolphin kicked downward. Only after her fingers touched the bottom did she propel herself up again. The fog swirled in dissipation as she broke through the surface. The first sound she heard was Alan's laughter.

"You coming in now?" Alan asked Clint, who didn't respond.

Clint looked away. Lorraine knew their time together was limited, but she wanted to have some fun. Even still, maybe she should climb out, towel off, and sit beside him. But the night air was cool and the water felt warm. Plus, they had spent so much time together that summer and in the years before. They would have plenty more in the future. What was the harm in spending a few minutes with another friend? Especially after Clint had the nerve to side with her mother, the woman she could never seem to fully please.

"You up for a contest?" she asked Alan.

"I've seen you dive. So, no."

"But have you seen me cannonball?"

"You?"

"Yeah. Me."

The two treaded water as they sized each other up.

"How big of a splash can a little thing like you make?"

"There's only one way to find out. But you first."

Alan looked at her for a moment before swimming to the side of the pool and climbing out. He enlisted the junior high girls to judge the competition, stressing that splash over form would determine the winner. All the while, Clint glared from the pool's edge. Lorraine felt her stomach flip briefly, Clint's annoyance sharp in the chilly air. But she ignored it as Alan climbed the steps of the diving board, slicked back his hair, and walked to the end. "You sure you're up for this?"

Lorraine nodded in defiance before hollering, "Let me see what you got."

Alan bobbed four times at the end of the board before jumping into the sky, tucking both legs, and falling into the water below. White foam exploded outward as he sank to the concrete bottom. The water still rocked against the sides of the pool when he resurfaced.

"Not bad," Lorraine said.

"You really think you can do better? I mean, we can call it off now so you don't embarrass yourself."

"Oh, I won't embarrass myself."

Lorraine didn't look at Clint as she walked to the diving board. She twisted and squeezed her saturated hair, leaving a trail of sprinkles that soaked into the concrete and disappeared within seconds. Even with the lights shining onto the pool that night, she could still make out the brightest stars, glimmering above her.

Despite Clint, she walked onto the diving board because she wanted to. Had her mother been there, she probably would've wished that her daughter would stop playing games with other boys and be more ladylike.

Lorraine smiled as she walked onto the board, her toes pressing against the gritty teal plank that bounced and bent toward the water as she walked farther toward the edge. She pumped her legs up and down, springing into the air until she had the lift she wanted. Then she launched herself toward those glimmering stars. She tucked one leg into her chest and pointed the other in front of her moments before her body plunged into the water, which exploded and spewed in all directions. Clint flinched as some of the spray reached his lounge chair.

The judges didn't need to declare a winner. Even Alan knew he'd lost. Everyone clapped. Everyone except Clint.

Lorraine knew he was disappointed, but so was she.

Clint didn't say anything about being upset when he dropped her off at home that night, but he did remind her of the surprise he had for her.

"You're really not going to give me a hint?" she asked, trying to lighten the mood before getting out of the car.

Clint looked at Lorraine. The dashboard lights lit up the left side of his face as the right side remained in darkness. He paused for a moment, as if considering what to say. Lorraine noticed that he seemed to enjoy knowing more than her, holding it over her head.

"Please," she said.

"It'll be a night you won't forget."

That's all he would say and Lorraine decided not to beg, knowing that begging was not becoming of a lady. She shook her head in frustration, but Clint pulled her close to him, pressing his lips into hers.

"You know I love you," he said.

Lorraine gathered her towel and grabbed the handle. As the door opened, she shivered from the cool breeze, her hair still wet.

"I know," she said, exiting the car.

And she did know. She never doubted his feelings for her. For the most part, she didn't question how she felt about him either. Though she didn't give it a lot of thought, at least not anymore. She had a lot to focus on with high school and then college, but the longevity of their relationship wasn't something that needed her immediate consideration. She knew they would be apart for a good portion of the school year, which she assumed would give her more time to study, more opportunity to achieve being valedictorian. Once she had done that, she could figure out what came next. For now, why think about something so far into the future? She let her parents play around with those ideas while she focused on what it felt like to do what she wanted, to walk to the end of the diving board and take a leap.

# CHAPTER THREE

---

If you asked Betty Delford why Eugene chose to build their home on that specific lot in Sunnymede, she couldn't have given you an answer. It wasn't the biggest, nor the one with the best view. But he hadn't asked her opinion on the matter. In fact, he had chosen the lot and signed the contract before he drove his wife and toddler to the piece of property to show them where their new home would be constructed. That day, as two-year-old Lorraine climbed over mounds of softened earth, Mrs. Delford looked around the rectangle, wondering how a house would fit within its borders.

She didn't ask questions; she simply took inventory of their rental home and made checklists of items that would be needed to make their new house their home—a larger davenport for the living room, a desk now that Mr. Delford would have a home office, and a swing set for the backyard, if she could talk her husband into it.

After moving in, the Delfords watched what had once been acres of forest and field owned by a farmer turn into an excavated and newly constructed neighborhood of mostly young families. The development continued for a few years before progress stalled. A few empty lots still dotted the neighborhood, and their road dead-ended into the remaining woods, not having a reason to go any farther.

It still bothered Betty that the development was never fully finished. And don't get her started on the acres of clearing that stood tucked away within the woods at the end of the road. She didn't mind the open field as much as the remains of the farmer's house, barn, and a few outbuildings. Weeds grew through the driveway's dirt path, and tree roots stretched to hide the existence of an entry as the farmhouse melted from memory and decayed into disrepair.

Betty learned of the house's existence one summer afternoon nearly a decade ago after Lorraine and a few other bored neighborhood kids followed a black-and-white tuxedo cat into the woods. The kids swore to not tell their parents what they had found, wanting to keep the discovery a secret, but when Mrs. Delford asked Lorraine why she was gathering bits of leftover ham into a napkin, she told her mother about Figgy, the cutest little kitten, who reminded them of Figaro, the cat in *Pinocchio*. And when she asked where the cat was, Lorraine told her about the clearing. The girl's mind had been too trained for truth for her to be able to report anything less.

Mrs. Delford asked her husband to do something about the house. The homeowners' association had discussed the nuisance, wondering how to convince the town to tear it down before vagrants or hoodlums or vermin could take up residence. But discussions never went any further because they all knew that they'd chosen a safe and secure neighborhood, one where things like that wouldn't happen. And there were other things to take up time and funding: new loungers at the pool, flowers at the front entrance, the annual Fourth of July BBQ. So the house had been untouched until Figgy had shown the curious kids the way.

But Betty's concerns went beyond vermin and vagrants. She knew teenagers lived in the neighborhood. She could only imagine what they might use that house for. Over the years, she had discouraged her daughter from going there, warning that abandoned houses were not safe places for girls, while Mr. Delford laughed off her concerns, saying the kids needed space to explore.

Lorraine was quite aware of Mrs. Delford's feelings about that place, but she never fully understood what her mother thought they would get up to. Of course, her mother never gave the details of the teenage trysts whispered about among her lady friends. Nor did Betty tell Lorraine the stories of hippies and beatniks, drugs and free love that she heard about on the news. They were enough to make her clutch her pearls. She never spoke aloud her concerns that a place with no supervision could permit practices like that to take hold.

So, imagine what Betty Delford would say if she knew Lorraine's boyfriend chose that very location for his planned "adventure" with her daughter.

The evening of Clint's promised surprise, Lorraine had rushed out the door, too excited to give Clint a chance to come in the house to say hello to her parents. Since the night before, Lorraine had tried to guess what Clint had planned—perhaps dinner at a restaurant downtown, the type that required a reservation, or maybe even the playhouse for a live performance. She chose to wear his favorite outfit of hers—the fit-and-flare robin's-egg-blue dress that gave her shape that she didn't have on her own.

As she walked down the front steps, Lorraine headed to the car, assuming they would be driving somewhere. But Clint said, "Let's walk instead."

Lorraine paused. "Where are we going?" she asked, as her dress sashayed around her, sounding like a rustling sleeve of soda crackers. Perhaps she should've chosen a different outfit.

"On our adventure." He pointed down the street to where the sidewalk ended at the trees.

"What?" Her anticipation changed to confusion.

"You'll see," Clint said. He grabbed her hand and led her down the street they knew well.

Lorraine stopped. "Maybe I should change."

"No! You're fine, beautiful," Clint said, tightening his grip on her. "As beautiful as I've ever seen you."

Reluctantly, Lorraine walked along beside him, her excitement having deflated. They ducked beneath a tree branch and stepped onto the path that they had traveled countless times before. If asked, she wouldn't have described a field hidden within trees at the end of her own road as a particularly adventurous destination. Of course, the adventure he had planned had less to do with the land and the house upon it. But she didn't know that yet.

As the trees gave way to the clearing, Lorraine saw something on top of the hill. She couldn't make it out immediately, but as they walked closer, she spotted a picnic: a blanket, a basket, and two candles sitting atop the rise.

"You did this for me?" she asked.

"For us."

*Us.*

He hadn't given her a night on the town, but he had done something special for her. As the candles flickered in the gentle breeze, Lorraine's heart warmed. She looked at Clint, his eyes sparkling as he watched her. They had been attached for a while, but with him about to leave, she realized that in some ways, she had started thinking of them as individuals once again, probably around the same time her heart had stopped flipping when he'd reach for her hand. Standing in the clearing that night, she remembered how she had first felt when she had agreed to go steady.

Clint took Lorraine by the waist and drew her into his embrace. "You know I love you." Then he leaned in and kissed her and kept on kissing.

Once he paused to catch his breath, Lorraine stepped back and suggested, "We better get to our picnic before the ants carry it away."

He had prepared a feast of pickle loaf sandwiches, potato straws, and his mother's infamous green goop salad, as the Delfords called it. Judy Claiborne insisted on bringing the concoction of lime gelatin, cottage cheese, crushed pineapple, and horseradish to every carry-in, regardless of the fact that no one outside the Claiborne family seemed to enjoy the dish.

During their dinner, they took turns sharing stories of their past—trading memories, like the time they held a funeral for a squirrel who met his untimely death when attempting to cross the road. Or the time when it had snowed and they took to the streets with their inner tubes, creating a chain ten kids long that snaked down Clint's street. Or when the neighborhood bully was picking on Clint, and Lorraine walked right up to the boy and stomped on his foot.

"You've always been fearless," Clint said. "Do you remember that time you dared Alan to touch the electric fence?"

They recalled how Alan walked up to the fence and went for a full-out grasp, grabbing it with both hands. Everyone had watched in silence until Alan started shaking and convulsing. They had all screamed until Alan let go and turned around laughing, calling them fools for believing the fence still worked.

When Lorraine asked Alan if he knew it was off, his eyes grew wide and he shook his head back and forth, "Nope. No idea." When she asked him why he did it, he said, "What am I supposed to do if someone dares me?"

As Clint and Lorraine reminisced, Lorraine picked at her sandwich and did her best to avoid the salad, never having been much of a fan of either of those items—even though she knew they were Clint's favorites. As dusk continued to settle, the candlelight spread a warm glow across the picnic blanket.

Nearly done with their makeshift meal, Clint scooted closer to Lorraine. "You remember our first kiss?"

"Of course," she replied. She stretched her legs out in front of her, her dress rustling with the movement, and leaned her head against his shoulder.

"You remember where it happened?"

Lorraine looked at the old farmhouse in front of them. The wooden siding had weathered years ago, giving the house a gray, ghostlike appearance. Nearly all the windowpanes had been broken out over the past few years as kids made wishes and threw rocks, believing that shattering glass somehow sculpted dreams.

The evening of that first kiss, Lorraine and Clint had been in the clearing with friends. Clint had closed his eyes, made a wish, and launched the rock. Seconds later they heard glass breaking. That was when he took fifteen-year-old Lorraine's hand, turned to her, and kissed her, a nervous peck pressed into her lips as the moonlight washed over them.

"How could I forget?" she asked.

Clint stood up and took Lorraine's hand, leading her to the house. They had been so absorbed in storytelling that they hadn't noticed how much the sun had set already. A faint and final orange glowed above the tree line, illuminating and outlining the branches, silhouetting the forest of spindly pines and oaks fighting to sprawl their branches in an effort to create a thick, green canopy.

"I'm not sure there's any glass left to break," Lorraine said as Clint picked up two rocks, then handed her one.

"I think we can still find some. Look there," he said, pointing to the second-story window at the front of the house. "There's part of a pane in the corner. You go first."

Lorraine closed her eyes. She thought of the stars and the moon and wondered what it would be like to touch a crater or a bit of moondust, let it slip through her fingers, and disperse beneath her feet with each step she took. She wanted to stand on the surface and look back to earth to see what it looked like from a distance, its clouds marbling the blue, brown, and green masses beneath. She inhaled, opened her eyes, and threw the rock to the top window near the front of the house. A moment later glass shattered.

"Nice shot!" Clint said.

He then closed his eyes, made a wish, and took aim. But instead of them hearing glass break, the rock hit the wooden siding and fell to the ground.

"Let me try that again."

He tossed a few more rocks, each failing in similar fashion, before turning to Lorraine and saying, "Glass or no glass, here's what I wished for."

He reached into his pocket and then got down on one knee in front of Lorraine. She wondered if he was searching for another rock.

"You know I love you." Clint grabbed Lorraine's hand as she tried to make sense of what he was saying, of why he was on the ground in front of her. "And I want to spend the rest of my life with you." Lorraine nodded her head slowly. "I know we still have time before we can really get married, but I want to give you this now."

Clint let go of Lorraine's hand, his own beginning to shake as he opened a small box. The sky overhead continued to darken, and since they had stepped away from the candles, Lorraine had to squint to make out what Clint held. There in front of her, she saw a thin, gold ring with an opal in the center nestled inside the box. It reminded Lorraine of something her mother would wear.

Lorraine stood speechless. *Did he take it from Mrs. Claiborne's jewelry box?* she wondered. Too many thoughts raced through her head as her breath quickened. He knew she still had a year of high school to go. *Was he really proposing?* Of course, it was assumed that they would eventually get married. Everyone thought that. So far she had gone along with that assumption. While she envisioned parts of her future as being unconventional—at least when compared to her mother and others, like the Sunnymede Sisters—she assumed marriage and children and suburban life would be part of who she would become. Just not *all* of who she'd be. Since Clint tolerated her notions of career and adventure, he seemed like the appropriate candidate to marry. But she hadn't anticipated officially yoking herself to that future before she was even eighteen.

"It's not an engagement ring. It's a promise. For the future." Clint's words slowed Lorraine's sprinting thoughts.

"A promise ring?" The words came out louder, more astonished than she had intended. "We're just...young. We still have time."

"We do!" Clint agreed. For this to be a promise ring, he felt he needed to speak to Mr. Delford first, but he couldn't quiet his nerves enough to do that. Not yet. "Call it a going-away gift. I don't want you to forget about me."

Lorraine chuckled, finally exhaling, breathing, heart rate slowing. "You know I wouldn't."

Clint shrugged. "You might. I wanted to make sure you didn't."

He really was a sweet boy, the quietest one in the group when they were kids. He didn't stand out like Alan—the jokester, the rebel.

Clint took the ring from the box and reached for Lorraine's hand.

"Are you sure?" she asked, still searching for what to say. "We can wait."

"It's just a gift, Lorraine. Nothing more."

The word *promise* echoed through Lorraine's mind. She heard what he had said about it being a gift, but she still wondered about the implications and if he attached more promise to it than what he was saying out loud.

"Here." She pulled back her left hand and gave him her right one instead. "This one."

As he pushed and twisted the ring onto her finger, her mind tried to assure itself that even with the ring, they weren't rushing into anything, but her gut didn't agree. Maybe someday they would be married. And she was okay with that. He was a good boy from a good family. He loved her. But this was only a gift.

As he coaxed the ring into place, he said, "You're going to do big things, Lorraine Delford." He stood up and dusted off his knee. "You're so beautiful. So smart. And I don't want to lose you."

Then Lorraine's heart fluttered again. He swept her away with his belief in her and reminded her of the "us" she had forgotten.

Clint stepped toward her and pressed into her, his arms holding her firmly, his body shaking enough for Lorraine to feel it. He began kissing down her neck, his one hand moving up her back to support her as she leaned into it and lifted her chin to the night sky.

They stopped kissing and Clint stepped away. "Hold on. I'll be right back."

As he ran back toward their picnic, Lorraine looked down at her hand. The clouds shifted, revealing the moon so that its light reflected off the opal. She fussed with the ring, moved it and twirled it around, trying to make it feel a bit looser, less weighty. But no amount of twisting or turning would lessen the pressure. She told herself that he meant well. It was kind of pretty. She'd get used to it. With her attention on the ring, she didn't see Clint running back to her, the blanket in his hand, until he was already beside her, catching his breath.

"Come on," he said, walking her to the front steps of the old house.

She hesitated for a minute. "Wait—"

She liked leaving the old house as it was, not disturbing it by leaving their mark on it. Sure, she'd broken windowpanes, but she had never crossed the threshold, nor intruded into what used to be someone's home.

"It's okay," he said.

The steps creaked beneath them and the porch planks sagged with each step they took. Dirt-covered glass littered the porch and crunched beneath their feet. The front door opened with little effort as Clint pushed against it, revealing what had once been the front hall. The roof and the second floor had long since collapsed in that part of the house, creating a skylight. Moonlight shined into the hall as if it were nature's chandelier.

Clint stepped inside first and laid the blanket on the old wooden floor. He sat down and invited Lorraine to join him.

She hesitated.

"Come on! Where's your fearlessness now?"

"Can't we stay outside?" she asked.

"It's quieter in here, not so chilly."

She hadn't noticed it being loud or cold outside, but she followed his direction and sat down beside him. She let his momentum push her to the ground. Her dress rustled as he pressed his body against hers. It wasn't like this was completely new to them. They had spent time sprawled across the front and back seats of his car. That summer especially, they had developed a habit of stopping by a quiet parking lot that seemed private enough for a few minutes of necking.

But something about this evening felt different.

Lorraine began twisting the gold ring on her finger with her thumb, twirling the object that felt foreign on her hand. She knew her mother wouldn't approve of accepting such an extravagant gift, especially when it wasn't even her birthday. She also knew that her mother would not like them being alone like that. She wondered if her mother ever fully trusted her. *How many times had she been so hard on her? Didn't she know what a good girl Lorraine tried to be?* She had proved herself responsible enough to save a life. She could make certain decisions for herself. *Plus, what was the harm in a little necking?*

At some point, Lorraine stopped debating. She stopped thinking about that ugly opal. She stopped looking at the moonlight chandelier above her or feeling the scratchy blanket beneath her back, and she simply let the moment carry her away from her thoughts. She escaped to a place beyond the warnings and rules her parents had given in such vague and incomplete language. In many ways, Lorraine could be forgiven for her ignorance. A bright girl, such as she was, could still be naive enough to lose herself in another's body without fully realizing that's what it was. Because in all her years, no one had been capable of actually saying—much less explaining—sex to her. Even still, she figured enough to know they shouldn't be doing what they were about to do.

But she also knew she didn't care enough to stop either.

Lorraine got lost in the feeling, the escape, the moment. Her body overruled her mind and quickly shut down questions of if-they-should or what-may-be. She let him remove her underwear, and she didn't get up and leave as he unzipped his pants. She let him lie on top of her and continue to kiss her before he lifted her skirt and fumbled around before maneuvering himself into position.

Within a few quick moments, Clint groaned and collapsed beside her on the blankets.

As they caught their breath, she looked through the opening in the ceiling. A star flickered and darted from view, leaving a brief tail of light.

"Did you see that?" she asked, but Clint didn't respond as he lay beside her, his eyes closed, his breathing beginning to slow. "That falling star, did you see?"

Clint rolled over, draping his arm across Lorraine's body, his hand resting on her still-exposed breast. "What star?"

He didn't try to look. He didn't even turn his head or open his eyes to see the sky. He shifted his head to rest on Lorraine's shoulder, further holding her to the floor as he relaxed for a few moments.

Through the accidental skylight, Lorraine watched a handful of stars twinkle overhead, wanting to give more attention to them than to think about what had just happened. How strange it had felt. How uncomfortable she now was. But Clint seemed satisfied, so she stared in silence.

Lorraine snuggled into Clint's warmth, watching the ancient shine of those stars. She knew little about those celestial bodies, not yet realizing that the light she saw had been cast thousands— maybe even millions—of years prior, taking a vast amount of time to stretch across the universe and catch her eye at that particular moment.

On the floor of that dilapidated farmhouse, she didn't understand how the past connects to the present and impacts the future. She didn't need to know that yet. For that moment in time, Lorraine breathed and smiled and dreamed, unaware that the minutes-ago past had already begun to knit a new and binding future.

# CHAPTER FOUR

In the weeks after Lorraine surrendered her virginity on the floor of the farmhouse, she couldn't quite shake the melancholy that hung as heavy as a water-soaked beach towel. If she had been taught to trust her intuition, she may have picked up on the early indications. Instead, she ignored the first signs, lost track of weeks, and found other excuses to explain away her exhaustion and nausea. Especially since she only knew what she had been taught, and lessons built on protecting innocence often bred ignorance, even in smart girls like Lorraine.

She struggled to be excited about her senior year, blaming her lack of energy on summer having turned to fall. She missed her job, and she couldn't help but think about it during class when her mind would wander from her studies and turn back to the freedom and fun in the sun. She supposed she should also be missing Clint. Well, she did miss him. She missed him at the supper table most nights or in the quiet of the evening hours. But while at school, she had other friends and distractions so she didn't spend much time thinking about him.

Whatever was going on with Lorraine, she handled it the way she had learned to handle most things: ignore it. Will yourself to feel otherwise. Or better yet, don't feel at all. Be stronger and more capable, and all would be well.

It was only in the quiet moments when she was alone in her room that she began to worry.

She was thankful that Alan had offered her a distraction one Friday night by inviting her to the football game. He didn't so much invite as demand that she get out of the house. Kickoff was moments away by the time they arrived, the crowd restless with anticipation, the bleachers nearly full of fans: upperclassmen in sweaters, girls in skirts, parents on the edges of their seats as they cheered for their boys on the field. The cheerleaders stood ready, armed with pom-poms to do their part in bringing home a victory that night.

Alan and Lorraine climbed the bleachers, searching for empty seats in the sea of fans. They found enough space for two near the top of the student section. From there, the breeze blew Lorraine's ponytail and rustled her bangs. They squeezed between a few freshmen, their shoulders and thighs having no choice but to touch.

Alan turned toward Lorraine and spoke directly into her ear. "Sure you're not the cheerleader type?" He pointed at the girls shaking their pom-poms, rallying the home crowd during kickoff.

"Me?" Lorraine laughed.

"Yeah."

"Why?"

"Valedictorian, homecoming queen, cheerleader—seems like some sorta trifecta right there."

"You think I want to be all of those things?" Lorraine asked. At that point, she was starting to become uncertain about earning the one title everyone assumed was hers. For the first time in her life, she was having a hard time finding the motivation to achieve what she had put her mind to. Her grades were still fine, but she feared that could change if she couldn't shake the overwhelming exhaustion she had been feeling for weeks now.

"Do you not know me?" she asked.

"Sure. Lorraine Delford: the brains and beauty of Mecklenburg High." She could feel her cheeks reddening. Alan often spoke his true thoughts, which sometimes meant complimenting Lorraine. As much as she knew that, he still sometimes embarrassed her, especially when most other people believed in the unwritten code that compliments should be hard-earned and rarely spoken. "I think that's what I'm going to call you—BB."

"BB?"

"Yeah. Brains and beauty."

Lorraine shook her head and hoped the color was starting to fade in her cheeks, but she was beginning to feel a bit dizzy, perhaps from the height of the bleachers. She had been feeling that way a lot lately. She blamed it on nerves, not that she'd ever had a case of them before. Not like her mother. She remembered seasons when her mother took to her bed for days at a time. As a child, Lorraine didn't really understand why, and any questions she asked were met with silent looks. She learned to not expect her mother to be in the kitchen or even available for the time it took her to sort out her nerves. Then, she'd join the family again as if the hiatus had never taken place. She learned that women were delicate creatures, as her father would say. And she vowed to not be so fragile, not like her mother.

"I don't know," Lorraine said. "I kind of like Delford."

"Yeah?" Alan asked.

"Yeah," she said. "You're the only one who calls me that."

"Now I'll be the only one who calls you BB." Alan reached into his pocket and pulled out a handful of sunflower seeds. He popped a few into his mouth and continued. "It's a good thing you don't want to be like them anyway."

"Oh, yeah?" Lorraine asked.

He spit a shell onto the bleachers and said, "Yeah, they're all a bunch of phonies anyway." That had become one of his favorite words ever since reading *The Catcher in the Rye* earlier that summer. Lorraine guessed it was the only book he had ever willingly read. "You're better than that."

"How so?" Lorraine knew Alan saw her differently than the others, perhaps because she saw him in ways the others didn't. When someone took the time to notice him, he rewarded them with loyalty others didn't think he possessed. She knew he valued her as a friend, but she didn't fully understand why he seemed to admire her—another trait that would surprise others.

"Come on. You know you're not like the rest of them." Alan nodded to the crowd around them. "What you say and do, it's what you believe, who you really are. I never have to guess if you're being honest with me. You're one of the good ones."

Alan bumped Lorraine's shoulder. She thought about how much she had considered staying home and was glad she had decided to come after all.

"Thanks for bringing me tonight," she said.

"It's about time you got out of the house. What have you been doing anyway? Homework? Knitting? Crying over Clint?" Alan leaned in close and teased, "He's not worth those tears, BB."

Lorraine swatted at Alan. "Oh, be quiet!"

Alan's laugh carried over the sounds of the crowd, causing a few people to turn in their direction. He paid them no attention as he reached into his pocket, grabbed more sunflower seeds, and offered them to Lorraine. She hadn't been very hungry lately, but she decided to take one anyway. She reached her hand toward his.

"Whoa, BB! What's this about?"

At first she didn't know what he meant and then Alan grabbed her right ring finger and touched the opal. She had worn the ring every day since Clint had given it to her. She had to since she couldn't easily remove it. No one other than her mother had commented on it. Mrs. Delford had inspected the ring closely after she first noticed it, her expression somewhere between surprise and concern. Lorraine told her Clint meant it as a gift and nothing more.

"He's a good boy," Mrs. Delford had said. "But don't rush into anything."

Lorraine, for once, agreed with her mother.

As Alan held on to her finger, she recovered quickly and joked, "It's called a ring, Alan."

Alan scowled at her as he spit out another shell.

"The bigger question is where did you get it?"

Lorraine didn't know why she suddenly felt embarrassed, but she didn't want to say that Clint had given it to her. She and Alan were friends, but he and Clint were a different story.

"It was a gift." She shrugged.

"From a certain Joe College?"

"Maybe."

"Please, Lorraine." Sunflower seeds nearly escaped his mouth as he spoke. "Tell me you're not engaged."

"In case you didn't notice, this is my right hand." She held up her left hand to emphasize her point. "If it was an engagement ring, it would be on this finger."

"Doesn't seem quite your style," Alan said.

"'Cause you know me so well?" Lorraine started to laugh, but then she turned to Alan.

The two looked at each other, staring in silence as the home crowd jumped to their feet, arms raised, voices roaring. They missed seeing the receiver—a boy in Lorraine's fourth-period class—run the ball into the end zone for a touchdown that put them in the lead. Lorraine and Alan remained seated in the mass of cheers as the bleachers beneath them shook with the celebration.

Truth be told, he did know her well. She'd never understood how; she just knew that he did. In that sea of people who didn't notice either one of them, she felt something that surprised her. As a breeze blew her hair and chilled her, she wanted Alan to wrap his arm around her and hold her, if only for a moment. The thought made her blink and look away, embarrassed by a notion she couldn't believe she had allowed to cross her mind.

Once the fans settled back into their seats, an even murmur returning to the stands, Alan whispered, "It's okay to want something different."

"I know," she said. But did she mean it?

———

Half of the senior class was at the drive-in after the game, radios blasting with Ricky Nelson crooning from the speakers. The honk of car horns as the train of upperclassmen pulled into the station, mixed with the smiles and cheers that erupted every time a football player joined the crowd, let the staff know that Mecklenburg High had pulled off the win.

Lorraine hadn't been to the drive-in yet that school year. As she and Alan sat in his car with the windows down, she wondered what exactly she wanted to do. She could hop out and walk over to their classmates. She could strike up a conversation or congratulate the team on their win. But at the moment, she felt like simply sitting behind the windshield and observing, much like Alan usually did.

That's where the two of them remained as they waited for their order, and even after the carhop skated back to them with their milkshakes balanced on a tray held above her shoulder. Neither of them spoke as they sipped their drinks and watched their classmates out the front window.

After only a few sips, Alan put his shake back on the tray. Lorraine wondered if he was ready to leave, but instead of starting the car, he turned around and leaned over the back seat.

"What are you doing?" she asked as he bumped into her shoulder. He didn't answer, but instead fumbled around with something in the back seat, something Lorraine couldn't see. But soon enough she heard the crackle before the sound filled the car.

"What on earth?" A giggle escaped with the words. As Alan faced forward and started drinking his shake again, Lorraine looked in back to find a portable record player. "Is there something wrong with the drive-in's music?"

"It's The Rolling Stones." Lorraine raised her eyebrows at Alan, waiting for a response to her question. "*The Stones.*" She still didn't understand. "This is way better than that crap about stars shining bright and then he kissed me."

Lorraine shrugged her shoulders and shook her head. She had never minded The Crystals or any of the tunes that played through the drive-in's speakers, but leave it to Alan to feel differently.

"Tell me you know this song," he said.

Lorraine listened to Mick Jagger's voice coming from the back seat of the car, but she didn't recognize the song. The two sat side by side, not saying a word as they listened to Mick sing about time being on his side.

When the song faded, Lorraine admitted, "I've never heard that before."

"Oh, BB. I have so much to teach you."

Alan held Lorraine's gaze. He looked as if he wanted to say more, so she gave him time, but the longer she waited, the more she wondered what he would say. She assumed he had another joke to crack, but the longer the silence, the more she began to fidget. Not even an hour ago, she had found herself wanting him to put his arm around her, and now she sat wondering if he felt the same way.

Unable to take the silence, she asked, "What?" Again, he hesitated. She shifted in her seat.

"Nothing," he finally said.

Alan reached into the back seat and reset the record player. Lorraine thought it best to not press him to say something she might not be ready to hear. She pushed the thought from her mind and settled in to listen to The Stones, the rhythm, the self-assuredness of Mick having time on his side. She felt the beat and kept her ear tuned to the electric guitar as the music drowned out the sound coming from the outside speakers. She got lost in the rhythm as they sat in the car and watched their classmates.

When she and Clint had stood together at those picnic tables after games or on weekends, time did seem to be on their side. But as the lyrics repeated, she didn't feel Mick's optimism. She wanted time to still be on her side, but something now felt different. Instead of time marching on as it always had, she felt as if she was falling toward a future, a feeling she couldn't explain.

She leaned her head against the window and looked up.

"You're always looking at the stars, aren't you?" Alan shook his head and slurped up the final sips of his milkshake. "Honestly, I don't know what you see up there. Nothing more than darkness and distant dots."

Lorraine kept her forehead pressed against the cool window and started talking before she even considered what she was about to say.

"You remember back in eighth grade, I had that spell of strep throat?"

"Not really."

"Remember? I was out of school a lot that winter and into the spring." Alan didn't recall, but it didn't matter. Lorraine continued. "One of those days I was home sick. It was still morning and I was lying on the couch, already bored from having to be home again when Mama turned on the TV and the news was on. They were showing the Mercury flight, the one with Alan Shepard?" Alan shook his head, not remembering. "The first American in space?"

Alan shrugged. When Lorraine didn't continue, he gave a drawn-out "Okay," wondering what she was talking about.

"I lay there on the couch"—she decided to move on—"and I watched this rocket ship, this big, white booster thing with a tiny little capsule at the top. As they counted down, the engines started. Smoke and fire came out of the bottom until that whole thing lifted off the ground and into the sky with Mr. Shepard right there on top. And I watched him fly up through the sky, above the clouds, into space. Can you believe that? Space!"

Alan looked at Lorraine in the same way she had wondered about his fascination with The Stones. Lorraine sat up in her seat as her voice picked up speed. "Space! This guy was on earth one minute and out of the atmosphere the next. For fifteen minutes, he floated along in this tiny little capsule thing and then? Then he came back down. Into the ocean. Just like that. Space one minute, earth the next. They showed the video of it all, but I know we didn't see the same things he saw. We couldn't. And I just wanted to know: what did it look like? What did it feel like? Then a few weeks later, President Kennedy talked about the Space Race and putting a man on the moon. The moon!"

Alan watched Lorraine as she got lost in her own story. When she finally paused, he teased, "So that's why you like to look at the stars? 'Cause Jack Kennedy wanted to stick it to the Soviets? Beat the commies to space?"

"No! Not exactly. It's just when I saw that and then I heard the president, I started wondering what it'd be like."

"What would *what* be like?"

Lorraine pointed at the sky, not sure that words could be clearer.

Alan asked, "You want to go there? To space?"

The question struck Lorraine square in her chest. Her breath paused as her mind began to question if she had said too much, too foolishly shared an unrealistic dream. Before she could chastise herself for being a fool, Alan said, "That's a hell of a dream, BB. And if anyone can do it, it's you."

A jolt of energy coursed through Lorraine. She shouldn't have doubted Alan.

"Have you ever wondered what it'd be like to be an astronaut?" she asked, hoping to find someone who had imagined the same.

"Honestly?"

"Yeah."

"No. In no way have I ever thought about that."

"Never? Really?" Lorraine didn't know how someone hadn't wondered what it would be like to stand in a completely different place, another world, one where no one had gone before. "Someday, I want to go to the moon."

The two friends looked at each other. For once, Alan didn't respond right away. He simply smiled. She wished more people knew the Alan she did, the one who didn't laugh at ridiculous dreams. But he wasn't the type to waste his time convincing others to like him.

When the music cut out, Alan placed both glasses on the tray before reaching in back and resetting the record player. They didn't bother each other with chitchat on the drive home. Lorraine rested her head on the window beside her, watching the stars above, as the steady rocking of the car nearly lulled her to sleep.

As Alan pulled up to the curb in front of Lorraine's house, he put the car in Park and said, "Promise me one thing."

"What?" she asked through a yawn.

"That you'll wave to me on your way to the moon."

Lorraine couldn't stop a grin from growing.

"Of course."

As she walked to her front door, she realized that she felt better than she had for weeks: no nausea, no oppressive exhaustion. She thought about the evening and their conversation. She had surprised herself at what she had told Alan, but he always had a way of getting her to say more than she intended to. She didn't think of what she had told him as having shared a secret. Instead, she had let Alan in on a dream. Secrets were another matter, and one that Lorraine was about to learn quite a lot about, especially since one growing secret was too far along to do much of anything about.

# CHAPTER FIVE

Lorraine knew what drowning felt like. Of course, no one knew that when Lorraine had saved Barbara Ann earlier that year. And no one knew what happened that typical summer day some eight years prior when it was Lorraine sinking below the waterline. She never told anyone, especially not her mother, who always told her that curiosity would kill the cat. It nearly did as much to Lorraine that day.

It started like any other summer day, the humidity high, the heat relentless. No breeze came through the windows, and even the shade of the bigleaf magnolia tree didn't offer enough relief. The neighborhood pool was still a year away from being completed. Lorraine had walked out the door with the intention of heading toward the woods, thinking maybe some neighborhood friends would be gathering along the trail, maybe even heading back to the farmhouse. But, she changed her mind once she got out there. Instead, she decided to hop on her bike and venture down the dirt road of the new subdivision that was being developed across the street from her neighborhood.

No construction workers were there that day. Maybe the heat was keeping them from their work. The land had only been partially cleared by then, enough to be a two-track dirt trail to clear trees before the digging and building could begin. Lorraine rode around the clearing, circling in the carved-out cul-de-sac a few times before the glittery reflection caught her eye. Through the trees, a pond sparkled, beckoning her to come closer.

Standing at the water's edge, Lorraine watched the cranes dipping their beaks into the water, ducks diving their heads in search of lunch, fat frogs leaping into hiding when she got too close. With barely any breeze that day, the pond's top stayed mostly still and glassy. Perfect conditions for skipping rocks. She found smooth ones, shoving them into her pockets before climbing on top of a downed tree that hovered over the water.

Balancing her way along the log, she brought her arm back in full force, ready to launch a rock across the still top when she saw a large fish come to the surface in the path of her pebble. Not wanting to hit it, she tried to stop her momentum. But, as she attempted to change the rock's flight path, she heard a crack beneath her.

The tree broke from its stump and plunged into the pond, taking Lorraine with it. She had just enough time to gasp for air before she submerged beneath the once-calm waters. She entered in a panic, her forehead scraping along a broken branch, and as Lorraine was forced below the waterline, she could either sink or swim. If only she knew how to swim.

Lorraine sank below the surface, surprised by how deep that seemingly small pond actually was. She looked above to see the light of the day rippling across the water's top. She propelled herself toward it as best she could. As she broke the surface, she gulped air before bobbing down again.

While her body continued to propel, gasp, and sink, her mind sped up, searching for a way out, unable to think of anything other than survival. No one could help her, not when the pond was along the back edges of a construction site, surrounded by trees and nearly a half mile from any residence.

Even the wildlife had left her. It wasn't the fall that sent them away as much as the splashing and gasping. The cranes and other birds had taken flight for quieter surroundings. The fish had darted to the bottom. The squirrels tucked into the tops of trees beyond sight. There was only one way for her to get out of that water: on her own.

In the moments that her body ached for breath, her mind demanded she save herself. She stopped focusing on the cool water, the needles in her lungs, the pressure that seemed to want to push her to the bottom of the pond. She recalled images of Olympic swimmers and did her best to imitate them.

She extended one arm before pulling it back and reaching with her other one. She managed a hybrid of a dog paddle and a treading-water motion. It was enough to keep her head above water, her lungs breathing, as she swam toward the edge. She drew herself close enough to the fallen tree to grab ahold and catch her breath. She held on for a few minutes, breathing and gathering herself before she moved toward the edge and pulled herself out.

As she sat on the shore, she watched the ripples she had created calm and disappear. Other than her soaked clothes, matted hair, and bleeding scrape on her forehead, no proof of her near tragedy existed.

The birds came back. The squirrels climbed down trees. Turtles poked their heads above the water's surface. Life continued.

Despite the heat of the day, Lorraine shivered. She drew her arms around herself as her body shook and teeth chattered from the rush of adrenaline. She had pulled herself out. She had escaped. Barely, but she had done it. She wanted to both smile and cry. She had saved herself, but she had nearly lost herself, as well.

By the time she returned home, she was mostly dry. She snuck up the stairs as her mother put lunch on the table. Mrs. Delford didn't notice when Lorraine reemerged from her room in different clothes. Of course, she did notice Lorraine's matted hair and the mud under her fingernails that would not come out no matter how much she scrubbed, assuming her daughter had spent the afternoon running through the woods with the neighborhood boys—always with the boys and never with the little girls who remained satisfied playing house or having a tea party.

And she noticed the scratch on her daughter's forehead, the one that would leave a scar, the blemish that would not fade regardless of how much cream Mrs. Delford demanded Lorraine apply. She told her mother she scraped it on a tree, which was true, but she didn't say it was a forever reminder of the day she ventured out too far.

No one knew what happened that day. Lorraine thought about telling her parents, but she didn't know what they would think about her wandering into that place all alone. So, she said nothing, not even when the neighborhood pool opened the next summer and, to her parent's amazement, she somehow knew how to swim on the first day.

That was the first secret she kept from her parents.

The second happened in the old farmhouse that night with Clint.

But some secrets, despite our desperation, just won't stay kept.

# Part Two

## GRAVIDA

# CHAPTER SIX

Lorraine's third secret began growing before she even knew it existed.

The truth of the trouble Lorraine was in became more real with each passing day and week. Her exhaustion continued. Her nausea came in waves. Her breasts and belly enlarged, subtly, but enough for her to notice. Ignorance may have been the stronger force for the first weeks, but finally physical evidence won out. Especially when she took into account her missed menstruations.

Faced with such proof, a girl in her position could have reacted in a variety of ways. Denial. Embarrassment. Shock. Maybe even contentment, though rarely, and certainly not for a girl like Lorraine who had both a reputation and a future to uphold. When faced with the empirical evidence from the calculation of missed cycles, Lorraine relied on logic. Well, first she counted and recounted the weeks since her last monthly, and then she did deny the possibility for a bit. She wasn't that type of girl. This couldn't have happened to her. Only loose girls found themselves in this predicament, not a good southern girl like herself.

But when shock didn't make her stomach stop growing, she chose a different type of denial: strategize. She needed to come up with a plan. She could smile and pretend all was fine in the meantime, but surely a solution would present itself. After all, her father had always treated her as if she wasn't like other girls. He made her believe that there was nothing she couldn't accomplish if she put her mind to it. So, she put her mind to figuring out how to have it all: the diploma, the career, and, she supposed, the family.

The first step, she decided, was to tell Clint. Her practical mind reasoned that together they could figure out *this*. She refused to actually say the word *pregnancy* aloud, let alone think it. They already planned on marriage. She had a ring to prove it, but now the opal would be more than a promise for sometime in the future. And that would be fine. Everything would be fine. After all, her parents got married quite young as well and look how that had worked out. They didn't get college degrees first and marry second.

One part of the plan that she chose to ignore was high school. She knew what happened to wayward girls. Not that she was a wayward girl. It had been only that one time. It was an accident. That didn't mean she was like those *other* girls, the ones who disappeared from school. The ones everyone whispered about until they faded from memory or became cautionary tales. The girls they sent away.

For now, she focused on the first part of the plan: tell Clint. She would do that as soon as he arrived home for Thanksgiving break. And then they'd go from there. It would all work itself out. Because it had to.

---

Clint drove to Lorraine's house for supper his first night home for break. She heard the rumble of his car out front and ran to the porch, careful to close the door behind her. As he walked toward her, she placed her hands on her stomach. It had been a tight ball all day, a combination of excitement and nervous anticipation. She had a plan, but her nerves made her question if she could actually say the words to him because once she spoke them out loud, the secret would no longer be hidden and, in some way it seemed, it would also finally be true.

Lorraine stood at the edge of the front steps. She fidgeted her fingers as Clint walked up the sidewalk. He looked the same and yet different, his stomach a bit rounder, his hair shorter than when he'd left for school. Even his expression seemed different, almost formal, not as relaxed in some way that she couldn't quite put her finger on. As he got closer, he stretched out his arms and a full smile lit up his face, making him look a bit more like himself. She couldn't help but laugh. Her stomach relaxed and she exhaled. For the first time since before he put the ring on her finger, she felt a sense of rightness.

He looked her over from head to toe. Once again she was wearing his favorite dress—the robin's-egg-blue one. The buttons pulled a bit more across her chest than they had the last time she wore it on that night in the clearing.

"Aren't you a sight for sore eyes?" he asked.

Clint couldn't wait to grab her. He still had one step to go, but in his impatience, he reached forward and pulled her into an embrace. Him standing a step below her put them closer to the same height. As he wrapped his arms around her waist, she hugged him around his neck, resting her arms on his shoulders. They kissed without thinking of her parents or the neighbors or wondering who might be watching.

Clint's arms drew Lorraine ever closer, holding her tighter, as he whispered, "I've missed you so much."

Lorraine planned to tell him the news after supper. She didn't want to ruin his appetite or force him to make conversation with her parents after hearing such life-changing information. But as he held her, she questioned her strategy. She had been holding on to the secret by herself for so long that she wanted to share the burden with someone. She told herself to be patient and stick with the plan. Now wasn't the time.

But Lorraine would have to wait longer than she wanted to. After dinner, Clint insisted they drive around town. He said he wanted to see if things had changed in the few months he had been gone. And, uncertain of exactly how he'd react, she didn't think she should share the news while he was driving.

They cruised the main drag, Lorraine in the middle of the bench seat with Clint's arm draped around her shoulder, the weight of him forcing her to slouch in her seat and lean in to him. They both knew nothing had changed in the time he had been gone, at least nothing visible within the town. The movie theater looked the same. Mecklenburg High was still exactly like it had been. Even the drive-in had the same cars and the same people gathered, the same carhops skating through the parking lot with trays full of sodas and milkshakes and fries.

Instead of stopping in, Clint drove back to the neighborhood. But he didn't take her home. Not yet. He pulled into the parking lot of the neighborhood pool, turning off his headlights as he parked beside a dense and sprawling bigleaf magnolia tree, so passersby wouldn't see the car in the otherwise empty lot. He kept the engine running, the radio playing and lighting up their faces.

Lorraine's heart began to pound in her chest. Her head began to spin. Now was the moment to say what she needed to. She swallowed hard. Inhaled. Closed her eyes and exhaled. But before words came out, Clint began to kiss her.

"You don't know how much I've missed you," he said before she could say anything. He leaned in again for another kiss, but she turned her cheek to him.

"Maybe we should talk."

As she leaned away, he took it as an invitation to draw closer. "Sure. But this first."

"But—"

"Do you know how much I've wanted this? Ever since that night."

Lorraine let his momentum lay her down across the front seat of the car. She let him kiss her, unbutton her dress again, before he explored beneath her skirt. She knew they needed to talk; she knew she needed to tell him. She didn't want to keep the trouble to herself anymore and who else was she going to tell? Certainly not her mother, at least not until she had spoken to Clint and they had gotten things figured out. She had it all worked out, or at least some of it.

She needed to tell him. She knew she should stop him from progressing into what they were about to do. But she couldn't seem to get a word out. Plus, what was the point just then? What harm would it do? They were going to be husband and wife soon enough, and a family not long after that. And as much as she had been both excited and fearful about this moment of reunion, now all she felt was excitement and certainty and optimism. Their closeness gave her hope that all would be fine. As long as she was in his arms, nothing bad could happen. Their life as planned would simply start a bit sooner. But it would start. And they would love each other and live happily ever after. She'd tell him about it soon enough, but for that moment, she'd let him embrace her, touch her, love her.

---

Clint had nearly been asleep beside her on the bench seat before she uttered the words. She told herself she would say it as soon as it was over, but she waited a few minutes. She waited until her body began to shake and sweat began forming on her upper lip. She waited until she felt the bile begin to rise in her stomach. She waited until her body nearly exploded from the secret keeping.

"I think I'm pregnant."

That was the first time she had said it out loud. It was the first time she'd even used the p-word to describe herself. Even in her mind, as she thought of her condition or what was happening or what was to come, she hadn't called herself *pregnant*. She supposed she could still find respect for herself if she thought ahead to the moments of motherhood instead of the consequences of indiscretion.

Clint was now fully awake. As the revelation hung heavy in the air, he bolted upright, scooting away from her, a gulf of emptiness between them in the front seat of the car as the radio continued to sing to them. She watched the range of emotions appear across his face, her stomach knotting more than she ever knew possible. Clint never was one who could hide his feelings. His expressions spoke for him. Even before he worked up the courage to ask her out, his blushing cheeks had long ago told her how he felt. Lorraine sat stone-still on that front seat, her eyes pleading for him to understand, still uncertain of what he would say, if he would accept their fate. If he would still love her.

Lorraine had thought through how she would tell Clint. The conversation played in her mind every night before bed and every distracted moment during school. She knew what she would say. And she thought she knew how Clint would react. At first, he would be quiet. She would give him a moment to absorb the news. Change never came quickly or easily for him. She would wait until he processed the information. When he began to smile, that's when she would reach for his hand, when he would turn to her and they would kiss as an engaged couple for the first time.

But she hadn't anticipated the nervousness that permeated every inch of her body while she waited for him to respond.

Just like when she had to approach her father about becoming a lifeguard, she knew she had to be strong, that she would need to lay out the facts and give him a moment to think things over, to lead quietly and submissively, as her mother taught her. But just like with her father, Clint would come around to seeing things her way. He would come to celebrate the start of their family. He had to.

She had planned. But she hadn't accurately anticipated how hard it would be to lay out a step-by-step process of how they should get engaged, have a wedding over Christmas break, find a house, and move in together as a happily married couple before he returned to classes in the new year. She'd figure out a way to finish high school and then she could go to college, too. Her mother wouldn't think that was a traditional way of doing things, but Lorraine's mind was made up.

The four words she had muttered to him took more strength than she had anticipated. And as they burst out of her, they left behind an oppressive feeling of shame. Sitting in the silence, watching him process the information, she ached for him to respond, and she questioned everything about her plan. And herself.

It turns out that she hadn't accurately anticipated his response.

"That's impossible." Those were Clint's first words. "We only did it that one time." That was his next line of denial. His voice wobbled with anger and confusion, but she didn't hear any hints of shame, what she most felt in that moment. Then came more denial as he said, "You said you 'think' you might be pregnant. You don't know for sure."

She had said that word, maybe in an attempt to ease into the new reality, but the truth was that she knew for certain.

"I do know." The words squeaked out as Lorraine fidgeted with the ring he had given her. Her fingers brushed against the skirt of her dress, rustling the material as one song faded into another. She wondered if he asked for the ring back if she could even get it off. But he wouldn't do that. He loved her. This ring would simply be replaced by another one.

"You can't know," he proclaimed, as if he better understood her body than she did. "A doctor needs to tell you."

"I can't go to a doctor." She projected her voice, no longer squeaking, but instead declaring what she knew and he hadn't thought to consider. "Not without Mama knowing. And I wanted to tell you first."

Plus, she knew without a doctor telling her. She didn't know how much more to say to Clint. He didn't want to hear about missed periods and cycles. Besides, that's not what girls should be talking about with their boyfriends. She didn't talk about that sort of stuff with her girlfriends, not even her mother. But she wasn't guessing. She wasn't making this up.

Her hands instinctively went to her stomach and began rubbing it. She was surprised that no one else had noticed yet. When Clint first hugged her with his arms tight around her waist and his stomach pressed against hers, she thought for sure he felt it. As he lay on top of her just moments before, she thought he noticed the bump, the swelling, the stomach that now protruded. But he hadn't.

Other than a bit of added weight, tiredness, and nausea, Lorraine didn't feel pregnant. She could go entire hours forgetting that a baby existed inside of her. She always imagined it would feel different, more obvious, not so easily overlooked.

"None of this makes sense," Clint said. He stared into the distance—through the pine trees, over the top of the picket fence, and past the neighboring Cape Cod cottage, looking through it all. "This isn't supposed to happen to us. This isn't who we are."

And who were they? Really? Lorraine had been asking herself that question over the past weeks as she had wrestled with this knowledge in solitude. She was BB, as Alan said. She knew it was a joke, but she also knew that he meant something by it. She was going to be the valedictorian, the first girl in Sunnymede to lifeguard, the first girl to dream of being something more than a housewife and a mother. And yet there she was, in a parked car, trying to figure out who she was more upset with—herself for getting into this trouble or Clint for not yet knowing what to do about it.

"Well, I guess there's only one thing to do." He finally turned toward her, reached for her hand, and said, "We have to get married."

Lorraine looked at him, searching the expression on his face to know if he meant it. She looked into his blue eyes, and while she didn't see the excitement she had earlier that evening, she saw resolve and assurance.

"Really?" While the knots in her stomach loosened, they didn't fully release. She thought she'd feel more hopeful or, at the very least, relieved.

"Of course." He kept holding her hand but turned his gaze from her to the darkness outside the car. "We were going to anyway. So why not?" Clint continued, "But, let's not say anything this weekend. Let me get back to college and figure out things."

She thought she would want to hug him. She thought she would want to put her arms around his neck and kiss him. She thought that would be a moment of delight, of hope, of answered prayers. But he remained on his side of the car and she remained on hers. His arm bridged the empty space between them, his hand cold against hers, her heart more unsettled than she had thought it would be.

His plan was a bit different than what she had imagined. She assumed they would tell their parents that weekend. But she could adjust. The fact that they agreed they should be married sooner rather than later, surely that was a sign that all would be well, that all would be figured out, that happily ever after would begin sooner than expected. But in the darkness of the car that night, the heaviness in her heart, the twist in her gut, the shame consuming her mind threatened her ability to believe in such naive notions.

# CHAPTER SEVEN

Clint really didn't need more coffee. Truth be told, he didn't even like the black drink, but he began trying to tolerate it after starting college. He was a serious man now, so in some sense, it seemed like he should drink it alongside his peers in between classes. Since Lorraine had shared the news, he began to want it more. He tried it with a little cream, then some sugar as he worked his way up to a lot of both. Susan, a waitress at the diner and first-year student at the secretarial school nearby, always gave him a hard time about his habit.

"Seems more like candy than coffee," she'd say to him more often than not after she'd warm up his cup and watch as he'd douse it with more cream and sugar to make it tolerable.

The diner—and Susan—had become part of Clint's routine early in his first semester at college. It started when some of the guys invited him to breakfast one Saturday morning. With a warm smile and a few flirtatious winks, Susan caught Clint's eye and his hankering for coffee started soon after that breakfast.

Clint made it seem like he had acclimated to college well enough, but sometimes he needed to get off campus and away from the other guys, especially as the semester wore on and his grades dipped lower than they had ever been. He hadn't told his parents; no sense in worrying them yet. He certainly didn't tell

Lorraine. She wouldn't understand his struggle, and he certainly didn't want her pity. Plus, she had her hopes up about college, and he didn't want to burst them. But college wasn't what he had expected. His roommate smelled. The guys were all slobs. The professors had unrealistic expectations, and the amount of work was crushing. He needed to keep his nose to the grindstone and eke by the next few years. Then he could get an office job like his dad and be set for life.

Until Lorraine threw a wrench in his plans.

He hadn't gotten much sleep since she had told him she was pregnant. He couldn't believe what she had said. Didn't she know he needed to focus on classes? That college isn't high school? That good grades don't come as easily? He didn't need to deal with this. Not then. But she hadn't given him a choice.

He had hoped Susan wouldn't be at the diner that afternoon. He needed to be back at the dorm studying, but he couldn't make the call from there. What if one of the guys walked by and overheard? He couldn't risk it at the library either. He figured the pay phone outside the diner would be the most private location.

His hands shook as he sat at the counter. He'd only taken a sip of coffee so far, not even enough for Susan to be able to top it off. His hands shook less from the caffeine and more from the anticipation of the call he needed to make.

Susan seemed to be in a chatty mood that day, which typically wouldn't bother him, but he wasn't there for pleasantries. He wasn't there to tickle her funny bone in a way that would elicit one of those laughs that always made him smile in return.

"Clinton?" She insisted on calling him that. "You alright today? Don't seem quite like yourself."

He couldn't handle small talk right then, couldn't handle seeing that smile of hers either.

"Yeah, just need to make a call. I'll be right back." He took one more sip, hoping it would give him a bit of courage.

As he walked outside, he fidgeted in his pocket in search of the change he needed. He hoped Lorraine would answer. He didn't want to talk to Mrs. Delford. As luck would have it, Lorraine was there and waiting as she had been every afternoon since he'd gone back to school. It had taken more than a week for him to call her. Each afternoon as she sat at the kitchen table and tried to focus on homework, her anticipation of the phone ringing grew more urgent.

Christmas was only a few weeks away. She had planning to do, a dress to purchase, hairstyles to consider. Plus, she should pack up her room so she could move into their apartment right away, but she couldn't do any of that until her parents knew, and that conversation would happen only after Clint got back to school, figured out their housing situation, and worked out any other details he needed to. But they had spoken so little that Lorraine didn't know what he had sorted out so far.

On that afternoon, she leapt from her chair to grab the phone as soon as she heard the first ring. Mrs. Delford had gone upstairs to put away laundry and gather more yarn, so there was no need to rush, but Lorraine couldn't help herself. She wanted this feeling of living in the in-between to end. She wanted to move on with next steps and thoughts of the future instead of the weight of the present. If she had something to actually do, to accomplish, then she wouldn't have the time to think about what they had done and what had happened and what everyone would say as a result.

Once he was sure he had Lorraine on the other end of the line, Clint gave her the instructions: "You need to get your mother's car and drive up here Friday."

"What?" Lorraine looked around the kitchen. The winter chill had set in, and as much as she wanted to stay in the warmth of the house, she knew it was best to head outside. Her mother had come back downstairs and presently sat in her armchair in the living room to take up her crocheting before she needed to finish supper. And Lorraine suddenly knew this was a conversation that couldn't be overheard.

Thankfully the kitchen's phone cord had reach. Though still a tether of sorts, it stretched a distance, thanks to her mother frequently cradling it beneath her cheek as she pattered around the kitchen. As Lorraine opened the door, a cool breeze blew in, but the importance of the call forced her out the door despite the chill.

"You need to be here by lunch on Friday."

Lorraine smiled. She felt like she was breathing again for the first time since she had told him. "You have things in order?"

Clint cut her short, "Yeah. You'll get the car, right?"

Lorraine pulled her cardigan tight around herself, trying to keep the cool away from her body. "How am I supposed to do that?" She wondered why she needed to drive up there. Maybe he had a place to show her. Maybe he'd found an apartment for them. She wondered how many rooms it would have. Would there be a window over the kitchen sink so she could look into the backyard as she washed dishes? Would there be a backyard at all?

Clint dropped the receiver from his ear down to his hip. He

inhaled and closed his eyes for a second before putting the phone back to his ear to continue. "I don't know. Listen. I have a—" He paused and looked around, making sure Susan hadn't followed him onto the sidewalk. He waited for a couple to pass by before he continued. "A fix. But you have to be here Friday."

The apartment must've been a great one, Lorraine thought, sensing the urgency around her being there on time.

"Mama grocery shops that day, so she's not going to let me borrow the car. Plus, I have a science exam."

"Lorraine!" A man paused and looked at Clint who smiled before proceeding in a hushed tone. "I've found someone who can help. I've figured out that much. You need to figure out how to get here. And don't worry about money. I've got that covered."

She hadn't thought of money until he said that. "Money? For the apartment?"

Clint's voice rose again so that another passerby looked his way. "Apartment? What are you talking about?"

"I thought you had a place for us."

"A place? No! I have…a—" He glanced around him, noticing a couple walking by. "It's a—" He held the receiver so close to his mouth that his lips touched it as he whispered, "A fix."

Clint hoped he had said enough. He couldn't say much more, not there on the public pay phone with listening ears on the line or passing by at any moment. They may have been strangers, but what if Susan walked out of the diner just then? Surely Lorraine could understand what he meant by "fix" well enough for her to know what needed to be done to get out of this trouble she was in.

"Clint, I don't—"

The operator interrupted, requesting more change to continue the conversation. Clint didn't want to talk any longer than necessary, so he said, "Just get here. Friday. By noon."

He slammed the phone back onto its cradle. He closed his eyes for a moment and realized how cold, exhausted, and angry he was. Maybe the rest of that coffee would give him the energy he needed to start writing his essay for history class. But after that back-and-forth, he couldn't bring himself to go back into the diner. He couldn't smile and make small talk with Susan. He figured he'd settle up with her later, give her an extra big tip next time. Surely walking out on one cup of coffee wouldn't be a problem. He didn't trust himself to go back in just then. He didn't know what he'd say to her or how much he'd let on. He liked the relationship they had, and he didn't want it to change. She was fun. Cute. Less complicated.

But at that moment, Susan mattered less than the timing of the events he had arranged. He hoped Lorraine understood. She had always been the girl he could count on. For the most part. There was no denying her defiance at times, but when it mattered, she always came through. He had to trust that she would come through this time, too. His future depended on it.

———

As Friday approached, Lorraine tried to convince her mother to let her drive to school. She didn't like lying to her mother, but she couldn't tell her the truth. She closed her eyes and uttered a message aimed at God. She just hoped He was listening.

When she finally worked up the nerve to talk to her mother, Lorraine made up a story that she needed to be at school early for her science exam, to which Mrs. Delford said she could walk. When she said the spirit club needed her to take in some large posters, Mrs. Delford said that surely Alan's car had enough space to transport them. Her final attempt took more of a personal approach, explaining that she wanted to pitch in more around the house and help out. She wanted to ease her mother's burden by picking up the groceries on her way home from school. Of course, Mrs. Delford had never been one who enjoyed mixing up routines, so she simply shook her head and laughed at her daughter, wondering what on earth had gotten into her.

Lorraine tried to call Clint at school to tell him, but he never seemed to be around the dorm when she called. She left messages with various guys, but Clint never called back. So, on the Friday that she should've been looking at their future apartment—or so she thought—Lorraine went to school. She took her science exam. At the end of the day, Alan drove her home as usual. As she sat at the kitchen table and got a head start on her homework for the weekend, Clint called.

"What the hell, Lorraine?" Thankfully her mother wasn't in the kitchen when she answered. "Where were you?"

"I told you I didn't think I could get the car."

"That's all you had to do!"

Lorraine walked outside, trying to wait to close the door behind her before she yelled back at Clint, "How?"

"I don't know! I got the appointment. The least you could do was that much." No one spoke for a minute. Clint's voice dropped low in defeat and for the sake of privacy. "The doctor could only fit you in today."

"Appointment? Doctor? What are you talking about?"

"He was doing me a favor. He said you're getting too far along. We shouldn't wait. That's why you had to get here today."

Lorraine sat down as she struggled to comprehend all he said. He hadn't wanted her to look at a place. He had wanted to take her to a doctor, a doctor who would fix her situation. The weight of his words pulled her onto the cold concrete of the back porch. It took her a minute to figure it out. She thought he had wanted a family. But instead he wanted to end what they had created together.

It took her a minute to find her voice, but when she did, it burst out of her. "That's how you were fixing things?" Surely her mother could've heard her yell from inside the house, but she was too upset to care.

"What did you expect?"

*An apartment. A marriage. A family.* She thought all of those things, but said, "What we'd always planned to do."

"Planned?" As he laughed, he ran his fingers through his hair. He held on to the ends and pulled, so that the pain gave him something else to focus on for a second. "We never planned on this."

"Maybe not like this." Lorraine rubbed her stomach. "But we can figure it out."

Clint closed his eyes and shook his head. He'd run all the calculations. He'd looked at the cost of apartments. He'd searched the want ads for a job he could do while he finished up college. But who was he kidding? He was barely making it through his first semester as it was, and he didn't have a wife and child to provide for. "No, Lorraine. Remember you said you trusted me? This was the only way."

"It's not! I'm sure it's not! I'll talk to my parents. They can help. I know at first they'll be mad, but like talking them into being a lifeguard, it'll work out."

Clint closed his eyes and shook his head. He spoke slowly and quietly. "Lorraine, this isn't a summer job. This was a mistake."

Lorraine hugged herself in the quiet of the backyard. She closed her eyes and was reminded of that night: the candles, the blanket, the moon shining through the ceiling. She felt the pressure, remembered his urgency, his breath humid against her neck as he shook and groaned and collapsed beside her.

"But it doesn't have to be," she said.

Frustration erupted from Clint in the exhale of a laugh. "You've always been a dreamer."

Lorraine misunderstood his meaning. She thought she was about to convince him. With optimism, hope, desperation dripping from her voice, she said, "We can do this. Together. It'll be our adventure."

But it took only one word to steal all hopes from her: "No." Clint paused for only a moment before spitting out the phrase he had been wanting to say but hadn't found the confidence to until that moment. "If you want to keep it, you're on your own."

"What? You don't mean that." Like the moment she fell into the pond, panic engulfed her. She had never considered a scenario in which Clint would walk away and leave her alone. Why would she? They were practically engaged. She couldn't believe what she had heard. Maybe it was a bad connection. Maybe if they were together, in person, looking into each other's eyes, he wouldn't be saying this. She had to do what she could right then to save their relationship, their future.

One sentence flowed into another, not giving Clint space to

respond, as adrenaline raced through her body. "I'll take care of things here. When you get home for Christmas, I'll have it figured out." As usual, she knew she would have to be the one to handle the details, get everything in place. She could do it; she had to do it. "I'll make the arrangements. We'll have a small ceremony before Christmas, right when you get home for break. That'll give us a few months to get moved in and settled before—"

She couldn't talk fast or loud enough to drown out Clint's retort. Lorraine couldn't see his face, but she heard the exhale come through the phone receiver and that was when she paused. In some contexts, it could sound like a laugh, maybe a chuckle, but this sound dripped with sadness, frustration, and defeat. "For someone so smart, you can be pretty dense sometimes."

Clint had never been perfect, but she knew she hadn't been either. As different from one another as they had always been, that last statement infuriated her more than anything else he had ever done or said to her. Some girls may have cried at such a statement. Some may have simply shrugged their shoulders. But a chasm opened within Lorraine, and while she wanted to scream at him, any words she thought she could say fell into that void. All hope and excitement of what could have been, the confusion and shock of what he had said, the anger and rage at his nerve to be so selfish fell into the depths, so that all she could do was sit on that cold concrete and listen without reply as two words tumbled out of his mouth so softly she could barely hear him.

"Bye, Lorraine."

As the phone went dead, Lorraine sat on the ground shaking, not because the cold cut to her bones, but because it was the only way her body could react to what she had just heard. When her voice gave out and her mind still tried to put together a puzzle that Clint had apparently given up on, her physical body was the only thing that seemed to understand the truth of what had happened. Her body shivered and shook until she forced it to pick itself up, walk back into the kitchen, and eat supper as if her world hadn't just collapsed around her.

# CHAPTER EIGHT

Beginning when she was quite young, Mrs. Delford dreamed of being a dancer. She didn't just dream; she earnestly believed she could do it. It started when her aunt took her to see Shirley Temple on the big screen. Betty sat at the edge of her folding seat the entire length of the film, spellbound by a girl who looked to be roughly her own age at the time. She watched this girl act, sing, and dance, holding her own with the adults on screen with her. Betty watched Shirley's banana curls bounce with each tap of her foot and spin of her body.

After that day, she begged her mother to put her hair into ringlets. Betty spent her days dancing and flitting around her house and yard, but for a girl born in the Depression era which morphed into the war effort, frivolous things like classes and lessons and practices were not a possibility. She never did get a pair of tap shoes like she asked for each Christmas. Her mother said that soda bottle tops stuck into the soles of her shoes sufficed just fine.

While her dreams may have included tap shoes and costumes, the reality of her life left her standing in a housecoat and head-scarf that held her curlers in place. As Mrs. Delford washed her husband's breakfast dishes, she tapped her toe to the music that played from the transistor radio. Mrs. Delford wondered if she had ever told Lorraine about her childhood dream. But of course she hadn't ever mentioned it. Why would she bother talking about childhood nonsense? Her daughter had her own notions that would go no further than her hopes of being a dancer. She didn't need to foster silly thoughts of becoming something else.

The time on the clock caught Betty's attention and pulled her back to reality. She turned off the radio, a bit embarrassed that she had allowed herself to get lost in girlhood foolishness. She should've been waking Lorraine. That girl could not seem to rouse herself in the mornings anymore. Mrs. Delford wondered how she'd fare at college next year without her mother's watchful eye making sure she woke up on time, did her homework, and completed any necessary chores.

Lost in those thoughts, Mrs. Delford didn't know that Lorraine had been standing in the opening between the dining room and kitchen for a few minutes already. She didn't know that her daughter had been watching her in what seemed to be a happy moment as the radio played music from what felt like a lifetime ago.

Lorraine stood in the doorway and took a mental snapshot of the scene to hold in her mind before she upended their lives. For a moment, she'd caught her mother enjoying a few minutes of bliss, a rarity for a busy bee like Mrs. Delford. Lorraine thought that if her mother was more carefree, maybe they would enjoy each other more.

She knew she couldn't wait any longer. After that call with Clint, she had to be the one to handle the situation. She couldn't remain silent anymore. With her stomach continuing to push against her clothes, she needed to say something before it became any more obvious.

With as much bravery as she could muster, she said, "Mama." She had only uttered two syllables, but her voice cracked between them, not even strong enough to hold them together in one certain word.

Having thought she was alone, Mrs. Delford startled. "Lorraine! Do you know what time it is? You're going to be late. I honestly don't know what has gotten into you this school year. You used to be so prompt. I don't know how I haven't gotten a call from the principal about your tardiness."

More words would've escaped her mother's mouth that morning if tears hadn't started streaming from Lorraine's eyes just then. Her mother grabbed a towel and wiped the dishwater from her hands before walking to her daughter.

"What's wrong?" she asked, touching her wrist to her daughter's forehead before pinching Lorraine's earlobes. "I don't feel a fever. Are you sick? Not feeling well?"

And that's when her mother felt it.

As she continued to look over her daughter to diagnosis the pain, the problem, the disease that had afflicted her, she moved her hands from her daughter's throat and downward to her stomach. Instead of feeling the flatness, the athleticism that had been so evident when she donned her lifeguard uniform, she felt a firm, solid, rounded bump.

And everything got quiet.

Her mother stopped chattering. She took a step back, looked into her daughter's eyes, and shook her head from side to side as she began to mutter again and again. "No. No. No." She treaded backward into the kitchen, her "no" becoming more emphatic, her head shaking harder so that her curlers began to loosen. "This can't be." She backed into the kitchen counter, gripping it so she wouldn't fall to the floor as she tried to make sense of what was happening.

Lorraine remained still, other than the tears that built in her eyelids before tumbling down her cheeks. She said nothing. She stared at the speckled linoleum as she both waited for and dreaded what her mother would say next.

"How could you?" The force of the words brought droplets of spit along with them that flew from Mrs. Delford's mouth and landed on the kitchen floor between them.

Lorraine couldn't remain silent anymore. Her sobs became audible as she closed her eyes and shook.

Mrs. Delford pushed away from the kitchen counter, walked to the table, grabbed the back of a chair, and then threw it across the room. She grabbed hold of her scarf and tore it from her head, a few curlers falling to the floor as she did so.

"How could you do this to us? What were you thinking? Did we not teach you better?"

Lorraine's legs felt weak as she began to sob, "I'm sorry, Mama. I'm so sorry."

"All your life that's what you've been saying. You never could listen. Always had to do exactly what you weren't supposed to do. And now this."

Her mother began pacing the kitchen, shaking her head, not looking at her daughter. Lorraine's legs continued to wobble, but she stood still, wiping away her tears, not able to predict what her mother would do next, but she knew enough to stay quiet.

Finally, her mother paused. She whipped her head in Lorraine's direction so quickly that a few more curlers fell from her hair and dropped to the floor. "When did this happen?"

Lorraine started to shrug her shoulders, but she knew there was no use in hiding anything anymore. "Before Clint went to school. The day after I saved Barbara Ann."

Mrs. Delford stared at her, unblinking, unforgiving. Hadn't she told Eugene that their daughter shouldn't sit around half-naked all summer? She began to shake, but refrained from yelling. Instead she began counting on her fingers.

"When was that? August? So, that would mean—" Betty mumbled to herself, forgetting for a moment how late in the year it was, forgetting that Thanksgiving had happened and Christmas was around the corner, hoping that it was still September and the girl was mistaken, didn't know any better, was confused and nothing else. Then she realized that Lorraine had already completed her first trimester. *If* she was pregnant, she had, at least. Betty had to hold on to that *if* for as long as possible. What did the girl know, after all? But hadn't Betty noticed already? Hadn't she seen the girl's cheeks rounding and her stomach growing despite how little she had been eating the last few months?

Betty hated to ask the next question. She never did like talking about such things, but she knew she needed to. The answer would be key.

"When was your last monthly?"

Lorraine looked at the floor, took in a breath first, and then said, "July."

*Shit.*

Betty closed her eyes and shook her head again. Surely it could be something else. Indigestion, stress, too many milkshakes and fries at the drive-in. She knew she needed to plan in case it wasn't, but until they saw a doctor she needed to get a handle on the situation.

"Did you tell Clint?"

Lorraine nodded yes.

Of course, she had, but Betty wished this information had been contained to only the two of them.

"When's he coming back?"

"Christmas break."

"What is today?" Betty looked toward the calendar. "We have, what? A couple of weeks? We can plan something for Christmas."

"Something?"

Mrs. Delford looked at Lorraine. "Yes. If you're really… with…in this situation, then yes. We need to plan a wedding. Something small. Nothing big."

Lorraine gave up trying to stand and sat down at the kitchen table. She put her head in her hands. In some way, admitting the next part felt harder than saying she was pregnant. Lorraine still couldn't believe that the boy who claimed he loved her, the one who had initiated all of this, had so easily walked away and left her all alone. She gulped and forced the words out. "He won't, Mama."

"What?" So many thoughts were racing through her mind that Mrs. Delford believed she had misheard Lorraine.

"He said…" Lorraine hiccuped a few times before she finally said, "I'm on my own."

Mrs. Delford grabbed another kitchen chair. Lorraine thought she would throw that one as well, but instead her mother held on to it, her knuckles turning white from straining. Mrs. Delford kept her head bowed, shaking it back and forth as she growled, "I can't look at you right now. Go to your room."

"But, Mama, I have school."

"School?" Mrs. Delford lifted her head to look at her daughter. Her curlers shifted from her face, down toward her neck, a few more loosening enough to fall to the floor with a clatter. "Not anymore."

"But, Mama!" Lorraine's voice rose to a pitch she hadn't spoken with since she was a toddler. "I have to go. I have to graduate. Be valedictorian."

"They have rules."

"But, Mama! I have to!"

As her daughter began to yell, Mrs. Delford's voice remained low and even, letting Lorraine in on the reality of her consequences, "That's all over now." As those words settled over Lorraine, weighing her down, pressing on her shoulders so she wanted to slump and collapse onto the kitchen table, her mother had one last thing to say to her. "Get out of my sight."

Lorraine went to her room. She closed the door behind her, leaned against it, and slid to the floor. She looked around her room, the walls painted pink, the 4-H ribbons hanging from the bulletin board, the Bible on her nightstand with the lamp above it glowing warm. Her walls were void of posters, but not by her choice. She had wanted to hang images of Bobby Vinton, Ricky Nelson, even Alan Shepard from magazines and newspapers. But her parents didn't like the idea of idols being hung on her walls. At that moment, she was glad those portraits weren't looking back at her.

She should have been leaving for school soon, but that was no longer an option. If she couldn't finish high school, she couldn't be valedictorian, couldn't go to college, would never go to space. At that moment, huddled on her worn pink carpeting, she had nothing left. No boyfriend. No future. No hope. Only shame.

# CHAPTER NINE

Eugene had no idea what was happening in his house. He had noticed that both his wife and daughter had been quieter over the last few days and that Lorraine headed to her room immediately after finishing her supper. But he hadn't noticed that she barely ate anything and spent most the meal pushing food around on her plate. Nor did he have any clue that she hadn't been attending school.

He assumed some of the quiet came from Lorraine focusing on her studies and Betty busying herself with organizing Christmas bake sales, food baskets, or whatever else. He couldn't keep up with everything she and the ladies tinkered around with. He was just glad she had something to do, which would come in handy next year when their only child headed off to college.

He knew he shouldn't be too prideful of Lorraine, but he couldn't help himself. She was growing into the good girl he and Mrs. Delford had worked so hard to raise. Of course, at times she had been a handful, for Betty especially, but their careful and attentive parenting had paid off. He knew she'd be a great wife and mother someday, and while school didn't matter as much, it didn't hurt that she was good at that, as well. He only had one child, so he let her carry the expectation he would've held for a son, had they been so blessed. He'd have to work to not spend Lorraine's entire graduation ceremony grinning from ear to ear.

Little did he know, that wasn't something he needed to spend time worrying about.

While being valedictorian was out of the question since school wouldn't allow a pregnant girl to attend, Mrs. Delford was doing all she could to save the family's reputation. That's why she told her daughter to stay in her room and away from the windows where neighbors might spot her. That's why she called the school and said they had a family emergency and Lorraine would be absent for a while, until the situation was resolved. That's also why she drove to the drugstore across town the afternoon Lorraine confessed her immorality and purchased her daughter what she hoped would be a solution: Lysol and a douche.

She instructed her daughter to do it daily until her cycle came and all of this could be put behind them. But, when Lorraine's period didn't start, Betty finally phoned a doctor. She had given up hoping years ago, a childish practice that had no purpose in adulthood, but she still held on to a thin thread of optimism that perhaps something else had stopped Lorraine's monthlies from coming. Of course, the ever-rounding belly seemed like an indicator, but perhaps some sort of growth—cancer maybe—was still a possibility.

When she had spoken with Dr. Harris, he sounded as though he could be discreet. He had asked her what they had tried, assuming this child hadn't been planned. When Betty told him that the Lysol failed, he wasn't surprised. Nor was he shocked when she told him that the father had walked away. He assured her that he had seen many girls in similar predicaments and knew how to handle the situation with the delicacy it required. She had to take him at his word. She had no other option at that point.

Before the appointment, Lorraine had been instructed to let her mother do the talking; she would handle the situation. So, after changing into the gown, Lorraine sat at the edge of the exam table, her ankles crossed and swinging back and forth as the doctor and her mother talked about her as if she wasn't there.

Lorraine listened to their conversation, ready to speak if they asked her a question, but they continued as if her presence wasn't necessary. She didn't mind. While she had enjoyed independence when she could handle a situation, she knew she couldn't manage this pregnancy by herself, let alone whatever came after that. She refused to think about what would happen at the end of the pregnancy, avoiding all thoughts of a baby because she could not bring herself to imagine single motherhood—a foreign concept. In the doctor's office, she did her best to politely smile and nod, but all she wanted to do was go back home, crawl under the covers, and sleep until this nightmare ended. If only this was something she could wake up from.

"Please lie back." Dr. Harris finally spoke to Lorraine.

The doctor grabbed a contraption Lorraine had never seen before. It had two earpieces and a horn that he positioned in the center of his forehead like a unicorn. He leaned toward her, pressing the device into her stomach. Lorraine shivered as it touched her skin. Dr. Harris pressed the fetoscope into her, pausing before moving it to another place. And then another. And another. With each hasty movement, Mrs. Delford hoped that he wouldn't find a heartbeat. But then he paused and listened and counted before he stood up, pulled down Lorraine's gown and officially pronounced her pregnant.

"You're sure?" Betty's voice quivered. She pulled at a hangnail. The pain barely registered as she ripped it from the side of her thumbnail.

The doctor nodded in the affirmative, looked at her over the top of his spectacles, and said, "There's no doubt."

Both Delford women exhaled, releasing the shared thin thread of hope they'd foolishly been clinging to.

"How far along would you say she is?"

"Definitely through the first trimester, four-and-a-half, five months given her last cycle."

The doctor reached for Lorraine and helped her sit up. He listened to her heart and lungs, checked her ears and eyes before saying that she seemed healthy. Despite that diagnosis Lorraine felt sick. Tired. Defeated and deflated.

"Two pieces of advice," the doctor said. "First, stop using the Lysol. The girl's got a contact burn. If it hasn't worked yet, it's not going to."

Mrs. Delford blushed. "I'd heard it could work."

"If it did"—the doctor chuckled as he removed his glasses and tucked them into his coat pocket—"I'd have less business." Then he went back to what he was saying before Mrs. Delford had interrupted. "Second, given the situation and timing, this is your best bet."

Dr. Harris handed a pamphlet to Mrs. Delford.

"They understand the importance of anonymity," he said as Betty looked at the cover of the brochure. "They know how to make all of this go away so she can resume life. Get back to how things used to be, like none of this ever happened."

Lorraine's ears perked up. She wondered how a place could make that possible. She certainly wanted to know more.

"They take girls for their last three months," the doctor continued.

"But it might be less." Lorraine, hopeful that the doctor truly did have a solution, spoke for the first time. Both the doctor and her mother looked at her. "You said the last three months. But I was early, right, Mama? So maybe this one will be, too."

Lorraine relaxed, only just a bit, for what felt like the first time in months. If this baby would come early, then maybe they could hide this enough for her to get back to school, finish her senior year, be valedictorian after all. As she sat on that exam table, she swung her feet back and forth, finding a new string of hope to hold on to.

———————

Most afternoons, Lorraine studied the few textbooks she had brought home with her, giving herself assignments to keep learning so when she finally returned to class, she would not need to catch up. But that afternoon, Lorraine studied the brochure instead of the schoolbooks.

*A place that cares*, the front cover said above a sketch of a building that reminded her of a smaller version of some of the dorms at the University of North Carolina. The inside of the pamphlet told how the girls could rest and relax in the comfort of professionals. Apparently, the home provided routine checkups, direction and guidance, and a good beginning.

A good beginning was exactly what Lorraine wanted for herself. And the baby, too, of course. When she had first realized she was pregnant, she assumed that beginning would be as a family with Clint. She had been okay with that. She had imagined it enough to believe it could work. But over the last few weeks, she had tried to dream a new dream. The trouble was, she couldn't. There were a lot of things Lorraine believed she could do, but raising a baby without Clint was not one of them. How could she finish school? Go to college? Have a job? Pay the rent? She couldn't do it alone. And she wasn't sure she even wanted to try.

But this home for unwed mothers, this had potential. This could be a place where she could bide her time, where she and the baby could be cared for. And, as Mrs. Delford had to explain to her on the way home, a place that could find a family to care for the child, a chance to be loved instead of labeled illegitimate.

Lorraine didn't fully understand the details, but she assumed she could trust the adults who were making the decisions. She could go live at the maternity home for her last trimester, spend that time away from nosy neighbors and watchful eyes. She could give birth with privacy and then return home as if nothing had ever happened. And that was exactly what Lorraine wanted.

Alone in her room, she began to dream again. She chose to think more about the maternity home and what it would be like, treating it in her mind like a sort of college experience, an adventure she'd soon be embarking on. After all, the only picture made it look like a dormitory. While the pamphlet said nothing of school, she assumed they had something to offer the girls as they waited for their lives to resume.

But first, there was something she needed to do. She didn't want to do it. She had hoped her mother would take care of it, but Mrs. Delford told her on their way home that afternoon, "You made this mess. You need to clean up after yourself."

Cleaning up meant telling her father.

As the clock ticked ever toward the supper hour, Lorraine tried to prepare herself for the conversation. She tried to think of the words to say. She tried to view this as a presentation, a report she needed to give, but unlike any school assignment, she had already failed this one. Regardless of what she said, her father would never look at her the same again. This was so much bigger than the time she had to confess to coloring with crayons on her bedroom wall or when she ran out of gas on her way back from the movies. Those had seemed like major infractions at the time. What she wouldn't give to be in one of those predicaments instead of this one.

That evening after the prayer, Mr. Delford placed his napkin across his lap and was poised to serve himself a piece of meatloaf as if it was a typical supper.

Lorraine tried to swallow down the nausea. She buried her hands in her skirt, filled her lungs with as much air as she could, and let the words flow before her nerves could pull them back into her: "Daddy, I'm pregnant."

She looked at her father. She waited for a response. She continued to force down any emotions, bile, light-headedness.

But her father didn't respond. He sat still. His hands on the table. His eyes on Lorraine. No anger. No laugh. No disbelief. No questioning of what he had heard. The room remained silent other than the tick of the clock on the wall.

Lorraine watched her father, who stared at her, his face red, his eyes large and unblinking. He shook his head slightly, from side to side, his eyebrows furrowing and unfurrowing as if confused. Finally, he turned to his wife and said, "What?"

Mrs. Delford simply nodded her head yes.

"How's this possible?" he asked.

Lorraine didn't know either. Even having been in the moment that started all of this, she still couldn't believe it had ever happened. If only she had known more, then maybe she would've found the voice to stop it. To say no. To choose otherwise.

Unable to bear the silence of the room anymore, Lorraine decided to move the conversation from the confession to one of a solution. "It's okay, Daddy." The words came out meek, barely audible, fighting to stay inside. "Dr. Harris told us about a maternity home—"

Mr. Delford stopped her. "It's *okay*?" he asked, drawing out the last word. He shook his head, not understanding what his daughter had just had the audacity to say to him. "It's *okay*?"

Betty reached for her husband's hand. Her touch startled him, quieting his questioning.

"That's not what I meant." Lorraine wished she had better prepared for this, thought it through more instead of haphazardly blurting it out. "I mean, it will be okay. This place will help." Lorraine pulled the brochure from her pocket and held it in the air.

"What's she talking about?" Mr. Delford asked his wife. "Where's Clint?"

"At school," Mrs. Delford replied.

"I know that much! But where is he in all of this?"

Lorraine spoke up. "He doesn't want anything to do with this." *With me*, she thought. She wished she could remove the ring and any trace of Clint, but as much as she tried, her fingers were too swollen to wiggle free of it. But a different reminder of Clint clung to her more.

At some point, the swelling would decrease and she could be free of the ring, though she'd never wiggle free of the baby who was half made up of Clint. No amount of effort or time could remove all traces. Not from her body, or her mind, and especially not her heart. But a combination of optimism, ignorance, and self-preservation prevented her from understanding that just then.

Mr. Delford slammed his hands on the table. He stood up and walked behind his chair. Lorraine wondered if he'd throw it across the room like her mother had done.

Lorraine tried to speak again, but her mother held up her hand, warned her to be quiet, to let Mr. Delford think for a minute.

"And who's this doctor?" he asked, still holding on to the chair, using it to keep him upright.

Betty responded, "He's a doctor I found." Mr. Delford's eyes grew wide. "Don't worry; he's on the other side of town. Listen, by now, I had no choice. I didn't find out all that long ago. With Clint and given how far along she is, I didn't have an option."

"And what's this home? How much is that going to cost?"

"Eugene," Betty began, "we have savings."

"For her college."

"And wedding. But now it will go to this."

Lorraine hadn't thought of money, but why would she? She had simply been searching for an answer to take all of this away. She hadn't thought of what it would cost. But hearing this now, she wanted to protest, to speak up, to save that money for college after all of this was done. She would rather stay hiding in her bedroom than go to the maternity home if she had to choose between it and college. She wanted to speak, to interject, but as she tried to tell them, her mother shot her a look, warning her again to not speak.

"But—" Lorraine tried to begin.

"No. Ma'am." Mrs. Delford warned.

Lorraine's shoulders slumped. As angry as she was at Clint, she still wished she could reach her foot under the table and tap his for comfort.

After a few minutes, Mr. Delford sat back down. No one spoke. No one moved. No steam curled off the meatloaf or green beans. All was still and silent until Eugene looked at his wife and reached his hand across the table to her. She met his hand with hers. They held on to each other, their eyes brimming with tears.

"What are we going to do?" he asked.

Betty shrugged her shoulders and said, "This is the only thing we can do. We'll send her away. Tell everyone she's gone to help Lois with the kids. You know everyone will believe it. The woman's always got her hands full, needs help with all those kids, especially now with the baby."

Lorraine watched her parents, feeling like an observer, an intruder.

"It wasn't supposed to be like this." Emotions choked Eugene's words so that he spoke with a whisper. "She had so much potential. Was going to be valedictorian."

"But I still can," Lorraine interrupted, interjecting herself back into the room. She waved the pamphlet in the air. "I can finish school here. Still graduate. Go to college in the fall."

Ignoring his daughter, Eugene released his wife's hand and sat back up in his chair. "It's all over."

"But—" Lorraine raised her voice, demanding they hear her. Her dream didn't have to die, if only they would listen to her. "After I get back—" she began to say.

"No," her father said, his tone low and even.

"But—"

Eugene's hand pounded the table again, clattering the forks on their plates, the serving spoon in the mashed potatoes, as he said, "You should've thought about that before you got yourself into this trouble. If Clint was man enough to clean up his mistake, then this would be a different conversation. But he's not. And you think Mecklenburg High is going to let you waltz back in to graduate, to still be head of the class, to give a speech at graduation as if you're a role model? No! They don't let girls like you do that!"

"Girls like"—the last word hurt too much to say, but it hurt even more to hear it come from her father's mouth—"me?"

Mr. Delford stared straight at her. He couldn't decide what emotion to express—anger, hurt, disappointment, embarrassment, shock—so he sat stone-still, barely blinking, hardly breathing. As Lorraine stood from the table and walked out of the room, he reached for the cold meatloaf and scooped a piece onto his plate. But he didn't take a bite. He put his elbows on the table and rested his forehead in his palms. He had been so hungry when he had gotten home, but he didn't seem to want to eat now. *How could this be happening?* he wondered. Wasn't it just the other day that she was showing him how high she could swing in the backyard, or he was teaching her to bait a hook, how to drive a manual transmission, or watching her stare up at the meteor shower? He'd had such hopes for her, that she would be different. But now, his little girl was one of them.

He left the table, made a phone call from his office, and walked out of the house without saying a word to Betty. She went to bed without him that night, but the smell woke her when he finally came home. She hoped he had simply taken up smoking again. But instead of asking, she turned to her nightstand, shook a sleeping pill into her hand, and escaped until the sun roused her in the morning.

# CHAPTER TEN

The new year came and went. One day rolled into the next, an endless amount of mundanity, a purgatory of Lorraine's own. Her parents carried on with their lives. Her father worked as usual, and her mother kept busy with housekeeping, volunteering, and organizing the Sunnymede Sisters as she always had. They had appearances to keep up, narratives to spin, images to uphold. They stood united in their refusal to allow their daughter's waywardness to destroy the status they had achieved.

All the while their daughter sat paused in her bedroom as one day melted into the next, a constant blur of inaction, other than her stomach continuing to grow. Each sunrise and sunset brought her closer to the day she would leave for the maternity home. After that, things would go back to normal. That's what they said. But she knew it would have to be a different kind of normal, one where she fought even harder to make her way to college.

Lorraine had mastered the ability to live without being noticed. She continued to obey her parents' rule that drapes must be drawn and lights not permitted, but the evening before she was scheduled to leave, she became too distracted to follow all of their rules.

Her parents had a meeting at church, so they tasked her with cleaning up after dinner, wiping the table clean, scrubbing out the roasting pan. When the dishes were done and the house was quiet, she could hear the hoots of two owls calling to each other. Lorraine grabbed her father's jacket from the coat-tree by the door, wrapped it around herself, and walked out the back door.

She breathed in the fresh air, picking up the scent of the pine trees on the other side of the fence. Goose pimples sprang up on her arms in response to both the delight of the smell and the coolness of the breeze. A gust blew across her face, sweeping her hair up and away. She hadn't thought to put shoes on—an unnecessary item when her territory existed within four walls with a roof above and carpeting below. She felt the grass beneath her, wiggling her toes so they could feel the blades again. She could hear the rusty chains of the swings groaning as they blew.

Lorraine walked to the swing set and took a seat, listening to the owls speak to each other, their hoots echoing through the woods on the other side of the fence. She wrapped her father's jacket around her, protecting herself from the chill as she swayed back and forth, closing her eyes and breathing in her surroundings. The night was a good one for stargazing.

She thought back to that night when she was five years old. When Lorraine looked for her father that evening to kiss him good night, she found him on the darkened back patio, rocking alone in the glider, watching the sky.

She skipped toward him asking, "What're you doing?"

"Watching the Tears of St. Lawrence."

"What?"

Lorraine had no idea what her father meant or why he sat alone in the backyard without the porch light on.

"Come here," he said, tapping the seat beside him. Lorraine plopped herself down on the glider, leaning in close, feeling the warmth of both his body and the humid August air. Mr. Delford wrapped his arm around her and pointed toward the sky.

"Watch."

Lorraine looked skyward. But then a mosquito tickled her arm, demanding her to swat away the nuisance.

"Did you see it?" her father asked.

"See what?"

"Look and be patient," he told her.

Lorraine wiggled and swatted as another mosquito attempted to land on her, but as her father tightened his arm around her shoulder, she calmed and stared into the night sky along with him.

The moon was barely a sliver, reminding her of a glowing fingernail in the sky. If she looked hard enough, she could see the outline of the full circle, a faint glowing that pulled her eye from the lit crescent. There wasn't enough of the moon showing to see the varying colorings, the grays and the creams, and the big, dark circle she would stare at when it was full. Her father had once explained that dark spot, Oceanus Procellarum or Ocean of Storms, he had called it. Some scientists believed an asteroid caused it, but they didn't know for sure. Perhaps once astronauts stood on the moon and examined it for themselves, they would have more answers.

Then, out of the corner of her eye, she saw it. Something move. Something flicker. A light shoot across the darkness, a tail burning out behind the bright speck.

"I saw it!" Lorraine bounced in her seat. "What was it?"

"A shooting star."

"Shooting star?"

"Yes! And there goes another one." His finger traced the light that glided just over the tops of the trees. "And another!"

They sat like that, together, pointing and watching and delighting in the meteor shower together until Mrs. Delford called Lorraine to bed.

---

Listening to the owls that cold January evening, Lorraine looked skyward. The St. Lawrence meteor shower had been months ago, around the same time as that consequential evening with Clint. She realized that it had been a few years since she and her father had watched the meteor shower together.

She thought of how, during those times together, her father would express amazement and awe at how even the moon had been carefully created and carved. He believed that God created everything in a week. All of creation made within six days, to be precise.

Alone on the swing that night, a pregnant Lorraine wondered what she had so many times before: How was that possible? Why would that be? Why would a God so big take so little time in making something so massive and extraordinary and endless? When she asked her father those questions, he simply said, "Because that's what God decided to do." That response satisfied her as a five-year-old, but the older she got, the more she began to wonder for herself.

A chill cut through Lorraine. She pulled the jacket tighter, her arms bumping against her stomach. She continued to rock back and forth as she wondered if she agreed with her father, if she believed the same as him, if maybe he was wrong.

Distracted by her thoughts, Lorraine didn't hear the first signs of his presence. It wasn't until he stepped on a dead branch that snapped under his weight that she realized she wasn't alone.

"Of all the places I thought you could be, the swing set wasn't one of them."

At first she startled. Gasped. Considered running to the house. But she knew the voice. She welcomed it. She wanted to jump the fence to embrace him, but her mind brought her back to reality. She tightened the jacket around her and looked in all directions to see if anyone else had noticed her.

"Alan!" Her voice filled with both excitement and uncertainty.

Alan stood on the other side of the picket fence, one hand huddled in the pocket of his leather jacket while the other brought a cigarette to his lips and inhaled.

"How are you, BB?" he asked.

"A bit chilled, to be honest."

"Well, you are barefoot."

Lorraine looked down at her feet and exhaled a chuckle of recognition. She wanted to ask what he was doing there, but she was afraid he'd ask the same of her, so she tried another question. "You're still smoking?"

"Guess the Old Man couldn't force that one out of me."

"I'd never seen Clint so sick," Lorraine recalled. "What was that? Two, three years ago?"

"Something like that," Alan said, sounding as if he wasn't in the mood to tell histories just then, didn't want to go further down memory lane to the time when his grandfather had caught him, Clint, and a few other neighborhood boys smoking. He forced them all to smoke an entire pack, one cigarette after another. All of the boys ended up sick, all of them swearing to never have another cigarette in their lives. Everyone except for Alan.

"I'm glad you're home," he said, preferring to talk about the present instead of the past. "I've missed you."

"Careful there." Lorraine tried to keep the conversation light. She didn't know exactly what her mother had told Alan that first morning Lorraine didn't need a ride to school, but since he trusted few adults, she doubted he believed it. "You're sounding sentimental."

Alan shrugged and asked, "You alright?"

They looked at each other in the darkness, the fence separating them, one standing at the edge of the woods, the other swaying barefoot on a swing. Just enough light shined from the moon so that Lorraine could see Alan's eyes as they held her gaze. She had a moment to decide how she'd proceed, what she would say, how much she trusted Alan, how much she trusted herself.

"Yeah," she said, deciding to continue the story her parents had woven. "Aunt Lois's has been crazy, you know, all those kids. I came home for a few days. Will be heading back soon. That's why you haven't seen… Why I'm not… Why I haven't been at—"

Alan exhaled a puff of smoke as he said, "It's okay, BB."

Neither spoke for a few minutes. Even the owls stayed quiet. Typically the silence didn't bother Lorraine, but she had spent enough time in solitude recently and she was forgetting how to be quiet with other people around. Plus, truth be told, she wanted to say something. She wanted to speak up. She knew the bargain she'd made with her parents, or the one they had informed her of. She had for the most part agreed to it, but Alan had already seen her, so what was the harm? She could say more. She could trust him. If there was anyone she could trust, it was him.

"I'm going to be going away," she said. She looked to the ground and rocked back and forth, not looking at Alan as she spoke. "For a while. A few months."

He took a long drag. Smoke curled and shifted as he exhaled and said, "I figured." While others may believe the Delfords' story, Alan knew in his gut that only one thing would keep Lorraine from her senior year of school. He didn't want to believe it, but finding her in the backyard that night, seeing her swollen face, even with the coat draped around her, she couldn't hide the truth from him. Damn Clint for doing this to her.

Alan didn't have it in him to crack a joke then. He didn't know if he could tease her or make her laugh or lighten the mood. Of all the girls, why did it have to be her?

Beams of headlights swept across the backyard, illuminating Alan's face for a mere moment, but long enough for Lorraine to see his eyes glistening. She had been expecting a joke, not sadness.

With no time to stall, Lorraine jumped from the swing, keeping the jacket closed around her belly, knowing that the light had come from her parents' headlights as they turned into the driveway.

"I've got to go," she said.

Before she could sprint away too quickly, she heard Alan say, "I'll be here when you come back."

She made it into the house before the car was fully in park. She hung her father's jacket on the coatrack and ran up the stairs, escaping visibility as they walked in the door. Had either of them checked on her, they might've asked why she was out of breath, her cheeks red, her hair windblown. But checking in wasn't part of the routine anymore.

With the moonlight spilling into her room that night,

Lorraine thought about Alan and their conversation. She had missed him more than she had realized. She thought back to that look in his eyes. It wasn't just sadness. It was empathy, something that no one else had offered her those last few months. And then his promise to be there for her. Perhaps she had underestimated Alan, as well. She was probably his closest friend, but she still hadn't understood his deep loyalty until the moment she needed it most.

Then, she thought about the Tears of St. Lawrence. The first time she had sat beside Mr. Delford and watched the stars shoot across the black void overhead, she had delighted in the light show. She had never seen such movement and streaks. The stars had always remained steady and true. The North Star always in the same place at the same time, always just as it should be.

But the night her father used the term *shooting star*, a new notion shook her five-year-old body.

*Stars can shoot?*

*They can fall?*

*They can go from twinkling to nonexistent?*

*If it could happen to those stars, could it also happen to this blue planet that sustained them?*

In the weeks alone in her room, hidden away from the life she had known, Lorraine felt like a shooting star, falling from grace, plummeting toward nonexistence. She knew that feeling. She had experienced it in the pond the afternoon she nearly drowned, when she sank to the bottom, and the depths of the water darkened the daylight. And like that afternoon, she was starting to realize that if she was going to survive, she was going to have to save herself.

# CHAPTER ELEVEN

The day Lorraine Delford went away, a thin layer of snow covered the road, sidewalk, and trees. It wasn't a lot of snow, but it was enough to provide a thin coating. On a typical day like this, she would've rushed outside to hold it, taste it, roll around in it before the sun rose and melted it away. Southern snow days didn't last long. But one thing southern snow days did do was quiet the world of typical goings-on. Work stopped, grocery store runs waited for another time, golf courses were closed, and extra cups of hot chocolate were sipped.

Her mother didn't have hot chocolate waiting for Lorraine at the breakfast table that morning of departure. Instead, there was a glass of orange juice and a few pieces of cinnamon-sugar toast. Her mother had not increased Lorraine's food portions during this time. After all, there was no use in putting on too much weight. She'd need to get back to her regular figure quickly.

After breakfast, Lorraine grabbed the bag she had packed the night before and walked out the garage door. The car was not warming in the driveway as it usually would be on a cold morning like that one. It was still in the garage, the engine not yet running, the garage door still shut tight. Lorraine began to walk to the passenger side of the car to get into the front seat, but her dad said, "Back seat. On the floor."

Lorraine stopped and looked at her parents. They had kept her in hiding inside their home, but in the car? On the floor? With a cantaloupe for a stomach?

"At least until we get out of town," he said.

Lorraine squeezed between the lawn mower and the car, trying to walk her way through the narrow opening. She pulled the car door open, but it had little room to move.

"Can't you back it out? I can barely get in."

"The sun's nearly up. Do you know how many neighbors might be outside grabbing their newspapers right now?"

Lorraine took a breath in and hunched her shoulders forward, hoping that would cause her stomach to go inward enough for her to squeeze through the opening. Both her back and front sides brushed against the door opening as she pushed her way into the back seat. Her mother motioned for her to get down on the floor as she said goodbye to her husband with a kiss. A moment later Mr. Delford opened the garage door, got into the driver's seat, started the engine, and backed the car out of the driveway. Lorraine could only see the snow-covered tree limbs through the windows and the first colors of morning light starting to brighten the sky. She couldn't see if her mother was standing on the steps in the garage waving at them as they left, but she was pretty sure she wasn't.

Lorraine could sense when they were leaving the neighborhood, heading by the shopping center and along the highway. Her father drove slower that morning, thanks to the snow still covering the roads. She wondered if there was much traffic but doubted many others had ventured out yet that morning. From the floorboards of the back seat, she watched the snow-outlined trees flash by, one after another.

By the time her father told her she could sit up in the back seat, the sun had begun to shine and the wintry accumulation had already started dropping off the tree branches and melting off the roadways. Any signs of snow that had been there that morning were melting away into a different form so that those who hadn't seen it first thing that morning wouldn't have even known it existed.

---

They drove for a few hours before they arrived at the home for unwed mothers. Lorraine took in her surroundings as they turned down the long drive lined with massive, wildly branching live oaks on both sides. The trees reached and twisted, covering the path as if hugging and protecting a secret place, one that came into view as the drive curved into a circle and pointed its visitor back to the road.

As Mr. Delford pulled up next to the curb and parked the car, Lorraine looked out the window at the two-story brick mansion that she had seen in the brochure. It both impressed and fright-ened her. The perfectly lined-up windows—all symmetrical, all the same—gave it an appearance of order, an even appeal, but the cold brick and largely intrusive front porch added a layer of forboding. Typically, southern porches welcomed conversation over slow sips of cold drinks, but this porch darkened the front of the house, hiding the front door from view, creating a cave to the entrance of the mansion.

A woman, clipboard in hand, stood at the top of the stairs where the afternoon sunlight landed. Her gray wool skirt hung to the middle of her shins, revealing a small portion of her white stockings beneath. A white turtleneck was layered beneath her V-necked sweater, the gray color slightly lighter than that of her skirt. Both tops were tucked in with a black belt securing everything in place. Her brown hair was pulled back in a tight ponytail, except for her bangs, which hung in one, long curl high across her forehead.

The woman squinted and pushed up her silver-rimmed, cat's-eye glasses, positioning them higher on her nose. As Lorraine got out of the car and walked up the stairs, she noticed small rhinestones lining the tops of the rims, a stark contrast to the woman's otherwise drab appearance.

"Mr. Delford, I'm Miss Mahoney, the social worker and resident housemother here." She spoke with purpose in an even tone meant to relay information, not pleasantries. "I spoke with Mrs. Delford by phone?"

The two shook hands, though neither bothered to say it was nice to meet the other one. Nor did anyone turn their attention directly to Lorraine.

"That's her only bag?" Miss Mahoney asked, while making a note on her clipboard.

"Yes."

"You are welcome to come inside, Mr. Delford, or you can choose to leave us now. Whichever you prefer."

Trying to distract herself from the nervousness that tightened her stomach, Lorraine wondered what was on the other side of the large wooden doors. The windows were positioned high on the door to not give away any hint of what was going on in the interior of the building. Lorraine imagined that at some point in this building's history, those doors had opened to reveal a party where neighbors and guests gathered in their best dresses and suits to dance and celebrate. *How many years ago must that have been?* she wondered.

"I believe you can get her settled," her father responded.

"Certainly. I'll give you a minute?" Miss Mahoney said before she pushed against the wooden door. As she walked inside, Lorraine strained to view the entry and see who else was inside, but all she saw was emptiness before the door creaked closed.

Mr. Delford lifted his hat and turned to his daughter without making eye contact.

"Just do as they say." His voice cracked, but he did not look at his daughter.

Lorraine nodded, but he didn't see her. She wondered if they would've felt as nervous had he been dropping her off at college, her beaming with excitement ready to settle into her dorm room while he struggled in a moment he hadn't expected to be quite so bittersweet. In the other version of her life, she would have embarked on a new adventure away from home in a different town. She knew she didn't have too many more dinners around the table with her parents. She knew she didn't have many more nights watching *The Dick Van Dyke Show* with her father. But she never imagined that the break would come so quickly, so completely.

Mr. Delford shifted his feet, the porch planks moaning beneath him. He rolled the brim of his hat in his hand. Lorraine noticed new laugh lines along the sides of his eyes, though she doubted laughter had caused them. His salt-and-pepper hair showed more salt than pepper.

When her father didn't speak, Lorraine said, "I will, Daddy." She meant what she said, at least in that moment she did. But her father still wouldn't look at her. Desperate to earn back his respect, she reached out and touched his arm, offering him comfort. "It'll be over soon."

Mr. Delford finally looked at his daughter. She had no way of knowing. She thought those were the words he needed to hear, and maybe she did believe them for herself. If only she had listened to them. If only she hadn't done any of this, then so many other things would be different.

Her father put his hat on his head and reached into his pocket for his keys. He didn't hug her. He didn't kiss her. He didn't touch her at all as he stepped past her and walked down the stairs to his car. She wanted to chase after him. To hop into the car and leave along with him. At the very least, she wanted to hug him, hold on to him, have him reassure her that this would all be over soon enough.

But instead, she stood at the edge of the porch and yelled, "Daddy!" He paused but didn't turn around. She had told herself that morning to be strong. To put one foot in front of the other and do what was necessary, but as she stood alone at the precipice of this strange place, she couldn't be brave. The emotions she had tried to ignore flooded her body, sending a swell of fat tears that began to pool heavily at the brims of her eyelids. "I'm sorry!" she yelled.

Her father finally turned to look at her. She wiped away the tears, hoping he didn't see them. She stood ready to run down the stairs and leave if he invited her to. Instead, he looked at the girl he had taught to ride a bike, the one he had comforted when she had lost balance and skinned her knee. He saw a girl he no longer recognized. Hadn't he taught her to listen and obey?

Didn't she know that they parented her for her own good, so she could be different? He wondered what more he could've done to prevent them from being in this predicament. He wanted to love her—surely he still did—but this situation made it all so much more complicated.

With a tone as cold as that snowy morning had been, he looked into her tear-heavy eyes and said, "It's too late for that."

Lorraine's body had been poised to leave but stayed rooted in its place and began to tremble. If her father had taught her anything over the years, it was to stop emotions from showing. While her heart cried out to her to ignore him and run to him, her gut responded with the obedience it had learned over seventeen years. She wanted to scream, but instead she wiped the snot and the tears from her face. She stood tall, her legs shaky despite her best efforts to remain still, as her father started the car and pulled away without even waving or looking back.

Hearing the engine start up, Miss Mahoney opened the door to the maternity home and ushered the girl inside. Lorraine distracted herself by taking in her new surroundings, including the grand staircase that started on both sides of the foyer and joined together in a balcony above her. She looked up at the chandelier that hung in the entrance, that somehow looked dim despite its crystal embellishments. But it was the smell that she most noticed. She couldn't identify it. It wasn't a smell of home or even cleanliness. It had an emptiness to it, a sterile quality, not fragrant and inviting. It got caught in her throat and made her cough, which only made her inhale the scent even more.

"As I said, I'm the housemother," Miss Mahoney reiterated as she turned to the right and began climbing the stairs. "We have a few rules for your stay," she continued, expecting Lorraine to keep up. She held one finger in the air. "First, don't share personal information. Use first names only. Don't mention your hometown, school, none of that. Second"—she flipped up another finger—"you're not here to make friends, and third"—another finger shot up—"forget this ever happened."

*Nothing personal?*

*Don't make friends?*

*Forget this ever happened?*

Lorraine's legs felt like lead as she took one step after another, trying to absorb that information, make sense of the rules, understand why those would be so essential for the next three months—or less, hopefully, if things started early. She knew that place was there for medical care, but she didn't understand why there would be rules dictating friendship.

They reached the second story as Miss Mahoney finished with the rules and showed her to one of the six bedrooms. "Choose whichever empty bed you want. Supper's at five. Lights out at eight. I'll see you in the morning. We can discuss plans."

Miss Mahoney's ponytail swung and swayed as she turned and left the room. Lorraine listened to the *clip-clop* of the woman's shoes walking back down the hall, the same way they had come. Out of the four beds, two looked to already be claimed. She could choose the bed closest to the doorway or nearest the window. She chose the one with the view.

She walked to the bed, put down her overnight bag, and plopped onto the mattress. It sprung back, wobbling until it adjusted to her weight. She looked out the window, thinking that maybe she'd see the taillights of her father's car, perhaps stalled in the driveway, perhaps still waiting for her to come back home, but all she could see were the winding, twisting branches of the live oaks hovering over the drive and blue lighting up the sky above.

She reached for her bag, her mattress again moving on the shaky frame. She unzipped the satchel and pulled out her only friend: Brown Bear, the stuffed bear her father had won for her at the county fair years ago. The bear slept with her for years after that, always there to comfort her, laugh at her jokes, stargaze alongside her. But at some point a few years back, she no longer reached for him at bedtime and eventually he got moved into the closet, lost and forgotten until she discovered him under some shoes and an old raincoat a few weeks ago. She began sleeping with him again, and when her mother told her to pack a bag, she placed him on top, careful not to catch his fur in the zipper.

Together in this new place, Lorraine gripped Brown Bear and whispered, "Looks like you're all I've got."

Before the sting of tears could even start, she felt a flip. A move. A thrust from inside herself. She let go of her bear and put her hand on her stomach, pushing where she'd felt the movement.

And then another twitch happened.

Lorraine sat on the bouncy bed in this foreign place, alone in a room with an odd smell, but she didn't notice any of it at that moment. She put both hands firmly on her belly. She held her breath until she felt movement again. What a strange feeling, a sort of muscle spasm from deep inside her. She kept her hands on her stomach, waiting for the next one. After a few more twitches, the movements stopped. So, she reached for Brown Bear, snuggled him close, and let her exhaustion sweep her into sleep so she could forgot for a moment why she was there.

# CHAPTER TWELVE

As Lorraine wrapped her body around Brown Bear and drifted off to nap in this new place, in another town, Clint sat at the counter, waiting to catch Susan's attention. He didn't need coffee that late in the afternoon, but he used the drink as an opportunity to talk with her, and he knew that she had more time to chat before the dinner rush.

He'd thought about asking her out for a while, since things had ended with Lorraine, but he hadn't yet worked up the nerve. He realized he hadn't had to put himself out there like that since, well, years ago. There had also been the girl at the dance that his roommate had set him up with, but no asking was involved since his friend walked the girl over to him, made the introduction, and then suggested they dance. While Clint had enjoyed her company that evening, nothing went beyond that one night.

Things were different with Susan. He knew her well enough by that point, but he still didn't know what she would say. He wondered whether he'd have to find a different diner to hang out at if she turned him down. Or maybe he'd spend more time around the dorm. The guys had been asking about him, but ever since Thanksgiving, he couldn't get quite as excited over their shenanigans as he had before.

"Got another exam coming up?" Susan asked as she poured

him a cup of coffee without asking what he wanted. She stopped pouring with enough space left for him to add the cream and sugar.

"Not this week," he said. He held her gaze for a few seconds before he looked down. He stirred so that the cream morphed into light swirls that twisted and twirled as they shifted and incorporated into the drink.

On the way over, he had rehearsed the words he would say, but with her standing in front of him, her long, thick eyelashes batting with each blink, he couldn't remember what he had settled on. Instead he asked, "Do you like movies?"

Susan giggled and told him of course. Her laugh always made him smile and put him at ease. He took a deep breath, and before he could think about it any longer, he said, "Want to go to the Saturday matinee?"

He didn't say what was showing and she didn't ask. Honestly, neither one of them really cared. All they wanted was a chance to be together without a counter between them.

Susan told him she'd love to before the bells on the diner door clanged with the arrival of a family seeking a late lunch. Before she walked away to greet her new customers, she and Clint worked out the details. He hadn't felt such a rush of anticipation in a long time. He placed his hand over hers as he said a quick goodbye. He hadn't taken a drink of his coffee, but he figured it was best that he leave sooner rather than later, giving himself less time to make a fool of himself before their first date.

As Lorraine woke from her nap on the strange bed in a strange place in a strange town, Clint pulled on his coat and walked out of the diner. He didn't feel the cold. He didn't zip up his jacket.

He walked down the street smiling as he thought of Susan and Saturday and things to come.

---

The sun had begun to set by the time Lorraine woke. She hadn't planned to nap. She didn't even think she could in such a strange place, but she was glad she had, until she saw the time on the alarm clock across the room. She walked over to the nightstand to get a better look, hoping she had misread it. She hadn't. She had been told that dinner would be served at five o'clock and she had missed the beginning by two minutes.

As much as she knew she should hurry to the dining room, she took a moment to examine a strip of pictures on the nightstand. Lorraine picked up the frameless photos, all four still connected. She remembered how she and Clint had huddled together in the booth at the fair, smiled as the camera flashed, and then waited for the images to come spitting out the side of the booth. They had divided the photos among them. Hers were still tucked inside the mirror of her vanity.

Lorraine held the photo strip and looked at the boy and girl who sat close together, smiling brightly. They seemed to be about her own age, as happy as she and Clint had been. The girl had wild hair of a color Lorraine couldn't identify in the grayscale image, but she noticed how one front tooth overlapped the other, as if hugging it tightly. The clock added another number, so Lorraine put the photos back in place. Her stomach rumbled, angry that it had missed out on lunch. But her bladder cried louder.

As she walked out of her room, she looked around the second-floor landing. On each side were six equal doors, all presumably leading to bedrooms much like the one she had just exited. Opposite the staircase were two doors: one small and to the side, and the other larger and with the sign "Restroom" above it. She quickly waddled to the bathroom, relieved to reduce the pressure. Her stomach bumped against the sink when she turned off the water from the faucet.

She thought she heard voices off in the distance, but before following the sound, she looked in the mirror and repositioned her hair, smoothing it as best she could without a brush. She ran her fingers over her eyebrows, knowing that she'd soon be making a first impression or at least assuming that would be the case during supper. She widened her eyes and ran her fingers along her eyelashes, pulling them upward, hoping that motion could suffice for a lack of mascara. After she groomed as much as possible with only her hands, she took a final look in the mirror, straightened her dress, and walked out of the restroom.

When Lorraine came to the staircase, she paused for a moment, looking past the chandelier to the windows behind it. No window coverings hid the outside world from her, but the branching oak trees shielded the neighbors from seeing the home's inhabitants. She stopped and looked for a moment. The skies had already darkened, looking more navy than the cerulean blue she often saw during the early evening hour on the East Coast. The lampposts along the drive flickered on, but the trees crowded them so that only a small amount of warm glow could be seen. She tried to make out the street and neighborhood houses they had driven by on their way in, but the trees blocked any view of local life.

She held on to the wooden banister and took the stairs

slowly, looking again at the chandelier, taking in the trim work that defined shapes and symmetry from the floor to the ceiling, imagining for a moment what it would be like to walk down that staircase in her prom or wedding dress with her family waiting in anticipation and awe below. Though Lorraine knew nothing of the mansion's history, she assumed it had been repurposed over the years, once meticulously crafted, now showing cracks in its plaster ceiling, gashes in the woodwork, and paint peeling from the walls. She could still sense the beauty beneath the surface, even if the building was no longer loved and cared for as it once had been.

Lorraine continued down the stairs and followed the sound of dishes clinking and the aroma of food. She was the last to arrive in the dining room. With the room full of girls came a chorus of talk. Voices flooded the space, bouncing off the walls and the ceiling. It had been months since she had heard so much conversation.

The group of girls—maybe twenty or so—looked to be about her age, some sitting around various tables with small metal trays topped with a red apple, a mound of mashed potatoes, and something that resembled a slice of turkey covered in gravy. No one gave her directions, but she saw the line of girls waiting to receive their meals before finding a table. All of them had stomachs shaped like hers.

The scene, the sounds, the smells all reminded Lorraine of her high school lunch hour. She paused for a moment, closed her eyes, and breathed it all in. She hadn't realized how much she had missed being a part of a community until then.

But unlike in her high school cafeteria, she had no idea who any of these people were. Nor did she know where she was going to sit. As she stood in line, she watched the tables fill, the girls seeming to know exactly where they should go as they took their trays and flitted off. Lorraine started looking around, coming up with a plan. She would find a table with a girl she thought looked nice and decide that she'd go sit there, but then another girl would beat her to it. So, she'd mentally choose another chair. This game went on and on until she reached the front of the line. She took her tray and turned to the room, seeking a welcoming face or at least an empty chair. That's when she saw the arm raise, the hand wave, and the girl jump up from the table.

"Hi! Hello! Over here! Here's a seat!"

The girl's long, red curls bobbed as she waved, and she didn't stop waving until Lorraine arrived at the table.

"Here! Sit here! Beside me!" Lorraine pulled out the chair and sat down. "Are you our new roommate?"

"I think, maybe." Lorraine had no idea who she was sharing a room with, but this girl did resemble the one in the pictures. Her cheeks were a bit fuller now, but her hugging front teeth looked the same. By looks alone, Lorraine guessed they were close to the same age, but something about her demeanor made her appear younger.

"Oh, I hope so! Miss Mahoney said a new girl was coming today, and I was hoping we'd get another roommate. We've had an extra bed for a bit now. I mean after what happened with Janet and all—"

"Mirabelle!" the girl across the table from her snapped. "Let her sit down." The girl's dark hair draped her cheeks, hiding most of her face but allowing enough space for Lorraine to see her roll her eyes. Matter-of-factly, she continued, "She gets excited about new people."

Lorraine finally sat down, scooted her chair in to the table, and barely had her napkin spread across her lap before the excited girl continued. "I'm Mirabelle and this is Denise. Who are you?"

"Lorraine Del—"

"Nope," the quieter girl interrupted. "Only first names."

"Oh," Lorraine paused. "I forgot."

Mirabelle pushed forward. "That's okay. Sometimes I forget. Or I used to. When I first got here. Guess now I'm just used to it. I don't know. It's so nice to meet you," Mirabelle said as Denise offered a nod and a small wave before going back to her meal. Mirabelle took a few bites of food between words, but soon she pushed her tray back from the edge of the table and took up a crochet hook.

Lorraine reached for her spoon and noticed her hand shaking. She hadn't expected to be nervous about meeting new people, but something about Denise made her feel uncomfortable, as if she needed to make the right first impression. On the other hand, Mirabelle seemed warm and inviting. She decided to put her attention there.

"What are you working on?" Lorraine asked.

"A blanket. Do you like it? I couldn't decide on pink or blue. I thought about going with yellow, but then I knew, something told me and I just knew. I felt it. Do you know what I mean? So, I had started on the yellow, but then when I felt it, well, I just unraveled that yellow and took up the pink instead. Can you believe I didn't even know how to crochet before I came here? Mrs. Belmont meant for us to make dishrags, but there's no fun in that. This is much better. Much bigger. I've been working on this since I arrived. It's growing every day. I hope I get it done in time."

Mirabelle held up the blanket. She had to stand for Lorraine to see the full size of it. She held it just below her nose and the length of it fell to below her stomach, protruding out and around her bump.

"You just learned how to do that?" Lorraine asked, feeling a bit more at ease, her hand no longer shaking as she ate her supper.

"Yeah. When I got here. Do you think she'll like it?"

Mirabelle didn't explain who "she" was, but they all knew. And judging by the size of Mirabelle's belly, she was a few weeks farther along than Lorraine, a bit closer to going home and getting on with her life.

"It's beautiful. She'll love it."

Mirabelle's hands worked quickly as the girls talked through the rest of supper. She told Lorraine she'd answer any questions she had, but the stories tumbled out one right after another in such a way that Lorraine hardly had time to ask anything at all. But really the ramblings were more observations than stories themselves. While Lorraine wanted to better understand this home and these new people, Mirabelle gabbed on about how she had never met someone named Lorraine before, how she found the hardest part of crocheting being the constant counting, how she was thinking about growing out her bangs, how she misses her cat and hates turkey ever since her mother made her catch her favorite one for their Christmas meal. Lorraine sat and listened to the girl, devouring every bite of her dinner. She hadn't realized how hungry she had been.

After they finished eating and washing up their own dishes and wiping down their tables, the girls had less than two hours before lights out.

"Do you want to watch television?" Mirabelle asked. "We have a television in the common room. I'll show you if you'd like. Do you know the room? It's where we meet with Mrs. Belmont— she's the one who taught me to crochet! Well, Mrs. Belmont calls it the salon, but no one else does. I guess she likes to use fancy words like that. But everyone else says the common room. I think that's what it says on the sign by the door. Have you seen the room? The big one. With the tables? And the TV? Just across the hall there." She paused long enough to point.

Denise used the momentary pause in Mirabelle's quick flurry to offer a different idea. "Maybe she'd like to get settled."

Lorraine wasn't sure she needed to get settled, but heading to the room sounded like a better option than the common room full of new faces. "Actually, getting settled sounds good."

"Oh! Good! Yes! Let's go back to our room!"

With that Mirabelle skipped into the foyer. As they came to the staircase, she chose the stairs to the right of the front door, while Denise went to the left.

"Denise!" Mirabelle warned. "You know you're not supposed to."

"Who's here to stop me?" she asked as she climbed the stairs and got to the landing before Mirabelle did.

Mirabelle answered Lorraine's question before she could even ask it, "Miss Mahoney says there's a right way and a wrong way for all things. The right way to go up the stairs is this side. The right way to go down is that side."

It seemed that perhaps Miss Mahoney had more than three rules.

Lorraine was winded by the time they reached the top, and even though the other girls' stomachs were bigger than her own, they were not as out of breath as she was.

"Miss Mahoney says the exercise is good for us, for what's to come."

"It's payback," Denise said just loud enough for Lorraine to hear.

"Payback?" Lorraine asked.

"Oh, Denise." Mirabelle turned to Lorraine and said, "She doesn't mean that."

"For our moral failings," Denise said, ignoring Mirabelle, her voice void of expression as if Mirabelle had claimed all the excitement available.

Mirabelle was the first to walk into the room, but she stopped suddenly and with a gasp. "You don't want that bed," she said.

"Why?" Lorraine wondered what could be wrong with the bed. It had seemed perfectly fine to her, and Miss Mahoney had said she could choose for herself.

Denise pushed past her and also paused before saying, "It's fine. She can take whichever bed she wants."

Mirabelle turned to Denise and lowered her voice, as if trying to not let Lorraine overhear, "But that was Janet's bed."

"There's nothing wrong with it."

"But what if it happens to her, too?"

"What happened?" Lorraine asked, wanting to know who Janet was and what this girl had to do with her bed and Mirabelle's concern, but her roommates didn't answer her question.

"We've talked about being superstitious," Denise said before turning back to Lorraine. "Either bed is fine. I don't blame you for wanting the one closer to the window."

Lorraine wanted to know what had happened. All of this talking amongst themselves reminded her that she was the new girl and she had a lot to learn. "Is there something wrong with the bed?"

"No," Denise said, waving off Lorraine. Mirabelle squeezed her lips together as if trying to stop words from bursting out of her. "It's fine. Mirabelle has a way of getting worked up about things."

The redhead smiled, tilted her head to the side, and said, "I do." Then she went on to tell Lorraine all about the morning and evening routines, the chores they were expected to do during the day, and the weekly trips to town. The girl talked until the lights clicked off. Lorraine still didn't get the information she wanted, but she figured she had plenty of time.

That night, Mirabelle was the first to fall asleep, but even in her sleep, her chatter continued. It was a quiet mumbling, almost a giggle at times, while Denise fell into low, rhythmic breathing. The window shades were rolled high to the ceiling, too high to reach without standing on the windowsill and balancing on tiptoes, though rounded stomachs stopped that from being a possibility.

Lorraine didn't mind the shades being open. As tired as she was, she couldn't fall asleep, so she looked at the night sky. She searched for stars but only saw a blockade of clouds reflecting hues of orange thanks to the streetlamps. She longed to see what was hiding behind the cloud covering. She tried not to think too much about this new place, about Miss Mahoney and other possible rules to come, about the girl Janet and whatever had happened to her.

That night, Clint lay in his own bed a few hundred miles away. Neither of them knew where the other one was. Only one of them thought of the other. Clint drifted off to sleep with a smile, anticipating his date to come, while Lorraine realized that she had somehow learned to cry silently in the dark so she wouldn't wake her roommates.

# CHAPTER THIRTEEN

Miss Mahoney shuffled papers around her desk as she waited for the new girl to show up. She should be thankful for the girl's arrival and the chance to fill another bed and another set of waiting arms. Just the other day, she listened to a woman at church tell her of her family troubles. Hidden in the shadows of the church hall during coffee hour, the woman whispered her anxiety, longing for a baby of her own, angry with God for all these reckless girls who seemed to so easily manage what this woman and her husband couldn't. She didn't use those words, but by now Miss Mahoney had seen enough desperation in the eyes of wives to know the truth lurking beneath the muttered heartaches.

Miss Mahoney didn't understand it either. But she had long since stopped asking why these girls in her maternity home, and others like it, could accomplish what good, committed couples couldn't. She consoled herself with the notion that when God closes a door, He opens a window. And she was happy to help pry open that window and let the sweet breeze in for those wives who wanted desperately to become the mothers they deserved to be.

It seemed that this new girl's placement would be an easy one, much easier than the ones who still required convincing. Given this girl's upbringing and education, Miss Mahoney already knew multiple families who would scoop up the baby in a heartbeat.

Of course, she was getting ahead of herself. First she needed to go through the motions. She had to start the conversation, make the girl feel like she was in control, give her the option without mentioning other choices. After her multiple years as a housemother and with as many girls as she had overseen, she knew the routine. Plus, the girls with the most urgent and adamant parents were typically the easiest to make conform. If the tone of the mother's voice on the other end of the phone was any indication, this would be just such a case.

Even with a bright sun filling her office with natural light, Miss Mahoney had struggled to wake that morning. As she sat at her desk, the steam swirled high and thick off the top of her coffee. She knew she should give it time to cool, but she couldn't wait any longer. She held the drink to her lips and blew, but it burned the tip of her tongue. As she reacted, her hand shook so that a few drops spilled from the cup and onto the folder on top of a pile of papers.

Miss Mahoney swiped at the mess and then wiped her hand on her skirt. She waved the folder in the air to speed up drying. In the flurry of the cleanup, she didn't hear the first knock at her door. Though she had left the door open by a few inches, Lorraine didn't dare enter without first being invited. She stood in the hallway, trying not to peek as she waited for the invitation, but the movement of the folder being waved in the air caught her eye. She knocked again.

"Come in," Miss Mahoney called. She straightened a few stacks and repositioned herself in her chair as Lorraine walked in. "You're late," she said without looking up.

"I'm sorry. I didn't know where to go." As with supper the

night before, she knew what time she needed to arrive, but no one told her how to get there. Thankfully, Mirabelle had finally pointed the way for her after breakfast.

She stood between Miss Mahoney's desk and a chair that looked like it had been dropped off at a rummage sale instead of being tossed to the curb. Lorraine waited to be invited to sit down.

Miss Mahoney looked up from the papers long enough to tell her to have a seat. She didn't offer any other words or instructions for a few minutes as she read the documents in the coffee-stained file folder. Rays of sunlight poured through the window behind Miss Mahoney. Those first rays had woken Lorraine that morning as they spilled in through the unobstructed window and roused her awake. She hadn't wanted to wake up then. She hadn't gotten much sleep thanks to the bounce of her mattress, Denise's snoring, and all the other sounds and silences of the home. Once the sun rose, she couldn't coax herself back to sleep. Instead she rested quietly, gazing out the window until she heard her roommates begin to stir.

The social worker continued to read the pages in front of her. Lorraine wondered what they said, assuming they had to do with her. She wondered what information this woman had collected and where it came from. Her mother? Probably. The doctor? Maybe. Lorraine sat up tall, leaned forward, and tried squinting to see if she could make out any of the words, but she couldn't. So, while she waited, she busied herself by looking around the stacks of papers, folders, and books covering every inch of the desk. She wondered how the woman could find anything. She looked around the small office, a den full of dark furniture, bookshelves, and filing cabinets. That closet of a room in the corner of a mansion was so crammed that she wasn't sure she would even be able to squeeze her body through the space alongside the desk to sit where Miss Mahoney sat.

Lorraine looked out the window. She could see two cardinals— one red and one brown—resting on a branch. A mister and a missus, she assumed, patiently waiting for a squirrel to leave the bird feeder, so they could get some seed for themselves. She watched the female cardinal perch on the azalea on the front lawn of the home. The green leaves and pink blooms would soon enough be returning, but for now the bush was a monotone earth color. The bird's brown body blended with the branches of the bush. *Why were the female birds not as beautiful as the males?* she wondered. She knew the brown existed for protection and camouflage, but she still wondered if that female ever felt a twinge of jealousy when she looked at her partner's radiant red feathers.

Miss Mahoney finally spoke. "You're twenty-eight weeks. Due April 25. No health risks. Seventeen years old and planned to go to college?"

Lorraine flinched. Hearing herself reported on in such a technical way was one thing, but the past tense of the final bit of information bothered her most. "Yes, that's correct. And, I *plan* to go to college."

Miss Mahoney looked up from the papers, making eye contact with Lorraine from over the top of her rhinestone glasses. The night before, Lorraine had guessed this woman to be older than her mother, but as she looked more closely, she didn't see the signs and wrinkles she had come to expect from a woman nearly forty years old. Her hair didn't yet show any streaks of white or gray. Sure, she could've colored it, but judging by her choice of style, Lorraine doubted that Miss Mahoney was the type to spend much time on fixing herself up in such a way.

Lorraine held the woman's gaze, waiting for her to ask another question or give her some bit of information. With each second of silence, she wondered if she should say something. Finally, she started, "That's why I'm glad to be—"

Before she could finish, Miss Mahoney's head whipped to the side. Something out the window to her left caught her attention. She swiveled her chair, her ponytail flinging sideways with the motion. She lunged at the window and banged upon it, her open hand smacking the glass.

"Git, squirrel, git!" Lorraine jumped as Miss Mahoney again yelled at the "filthy rodent!" through the glass before sitting down and slowly pivoting back to face Lorraine. "Go on?" the woman said, as if she had been conversing the entire time.

"Uh," Lorraine stammered—her mother wouldn't have been happy about the stammering—trying to figure out what to go on about. "That's why I'm glad to be here. Where you can help. So, I can finish high school, go on to college, study science, and so on." Words streamed out of her, while another part of her mind waited for Miss Mahoney to catch sight of another squirrel that needed reprimanding.

Instead, Miss Mahoney reclined and repositioned her glasses before looking down at the papers inside the folder. Lorraine watched the cardinals continue to hop from azalea bush to tree as she considered breaking the silence with more information, more clarity, but before she could continue, Miss Mahoney pursed her lips and squinted her eyes. "Yes, well, we are here to help?"

Her voice lilted up as if asking a question, as if giving the girl something to respond to, making her feel like part of the process. But Miss Mahoney didn't need collaboration from any of them. All she needed was compliance.

Lorraine heard her statement as a question. She tried to think of a response, but before she could say anything, Miss Mahoney leaned toward Lorraine, lowering her voice as if she had an important secret to share. "We know that mistakes happen, but we're here to help our girls get through those mistakes, help them get on with their lives."

Lorraine eased into the back of her chair, her muscles and breath both relaxing as she felt confident about exactly what the brochure had promised: a good beginning. For the first time in months, she began to feel that she had found a way through this trouble.

Miss Mahoney picked up on the body language; she loved the easy cases. With the best tone of care and comfort she could muster, she said, "We help lighten the burden. We give you a way for this short time, this hiccup, to stay in the past as you figure out your future. Is that what you'd like?"

Lorraine couldn't nod her head quickly enough. Finally, this woman—who once again banged against the window, telling another squirrel to "git"—could help.

As Miss Mahoney sat back down, she continued. "I'm so glad that we agree on this. So, all I need is for you to sign this paper right here." The housemother scooted a piece of paper across the desk.

Lorraine looked at the form, unable to avoid reading the words written large across the top: Release for Relinquishment of Parental Rights. At the bottom, she saw a line with an X drawn at the beginning. This form was somehow what was going to save her. She wanted to sign it quickly, but her stomach tightened, uncertain of what it all really meant.

"Your name on the first line. Date on the second." Miss Mahoney held out a pen.

"What is this?" Lorraine asked as she took the pen.

"Oh," Miss Mahoney shrugged her shoulders and continued, "it's just a formality." Lorraine stared at the paper. "You know, consent for treatment. Whatever's necessary. It's okay. Every girl signs this when they come here."

Lorraine looked at Miss Mahoney. She studied the woman's brown eyes, so deep in color that the irises blended with the pupils, nearly indistinguishable from each other. Miss Mahoney focused on the girl, on keeping her gaze soft, on not being the first to drop eye contact, on breathing deeply despite her desire to tell the girl to sign the damn paper already.

"Relinquishment," Lorraine read. "That means I'm agreeing to give up the baby?"

Miss Mahoney's smile became more forced. Her eyes blinked repeatedly. This girl was smarter than some of the others who came through the home. "Yes, it means we can help your baby have a fresh start, the start he deserves."

Lorraine leaned forward in her chair, her belly resting on her thighs. It had become so firm and solid, so round that she looked like she was hiding a volleyball beneath her shirt. She wasn't sure why she was hesitating to sign the paper. After all, this was why she had come.

"Will I get to meet... I mean, can I help find... Can I choose the parents?"

The smile dropped from Miss Mahoney's lips, but she maintained eye contact with the girl. "We have a way of doing things that's best for the baby, meant to give him the best start in this world that he can have. We have had hundreds of successful placements. We know what's best, so you can rest and relax while you're here without worrying one bit about having to make such decisions."

This woman acted like she wanted to help. Though she didn't know this Miss Mahoney, Lorraine trusted her parents who had sent her there and Dr. Harris who had recommended the home. As the social worker watched and waited for her to do what she had been asked to, Lorraine hesitated. She needed help, but a voice somewhere in the back of her mind offered a quiet question: Is this the only option?

Of course, it was, she reassured herself. Without Clint, she couldn't have a family. With a baby, she couldn't have college. Plus, she had no business raising a baby on her own. How would she support them? How would she make a home for them? How would she give up her dreams because of one mistake they had made? Clint certainly hadn't.

Lorraine scooted to the edge of her chair, held the pen in her right hand, and signed her name on the line.

Apparently, Miss Mahoney's initial impression had been correct; this girl was an easy case. Thank goodness because she still had that other girl who hadn't signed the paper yet, the girl with the crochet needle, stitching that blanket over and over again.

"Thank you," she said as she reached for the paper and tucked it inside the girl's stained folder. "Now, I want you to think about going home, getting the life that awaits you after this hiccup...

You know, college and—" Miss Mahoney didn't look at Lorraine when she said, "Who knows? You'll meet with Dr. Reese in a few days. Until then, chores and school will keep you busy."

"School?"

"Yes, every afternoon in the common room."

Perhaps this would be a good beginning after all. Lorraine had plenty of time to think about that while she scrubbed the toilets that morning. Apparently, chores worked in a hierarchy; the girls who had been there longer were given the preferred duties. Lorraine had been the last to arrive, which meant she was handed the rubber gloves, scrubbing brush, and toilet cleaner.

While Lorraine looked forward to school that afternoon, she couldn't help but think that she had missed something. But what did it really matter anyway? She was there so that the place could help. So that they could provide a good beginning, not just for her, but for the baby, as well. The adults around her seemed to believe they could do that, so why should she question it? As Miss Mahoney had said, this was a hiccup.

The thing is, Lorraine hated hiccups. She hated the involuntary contractions nearly as much as she hated being tickled. To stop them, sometimes she would hold her breath, drink water while plugging her nose, or eat a spoonful of peanut butter. But this hiccup wasn't over yet and no easy remedy would stop it, no matter how badly she longed to have control once more.

# CHAPTER FOURTEEN

Good southern women prided themselves on loving their neighbors and caring for the less fortunate. Some women organized potlucks and rummage sales, others donated old items, but Mrs. Belmont's form of volunteering was educating wayward girls.

It all started after Mr. Belmont passed away, leaving his wife with an abundance of time on her hands. She lived just down the street from the maternity home and one day while hanging laundry in her side yard, she saw the line of troubled girls walking into town. One look at those rounded bellies and sullen faces and she knew she had a new mission in the twilight years of her life: she would offer her skills and expertise to those less fortunate, more in need.

Soon she started teaching classes in the salon of the maternity home. Sure, it took some getting used to, seeing so many young girls in such a state. But after more than a year of teaching them, she now looked past their bellies and sin to recognize the potential within each of them. She never got to know any of the girls too well. They moved in and out of the home in somewhat quick succession, spending three months at most there. Of course, some stays didn't last that long. Thankfully she didn't need to concern herself with that sort of business. Miss Mahoney was the one to handle that, those late-night calls, the unexpected circumstances, the unpredictable emergencies.

Nevertheless, Mrs. Belmont tried to learn each girl's name, and she understood that yet another one would be joining them that day: Lorraine. She never knew their last names, and that was quite alright. She simply needed to know what to call them for the few weeks they'd be together until their lives parted ways—a way to make a connection, no matter how short-lived.

She did her best to prepare lessons that would engage each girl, get her excited, take her mind off her predicament. It worked for some, but others were a bit more fickle, like that Denise character, who seemed to carry a chip on her shoulder larger than her rounded stomach. The girl kept to herself for the most part. She didn't disrupt class, per se, but a sour attitude oozed from her. Nonetheless, Mrs. Belmont always welcomed her with an extra-large smile.

Miss Mahoney had told her that Lorraine seemed like a good girl, one who wouldn't give them any problems. From first impressions, Mrs. Belmont agreed with that assessment. The girl walked into the salon happy. Smiling. Dare she say, eager? But it took only a few minutes for confusion to set in.

In the middle of Mrs. Belmont's lesson, Lorraine raised her hand.

"Where are the books?" the girl asked before Mrs. Belmont could fully explain the lesson for the day.

"I'm sorry?"

"Books? Where are the books we'll be using?"

The girls all looked around at one another, confused by what Lorraine was asking, wondering what she had been expecting.

"We don't need books. I wrote out all the steps right here on the blackboard. You see, our lesson for today is napkin folding."

Mrs. Belmont could see the look of consternation cross Lorraine's face. *Napkin folding?*

As Mrs. Belmont explained, it was a task every housewife needed to perfect to be the best hostess on the block. Lorraine had been folding cloth napkins for more years than she cared to count. Her mother had long ago given her that task, showing her how to match corner to corner and apply pressure to each crease before beginning the next fold, but what did this have to do with school?

Lorraine's hand shot into the air. She waited for the instructor to give her permission to speak again before she asked, "When do we get to math? Or science?"

Mrs. Belmont chuckled. "Oh, bless, there's no math or science. Unless it has to do with baking."

"Then what kind of school is this?"

"Well, finishing school, of course."

*Finishing school?*

It turns out that Mrs. Belmont was there to transform wayward girls into domestic companions, not help them earn high school diplomas.

Lorraine raised her hand again to get clarification, but Mrs. Belmont ignored her, proceeding with her lesson. Lorraine leaned toward Denise and asked, "When's real school?"

Denise furrowed her brow. "What?"

"Like actual classes?" Lorraine tried to keep her voice low as Mrs. Belmont continued talking, but her frustration was making the words come out louder than she had planned.

Slouched in her chair, Denise held out her arms and pointed at the room around her. "This is it. Welcome to Maternity Home High."

*No. No. No.* This place was supposed to help, which meant continuing to take classes. How else was she supposed to graduate on time?

"Girls!" Mrs. Belmont hollered, then held a finger to her mouth and shushed them.

Lorraine slumped in her chair alongside Denise. She didn't raise her hand again. She didn't ask another question, not out loud anyway. She didn't want to believe that her parents had been right that pregnant girls couldn't finish high school. Miss Mahoney had said there would be classes, but Lorraine had failed to understand just what kind of school that could be.

According to Mrs. Belmont, a rectangle fold wouldn't please guests and make you the talk of the neighborhood, the much-admired hostess. Lorraine didn't care about napkins looking like swans or flowers or whatever shape Mrs. Belmont claimed they were. But she had nothing else to do, so she followed along with the instructions, her heart not even half-engaged in the exercise, her mind shifting between disappointment and anger. It was an activity her mother and the Sunnymede Sisters would've enjoyed, but Lorraine wanted more.

All the girls sat at tables, perfectly in a row, each attentively listening to Mrs. Belmont, their hands working nearly in unison to follow the instructions, complete the cloth masterpieces as directed. All except Mirabelle, who sat in the corner with the pink blanket spread across her lap, crochet hook moving about.

"Why isn't she folding napkins?" Lorraine asked Denise.

"She's working on the blanket."

"We don't have to do this?"

"Well, *we* do."

"So why isn't she—"

Denise stopped folding and looked at Lorraine. "Mirabelle's exempt."

"But—"

Denise scowled at Lorraine. She wanted to know more, but she didn't want to annoy her new roommate, still hoping to find her way to Denise's good side, if that existed, so she kept quiet.

The girls put their attention back on their napkins. Lorraine folded and pressed, flipping, turning, and pulling as Mrs. Belmont instructed. Around the room, the other girls did the same, together in unison. It reminded Lorraine of the women at the church back home gathered together for a potluck dinner, working in harmony to host an event, spoon after spoon dipping into the serving platter, plate after plate being filled. But in this room, there weren't any guests, no actual event, no immediate purpose behind their practice, just a bunch of strangers put together in one place thanks to similar circumstances.

"My, my," the teacher said as she walked around the room and stopped at Lorraine's table. The elderly woman leaned back, interlaced her fingers and rested her hands on her soft, round stomach. If she wasn't so advanced in years with silver hair in short tight curls, some would wonder if she was in the home because of her own predicament thanks to the size and shape of her belly. But it was genetics and a sweet tooth, not an indiscretion that gave her the plumpness she had.

Mrs. Belmont reached for Lorraine's napkin. "My! You're sure to be quite the hostess! Just look at that!" The woman leaned in, grabbed hold of the napkin creation and examined it closely. Her glasses hung on a chain around her neck. With one hand, she held the napkin and with the other, she placed her readers on her nose so she could better examine Lorraine's work. "I do declare this is perfection at its finest! Well, all except for this tail right here." She tugged a bit at the top. "Not bad, especially for your first day." As she walked past Denise, she muttered, "Perhaps you could learn a thing or two from your neighbor."

Lorraine looked at Denise's napkin, expecting to find a similarly finished creation, but instead she saw a rectangle. Denise sat with her hands folded as if done and satisfied.

"I can show you how," Lorraine offered.

Denise stared toward the front of the room where Mrs. Belmont had stood during the instruction part of the exercise. Her gaze looked as though she was reading the numbered steps that had been carefully printed across the chalkboard, but her eyes were focusing on those words as much as a teen focusing on his mother's request for the trash to be taken out while *American Bandstand* was on.

"I'm quite pleased with what I accomplished," she said without looking away from the chalkboard.

Lorraine reached for Denise's napkin. "But don't you want to—"

Denise's hand slapped the top of Lorraine's so that Mrs. Belmont turned back from examining another girl's folding. "I'm not planning to host tea parties anytime—"

Denise didn't finish her statement before a moan bellowed from a girl a couple of tables over. Everyone turned their attention to her. The girl remained in her chair, her shoulders rounding forward, her head angled downward. She kept her eyes closed, her breath held inside her. The girl next to her asked if she was okay.

Nearly a minute passed before the girl said, "My back. It

hurts." She put one hand on her lower back before another moan filled the room.

Mrs. Belmont sprang into action. She had seen this happen before in her time there. "Oh, Linda!" she said to the girl who was in pain before she told another girl to run and get Miss Mahoney. Quickly.

"A short class today," she said, dismissing everyone. "Go on about your days and I'll see you again tomorrow."

Denise scooted back her chair, ready to leave the napkin lesson behind, but Lorraine lingered, watching Linda. Even from the side, she could see the grimace, the pain, the eyes that she squeezed together.

Denise nudged Lorraine. "Come on," she said, as Mirabelle approached them.

"Look!" Mirabelle said, as she held the blanket to just under her eyes. It draped over part of her stomach but did not cover it.

Finally focusing on something other than the laboring girl, Lorraine said, "I think you're holding it sideways."

Mirabelle looked down at her blanket. "Nope. That's right. Top to bottom."

"That can't be right. It's shorter than when you showed me yesterday."

"Uh-huh."

"But you've been working on it all last night and today."

"That's right. But then I noticed this spot. It wasn't purling right. I thought I could let it go, but do you know what I saw every time I looked at the blanket? That purl. Turns out I needed to fix it. I had to fix it. This blanket will be my baby's forever, and how would I feel if it wasn't just right. What would she say if she looked at it and saw the mistake and wondered why her mother hadn't fixed it when she'd had the chance? Well, I couldn't live with that. So I started over."

"You started over?"

"Uh-huh." Mirabelle gathered the yarn and hook in her arms.

"You mean you removed a few rows and fixed the problem?"

"No. I started over."

"Completely?"

Mirabelle nodded and smiled. She had made a mistake and she had started over. She hadn't just fixed the error; she had unraveled every stitch before and after that one. Lorraine wondered how many times Mirabelle had done that already, how anyone could start over so completely.

Miss Mahoney walked into the common room, where the groans had gotten louder. Mirabelle gathered the blanket in her arms and stuck her fingers in her ears as she raced toward the steps on her way to their room.

The more the girl's noises carried through the home, the more Lorraine wanted to do the same as Mirabelle.

"Does that happen often?" she asked Denise. "In the time you've been here, have you seen that before?"

Lorraine knew that Denise had been there for a few weeks already. What she didn't know was that Denise had heard those sounds before. In fact, she had seen things far worse. More troubling. Denise said none of that then. "Some," she said before changing the subject. "Was school all you thought it'd be?"

"What? No. Not at all. I'm a senior. About to graduate, as valedictorian, in fact. Miss Mahoney told me there would be school. I thought she meant real class: math, science, English, not this. How else do we graduate?"

Denise shrugged. If school was the worst of this girl's concerns, Denise thought, then she definitely didn't want to hear about the incident in the middle of the night, the one that happened while the house slept. And if she thought that Miss Mahoney was a woman to be trusted, then this girl wasn't as smart as she seemed.

Back in their bedroom, Lorraine walked to the window to see Miss Mahoney guiding Linda down the front steps and into a car. She hadn't even known the girl's name until Mrs. Belmont had said it. Now she wondered if she would ever see her again, but more importantly, she longed to be her. Lorraine had only just arrived, and she couldn't seem to settle in. The rules, the smell, the incomplete information, and—dare she say?—lies. This wasn't what she had imagined when she had first looked at the brochure. She wondered what her parents knew, if they had expected a place like this. As she watched the car disappear into the tree tunnel, she wished she could be Linda, her time there ending. Her time in the future beginning.

# CHAPTER FIFTEEN

Nurse Jenkins had arrived before Dr. Reese that morning, as usual. She had organized the charts according to the order of appointments. One had been removed and another had been added since their last visit, yet another case in a never-ending flow of girls through the home. She knew Dr. Reese would want to stay on schedule that day, and she would do her best to make that happen. Neither of them wanted to stay in that basement exam room longer than necessary. She never was one to believe in ghosts, but something about that long, dark hallway and the sterile yet stale smell of the place always gave her a fit of nervousness.

But if they wanted to get out on time, they'd need this new girl to stop piddling around and get there quickly. The nurse already had the gown laid out and the instruments in place. Trouble was that Lorraine lingered at the basement door, working up the nerve to have another doctor examine her. Lorraine grabbed on to the railing and walked down the narrow staircase. What the front staircase had in grandeur, this one had in uncertainty. The squeaking wooden stairs reminded her of the first time she had walked up the front steps and through the doors of the old farmhouse, but that time she had had Clint to lead the way. This time she walked alone down rickety, barely lit stairs.

The ceiling hung low on the basement level, exposed pipes

running overhead and cold concrete beneath her feet. Nurse Jenkins waited behind an open door.

"You're late," the nurse said. She didn't bother introducing herself before giving Lorraine instructions to strip down and put on the gown. The doctor would be there shortly. "Let's not keep him waiting any longer."

Dr. Reese didn't offer to shake her hand when he walked into the exam room, even though she extended hers. He didn't call her by name, barely looked at her as his nose and eyes were hidden behind Miss Mahoney's coffee-stained folder that he flipped through, spending a few seconds on each page before moving to the next one.

Lorraine sat on the exam table, her legs crossed at the ankle, hands clasped in her lap. She had questions to ask the doctor, but she gave him time to read first, telling herself to be calm and patient, willing her heart to beat more slowly. The longer he took, the more she felt a draft coming through the back side of the cloth gown. She had struggled to tie it by herself and now feared she hadn't tied it tightly enough. She had done her best to reach behind and get each of the three ties shut as much as possible, as if a doctor who was about to examine her private area should be shielded from seeing her back exposed.

She reached behind her, pulling the gown closed a bit more, but it only fell open again when she repositioned. The paper covering the exam table crinkled with her movements, emitting the only sound in the room until the doctor said, "Let's take a look." He put down the papers and turned to her as she sat upon the table. "That means lie down."

Lorraine needed the support of her arms to help with the

transition. Her stomach didn't care for this sort of movement and demanded that she twist to the side ever so much. As her back finally met with the paper covering, her legs hung at an uncomfortable angle at the end of the table, her bottom nearly falling off.

"Dear, you're going to need to scoot up."

She did as the nurse requested, scooting until she was told she was fine. The nurse then placed her feet into the stirrups and lifted her gown to above her stomach. Suddenly she didn't care about her back exposure anymore.

She lay turtled on the table as the doctor felt her stomach, pushed against it, and then measured it. As he prowled over her, Lorraine looked to the ceiling. This room had white and black speckled tiles instead of exposed pipes like the hallway did. She studied the orange stain that bled through a tile, the shape reminding her of the over-easy eggs her mother made for her father's breakfast each morning, the darkest color in the center of the stain just like the yoke, with the white spilling outward.

The doctor's hands pushed against her stomach, his face so close to her body that his breath tickled her belly just as John's had caused goose pimples across her that summer during CPR training. It was the first day of lifeguard school, before the pool season was in full swing. She was the only girl in that training class, and when the instructor had said someone needed to be the test dummy, the boys all volunteered Lorraine, who had already assumed that she would be the one.

She lay down on the floor, and let each one of them take their turns feeling for the pulse in her neck and her wrist before placing their hands upon her sternum to replicate compressions. John's hands went the highest, though a few others brushed closely to the underside of her breasts. His were the only ones to fully come in contact with them and then linger there without apology. He was also the one to bow closest to her as he breathed out practiced breaths, slow and warm. He looked into her eyes and she focused on the ceiling tiles of the training room. She tried to remain calm, placid as her skin crawled from the violation.

"Now for the internal," the doctor said as if that gave enough explanation. He walked from her side to her feet, tapping on her knees that had remained glued together since he had asked her to lie back. "Relax. Open up." That was the closest to encouragement he offered.

Dr. Harris had not done this. Lorraine exhaled and let her knees drop as far to the side as they could. She fought the urge to tuck her gown down around her, to cover the area that no one had ever seen before, at least not since she had stopped using diapers. She watched the egg on the ceiling, focusing on the changing gradient of the rust color, trying not to think of what was happening to her, of what had happened to Linda the other day.

She gasped when she felt something cold enter her body. Her stomach tightened, her shoulders lifted off the table, and she looked at the doctor, who stood between her legs.

"Relax."

She tried to do what he told her to, but it was hard to relax when she was holding her breath, counting down until this humiliation was over. The longer he examined her, the more she felt pressure, like a need to pee, but she had done that earlier. It seemed too soon, but the feeling grew strong and more uncomfortable. She wanted to wiggle and adjust for relief, but she feared moving at all and risking being reprimanded again.

"You can sit up now," he told her a few minutes later.

The pressure released as the doctor stepped away. She pulled the gown down as far as she could, not even attempting to sit until she was properly covered. Sitting wasn't as easy as she had expected. She again had to roll to one side and use her arms as the doctor wrote something on the paper he had read through when he first entered the room.

"I'd say you're twenty-nine weeks. You only saw a doctor once?"

"Yes."

"All looks fine," he said as he closed the folder. "Measuring on target. Heartbeat's strong."

He began walking to the door without giving her time to ask anything.

"Doctor, wait!"

He stopped with his hand on the doorknob and looked back at Lorraine.

"I have a few questions."

The doctor kept his hand on the knob, shooting an impatient look at the nurse who shook her head in response. The fact that he hadn't left the room made Lorraine think that it was okay to start asking.

"What will it be… I mean, how will I—" Lorraine thought back to Linda, the girl who had gone into labor and never returned to the home. "What will it feel like?"

The questions fought to get out of her, more than she even realized she had. So many that she should've asked her mother, but she hadn't thought to. She wished now that she had asked about the day she was born. All she'd ever heard was that the pains started in the evening, her father drove her mother to the hospital, and she entered the world sometime in the early morning hours. "You didn't give me a wink of sleep that night. Nor the next day" was as much detail as her mother gave her. She wanted to know more about those "pains," about what happened after her father drove her mother to the hospital and before the doctor placed her in her mother's arms early that next morning.

"Whoa, whoa—" the doctor said, finally lifting his hand off the doorknob in an attempt to stop the flood of questions. "I can answer a few of those for you, or do my best, but not all."

"Why not?"

The doctor didn't appreciate the question. "You'll know when labor starts. It will feel like cramps. Strong cramps. It will take as long as it will take, hours, but we can't guess how many."

"How much will it hurt?" Of course, Lorraine knew it would hurt. Though she knew very little about birth, she at least knew that much. But until she saw that girl in the beginning stages of labor, she hadn't anticipated the intensity. What she really wanted to ask was: how will I make it through?

Dr. Reese reached for the doorknob and said, "Other questions can be directed to Miss Mahoney."

The door shut before she could ask anything else. She turned to the nurse, wondering if she might have answers. But Nurse Jenkins spoke first, her scowl telling Lorraine to not ask more questions. "Get dressed. Quickly. The doctor's a busy man."

With that, she was left alone in the basement room with no more knowledge of her situation than when she'd walked in.

Lorraine already had other questions for Miss Mahoney. She had been at the home for nearly a week and was surprised by how little contact she had with the woman. Lorraine had assumed she would be a mother type, active and involved. But she always seemed to be off taking care of something or someone else.

Still winded from climbing the stairs back to the main level, Lorraine decided to find Miss Mahoney. She hadn't given up hope to find a way to take classes. The housemother was in her office.

"Come in," Miss Mahoney said with a wave. She motioned to the chair across from her desk. "Move that box and you can have a seat."

Lorraine picked up the box, noticing a few of the contents: a robe, slippers, and hairbrush. But it was the framed photo on top that Lorraine couldn't stop staring at. She recognized Linda despite how different the girl looked—younger and happier. Less swollen and round, face not scrunched in pain.

"Sit it down there on the floor," Miss Mahoney directed.

Lorraine situated the box and asked, "Is she okay?" Miss Mahoney didn't answer, so Lorraine clarified. "Linda? Is she alright?"

The social worker cleared her throat and said, "I believe that sort of question falls under the personal information rule."

"Yes, sorry." Lorraine never liked being reprimanded by an adult, but she wanted to know what had happened. She hadn't heard anything about Linda since the day she had gone into labor. No one had seen her and no one seemed to know anything. Was she okay? How was the baby? Was she coming back? "I was just wondering if she's—"

"You wanted to see me about something?" Miss Mahoney redirected the conversation.

"Um, yeah—" Apparently Miss Mahoney was not looking to share information, so Lorraine decided to ask a different question. "How soon can I start taking classes?"

Miss Mahoney's head tilted, eyes squinted. "Classes? If you're referring to the finishing school, that's every afternoon, after chores and lunch are done."

"No, when we spoke before, you said we'd have school."

"Yes. Mrs. Belmont teaches helpful skills: crocheting, sewing, bridge. Maybe you already know those things, but some of these girls don't. And they will be necessary parts of life once you go home. Get back to normal?"

Lorraine needed more than tutorials on napkin folding, ironing, and place settings. It may have been a fine enough solution for the other girls and the typical life of a modern housewife, but not for her.

"No, I mean when will high school classes start?"

"I think you misunderstand. We don't do that here."

Lorraine scooted to the edge of her chair again. "But you said you take care of everything." Miss Mahoney's head tilted to the other side. "It's just…I was supposed to graduate this year. I was supposed to start college. I was supposed to—"

"Yes, there were a lot of 'supposed to's' in that sentence, and yet here we are." Lorraine flinched at the housemother's tone. Until then, Miss Mahoney had been patient and kind for the most part, but that response held an edge similar to the one she used with the squirrels.

Lorraine wanted to sink into the chair, but she reminded

herself to sit up straight. If Lorraine wanted an explanation as to the good beginning she had been promised, then she needed to stay strong and respectful. She could still have a couple of months in that home, and she didn't want to get on this woman's bad side, but she also wanted some answers, so she asked, "What am I supposed to do after this?"

The housemother scooted to the edge of her chair, sitting upright, her tone calming to congeniality once more. "I understand that this is all new, not what you'd planned for. We're here to resolve this situation. The rest is up to you and your parents to figure out, when you're home again. I suppose some girls find ways to finish school—" She frowned at Lorraine for a moment, implying just how low the odds may be. "But we don't do that here."

Heat rushed into Lorraine's cheeks. She thought back to when she first read the brochure, the image of the dorm-like building. She'd believed the place would give her freedom, and her mother had not told her otherwise. She had imagined her months there as a sort of precollege experience, but now she didn't know what to expect. "But, what *do* you do?" she snapped.

Miss Mahoney could see the frustration on Lorraine's face, her whole body melting into the chair, slumping into a posture of defeat. The home was not equipped to do what the girl was asking. But she didn't have the time or patience for this girl's persistence. She sensed that Lorraine would not relent until she gave her some sort of concession. It would be easier to shut this girl up now than continue to deal with her disruptions. Plus, what was the harm in a little bit of learning?

"There's a library in town. Within walking distance." Miss

Mahoney paused, taking a moment to devise a plan. "You can make weekly visits there to read and study. How's that sound?"

It sounded like a plan. Or at least the start of one. It wasn't what Lorraine had expected or desired. But in this place where girls like Linda seemed to disappear, Lorraine decided to take what she could get.

# CHAPTER SIXTEEN

Lorraine hadn't yet learned who to trust. Her first seventeen years of life had given her faith in a safe, comfortable, loving world. But these months of pregnancy had new lessons in store.

Miss Mahoney had told Lorraine to be in the foyer at 9:00 a.m. sharp, as soon as breakfast was done. She hurried to make sure she didn't miss the appointment that Miss Mahoney had arranged for her at the library. She was excited at the possibility of continuing her studies. She wished she had brought her textbooks to the home, but her mother didn't think it was appropriate for her to take school property with her, so she'd left them behind. Now she thought of the possible learning that could occupy her mind over the next couple of months.

That morning, she walked into the foyer and was surprised to see a few other girls there, milling around, chatting with one another as if they had nothing else to do. She assumed the rest of the girls would be going about their daily tasks, needing to dust, clean the stairs, wash the windows and the sheets.

As the clock ticked closer to 9:00 a.m. sharp, more girls gathered. The volume of the foyer began to rise with the chatter of the crowd. When Denise and Mirabelle arrived, Lorraine finally asked, "What are you doing here?"

Matter-of-factly, Mirabelle explained, "Getting ready for our weekly outing, of course!"

"Weekly outing?"

"Yeah," Mirabelle said. "When we go to town. Each Thursday morning. Well, if we earn it, anyway."

"Earn?" The word came out slow and low.

"Girls!" Miss Mahoney interrupted all the conversation. "Stay with your partner." She began going over rules. Lorraine had a hard time focusing on all the housemother said. She had thought she was the only one with a special arrangement. "Meet at the flagpole at 10:30 a.m. sharp. Under no circumstances are you to carry on a conversation, especially with a man, even if he seems quite the gentleman, especially if he seems a gentleman. And everyone must wear one of these."

Miss Mahoney held up a small gold ring between her fingers as the girls fell into a line and stepped toward the door one at a time. Lorraine automatically touched the opal ring on her own finger. Her fingers were far too sausage-like to remove it now. For the most part, she had gotten used to it, but every once in a while it would catch a strand of her hair, the pain reminding her of its unwelcome presence.

Lorraine followed her roommates, lining up behind them. One at a time, they moved toward the door. Each girl paused by the entrance before being waved outside or told to stay behind.

"What's happening?" Lorraine asked.

"Gotta be weighed first," Denise informed her.

"What?"

"Weighed. Gotta step on the scales and make sure you didn't get too fat in a week."

"Denise!" Mirabelle said. As they stood in line, she kept her arms around her belly, swaying as if dancing to music no one else heard.

"It's true," Denise continued. "She won't let you go if you've gained more than two pounds."

"No." Lorraine stood on her tiptoes to try to see if what Denise said was true. "Really?"

Mirabelle nodded yes. "Says we have to stay trim." She shrugged her shoulders and pulled on the cuffs of her shirt.

One by one, they waited for their turn. Denise stepped up first and seemed to meet with Miss Mahoney's approval. Mirabelle, on the other hand, didn't.

"Not this time," the housemother told her.

"Let me try again," Mirabelle said as she stepped off and then back onto the scale, but she still failed. "Maybe without shoes." She slid out of her shoes and tried again, but she couldn't seem to reach the magic number.

"Maybe next week," Miss Mahoney mumbled as she motioned for Lorraine to step up.

Mirabelle grabbed her shoes and began to sulk away.

"I'm sorry." Lorraine tried to console her.

Mirabelle turned and shrugged. "It's okay. It'll give me more time to work on the blanket."

"And chores," Miss Mahoney chimed. "Chores first."

Mirabelle forced a smile before walking back up the stairs.

Lorraine stepped onto the scale, and Miss Mahoney declared her within the parameters of permission. She handed her the plain gold trophy for apparently being properly trim.

Lorraine slid the ring onto her left ring finger. It was loose enough that she clenched her hand into a fist, fearing it might fall off. It was different than what she had imagined her wedding ring would look like—a simple, round solitaire with a silver band—but of course she reminded herself that this was not a wedding ring. This was a costume for a part that needed to be played so that they could go about town and act normal for at least an hour and a half.

With everyone properly weighed, the girls marched down the front steps. Lorraine continued her questioning as Denise lit a cigarette. "Has Mirabelle not been able to go before?"

Denise inhaled the first hit of nicotine for that day. As smoke billowed from her mouth and swirled through the morning air, she said, "Yep."

All in a line beneath the live oak trees, the girls walked through the front gate, across the street, and down the sidewalk of a neighborhood that made Lorraine's heart ache for home.

Along the way, Lorraine noticed a few women in their front yards, sweeping off porches, shaking out rugs, pinning clothes to their clotheslines. Each of these women had one thing in common: a look. They all paused what they were doing to watch the group of girls file by. They didn't wave. Didn't smile. Didn't move much at all, other than with their gazes. Their eyes followed that line of waddling ducklings led by Miss Mahoney, the mother of them all.

Lorraine couldn't help but wonder if they traveled in a group instead of a line, maybe they would've seemed more natural and normal. Maybe they wouldn't have been so obvious if they traveled as grown women tend to do. She thought of her mother and the Sunnymede Sisters. They may have traveled in a herd or a gaggle or a circle of chatter, but they didn't walk single file in a line like dutiful grade-schoolers. She tried not to think too much about her mother's friends, and especially not about what they would say if they saw a group of pregnant girls, the remarks and judgment whispered among them.

The line dispersed once they reached the flagpole downtown. Lorraine took a minute to look around at the various storefronts. Red and brown two- and three-story brick buildings with various sized awnings over the front doors lined both sides of the street. Smaller than Charlotte, the town put her in the mind of Matthews, a quaint town only twenty minutes from where her family lived.

She saw a five-and-dime, a corner diner, and a dry cleaner. A bit farther down was a movie theater, the marquee too far in the distance to see what was showing. Then she finally spotted the place she had come for: the town library.

She headed to the crosswalk and looked both ways. With the coast clear, she began to step into the intersection, but Denise didn't follow.

"Come on!" Lorraine waved, but her roommate remained where she was and shook her head. "Come on! To the library." Lorraine hoped her waving and motioning would light a fire under Denise. Time was of the essence.

"Why?" Denise finally responded.

"Rule number one: stay with your partner."

"I didn't realize we were partners," Denise said.

Lorraine took a deep breath before replying, "I don't see any other girls sticking around."

Denise finally agreed to walk across the street together, but refused to go inside the library. "I'll sit here and wait," she said, as she took a seat on the bench outside the main entrance.

Lorraine pushed the wooden door open, stepping into a vestibule before entering through a second set of doors. The library was empty at that time of the day. As she walked in, the smell of aging pages delighted her as much as the chlorinated pool on opening day. She took a moment to look around, but before the librarian could ask if she needed any assistance, Lorraine had figured out the arrangement of the books. Once you knew the numbering system, you could find any book in any library. Lorraine found comfort in that fact, that no matter what library she walked into, she could find what she was looking for.

She headed to the 500s and couldn't help but brush her fingers against the spines of the books as she walked through the rows of towering wooden shelves. She reached the section she wanted and carefully chose her first book *The Moon and the Solar System*. Then she chose another one. And another. She nearly removed more titles, but stopped herself. This was merely the first of many library visits. She could only read so much at a time, so she needed to pace herself.

As much as she loved the sciences and knew she needed to do more studying, she couldn't help but walk to the fiction section. Mr. Delford thought made-up stories were a waste of time, but Lorraine craved a novel—a chance to escape. She desperately wanted to get lost in a bit of imagination, if only for a while.

A good student, Lorraine excelled in her classes, always learning what was to be expected without being too inquisitive. But alone in the library, without the structure of a teacher or a syllabus, she realized she could finally read what actually interested her. Learn something that hadn't been chosen for her. Of course the danger was in the possible questions she could ask when she was free to learn for herself.

Lorraine gave herself permission to pull one book off the shelf. She knew just the one she wanted, the only book Alan had ever read. The one she had never been brave enough to read after her mother called it smut and the school library refused to carry it: *The Catcher in the Rye*. Lorraine tucked it between nonfiction books, as if it was contraband that needed to remain hidden.

She walked to a table, put her treasures upon it, and looked at the clock. She had little more than an hour before she had to be back at the flagpole. Not wasting any more time, she selected a book, opened it, and began leafing through the pages. Knowing she must devour as much information as she could in the amount of time she had, she flipped through pages full of text and photos. She promised herself that she would start with the vegetables (science) before giving herself a few minutes of dessert (fiction).

But the dessert kept calling to her. She could only focus on the science for a few moments before the pages of the novel demanded her attention. She opened *The Catcher in the Rye*. With each morsel of story she consumed, a hunger emerged. Much as a stray dog consumes the scraps of food that someone tosses their way or as a teenage boy claws at the sweater buttons of his girlfriend, she devoured Holden Caulfield's tale.

Lost in the depths of discovery, she didn't hear Denise approach. "You planning to spend all your time in here?"

Lorraine gasped. She jumped in her seat, flipping the book out of her hand, the edges of a page slicing her finger. She pulled back her hand and put her finger in her mouth. She began sucking on it, nursing the small amount of blood that came out.

"Guess that's why my daddy always said books were dangerous," Denise said.

This was the first time Denise had ever said anything about her family, had mentioned that she even had a daddy. Lorraine made a mental note to ask questions later, but for now she returned to her reading, still holding her finger in her mouth as Denise walked in the direction of the periodicals.

Looking at the time, Lorraine realized she only had a few minutes to check out books before she needed to get Denise and head to the meetup point. As much as she didn't want to say goodbye to Holden, she knew she could meet him again next week. Plus, she doubted that Miss Mahoney would appreciate such a book in her maternity home. If she wanted to keep coming to the library, she knew she needed to show the appearance of a dutiful student. So, she selected three books to tide her over until their next outing. She scooted back in her chair, the edge of her stomach rubbing against the table as she pushed herself to standing.

As she walked to the checkout, she smiled at the woman behind the desk. The librarian was not like most she'd seen before, especially Mrs. Mulner at their school, who was as old as most of the books on the shelves. She had been at that school since Clint's father had attended, her hair gray and fastened in a bun just the same then as it was now. But this librarian could be Lorraine's age, though Lorraine guessed she was most likely a few years older. Her hair, neatly brushed, hung past her shoulders, loose and carefree. Her skin was freckled, probably from sun exposure, just like Lorraine's.

"Let me help you with those." The librarian took the books from Lorraine. "Did you find everything you were looking for?"

"Yes."

The librarian turned the spines toward her.

"Wow. This is quite a stack. Not what women your age typically choose."

Lorraine took that as a compliment.

"Are you pursuing a degree?"

"Yes." *Kind of.* Lorraine hoped the librarian didn't ask too many questions.

"It's refreshing to see another woman interested in the sciences. What's your name?" The question caught Lorraine off guard. She had only been at the home for a week, but it had been long enough for her to already protect her identity. "For checkout?"

"Oh, uh, I've never checked out books here."

"That's okay. I'll get you set up. Name?"

"Lorraine." She stopped. The librarian paused, waiting to hear more. Finally, Lorraine continued, "Delford."

"Nice to meet you. I'm Ms. Whiler."

"Missus—"

"*Ms.* Ms. Whiler."

Lorraine had never heard of that honorific. All she knew was *Miss* or *Mrs.*, the latter being the desired and earned title, at least according to women like her mother.

"Well, Lorraine Delford, let me get you checked out."

As Ms. Whiler stepped away for a moment, Lorraine sensed someone behind her. Assuming it was Denise, who had vanished somewhere within the bookshelves, she said, "It'll be just a minute. I need to check out a few books."

A hand grabbed her elbow, and a harsh whisper replied, "What do you think you are doing?"

Lorraine twisted her neck, unable to fully turn around and see Miss Mahoney, whose grip grew stronger. She assumed she was meant to answer that question. "Checking out books."

"It's time to go."

"But—"

Ms. Whiler walked back toward them. "We're nearly all set."

Miss Mahoney's voice lilted higher than normal as a forced smile spread across her face. Though the librarian might've taken the smile to be politeness, Denise, who was walking up behind them, saw the veins protruding in the social worker's neck and knew the sentiment didn't match the feelings boiling beneath the surface.

"I'm afraid we don't have time for that today," Miss Mahoney said as she began to walk away, still gripping Lorraine's elbow.

"It will only take a moment," Ms. Whiler offered.

"Perhaps another day."

Miss Mahoney directed Lorraine to the exit and outside the library. She waited for both sets of doors to close and first checked to make sure no pedestrians were nearby before she said, "What were the rules?"

"Stay with your partner." Thankfully, Denise had come inside the library. "Meet back at ten thirty." They still had a few minutes. "Don't talk to men."

"No! Don't talk to anyone! And don't give out your name! House rules apply even on outings. I didn't realize I had to spell that out." Miss Mahoney looked at her watch. "I have to go gather the others. You two, head back now."

"I need to pee," Denise stated matter-of-factly.

"Manners!" Miss Mahoney snapped, as she rubbed her temples.

"Ma'am." Denise punctuated her statement.

"Fine. Just go. Quickly. Then head back."

The three parted ways as Denise walked back into the library and Miss Mahoney headed to the flagpole to meet the others. Lorraine considered going back in to get the books she wanted to check out, but the bulletin board in the vestibule caught her eye. She read the flyers that advertised things like an upcoming circus, a prayer group, and a fish fry, but what she noticed most was the flyer announcing GED classes. Tuesday and Thursday nights at the library, it said.

"Ready?" Denise asked as she walked out of the library.

Lorraine grabbed the flyer. She was ready, ready to learn more about what that flyer had to offer. She tucked it inside her skirt pocket, determined to ask Miss Mahoney about joining the class.

As she and Denise exited, a woman and her little girl approached the library door. Lorraine held it open for them and watched them step inside. The girl, not yet old enough for school, reached both her hands up to her mother, and without words, her mother picked her up, placed her on her hip, and walked into the library as the little girl rested her head on her mother's shoulder.

Seeing that flyer, the opportunity, the hope had filled her with delight. But that moment between the mother and daughter on their way into the library, that is what Lorraine thought about on her walk back to the home and as she scrubbed the toilets later that day. She couldn't stop thinking about that moment, the simple act, the symbiotic relationship between the two. She didn't realize yet that something else was growing, something no one had warned her about, something everyone hoped wouldn't happen because giving up is much easier if attachment never has a chance to take root.

# CHAPTER SEVENTEEN

According to math and biology, or what little Denise knew of either one, she wouldn't have to be at the home much longer, maybe six more weeks. Even still, the weekly outing always made her realize how easy it would be to step away and leave it all behind. Everything. The home. Her parents. The man who'd done this to her. Life.

She'd never much been like Mirabelle, not imaginative and optimistic like that girl, and as much as that girl's nonsense drove her crazy, she did sometimes wish she could be as carefree. Denise had already gotten closer to Mirabelle than she had expected, but after what had happened that one night, she'd let her guard down. She told herself she was helping Mirabelle. What she didn't like to admit is that they were supporting each other.

Then there was the new girl, Lorraine. She didn't talk as much as Mirabelle, but she still talked too much, more than Denise liked. Thankfully, she seemed to be enough of a rule follower to not ask too much personal stuff. While there were few things Denise and Miss Mahoney would agree upon, not getting personal was one of them.

Both of her roommates seemed to know what they wanted once they got out of that hellhole. Mirabelle couldn't wait for motherhood, while the bookish one wanted to study more.

Denise didn't want either one of those futures, but she couldn't figure out what she did want. Or maybe it was more like she couldn't figure out what future she could have.

Her father had always told her she had no sense. If there was one thing she wasn't going to do, it was prove him right by being foolish. She had no business dreaming or planning. More of the girls in that place could be better served by a healthy dose of realism. Like Lorraine.

In the days since coming back from the library, Denise couldn't help but notice a new optimism in Lorraine. For a girl who had gotten knocked up and left cold on the doorstep of that institution, Denise didn't know what she had to be optimistic about.

"The GED. It's a degree completion program," Lorraine told her, waiving a flyer in the air, as excited as a small child who had just been handed a lollipop.

"So?" Denise asked, while Mirabelle applauded for a reason she didn't fully understand, but Lorraine's excitement made it seem like the appropriate response.

"*So*, I can do this and still start college in the fall."

"You *want* to study?"

"Yes," Lorraine said as she brushed her hair. It had gotten quite thick over the last few months.

"The one good thing about this place," Denise said as she pulled on her socks, "is that I don't have to go to school."

"Well, finishing school," Mirabelle corrected.

"Yes, because apparently knowing the difference between a salad and a dinner fork is necessary."

"The salad fork has fewer prongs," Mirabelle whispered.

Surprised, Denise asked her, "How did you know that?"

"Mrs. Belmont."

"But you don't even do the lessons."

"I still hear things."

"I want to do this," Lorraine brought the conversation back to its original topic. "I need to. I just need to get permission."

"Good luck." Denise meant it as more of a warning than well wishes.

"What do you mean?"

"You think Miss Mahoney is going to give you permission to be away from the home, unsupervised? There's no way."

"Well," Lorraine put away her hairbrush and straightened the shirt that tented over her stomach, apparently designed to hide what was beneath it although no amount of fabric could do that, "there's only one way to find out."

---

Lorraine should've listened to Denise. But instead she went looking for the housemother as soon as breakfast was over. She found Miss Mahoney feeding birds in the back courtyard that was tucked inside a perimeter of gardens. Lorraine hadn't spent any time there before that morning. Much of her childhood had been spent outside, but the months of being hidden away in her bedroom had trained her to stay indoors.

A symphony of birds filled the air as Lorraine stepped into the courtyard bursting with unkempt bushes. A good decade past the need to shape and prune, the gardens had become a tangled jungle of camellias, azaleas, gardenias, and hydrangeas all intermingled, yet still surviving.

The pink and red camellia blooms had started to brown in a

sign that their season was about to pass. The azalea buds hadn't formed yet, but Lorraine knew it was only a matter of time before those bushes would be full of color, the sign that spring had come and that the temperatures would be warming before summer fully arrived. The South didn't need to wait for a calendar date for the heat to come on, the humidity to fill the air so thick that beads of sweat formed on foreheads as easily as on glasses of iced sweet tea.

And that's how Lorraine felt as she walked toward the bench where Miss Mahoney sat, like the outside of a glass of sweaty sweet tea. Lorraine didn't usually get nervous, but she hadn't felt like herself for months now and especially not since she had arrived at the maternity home. She was still trying to find her rhythm there.

Miss Mahoney reached into a brown paper bag and began tossing seed onto the ground, offering only a slight nod to Lorraine. Chickadees, blue jays, and cardinals swooped down to scoop up the food.

Lorraine sat down and waited a minute before finally breaking the silence. "Why do you feed the birds?"

"They need looking after."

Miss Mahoney continued watching the birds, intermittently tossing seed to the flock. She extended the bag to Lorraine, who took a handful. Instead of throwing it all at once, she took a few pieces into her other hand and threw only a couple at a time, aiming for the birds on the outskirts of the gathering.

"Guess I've been taking care of birds for a while now. I suppose it started when I was a girl," Miss Mahoney began. "There was this set of cardinals that would build a nest in the gardenia bush right outside our back door. Each year, they'd come back and lay two, maybe three eggs. That mama would sit on those eggs until they hatched. Have you ever seen a baby bird? I mean a baby just born?"

"Only in pictures," Lorraine said.

"They are so small and fragile, ugly as ever. Takes a few days for their feathers to come in. But that mama, she never cared how ugly they were. She'd feed them and sit on them until they'd grow too big for their nest and it was time for them to take off. And you know what she'd do? Every year, she'd let them go, knew what was best for them. Didn't try to keep them in her nest."

A squirrel ran into the middle of the bird party, trying to scoop up a few bits of seed, but Miss Mahoney stomped and clapped so it ran away.

"You don't feed the squirrels?" Lorraine asked.

"Those bushy-tailed rats? They're filthy pests, always trying to take what isn't meant for them."

Trying to work up the nerve to ask what she wanted to, Lorraine watched a towhee rustle on the ground, flipping and flapping through the fallen leaves as if angry with the unkempt ground covering. It fluttered around, rustling the leaves, kicking them up with its wings and beak, tossing leaves around as best a small bird could do. After a minute of this, it flew to a branch and perched, its orange chest puffing outward, all the while looking back at the spot on the ground that it had ruffled up. Then it dove back to the ground and started its rage all over again.

"I wanted to ask something," Loraine said, finally getting to the reason she was in the courtyard that morning. When she had asked her father for permission to lifeguard, she knew the answer before she asked the question. Because she knew her father, how to work him to get what she wanted. Or at least, back then she did. She hadn't yet figured out this housemother. During their first conversation, Lorraine thought she was there to help. But since then, the woman seemed less agreeable. Plus, with Denise's attitude, Lorraine didn't know what the answer would be. Lorraine knew that she could keep reading library books, but this was her last chance for a real educational opportunity. Without it, college in the fall was out of the question. And if that didn't happen, then what would she do?

Lorraine ignored the sweat beading on her forehead and said, "It's about the GED."

Miss Mahoney clapped her hands together, shaking off the dust from the seed and startling Lorraine, who sat on edge, waiting to hear her reply. "I told you we don't do things like that here."

"Yes, I know." Lorraine began to sweat even more. "But there are classes, two evenings a week in town, that I could take." She thought that if she explained the program enough, or at least what little she had learned from the flyer, then the social worker would allow her to break curfew. Unlike Denise, Lorraine trusted that this woman had her best interest at heart. After all, she had said she wanted to give her a good beginning.

"No."

That one word with only two letters delivered a sting similar to a belly flop. But like a child determined to learn to dive, Lorraine shook it off and tried again.

"I'd get all my chores done. Still attend finishing school. I could do it all."

"No." Another smack shook, stunned, silenced her. She wasn't used to hearing that word, especially when she thought through something, presented it well, explained how she could succeed. What she didn't realize is that those who had told her yes in the past did so because they loved and cared about her. But this woman didn't care about her like they did.

Miss Mahoney stood from the bench, walked toward the feeder, and shook the remnants of the seed onto the ground. Then she spoke in a hiss similar to the one she had used at the library, but this time they were alone, in the privacy of the gardens, with no concerns of a librarian or passerby eavesdropping. She didn't lower her voice. She didn't mask her annoyance.

"You really think I'd give permission for you, an unwed girl in your state, to walk into town alone at night to sit in a class with other people? Can you imagine what the townsfolk would say about that? I don't know what you think this place is supposed to be, but your parents didn't send you here so you could gallivant about town. They put you here to hide you."

The sting of those words radiated over every inch of Lorraine's body.

Miss Mahoney wrinkled up the paper bag and tucked it inside her skirt pocket as she said, "Quit dillydallying and get on with your chores."

The door no sooner closed than a congregation of squirrels scurried in to pick up the last bits of seed. Lorraine watched them, their tails twitching and swaying, as if communicating something, maybe excitement. Unable to pull herself off the bench just yet, she watched them as they picked up a morsel, sat up on their hind legs, and used their two front paws to bring the seed to their mouths and nibble away.

She watched them dart up the trees, following one high into an evergreen, where a large nest of leaves she hadn't noticed balanced at the very top, far away from any place a human could reach. The tree swayed in the breeze, the sun shining on its top branches as the squirrel sat high above the earth at a distance safe from interference. If only she could climb so high, but what she was learning was that with such height comes the risk of an even bigger fall.

# CHAPTER EIGHTEEN

Over the next couple of weeks, time passed in the home in both slow and fast ways. Girls came and went, each acclimating to the way of things, though like Lorraine, few completely adjusted. Lorraine marked the passing of time by the change of chores. As more girls moved out of the home, her duties progressed, with new girls taking over the ones she had previously done. She had graduated from toilet duty to sweeping the common room, polishing the stairs, setting the tables, and now cleaning the front porch. This was by far her favorite chore. Of course, who wouldn't prefer dusting rocking chairs to cleaning toilets? Even wiping away the thick, shimmering cobwebs on the furniture was preferable to being on her hands and knees shining the wooden staircase.

Bugs were everywhere in the South. Large bugs. Big ones. Some even bigger than hummingbirds. While Lorraine had come to expect finding them along the wooded trail or even caught in the filter of the Sunnymede pool, she did not appreciate them encroaching in her home, especially not her room. If she ever came across one at home, she'd call for her daddy, keeping an eye on the trespasser so she could point her father to the spot where it was hiding. He'd take care of the problem with his shoe or a rolled-up newspaper, whatever he could make use of. Then he'd clear away the debris and they'd go on with the satisfaction that the trespasser had been removed and their lives could get back to normal. Lorraine had always been okay with that arrangement.

The first time she cleared away a spiderweb on the porch and watched the inhabitant scurry out of sight, she couldn't help but wonder what her father was doing at that moment. With each web she cleared, she thought of him less and less as she became more capable of handling the duty on her own.

Sometimes, she would even allow herself to think of Clint, couldn't help herself from doing it as she ran the cloth over the rocking chairs. She thought back to the evenings on her parents' patio, sitting on the swing, certain of who they were and what was to come. That may have only been a few months ago, but it felt like a different life, one where she knew who she was, who he was, what they both wanted, and how they'd get it. While one of them was still walking that path of possibility, the other was on her knees, wiping the dust and dirt and pollen from the rungs of the rocking chairs.

The yellow pollen had just begun to show its spring presence. Lorraine knew that over the next few weeks, it would only grow thicker and more present, only require more persistent clearing. The beauty of the spring blooms couldn't happen without the thick layers of the dusty nuisance. As Lorraine wiped it away, the particles floated through the air and into her nostrils, causing her to intermittently let out sneezes that would echo through the porch and into the surrounding trees.

"Bless you," a voice said from behind her.

Lorraine gasped, first from the surprise and again when she realized who had said it.

"I'm sorry," Ms. Whiler said. "I didn't mean to startle you."

"That's okay," she replied as she tried to stand.

"Please, don't get up," the librarian said. Lorraine stood and dusted herself off, noticing the bag in the woman's arms. "Lorraine, it's good to see you."

Of course, the librarian knew her name. She had seen her every Thursday morning between 9:00 and 10:30 a.m., but they had never spoken about more than books. While Lorraine hadn't been able to take the GED classes, over the last month, she had continued her own self-guided studies during the weekly outings. Thankfully, she had successfully passed each test of the scale to make that possible.

"Ms. Whiler." Lorraine wiped her hands on her skirt, trying to stop the pollen from clinging to her. "It's nice to see you." Though she'd much rather see her in town, not on the front porch of the maternity home.

"I've come to drop this off, some items that I thought y'all could use."

While the two of them often carried on conversations at the library, Lorraine had never told the librarian where she lived, and they had never discussed her pregnancy. But only Lorraine seemed surprised that day on the porch of the home for unwed mothers. She crossed her arms in front of her, as if trying to hide the stomach that Ms. Whiler had already become quite familiar with.

"Thank you. I can get Miss—"

"No. That's quite alright. I'll leave it with you." Ms. Whiler put the bag on the ground. The wind rustled the sprawling oak branches and whipped through the porch, blowing the librarian's hair into her face. She tucked the loose strands behind her ear and continued. "Listen, I was hoping I might see you here."

"How did you know?" Lorraine asked. Their weekly conversations were what gave Lorraine purpose—a reprieve from her situation. Ms. Whiler had recommended books and introduced her to new theories and ideas. They had seemed like teacher and student. While they discussed math and science, Holden Caulfield, and *Silent Spring*, they had never discussed why Lorraine was there. Nor had they ever spoken about the pregnancy. And Lorraine had liked it that way, had felt normal. Standing on the porch that morning, Lorraine moved behind a rocking chair, holding on to the back of it, attempting to camouflage her middle section.

"I've been thinking." Ms. Whiler chose not to answer Lorraine's question directly. She had figured out the girl's predicament from the first time she saw her at the library, especially after she had seen that woman grab her by the elbow and direct her outside. "I enjoy our weekly meetings. You're quite bright and I know you're working to go to college." Lorraine preferred to focus on college and not mention that she hadn't graduated from high school. "I was wondering if I might be able to help."

The breeze again swirled through the porch, dispersing pollen through the air and into Lorraine's throat as she gasped with the thought of opportunity. She coughed and spoke at the same time, choking on her reply, excitement dripping thick from her voice. "Can you?"

"I'd like to try." Ms. Whiler smiled, amused by the pleasure her offer had given the girl. But then she noticed a change come over Lorraine's face, a cloud covering the initial burst of happiness.

Lorraine's stomach had leapt with relief only seconds ago, but now a sinking feeling replaced it. She knew she needed to be honest with Ms. Whiler, though the woman had already figured out she resided at the maternity home, so perhaps what she was about to say wouldn't be quite so surprising.

"There's something you need to know." She began to speak, swallowing hard and forcing herself to proceed. "I haven't graduated from high school yet."

"Oh." Ms. Whiler paused and Lorraine's stomach dropped even further as she waited. She couldn't read the librarian's response, and she worried that she might rescind her offer to help. "That's fine. What year are you?"

As Lorraine exhaled, a grin grew, the feeling of hope returning. While everyone else spoke of her in past or future, Lorraine noticed the present tense of the sentence.

"Senior."

"I assume your evenings aren't free for the GED class? I actually teach it in town." Lorraine shook her head no. "That's fine. We can work around it. I can help you get ready for the test."

The pollen still tickled the back of her throat, preventing Lorraine from speaking a complete sentence. "But"—*cough, cough*—"Miss Ma"—*cough, cough*.

Ms. Whiler assumed that woman might be an issue. She had seen that stern woman with the tight ponytail and attire as drab as her demeanor with the girls around town before Lorraine ever came into the library. The housemother always looked annoyed by her charges. Neither she nor any of the other girls had ever come into the library before Lorraine. Well, the quiet girl had been taking periodicals for a couple of months now, but Ms.

Whiler decided to let her be, assuming she had a need for the magazines and also knowing that the thievery would stop once the girl left the home.

"I can work out the details with Miss Mahoney." She'd prefer to not have to talk to that woman, but if it meant helping one of these girls have a chance at a future after this, then she'd do it. "If you can't meet more often, I can give you assignments, help you prepare for the GED. I'd guess you're not that far from being able to pass it. With some more work over the weeks ahead, I think you could get it done in time before, well, before you leave here."

"I'd like that." Lorraine's eyes glistened from the effects of the pollen. And hope.

———

Once she finished on the porch, Lorraine nearly skipped up the stairs to her room. Mirabelle had beaten her there. As Lorraine walked in, Mirabelle threw her pillow over the top of her bed, covering what had been laid out in front of her. Relieved to see Lorraine, she removed the pillow and resumed the work that had been occupying her.

"I didn't mean to scare you."

"Oh, that's alright." Mirabelle brushed her bangs away from her eyes. "I thought you'd be doing your chores."

"I just finished." Ms. Whiler's proposition had given Lorraine a burst of energy that helped her finish the job faster than usual.

Mirabelle took a pair of scissors in her hand and maneuvered them around a page that she had torn from a catalog.

"What're you working on?"

"Oh, nothing, really." With her scissors, Mirabelle carefully followed the curves of the picture, not simply cutting a square or a rectangle, but respecting the contours.

"Can I see?"

"Really?" Mirabelle smiled. "Denise called it foolish once, before she changed her mind. That was when Janet was here. Janet told her to let it be. Said we all should be so wishful. I don't know what she meant by that. Wishful. I mean I'm not looking out the window wishing upon stars or anything."

Lorraine's ears perked upon hearing that name again—the one Denise refused to say aloud. "Janet?" Mirabelle stopped cutting. "Who was she?"

"Oh, silly me. There I go saying too much." Mirabelle always said too much, so Lorraine wasn't sure why this was the moment she had gone too far. "She was our roommate. Before…before you came. She was so nice. Funny too. And she would help me with my collection."

"Your collection?"

"Yes!" As Mirabelle's lips turned upward, her cheeks plumped and her eyebrows curved into a relaxed and simple arc. Mirabelle held the paper up for Lorraine to see. Across it was pictures of all sorts of baby necessities: wooden cribs, woven bassinets, upholstered buggies, seersucker rompers, glass bottles, and even cotton diapers.

"Wow! You've put a lot of work into that."

Mirabelle smiled, then grabbed a glue bottle, dabbed a bit on the back side of a picture she had cut out, and added it to the collage.

"Yes. These are all the things I'm going to get for my baby. And only the best. See this buggy here? Isn't it beautiful? I can't wait to take her for walks in it. Can't you see it? The baby in the stroller, her pink blanket over her, keeping her warm? 'Cause we have to be careful to keep them warm enough. Babies need help like that. They need us to know what's best. And just look at what it says." She pointed to the description beneath the photo. "This buggy is the best. I'm gonna send this to Stuart so he can place the order and our baby will have what she needs."

Lorraine knew all about Stuart. While most abided by the rules, keeping personal details at bay, Mirabelle did not. She spoke of all things and all the time. She'd tell of her past, her rural home not far from Charleston, of running barefoot in her backyard, chasing the chickens; of her time with Stuart, how handsome he was and how much she longed for him to look at her again, see her, smile back at her. She'd tell about her mama's cooking—the fried chicken and low-country boil with shrimp fresh out of the ocean—and how she missed it, but how she didn't miss her daddy's yelling and especially not the moments when he was quiet, just the two of them, alone together.

But for some reason she didn't talk much about Janet.

Lorraine let Mirabelle talk, point to all the pictures, and show what made this choice or that better than the others that filled the catalog pages. Globs of glue moistened the paper and clung to Mirabelle's hands, and as she went on speaking, she began twisting her fingers together, nearly as if snapping, but instead of making a sound, the bits of dried glue pilled and dropped to the paper below, as if dead skin rained down on her shopping list.

"You've really put a lot of thought into this," Lorraine said.

Mirabelle smiled, her green eyes moistening as she bit her bottom lip. She began gathering the items, placing the scissors, glue, and catalog in the nightstand drawer.

"I just want to be ready." She closed the drawer and put her hands on her stomach, rubbing it in circles. "Only a few more weeks, and then I'll get to meet her."

Mirabelle had been counting down, but for a different reason than either of her roommates. Denise couldn't wait to leave. Lorraine looked forward to getting back on track. But Mirabelle wanted one thing: her baby. She seemed to enjoy being pregnant, anticipation and love growing with each day that went by.

On the other hand, Lorraine hadn't connected to her ever-growing stomach in the same way. She knew something was forming inside her. Everyone who saw her could come to that conclusion. And the movements, the kicks and twists and flip-flops that happened within her abdomen told her that something alive was in there. Yet her mind still avoided connecting that ever-growing bump with a baby. A person. A little human that was half her and half Clint. She may have felt it on a physical level, but beyond that, it was something separate. Something else. And why would she think any differently? Her mother hadn't talked to her about what would come after. Miss Mahoney and Dr. Reese didn't either. This was just a thing. A moment. And then she could get back to normal again. That's what they had made her believe—that she could make it through these nine months and then go on as if none of this had ever happened.

But as the weeks went by and the movements became more frequent, her mind could only protect her so much. Just the other night at dinner, she had been hungrier than she had realized. She scarfed down her Salisbury steak and could've eaten more, had she not been concerned about having to weigh in for the weekly outing the next morning. As she waited for Denise and

Mirabelle to finish, she began to feel the baby move. She had felt that before, but this time was different. This time, it almost felt like dancing. Lorraine put her hands on her stomach. She pushed against a mound of roundness, which then twitched and shimmied to the other side of her stomach. She pushed on that side, which made the baby jolt back again.

She sat in the dining room for a few minutes, lost in a moment with the growing baby inside of her. She didn't notice anyone else. She had lost track of the story Mirabelle was telling. She couldn't stop from pushing and feeling and smiling to herself.

Not noticing Lorraine, Mirabelle announced, "I've settled on a name: Rose. Isn't it pretty?"

"Yeah," Denise said with a nod.

"Lorraine, did you hear me?" Mirabelle asked. "Lorraine! What do you think of the name Rose?"

Finally answering her roommate, Lorraine smiled and said, "Beautiful."

Lorraine hadn't thought of a name, which she told herself was proof that she wasn't meant to be a mother. Not yet. A girl like Mirabelle thought of things like that. She thought to plan and prepare, to consider things like strollers and cribs. Perhaps Lorraine would've been thinking of those things had she and Clint gotten married. In a different life, she would've been preparing the nursery, having a baby shower.

But that hadn't happened. She couldn't spend her time thinking about it. Just like she couldn't allow herself to think back on her last conversation with Alan. She sometimes wondered if she should've said more to him. She knew she had to keep it a secret, but she never knew how isolating that would be. Plus, she recalled the sadness in his eyes. Perhaps he simply missed his friend, but Lorraine wondered if he had figured out more. Surely he didn't know the full truth, but she knew not to underestimate Alan and his ability to see what most others overlooked.

Watching Mirabelle, she saw in her a motherly instinct that Lorraine didn't have. It made sense that Mirabelle would want to keep the baby. But Lorraine couldn't. Her circumstances and plans didn't allow for that option. That's what she had been told. And it was what she still believed. For now.

# CHAPTER NINETEEN

Mary Jane Whiler could smell a rat. She had learned the skill at a young age, her sense now nearly as keen as an emaciated tomcat on the prowl. She noticed it the first time she ever saw that housemother with the girls, marching them through downtown, a constant scowl of disapproval stamped across her face. She knew it that day the woman grabbed Lorraine by the elbow and pulled her out of the library as if she were a tantruming toddler.

Like all townsfolk, Mary Jane knew the home existed. But unlike most of her neighbors, she pitied those who spent their time there. Most in the town felt the home was a service to loose girls who had gotten themselves into a mess, but more importantly, a blessing to families waiting to love a child of their own. But those people didn't consider the futures these women had ahead of them. Mary Jane had seen the threads that wove and bound that present reality to the shame—or worse—they would carry with them for the rest of their lives.

Mary Jane was only eight when her oldest sister, Charlene, had become pregnant. Charlene wasn't sent away. Instead, she ran away and eloped. Mary Jane was too young at the time to understand any of it. She remembered the yelling, tears, whispers, and arguments that led up to her sister leaving the family for a few months. Though what she remembered most was that Charlene never really came home. The woman who walked back in the house with a deflated stomach and crying baby was a shell of the bubbly, vivacious sister who had once given her piggyback rides around the backyard.

The first rat Mary Jane sniffed out was the man Charlene brought home and introduced as her husband, the father of the baby. Mary Jane knew from the first moment she laid eyes on him that he did not and would not love her sister, a boy too angry and immature to be a father and a husband. The bruises that Charlene attempted to hide each time they saw her proved that to be true.

Watching her sister disappear, Mary Jane chose a different path for herself. Instead of putting her attention on boys, she studied. Even in college, as some of her friends discussed women's rights and practiced free love, she already knew that love came with a very high price. One she was not willing to pay.

Now only a year out of college, Mary Jane watched the pregnant girls march into town every Thursday morning. She didn't want to pity them, but she feared the fate that lay ahead for them. If they weren't strong enough to break attachments, to think of themselves and their own future, much like her sister, their time to come would include sustained hurt and heartbreak.

She knew she couldn't help them all, but when Lorraine walked into her library, she thought she might be able to do something. The problem was getting past the housemother, who had a specific way of doing things and a singular focus for the girls in her charge: control them until they could hand over their babies and leave.

As long as Mary Jane had been in town, she'd known the

maternity home existed somewhere down the tree-choked drive, but she had never seen it, let alone stepped inside, until she had to. Clearly Lorraine wanted her help, and with an ever-looming deadline, Mary Jane needed to act quickly.

She didn't know what she expected to find behind those large, wooden doors, but what she saw looked a lot more typical than she had imagined. She had thought of girls all alone, sitting and waiting, the clock ticking toward birth and separation. Instead, what she found reminded her a lot more of dorm life—activity, conversations, and even a bit of laughter filling the air.

Taking a seat in Miss Mahoney's office, Ms. Whiler tried not to look at the mess, a haphazard nest spilling with books and papers. She decided to get right down to business, needing to get back to the library.

"I'd like to help Lorraine."

"Help?" Miss Mahoney didn't know why the librarian was in her office that morning; nor did she understand what the woman meant by helping. "That's a kind offer, but we have things all in order."

"Yes, I'm sure you do, but I can help in a different way."

Miss Mahoney, though a bit annoyed, was intrigued. It wasn't too often that people offered to help, other than donating stray items or taking up a church collection here and there. There was Mrs. Belmont who graciously gave of her time, but in the six years Miss Mahoney had been the housemother, no one else had volunteered. "How so?"

"I want to help her get her degree."

Miss Mahoney removed her glasses and rubbed her temples. Of course. That Lorraine certainly was a determined girl, singularly focused on her future. Miss Mahoney knew that she should be glad the girl had something to keep her mind occupied. That might lessen the possibility of reconsidering things.

"Oh, yes," she said as she put her glasses back in place. "She and I have spoken about that, but as I've explained to her, we don't do that here."

Through a fixed smile, Ms. Whiler continued. "I understand that. But that's how I can help. I offer GED classes two evenings a week—"

"I'm going to stop you right there. I'm well aware of what you offer the community, mostly men, I'm assuming? I'm sure you know that not everyone in town appreciates having these troubled girls in their community, examples of poor behavior for their daughters to see. We do our best to keep them off the street, away from view other than an hour and a half each week. Enough time for them to stretch their legs a bit while others are at work or school. I'm sure the town wouldn't appreciate them wandering around the streets at all hours."

"I'm not talking about all hours." Ms. Whiler paused, reminding herself to be casual and cordial, not condescending. "And I'm not suggesting Lorraine attend those classes. She has been coming to the library each Thursday for a few weeks now. She's smart. I'd like to see if she could come five days a week and I could work with her to prepare to take the exam."

"Five days? Oh, surely not. She has work to do around here. Chores and finishing school."

"I'm sure you can see how this could be more beneficial to her in the long run than dusting off the porch."

"Five days?" Miss Mahoney asked as she leaned back. She

didn't want to the let the girl go, to have her wandering into town alone and so often. "It's simply too much."

Ms. Whiler shifted in her chair, the leather squeaking with the movement. As much as she preferred straightforward conversations with only facts and pertinent information, she knew she needed to be more cunning and crafty. She needed to exploit Miss Mahoney's weakness: her pride.

"What you do for these girls... Well, it's admirable." Ms. Whiler paused to smile as she coaxed herself to keep going for Lorraine's sake. "A good Christian woman like yourself, surely you're doing the Lord's work here. And, well, I do believe that He has called me to do likewise." Bless her heart, was she really saying these words? "You see, this girl is different. And I believe we can be of greater help to her, give her something more than most girls need. What's the harm in the girl learning a bit while you wait for her baby to arrive? You wouldn't have to worry about any of it. I'll take care of it all. But to help like this, I need more time with her."

She had a point, Miss Mahoney realized. She didn't want to give such leeway. She preferred running a tighter ship, having more control, keeping the girls under her watchful eye at all hours of all days of the week. But maybe this woman could help keep Lorraine thinking about something other than the baby, keep her from getting attached to that child growing inside of her. She'd seen it before, girls who came in easily signing the relinquishment form, agreeing to give up their babies. But then time and movements and hormones, she could only assume, whispered into their ears and made them question everything. Made them think they could keep their children. Could you imagine? Thinking they could raise them as a single mother, give them love and care like they needed from a mother *and* a father. Like Mirabelle, who, now that Miss Mahoney thought of it, Lorraine did spend a lot of time with.

Maybe this arrangement could be a bit of insurance so that Lorraine wouldn't turn into one of those girls.

"How about three days?" Miss Mahoney asked.

"Three it is."

---

Lorraine nearly skipped to the library after Miss Mahoney told her the news. Before she left, she had to agree to complete all her chores when she got back.

"This is a special arrangement, and it can be withdrawn at any time. You must keep up with your duties around here, or there won't be any library time," Miss Mahoney warned.

Lorraine agreed and nearly hugged the housemother.

When she got to the library, Ms. Whiler already had a lesson plan laid out. She started by testing Lorraine, getting an idea of what she knew and what they needed to spend time on to prepare her for the exam. Ms. Whiler hoped Lorraine could learn enough in six weeks to take the test before the baby came.

The librarian believed her student could do that. She really was a bright girl, and Ms. Whiler had no doubt that she would do well in college. She had no way of knowing how much studying Lorraine did between their sessions. Her nose always in a book, as Denise would say. Mirabelle wished she would read less and talk more, but she was also the first to offer to help her friend when Lorraine slipped behind on keeping up with her chores.

Lorraine found Ms. Whiler easy to talk to. She listened and shared, encouraged and challenged. They both loved science and spent time talking about Valentina Tereshkova, a Russian cosmonaut and the first woman in space. While they celebrated the accomplishment, they lamented that the Russians had beat them to it. She updated Lorraine on the latest news out of NASA. She also kept Lorraine grounded, introducing her to the developing theory of plate tectonics.

"Alfred Wegener first developed this theory that all the continents once fit together like a puzzle, if we simply moved them around a bit," Ms. Whiler explained. "He called that land mass Pangaea."

"But, how did that happen?" Lorraine wondered, trying to make sense of how the puzzle had come apart.

"Continental drift," Ms. Whiler explained. "The continents moved apart from one another and they continue to move today."

She went on to explain how slowly these large land masses move, but how over time, lots and lots of time, a shift can be seen and evidence of that shifting can be found in earthquakes, volcanoes, and mountains. With that claim came the question Ms. Whiler had anticipated.

"But how can that be?" Lorraine asked, thinking about all the Sunday school lessons she'd had.

"Great question!" Ms. Whiler reached for a piece of paper. She tucked her hair behind each of her ears and began drawing a timeline across the paper, using hash marks to denote millions and billions until she came to the present day. She explained carbon dating and scientific research about theories of how old the earth is.

"But Daddy always said God made the world in six days."

"That is the literal interpretation of the Bible," Ms. Whiler said. "It appears that Mr. Wegener and others have different theories. That's what makes science so exciting! We can take ideas and test them and discuss and try things and see what results we get."

Moments like these are exactly why Lorraine treasured her time with Ms. Whiler. She was like no teacher Lorraine had ever had before. And she wasn't even a teacher. Not officially. But the woman knew so much, and she didn't seem bound to have to teach only certain specific things.

With their time for the day nearly over, Ms. Whiler began stacking the papers and books, handing Lorraine what she should take with her for further study. Busy with tidying, she let the words escape, "Guess that's why I've never much been the church type."

Lorraine involuntarily shook her head and second-guessed what she had heard. In all her life, she had only met a couple of people who didn't attend church. "What?" Lorraine asked.

When Ms. Whiler saw Lorraine's surprise, she realized she had said too much. She knew that Lorraine had been raised to believe in the Father, Son, Holy Ghost, and weekly attendance. On the other hand, Ms. Whiler had never needed to put blind faith into an invisible cosmic genie, nor did she desire to be a part of a religious social club.

"Oh, sorry," Ms. Whiler stammered. She had her feelings about the whole God thing, but she didn't need to bother Lorraine with those ideas. More pressing matters needed her attention. "You're doing great and I have no doubt that you'll pass without a problem."

Lorraine smiled as she relaxed. "Thank you."

"I mean it. You still have a few weeks to go, but the timing should work out perfectly, just before the baby…before you're due." While they had discussed grammar, history, math, and science in their time together, they both gladly avoided any conversation about the pregnancy.

"Good," Lorraine replied. As she gathered the books and prepared to head back to the maternity home, she continued. "And thank you. For all of this. I appreciate it." She did. Without Ms. Whiler, she didn't know how she would make it through her time there, and she certainly didn't know what she would do once she got home. "I've really been enjoying our time together."

"Me too."

Ms. Whiler gave Lorraine a different perspective, not just on learning, but on life. She had no husband, no kids, and seemed fine with that arrangement. From the best Lorraine could tell, she wasn't a member of any social clubs, societies, or church groups. And she certainly wasn't the type to be a Sunnymede Sister.

The two women walked toward the door together. Before leaving, Lorraine paused and asked, "Have you ever wondered what it would be like to go to space?"

"All the time." Ms. Whiler smiled. A patron rang the bell, beckoning the librarian. "Have a nice walk back. I'll see you in two days."

Lorraine had never met anyone else who had the same dream, wondered the same thing as she did. She held her books to her chest and walked back to the home as the breeze tickled her arms and legs. She watched the clouds float overhead, shifting and morphing as they journeyed across the sky.

Ms. Whiler had a different way of existing in the world. Lorraine had never thought about a woman not being a wife or a mother. Even as she would dream about space, she assumed that her husband and kids were somewhere in that picture. She just didn't know exactly where. She was a woman; being a mother was something they did. That's what she believed until she met the librarian. And somehow her future seemed to open up for her when she no longer thought about a husband and kids. No longer considered who she might date and what she'd have to eventually tell him some day.

Likewise, Ms. Whiler saw Lorraine's potential, her openness to new ideas, her thirst for discovery. She thought she had a kindred spirit in some regard, another woman who saw the world as she did, who didn't buy into the systems that so many women submitted themselves to. She thought Lorraine could be different, like her. That is, until the day she saw in Lorraine what both she and Miss Mahoney had feared would happen.

# CHAPTER TWENTY

Betty knew that her daughter's room didn't need to be cleaned, but she still found herself standing in the bedroom periodically. Betty knew what her husband would say, that she needed to be tough. To push down those feelings. To let the girl go. Lorraine would be back soon enough, though Betty understood better than Eugene that the girl would never fully come back, not in the same way. But how would he know that? He wasn't a mother. He didn't know what they had asked of her. But they hadn't really asked, had they? More like, expected. Demanded. Coerced.

Eugene had been spending more time at the office and meetings, coming in smelling like smoke when he would crawl into bed in the middle of the night. They didn't talk, not about the smoking, nor much else. How could they when he was gone so much? But even when they were together, they were both gone. Or they busied themselves with tasks and projects that neither one of them really cared about.

Eugene did a better job of acting, of continuing the role when they saw friends and neighbors, when they shook the pastor's hand each Sunday and he asked if they had heard from Lorraine. Betty could smile and nod, but she feared her eyes still told the truth.

Betty walked to Lorraine's bed and sat down. Home alone, as usual, the only sound in the house was the hum of the refrigerator in the kitchen below. She lay down on the bed, resting her head on her daughter's pillow as she curled her legs in toward herself. She had known that secret keeping is a lonely business, but this one was even lonelier than the others. She had wanted to visit or at least write to Lorraine, but Eugene had said it was best to let Lorraine be, as if fearing that if they contacted her, she would be reminded of family and want to start one of her own.

But Betty knew what Eugene didn't: the body kept score, in both seen and unseen ways. Lorraine would probably have the visual reminder of a misshapen stomach and stretch marks. She'd help Lorraine diminish both as best she could, but no amount of calisthenics or Jergens Lotion would fully remove them. Of course, the physical reminders were the least of her worries. The heartache would be worse. Betty already feared the annual reminder of a birthday without a reason to celebrate.

The Delfords expected their daughter to do something that went against nature, against motherhood itself. Betty hoped the girl's ambitions were strong enough to keep her focused, moving in a different direction. Betty knew she wouldn't have been strong enough to give up Lorraine, to hand her over and walk away. But she had to trust that Lorraine could do it. She was strong enough. She needed to be. And Betty Delford had to believe that.

The thing was, Lorraine was strong. But she was also tired.

So far, Lorraine had pushed through it all: aching back, pelvic pressure, engorged breasts, indigestion, and restless sleep. Some nights she even woke herself up snoring. She had never snored before in her life, not that she knew of.

At thirty-five weeks, she barely recognized herself in the mirror anymore. Her cheeks were more full, her hair longer and thicker, her shape more like Humpty Dumpty's than an hourglass. She didn't spend much time looking at herself. Each morning she'd rush to breakfast and down a few cups of coffee before hurrying through her chores and out the front door to the library on the days she met with Ms. Whiler. So far, it had all been working out. In part, thanks to Mirabelle, who pitched in and helped with Lorraine's chores when the coffee didn't seem to be enough to get her going and through her tasks in time.

"I'm happy to help," Mirabelle always told her, and Lorraine believed her.

"You need to slow down," was all Denise would ever say, but Denise seemed to live her life in slow motion, moseying here and there without any sort of purpose or hurry in her step.

It was in her third week of meeting with Ms. Whiler when Lorraine felt something. She couldn't quite explain it, but she felt a little off. She poured herself a third cup of coffee that morning at breakfast as Mirabelle told some story about a three-legged dog they once had.

"We called her Bubbles," Mirabelle explained.

"Bubbles?" Denise asked.

"Yeah, she was round and fat, like a big bubble about to pop. I don't know how those three legs held her up. Seemed like even four would have a hard time, but you should've seen her run! Well, all except for when she'd get going down the hill to the creek. Then sometimes her one front leg couldn't keep up with the back two. They'd get going too fast and she'd roll end over end, sometimes splashing into the creek before she could even stop."

Mirabelle laughed at the memory, but Lorraine remained

quiet. Come to think of it, it wasn't so much *Lorraine* who felt off. Something seemed different with the baby.

As Mirabelle continued talking about the day Bubbles tried to befriend a raccoon kit but ended up with a swipe across her muzzle, Lorraine put her cup of coffee on the table and placed her hands on her stomach, pressing from both sides.

At that time of the day and especially after having just eaten, the baby would typically be moving, pushing against her insides and outsides, shimmying around as if saying "thank you" for the meal.

But that morning she felt nothing.

Lorraine continued to press and hold, moving her hands to different spots, slowing her breathing so the only movement of her body that she could feel would come from the life growing inside of her.

But she still felt nothing.

She hadn't realized until that moment how accustomed to those movements she had become. They had gradually grown to be a part of her, but now that they weren't happening, she noticed their absence. And for the first time, she began to worry, not about her predicament or future but about her baby.

"Are you okay?" Mirabelle asked.

Lorraine had long since lost track of the conversation Mirabelle and Denise had been having. She didn't know when they had stopped talking and started looking at her, but at that moment, they were both watching her.

Mirabelle reached toward Lorraine and placed a hand on her arm. She asked again, "Are you okay?"

Lorraine felt foolish saying anything. She didn't want to make a big deal if everything was okay. Plus, she didn't want to draw too much attention to herself and risk Miss Mahoney not allowing her to leave for the library.

For all she knew, the baby was resting, sleeping, as she wished she still was. She figured she was simply being a bit overreactive. She took another sip of her coffee and said, "I'm fine. Just a bit tired."

That morning, Lorraine got to the library later than usual. She didn't walk as fast as she typically did. She took her time, but it wasn't exactly a leisurely stroll. She didn't notice the azaleas that were beginning to bloom, nor the first hummingbird of the season that scouted for nectar in the new blooms. She kept her eyes focused downward, at least one hand on her stomach the entire walk.

Ms. Whiler greeted Lorraine as usual as she walked into the library.

"I've got you all set up. I'll check on you in a few minutes."

Thankfully she was busy with a patron, so she didn't have a chance to notice how much quieter, distracted, and distant Lorraine was that morning.

Lorraine took a seat in her usual study carrel tucked in the corner of the library. Ms. Whiler had a lesson plan and books laid out, but Lorraine pushed them away as she took a seat. She closed her eyes and for the first time in months muttered a prayer.

*Dear God, let everything be okay.*

She placed both hands firmly onto her stomach.

*Protect this baby.*

In her eight months of being pregnant, no one had talked to Lorraine about the possibility of something going wrong. All anyone seemed to care about was what to do with the baby after it was born. So Lorraine had gone along, assuming everything was okay, and would continue to be okay, as far as the baby was concerned. But that morning, as she sat in the corner and waited to feel something, anything, a new reality hit her. Just like that night when she had learned that stars could fall, she now understood that it was possible that something could go terribly wrong.

*Don't let anything bad happen to my baby.*

She sat in silence. Not moving. No longer praying. Simply waiting. She didn't feel it right away. It still took a couple of minutes for her hands to sense the first pulse. Then a second one. And a third. She welcomed the feeling. At first she was delighted. There was something! There was movement! Her prayer had worked and her baby was okay after all.

Or was it?

The movement was odd. Different. It wasn't the usual jumps and jolts she typically felt. The beats continued. They were smaller. Consistent. A staccato rhythm that drummed from within her.

"Is everything okay?" Ms. Whiler asked as she approached Lorraine.

With tears in her eyes and panic in her voice, Lorraine whispered, "I don't know."

Ms. Whiler knelt on the floor beside her. She had been afraid this might happen, that Lorraine would go into labor too soon and not be able to complete the GED before going home.

"Do I need to call Miss Mahoney?"

"No. I don't think so. I don't know."

"What's going on? Tell me how you're feeling."

"It's not me," Lorraine said. "It's the baby."

"What do you mean?"

"At breakfast this morning, the baby didn't move, not like usual. And now, it's just weird. Here, feel."

Lorraine reached for Ms. Whiler's hand and placed it on her stomach so she could feel the pulses, one after another.

"Do you feel that? What is that? The heartbeat? It's never felt like that before."

Ms. Whiler withdrew her hand, relieved that labor hadn't started. They still had time. The librarian knew what was happening. Her sisters had been pregnant enough times for her to recognize that rhythmic beat.

"Hiccups," Ms. Whiler said, identifying the biological reason.

"What? Are you sure?" Could it really be that simple? Lorraine hoped so. Her eyes pleaded with Ms. Whiler for her assessment to be correct.

"Yes. You're sure you're feeling fine otherwise?"

Lorraine stopped and assessed herself for a minute. She didn't feel feverish. Her head, back, and stomach all felt fine, or as fine as they had been feeling recently. After all the worry and concern, she wasn't as tired as she had felt at breakfast that morning.

"Yes, I'm fine." Especially now that everything seemed to be okay with the baby.

Lorraine felt a combination of joy and foolishness. The fear of a moment ago had been replaced by relief, but she felt embarrassed by worrying about such a small, intrinsic thing as a hiccup. She had panicked over something so simple. What did that say about her ability to be a mother?

Ms. Whiler knew she needed to redirect Lorraine, who had gotten there late that morning and was already behind. But more important than staying on track was getting the girl's mind away from the baby.

"Hiccups are good." She hoped that fact would help Lorraine settle. "A sign that the baby's lungs are developing. Now, let's see how your work is coming along."

The librarian tried to refocus her, but Lorraine kept looking at her stomach and smiling.

"It feels so weird."

Ms. Whiler had no idea how it felt, but for the girl's sake, she needed to get her mind back to her studies. That task would be harder than she had expected. She had no way of knowing how occupied Lorraine had been with thoughts of the baby even before the concerns and worry of that morning. Ms. Whiler didn't know that over the last week or so, Lorraine, who she had thought was her kindred spirit, had started to think more about what was growing inside of her: fingers, toes, eyes, heart, even fingernails, and hair. It had taken months for Lorraine to get to that point, but the more the baby moved, kicked, turned, and now hiccuped, the more it felt like a whole, tiny person existed inside of her.

And that morning had also shown her something new: a concern and care for this baby. *Her* baby.

It only took a few moments of inactivity, a disruption to what had become typical, for the bonds of attachment to challenge the best-laid plans of the past few months and ignite a question in Lorraine's mind that everyone hoped she would never ask.

# CHAPTER TWENTY-ONE

As the rain tapped against her office window, Miss Mahoney stretched her neck from side to side, placing her right ear on her shoulder before bending her neck so the left one could do the same. That bed certainly wasn't the most comfortable. It was a step above what the girls had, the newest bed in the home, but that wasn't saying much. Of course, she hadn't taken on the role of housemother because of the accommodations.

When her daddy moved to serve another congregation, she had to decide whether to move with him to a new town or stay where she'd been born and raised and embark on some sort of mission. A husband hadn't yet presented himself, so she had few other options.

As much as she thought of staying with her daddy, she felt the calling, akin to the one her father had said the Lord had placed on his heart when he decided to devote his life to ministry. Of course, she couldn't follow in his footsteps—a woman in the pulpit in her Southern Baptist church! Could you imagine? She never dared to consider that a possibility.

After sitting in prayer circles and hearing the cries of wives with empty arms, she decided to make it her mission to take the trouble that some girls got themselves into and turn that to good for those who deserved a blessing. And the local maternity home seemed like the perfect place to do just that.

That morning in her office, Miss Mahoney stretched and yawned. She didn't have an appointment scheduled for a few more minutes, so she was giving herself permission to ease into the day. She knew she could be in for some hectic hours ahead, what with a few of the girls about ready to burst. She had to admit, she wasn't going to be sad when some of them left, especially that Denise girl. The girl was quiet, which Miss Mahoney appreciated, but she didn't feel she could fully trust her. She kept waiting for some sort of defiance. Thankfully she'd signed her paper the first day—with little hesitation, in fact—so at least that matter was settled. If only she could get that Mirabelle to do likewise. She had a couple ready to take the baby. Of course, she'd only given them the necessary information, not all the details. She didn't consider it lying, especially when the means justified the ends. As long as they were a happy family, that's all that mattered.

Miss Mahoney rocked back in her chair, not yet knowing her first appointment was about to interrupt her a few minutes ahead of schedule.

The door wide open, Lorraine paused before she knocked on the doorframe. She knew she was a few minutes early, but she wanted to get this routine check-in out of the way so she wouldn't miss out on any time at the library. She was looking forward to the walk, hoping the fresh air could relax her and help with a bit of indigestion that seemed to be more common those days.

Miss Mahoney was at her desk when Lorraine knocked, her chair swiveled toward the window. Lorraine waited for an invitation to proceed. As she did so, she noticed a door that hadn't caught her attention before, probably because it was behind the chair she sat in when she was in the office. On this morning, the door wasn't closed all the way. She could make out just a portion of the room and a bed inside it.

Lorraine wondered why anyone would choose to live there, choose to stay there, choose to limit her life to a cramped office and a small bedroom inside a home with so many rules. Though, she supposed, someone had to supervise, to be on call at night if anything happened. Mrs. Belmont went home, as did the cook and the nurse and certainly the doctor. Miss Mahoney only got one night off a week—Tuesdays. But that only amounted to a few hours after dinner and before bedtime. The rest of the time the housemother was on duty, her life and her calling too intertwined to be separated.

"I said come in!" Miss Mahoney's voice rose. Lorraine had apparently been too distracted to hear her, too busy trying to see more of that room—the bed with the rumpled blankets, the blank walls, the room even emptier than her shared room upstairs.

Miss Mahoney shuffled around a few pieces of paper as the girl took a seat in the chair opposite the desk, her back now to the hidden room. Lorraine gripped an armrest with one hand to slow her descent. The chair sat low and any amount of cushion deflated as Lorraine sat down. Springs pushed against the leather covering, poking into the weight of her body, causing her to shift around every few minutes to move the pressure from one area to another.

Miss Mahoney remained silent, which gave Lorraine time to realize how uneasy she felt. But maybe some of that was the bacon she had for breakfast, the grease coating her esophagus and stomach, her body wanting to emit a burp. She shifted in her chair, trying to stifle the urge, knowing this was not the place for such an impoliteness. In that moment, she thought about Alan. If anyone would've appreciated such an act, it was him.

"Thirty-five weeks," Miss Mahoney finally said. "Dr. Reese says you're measuring fine. Weight's good. Blood pressure where he wants to see it. Four to six weeks and then you'll be going home."

Home. Lorraine didn't allow herself to think of it too often, but she couldn't always help herself. How she missed her bed. Her dad's recliner. Her mother's cooking.

"It appears all's in order, so—"

These check-ins never lasted long, which Lorraine was typically okay with. She didn't particularly want to spend a lot of time in Miss Mahoney's office, especially when she'd rather be on her way into town. But that morning, instead of leaving right away, she decided to ask for more information.

"So, have you—" How did she say this? Could she even say it? "Did you find the... Do you have a family in mind?" She couldn't end that question with the words *for my baby*, though those were implied.

Miss Mahoney crossed her arms.

"It's just that I've been doing some thinking, wondering—" Especially since a few days ago when she hadn't felt the baby move and she felt the worry that only a mother can know. Since that panicked morning, she wanted answers to questions she hadn't thought—or cared—to ask until then.

"Now, you don't need to be doing any of that. It's quite alright for you to think and wonder all you want with Ms. Whiler. But I have everything taken care of here. You just go about your last month thinking about getting home and getting on with things. I'll handle the rest."

Lorraine heard what she said, but it wasn't enough.

"You said you're here to help. It's just, I've been wondering if help is always the same. I mean I know Denise, she wants to give up the baby, but then there's Mirabelle who can't wait to be a mother. And I've just been thinking that maybe there are different options."

Miss Mahoney sat up. She knew where this was headed. This is exactly what she had feared, why she hoped the librarian could distract the girl so she wouldn't start thinking these thoughts. She reached for the folder stained with coffee.

"Hmmm. Well, let's see here," she said as if they had been in the middle of a discussion that had nothing to do with what Lorraine had just asked. "Course since the first time we met, you told me about your future. What you hoped for. I've even gone so far as to make sure you could keep up your studies, letting you meet with that librarian." Miss Mahoney looked at Lorraine with her lips pursed.

"Yes, ma'am." The indigestion brought warmth and acid to her throat. She paused, swallowed, adjusted in her chair again. The two women held each other's gaze until Lorraine looked down at her hands. They rested in her lap with her fingers braided together around her stomach.

"And what about this college you're still hoping to attend?" A quiet smile faded from the housemother's lips. "I'm simply trying to help you do that, despite this…predicament?"

Lorraine looked out the window behind Miss Mahoney. Despite the rain, the cardinals still perched on the feeder, their feathers matted from the constant drizzle. She wondered why they didn't find shelter, some place dry to hide until the precipitation passed. She wanted to stand up, squeeze between the desk and bookshelf, and tell them to go home until the storm stopped.

Surely they could fill their bellies once the clouds swept away and the sun came back out. Hadn't they learned by now that the feeders would be full and waiting when they needed to eat? Hadn't they learned the rhythms, grown accustomed to the assurances? Yet they fluttered to the feeder as the rain dripped down, apparently not trusting in assumptions of how things had always been.

"I know all of this can be confusing, trying, even. But..." Miss Mahoney leaned forward, the weight shift causing the chair to creak as her demeanor changed. As much as she wanted to demand the girl not change her mind, she needed to rein this one in. And quickly. "I can see you have a bright future ahead of you. You've made the right decision, so leave it to us."

"But—"

Miss Mahoney couldn't let the girl say too much, ask too many questions, give too much thought to what options she might have. She lowered her voice and asked, "Wouldn't it be nice to go home without any shame?"

That last word landed on Lorraine's shoulders, pushing them down. She kept her chin up and her eyes dry, though the feeling that washed over her was so heavy that she should have cried, that she should have burst into sobs right there in front of that woman with the cat's-eye glasses.

It was that word: *shame*. That was what hit her and pushed her down into that worn chair in the tight, cramped office. That was the word that defined how she had been feeling for the past few months, during the quiet alone times, first in her bedroom, then in a place called a "home," but that felt nothing like what the word *home* actually meant, what she had been taught it had meant from the time she was in grammar school. She had been there long enough to know this wasn't a home, even if the sign said it was. That word trapped her in that moment, that season, that chair in that drab room.

Miss Mahoney gave her a few seconds to feel that weight before she stood from her chair, shimmied her way between the desk and the bookshelves, and slid in front of Lorraine. She knelt down and, with a flat hand, patted Lorraine's knee as if it were a drum. "There, there," she said.

Lorraine welcomed the touch, the bit of comfort. That word she said as she knelt in front of her; it was the same word said twice, the word she had wanted to hear her mother or father or Clint say for the past eight months, and yet the housemother was the first one to say it.

"I know this must be hard. You're a smart girl. You want to do what's best. So why not make a list?"

"A list?" Lorraine asked. She thought of Mirabelle. "Like a collage?"

"Uh," Miss Mahoney stammered, confused by the idea. "Most girls write their answers." She stood from her kneeling position, leaned against her desk, and crossed her arms.

"Oh, I thought you meant like what Mirabelle was doing." Miss Mahoney's head tilted to the side, like a robin's would do when searching for food. "With the magazines." Again, Miss Mahoney's head tilted. "Cutting out the pictures." Miss Mahoney's eyes squinted, eyebrows angled toward the bridge of her nose. Lorraine couldn't stop talking. "Pasting them onto the piece of paper. The collection, that's what she calls it. With baby items, what she wants to get for her baby."

Miss Mahoney grabbed a pen and a piece of paper, made a note, and then responded. "No. That's a…project…she's doing on her own. This is a list of reasons why you believe you would make a better parent, by yourself, to your child than a married couple, a mother *and* father would."

*Wait, what?*

Now Lorraine's head tilted, eyebrows scrunched together. Miss Mahoney didn't acknowledge the confusion; she kept right on going with her directions. "Sometimes when we write things down, we see things more clearly. So, take this piece of paper and pen, make two columns, one for you and one for the parents who pray daily for a baby to love. Put in each column the reasons each would make a better home for the baby."

She didn't want the girl to think too much about the baby. It was always best when it could remain in the abstract, but clearly the girl's mind had already been making a person of the thing. The list usually did the trick for a girl like this, especially a girl who had been raised the way she had.

Miss Mahoney walked back to her chair, straightening her drab sweater before sitting down. "I have another appointment now. We'll talk more later. For now, make the list."

Lorraine pushed against the arms of the chair to stand up.

"And one more thing. Please don't say anything to Mirabelle. I'll speak with her about her project."

Lorraine walked toward the staircase. She took each step slowly, her eyes on the empty piece of paper. She walked into her room. The rain continued to fall outside, droplets landing on the window, uniting with others as they zigzagged down the length before dropping out of sight. The room was darker than it typically was at that time of the day, but Lorraine didn't turn on the light. She didn't plan to be there long. This was simply a stop before leaving for the library, a moment to put away, to pause, to breathe.

With muted grayness consuming the outside world, a spot of color on the inside caught her eye. Upon the empty fourth bed was the pink yarn blanket, it's purled craftiness swaddled around Brown Bear, the only piece of home she had. As the raindrops zigzagged down the window, Lorraine tucked the paper and pen inside her nightstand drawer before walking past the pink display of hope and love that had been painstakingly knotted together once again.

# CHAPTER TWENTY-TWO

The home's inhabitants weren't the only ones with secrets to keep. Built in the 1700s, the home itself had a history. Long before it came to house unwed mothers, it sheltered generations of a family, stood throughout a war, hosted generals, and segregated the help from the hosts. Its grand Palladian architecture incited awe, while its secret passages kept servants accessible, yet hidden.

The girls of the home knew nothing of the history, architecture, or family whose name would be ever etched in the stonework above the stately front doors. They knew it merely as a temporary resting place, one they hoped to leave behind quickly and never think of again. Too lost in their own confusion and predicaments, few girls took the time to explore the home or the gardens or the passages hidden in plain sight.

So, it's no surprise that in her two months there, Lorraine had never thought about the wood-paneled door right beside the second-floor bathroom until the evening she saw Denise open it and sneak inside. Curiosity had led Lorraine to the pond in the new development the day she nearly drowned. On this evening, it coaxed her to open the door and follow her roommate. First, she gave Denise a few seconds' head start before she opened the door for herself. Behind it was a curving staircase leading downward—a tunnel tucked within walls.

She walked down one flight, the stairs narrow and steep, the walls nearly pushing against her shoulders, or so it felt in the hallway so dark that she could barely see her own hand if she held it in front of her face. She crept slowly downward, holding on to the railing for balance.

On her first day at the facility, Miss Mahoney had promised that climbing the stairs would help with her physical conditioning, but as her stomach had continued to grow over her weeks there, her breath seemed to be harder and harder to catch with each flight. It had required her to slow her pace and take longer to walk to the library.

Lorraine stopped for a moment when she reached the bottom. She knew from the hollow echoes of her footsteps and the musty smell that she had reached the basement, a place she visited only during her appointments with Dr. Reese. At the end of a dark tunnel, light entered through an open door as Denise stepped outside. Lorraine felt foolish following her this far, but she didn't feel like turning back now. Plus, fresh air sounded good to her, so Lorraine hurried to the door.

As she opened it, the breeze greeted her, whipping her dress so that the hem tickled her knees and the skirt nearly blew upward, revealing her undergarments. As much as she was trying to be quiet, she giggled with the surprise, and the door slammed shut behind her when her hands reflexively moved to cover herself.

Lorraine stepped onto the grass at the back side of the home, acres of lawn opening up around her, fenced off by a line of trees. She watched the silhouette of Denise disappear into those trees, and just as she had followed the feral cat down the wooded path that day so long ago, she followed her roommate, as well. The path opened into a clearing, like the farmer's land, but without the house or the memories.

With one hand, Lorraine held her skirt in place, while the other gathered her hair into a ponytail so she could look up at the sky without obstruction. She looked above herself, the sky clear and the stars turned on bright that night. This was the best view she'd had since she'd left home. Even through her room window, the leaves had begun budding and opening. While she welcomed the green signal that spring was coming, at night she found herself longing for the bare tree branches that she could peek through to see the stars overhead.

Left alone in a moment to see the moon and the shades of gray upon the white glowing orb, she nearly let herself realize how much she had missed it, had missed walking outside, breathing in the air, and admiring the night lights. She even missed her own bedroom, wondered if her mother had rearranged things while she had been gone. Hopefully, she hadn't. Hopefully, she would walk back into that room and all would be as it once had been.

But Denise interrupted the recollection.

"What the hell?" she yelled, too exasperated to remain quiet. It was the loudest Lorraine had ever heard her speak. The wind carried her voice through the clearing, but the trees and distance kept the sound from reaching the home.

Lorraine let go of her hair and used both hands to keep her skirt down, reacting with modesty as the breeze rattled her hem again. But her hair blocked her view as she looked around the lawn, trying to find her roommate, the voice she had gotten to know over her two months there even if she didn't know the person all that much.

She scooped her hair back into her hands, held most of it

behind her though a stubborn lock flapped around her face, but it wasn't enough of an obstruction to prevent her from seeing the orange glow near the center of the clearing.

She walked toward Denise, who sat in the grass, puffing on a cigarette. As she exhaled, a plume of smoke dispersed in the wind and swirled around the two girls. Before she took another drag, she asked, "You're following me?"

"I saw you open the door and was curious."

"So you were following me." Denise turned her head and blew smoke into the wind.

"Yes, well, no. I mean sort of. I wanted to see where it led."

Denise didn't say anything. She looked at Lorraine, the moonlight reflecting off her large pupils. "Why're you here?" she asked.

"I told you, I saw you and was curious."

"I get that much, but why are you *still* here."

Part of the reason was Mirabelle. The girl had been extra chatty that evening at dinner, which was something to say since the girl was nearly always talking, even when she was eating. Lorraine wondered what her mother, or Mrs. Belmont, would think if they saw the girl at the dinner table, her mouth full of food but words still fighting to get out. Sometimes Lorraine would have to gently remind Mirabelle to use a napkin to clear her chin of the food that hadn't stayed in her mouth.

But that night she was talking more than usual, excited that her blanket was nearly done again, showing everyone her accomplishment. Lorraine had been excited for her the first and even the second, possibly the third time that Mirabelle had made such an announcement. But the girl never tied it off, folded it up, and moved on to a new project.

She didn't want to gossip that night, didn't know that Denise would welcome that anyway. Though she'd spent the same amount of time rooming with both the girls, Mirabelle had spoken far more words during their stay than Denise had. Lorraine knew all about Mirabelle's boyfriend, but the more she talked, Lorraine began to wonder if *boyfriend* was the right term. Clearly there was a crush there, but when pressed for stories about their first date or when he asked her to go steady, Mirabelle grew silent or changed the subject or went on with a different observation she had to share.

Denise, on the other hand, Lorraine knew nothing about. She didn't know what town she'd come from, how old she was, how she'd ended up there. It wasn't that she didn't talk at all. It was just that most of what she said was trying to help Mirabelle or remind her of things.

So Lorraine didn't want to tell Denise that she needed a break from Mirabelle, though she desperately wanted to know if Denise felt the same way. Maybe that's why she was also in the clearing that night; she needed her own silence, and smoking was a way of finding that. So Lorraine simply said, "For the view."

Denise exhaled. Then she looked up to see what Lorraine meant by the view.

"That's what you wanted to see?"

Yes, that's exactly what she had been missing. In all the time sheltered away with a roof overhead, she had missed this. What's more, she had forgotten about it. She had been so distracted by other things—classes, chores, rules, studying, questions—that she hadn't sat under the expanse of the night sky for months, not since the night before she left when she last saw Alan. She had forgotten to look up.

A cloud passed over the moon and darkened the clearing. The wind quieted and tree frogs started chirping. Instead of filling the moment with her own humming, she took Denise's lead and sat there. Quietly. As the insects sang through the otherwise silent night, a question crept to the forefront of her mind: *What do I really want?*

Lorraine only permitted that thought to take up space in her mind for a moment. As the cloud that had been blocking the moon began to pass and the night sky grew light again, she hid that question behind knowledge she had accumulated over time.

"You see that gray mark there?" Lorraine pointed to the moon. "That sort of circle-looking thing?"

Denise looked upward, squinting, and tilting her head to the side. "That thing right there?"

"Yeah. That's the Ocean of Storms."

"There's an ocean on the moon? Like water?" This was the most interested Denise had ever been in anything Lorraine had to say.

"No. There's no water on the moon. It's a crater. And some day, before the end of this decade, astronauts will be able to see that up close."

Denise laughed. "You believe that?"

"Why wouldn't I?"

"You believe that there's actually going to be a rocket ship that will take people to the moon and back?"

"Yes." She had to.

Denise shrugged her shoulders, an expression Lorraine had seen her give Mirabelle countless times when she was done arguing, choosing not to pursue a conversation any further.

"Must be nice for those people," Denise said.

"Who?"

"The ones lucky enough to leave this place."

Denise put the cigarette to her mouth and inhaled, the tip glowing in the darkness and fading again as she exhaled.

"Have you thought about what you'll do after?" Lorraine asked.

Denise shifted to lying down, one arm bent so her hand could act as a pillow.

"You mean other than host tea parties and luncheons like Mrs. Belmont's teaching us to do?"

They both knew neither of those things would be in Denise's future.

"Sort of," Lorraine said. "I mean are you going to go back home? Get a job? Settle down with your boyfriend?"

Denise took another puff of her cigarette but didn't answer.

Lorraine had been thinking a lot about this lately, especially as her stomach grew ever bigger, pushing so that marks began to tear at the sides of her skin. She wondered if that would ever go away or if she would be left with the reminder for the rest of her life.

Lorraine decided to ask Denise her thoughts. "They keep talking about normal and tea parties and napkin folding. Then there's Mirabelle, who plans to marry Stuart and push baby Rose in a carriage."

The breeze rustled the trees, moving the branches so they creaked, but Lorraine could still hear Denise let out a low laugh.

"Yeah, that's what she wants."

"Don't you think she will?"

"Listen," Denise began, "there's a lot I don't know. I'm not like you. I don't read books for fun or ever. But one thing I do know is that Mirabelle would love that baby, be the best mom that baby could have."

*If that could be true for Mirabelle, could it also be true for her?*

Lorraine put her hand on her stomach. The baby leaned into it. Lorraine pressed against the spot where she felt pressure, held it for a moment.

"And what about you?" she asked Denise. "Don't you think you'd be a good mom?"

Denise let out a long puff of smoke. "Nah. Others are better at that than I would be. Guess that's why I didn't have a problem signing that paper."

"But," Lorraine asked, "what if that's not what we want?"

Denise laughed. "What're you saying? You want to keep the baby? You want to take home this crying, pooping, helpless little thing and you're going to what? Provide for it yourself? Take it to cheerleading practice with you? Push it in a buggy up and down the school halls?"

The questions kept coming. Lorraine knew the absurdity of what she had said. Lorraine had been told that after this, she could move on as if nothing had happened, go on to college or marriage or have a family of her own. That's why she was there. But what no one had told her was that the thing she couldn't see, the thing that kept growing and pushing against her, might not make it possible for life to get back to normal.

She had signed the letter of relinquishment the first day before she understood things, before she found herself laughing at the little person doing cartwheels on the inside and worrying when those movements changed. The more her stomach grew and the more the baby moved, the more she thought of the child as not just a temporary inconvenience and questioned what she had done. And the more she got closer to questioning if she could undo it.

"I don't know," Lorraine stammered. "It's just, the paper... I thought I had to sign it."

"They want you to think that," Denise said as she smushed the cigarette into the grass. "But not everyone signs. Mirabelle hasn't. Drives Miss Mahoney crazy, too. Kinda wished I hadn't signed it so I could piss her off, keep her dangling."

"Maybe you could unsign it," Lorraine said, offering Denise an option along with herself.

"Nah. No way she'd allow that."

"I guess we're not allowed to change our minds," Lorraine said, telling herself there was no need to rethink things because what was done was already done and there was no undoing it now.

Denise stood up and brushed her hands along her backside to remove any blades of grass that clung to her. "Sure ya can. Until that baby's born, she can't take it from you."

"But how? If we signed the paper already?"

"She can't do anything without that paper. So, sneak in and get it. I mean, if that's what you really want, figure out a way."

For months, this thing had seemed somewhat abstract and arbitrary, but those flutters and flips within her only brought dimension to a decision she thought she had already made. But no one had asked her what she had wanted. No one had laid out options for her. No one had given her a choice in the matter. The question was: If she had a choice, what decision would she make?

# CHAPTER TWENTY-THREE

Mirabelle's favorite shirt was the one with the big yellow bow. The entire shirt was bright, sunshine, canary yellow. Her favorite. The bow was long and floppy, the tails falling to the side of her rounded belly, framing it. Hugging it. Holding on to her baby.

She wore the shirt more often than she should, more often than she did her laundry. But she couldn't help it. It made her happy. And in that home, she needed reminders of happiness. Gloom had a way of creeping in, in the quiet times, the dark hours, the moments when no one else was around. But that shirt, whenever she wore it, acted like a shield, a protection, a barrier against anything bad.

She had found it in the donation box shortly after she had arrived, not long after Janet, but she didn't like to think about that, be reminded of what happened. That's where the shirt came in. The sunshine feelings it wrapped her in helped her forget about that night, the memories she'd shake out of her mind like clearing an Etch A Sketch doodle.

Nearly to the end of her three months there, her stomach kept pushing ever outward, causing the shirt's hemline to creep ever upward. But she wouldn't need it for much longer. She hoped, if she had any say in the matter, that she'd go into labor with that shirt on. Wear it to the hospital. Hold her baby girl while wearing it. Even tickle little Rose's toes with the satin bow.

She was wearing the shirt the morning she overheard Miss Mahoney through the floor vent in the bathroom. She was trying to wipe off the spaghetti sauce from the previous night's supper. She hadn't even noticed the spot until she caught a glimpse in the mirror. A speck the shape of Saturn landed to the left of her protruding belly button, with a few spots acting as moons circling it. She smiled to herself, thinking that Lorraine would get a kick out of it. She wished she had shown her, but she needed to get herself cleaned up before she got in trouble again for not cleaning her clothes.

Mirabelle thought she could use the hand soap to clean the garment—or clean it well enough to get by without Miss Mahoney making a fuss over laundry. She knew she needed to get around to doing that, but she had been so busy lately, what with helping Lorraine keep up with her chores, not to mention putting the final touches on her collection, thanks to the magazine Denise had brought her a few days ago.

She didn't mean to overhear things. With as much as she talked, few doubted she could even hear others over her own chitter-chatter. But when she turned off the faucet that morning, she heard Miss Mahoney telling Mrs. Belmont that she'd be going out that evening.

Everyone knew Miss Mahoney had an evening off each week, but everyone also knew the woman rarely took it. No one knew if it was because she had no social life or because she felt the house would cave in without her there. The truth was probably a combination of the two.

With that information, Mirabelle began to prance. She dabbed at the spot a bit more. It seemed faded enough, passable enough, so she ran out of the bathroom and down the stairs to find the others and share the news with them.

"Tonight! Tonight!" Mirabelle tried to contain her excitement to a whisper as she ran into the dining room, faster than any girl in her condition should be capable of doing. Denise and Lorraine were already at the table, silently consuming their biscuits and gravy.

"How many times do I have to tell you to take it easy on the coffee?" Denise asked as she took a sip of orange juice to wash down her breakfast. On some mornings, Mirabelle did drink a few too many cups, making her jittery and even more talkative.

"It's not that!" Mirabelle pranced, quickly realizing she had forgotten to pee when she was in the bathroom. She seemed to always need to pee. "Miss Mahoney won't be here tonight!"

"Well"—Denise slurped another sip—"that is reason to celebrate."

"It means"—Mirabelle crossed her legs and began dancing not just for excitement—"we can have a dance!"

Denise rolled her eyes and swallowed. "A Mrs. Belmont box step? No thanks."

"No! Better than that! The librarian, she dropped things off a few weeks ago. One of them was a radio. Can you believe that? A radio! We haven't had one for months, not since the last one stopped working. But now we do! And it picks up the stations. We know. We tried. So tonight after dinner, in the common room, we're gonna dance!"

Mirabelle was already doing her own dance in the dining room that morning. She stopped the moment she saw Miss Mahoney walking through the door and toward their table.

"How's everyone this morning?" the housemother asked.

"Fine," Lorraine and Mirabelle said as Denise groaned and shrugged.

"Mirabelle," Miss Mahoney began, "looks like you're in quite the chipper mood."

"Yes, ma'am."

Miss Mahoney watched her for a moment, not content with a good mood. "You seem…antsy. Is there a reason for this?"

Mirabelle squeezed her lips together. Denise and Lorraine both feared she would burst with the secret she had just asked them to keep. Finally giving in to the pressure, she said, "I have to go!" and ran from the room.

———————————

That night, the dining hall was abuzz with excitement. The girls dressed in the nicest outfits they had available to them, their napkins draped across their laps or tucked into their necklines to guard against possible stains and spills. Some had spent the afternoon styling one another's hair, pinning updos and attempting beehives with the limited supplies they had on hand. It was a ragtag attempt at a prom of sorts, but it was also the closest these girls would come to attending that type of dance.

Too eager to start their evening, the girls ate quickly and filed into the common room. Anticipation had filled the house that day as word spread, but now as they gathered together, they waited for someone to take the lead. Groups of girls, divided according to room assignments, gathered in various corners of the common room until the music started playing. The girls started swaying, tentatively at first, still locked into their cliques. As the music continued, a few brave girls, like Mirabelle, stepped into the center of the room and let the music move them, too free to be embarrassed by what others might think. Soon, the floor filled with others, all too happy to be nervous.

There was no Mrs. Belmont–approved box step. The girls

jumped and jived as they had learned to do at high school dances. They shook and shimmied as Ricky Nelson sang about girls around the world who he met as a traveling man. They twisted with Chubby Checker, they longed to be Peggy Sue, and as the night wore on and their inhibitions lowered, they partnered up for "Earth Angel."

Mirabelle grabbed Lorraine, pulled her close, and plopped her head on her roommate's shoulder without even asking if she wanted to dance. When the song ended, she looked at Lorraine and asked, "Do you think I'll ever be someone's earth angel?"

But she didn't really need an answer, didn't wait for one, didn't expect one. Instead, she immediately began singing and swinging, belting out that breaking up is hard to do.

Being released of the slow dance, Lorraine took a moment to sit down on one of the chairs that had been pushed to the outer edges. She looked around. From the shoulders up, the room of girls looked like any other room, any high school gym, any gathering of teenagers with smiles all around and laughter periodically rising in the air.

Even Denise lost herself in the moment of the night, of the normalcy and excitement as she held on to Mirabelle, swinging her in a circle before dipping her. The girls laughed as they danced, both working to catch their breath before walking to Lorraine, Mirabelle prancing and wiggling as she went.

"I have to go so bad!" she announced to Lorraine.

"Then go!" Lorraine said, wondering why she was still standing there, hoping the girl wasn't about to make a puddle of a mess on the floor at her feet. Mirabelle turned back to the dance floor as she continued to twitch with urgency.

"Okay. But I'll be right back." She waddled her way to the door and out of the room.

Denise and Lorraine sat beside each other on the chairs, watching the rest of the girls sway and swirl together. They remained silent for the rest of the song, other than laughing at some of the girls, especially the ones jumping and jiving, though it looked more like waddling and swaying.

They all lost themselves in the fun. They let the music carry them away, make them forget about why they were there, all gathered together in that place. For a few moments, they felt joy. Contentment. Peace.

But then the song stopped, and in the dead air before the next one started, they heard the screams reverberating through the building.

Denise and Lorraine knew who it was, what room it was coming from. They looked at each other and ran for the stairs as quickly as possible, as best they could.

When they got to their room, Mirabelle was on the floor, screaming, tears running down her face, her chin, her neck. Pieces of paper were scattered around her, in her lap, on the floor, held tightly in her hands. Denise ran to her.

"What's going on? What happened?"

Mirabelle would only respond in sobs and screams.

"Are you in pain? Is it time?"

Mirabelle's head dropped, her chin pointing to her sternum, her hair falling beside her cheeks. Between hiccups and gasps for air she whispered, "My collection."

And that's when she opened up her hands so the girls could see what she was gripping so tightly. There were segments of photos from magazines and catalogs, torn into small sizes, so small that to reconnect them would be more difficult than any puzzle ever created.

"I told you not to let Miss Mahoney find that," Denise snapped. She didn't mean to be angry with Mirabelle, but she had warned the girl.

"I didn't!" Mirabelle's voice screeched through the room, echoing off the ceiling.

"Then how did she find out?" Denise asked.

Lorraine inhaled. Her eyes grew wide and her pulse quickened. She had been the one to speak it. She had said out loud to Miss Mahoney that Mirabelle had been keeping a list. It hadn't been the same thing that Lorraine was supposed to be filling out for herself. But Lorraine hadn't realized that when the words came tumbling out of her in the housemother's office, a foolish admission in a moment of innocence that Miss Mahoney had used to break the heart of a girl whose heart had already broken so many times that it had taken a piece of her mind with it.

Through sobs, Mirabelle mumbled, "I don't know."

Lorraine watched the two on the floor of their room. Mirabelle sobbing in her hands as Denise scooped up the torn pieces of Mirabelle's wish list of all the things she was going to buy for her baby. Lorraine gingerly lowered herself to the floor, remaining silent, crawling around the room, pulling pieces from under their beds, wondering why this collection was against some rule, wondering if she could help put it back together or go back in time to keep her mouth shut, to not say what she did, not do what she did, not get her to a place where she was crawling around on the floor, picking up the pieces of choices she had made.

# CHAPTER TWENTY-FOUR

A place of birth is not always a place of joy, celebration, and optimism. Lorraine never realized that until the maternity home. And she still had only come to know that on a subconscious level. It's not that the home was a place of death—though it hadn't been void of that either. But hope wasn't one of its main characteristics, perhaps it was for the families who lived outside its walls, but it was not for the girls who lived within them.

The home had a way of breaking wills. And it didn't always take the full three months for that to happen. For some, that slipping of hope showed in withdrawal and silence. For others, it was tears shed in the middle of the night when they thought their roommates were asleep. For a few, it was the slipping into an alternative world where handcrafted baby blankets held purposes.

Mirabelle had served nearly her predicted amount of time there when she woke up panting in the dark morning hours. A few days after her collection had been destroyed, as she lay on her side, huffing and puffing and moaning, she fought for the last remnants of hope to not leave her. She fought to ignore the pains. She told her body to stop. She pleaded with the baby to stay put. She had spent hours repeating her pleas in her mind, but when the time between the pains grew less, she started to verbalize her prayers.

"Please stop. Please stop. Please stop." She pleaded a liturgy of urgency until the next contraction rose and her voice was taken from her. When the wave passed, she started all over again, "Please stop. Please stop. Please stop."

"Mirabelle?" Lorraine spoke before her eyes had fully opened. "What is it?" She barely got the question all the way out before her roommate's cries ignited a shot of adrenaline that pulled Lorraine from her bed and across the room.

"Mirabelle? Are you okay?"

Mirabelle didn't respond immediately, not until the huffing and puffing momentarily ceased. The girl looked up, her green eyes full of tears, and said, "She won't stop."

Lorraine didn't know how to respond, so she called, "Denise! Wake up!"

Denise stirred in her bed, wiping her eyes before realizing what was happening on the other side of the room. She ran to Mirabelle's side, looked her in the eyes, and asked, "Is it time?"

Mirabelle looked back and shook her head no, but couldn't get any words out of her mouth before the next round of moaning began. Denise rubbed Mirabelle's back and waited, and when it seemed like Mirabelle could talk again, she said, "You know it's time."

Mirabelle shook her head again, shaking loose fat tears that slid down her cheeks and onto her pillow.

Searching for some sort of solution, for some way to comfort and ease her friend's pain, Lorraine suggested, "Why don't you stand up?"

Both girls' heads whipped in her direction as they yelled, "No!"

They looked back at each other and Mirabelle pleaded, "Don't make me do it. Don't make me stand up."

Denise pushed her forehead against Mirabelle's. They closed their eyes and pressed into each other as Denise promised, "I won't."

"Promise me. Please!" Spittle shot from Mirabelle's mouth as she pleaded.

Denise leaned back, wiped off her chin, and said, "Everything will be okay. I promise."

Mirabelle couldn't respond before the next wave of pain consumed her. The only sound her body let her make was a guttural cry, a deep moan that scratched her throat.

As she recovered, Denise persisted, "We need to call Miss Mahoney."

Mirabelle's voice reached full volume, "No!"

Still on her knees, Denise put her hands on Mirabelle's cheeks and looked into her eyes again. "We have to. You know that. You know it's time."

"But—" Mirabelle's voice broke. "But I'm scared."

Lorraine stood beside the bed, wanting to help, uncertain of what to do, what she should do. She stood apart from the other two, wishing she knew how to participate and not simply observe. She wanted her mother just then. She always knew what to do, how to help, what a friend needed. But Lorraine stood helpless, wanting to grasp for something to hold on to, give her friend to hold on to, to pull her out of this pain and fright, but she stood there empty-handed. That's when she thought of Brown Bear. She found him on the floor, partially wrapped in the pink blanket.

"Brown Bear! Hold Brown Bear!" she said to Mirabelle. The

girl smiled at her as she took the stuffed animal in her arms. She held him tightly and put her sweat-soaked cheek on his until the next wave gripped her. She squeezed the bear in her arms as she let out a howl that bounced off the walls of their room. In a moment, the pain passed again. After she caught her breath she said, "But the doctor said I had more time. Another week."

"I know," Denise said as she rubbed her back. "I guess your little girl can't wait to meet you."

Mirabelle smiled again and Lorraine thought that finally she would allow them to get Miss Mahoney, but her smile faded and the look of fear returned as she grabbed ahold of Denise's hands and said, "But what about Janet?"

"That's not gonna happen."

"But what if it does?"

"It won't."

"It could."

"Not to you."

Mirabelle's breath caught in her throat again. She inhaled and exhaled, her cheeks scrunched, her eyes squeezed shut, and her entire body curled in response. When it finally relaxed again, Denise said, "Just keep thinking of your little girl."

Those were the last words Lorraine heard before Denise gave a nod and Lorraine ran out of their room and to the stairs. She pounded on Miss Mahoney's door until the housemother opened it, blinking as her eyes adjusted to the office light.

"What's—" she started to ask before Lorraine interrupted.

"It's Mirabelle!" Under no other circumstances would Lorraine have dared to interrupt the housemother—well, not under most circumstances—but this was not a time for her to wait patiently.

Miss Mahoney didn't ask for details or clarification. The look, the tone, the hurry, the disregard for unfounded rules seemed to relay the message clearly. Instead of going up the stairs, Miss Mahoney shuffled to her desk.

Lorraine stood in the doorway as Miss Mahoney disappeared into the bedroom. She emerged a few minutes later, tucking her sweater into her skirt. Lorraine expected her to run up the stairs and check on Mirabelle immediately, but Miss Mahoney took a brown leather satchel off the floor and placed a file folder, a pen, and a set of car keys inside of it. Finally, she walked out of her office with Lorraine trailing behind her.

Miss Mahoney strolled to the stairs, taking each one carefully. Even though they could hear the gasps for breath and the exasperation in Mirabelle's cries from down the hall, Miss Mahoney kept a slow and steady pace.

"Thank you, girls," she said to the crowd who had gathered around the room. "You may go back to bed." She looked at her watch and yawned. "Or about your morning."

Lorraine assumed she was speaking only to the other girls, those who weren't Mirabelle's roommates. But her assumption was wrong.

"Take your clothes and go on now," she told Lorraine and Denise, but neither of them moved. "Go on! Git!" she said.

Lorraine looked at Denise, who refused to leave Mirabelle's side.

"I said, go on now," Miss Mahoney repeated, but neither of them moved. Miss Mahoney walked to Denise and grabbed her by her arm. Denise jerked her arm out of the woman's hand and began stroking Mirabelle's forehead.

"I'll take it from here," the housemother said.

Denise stood up. Lorraine took that as a sign of compliance, so she walked to her drawer to pull out clothes for the day. That's when Denise whispered, "You and I both know why she's here."

Miss Mahoney crossed her arms over her chest, her cheeks fiery red as she hissed, "You mean why all y'all are here?"

Denise paused for a moment and looked toward the ceiling. She shook her head and caught her breath before looking back at Miss Mahoney. "No. Not like the rest of us. My daddy didn't cause this." Denise grabbed her stomach, smoothing out her nightgown to show what looked like a watermelon hiding in her nightshirt.

Miss Mahoney's arms came unclasped. She brushed at her hair, straightened her sweater, and stood a bit taller before saying, "Now we don't need to discuss such things—"

"You can deny all you want, makes the adoption easier if you do, but we both know the truth. That bastard did this to his own child. There's no way in hell I'm going to leave her. Not like this. Not to go back to him."

Miss Mahoney looked back at Mirabelle, who was coming down from another contraction, having been too full of pain to hear their conversation.

But Lorraine heard it. All of it. *It hadn't been Stuart?* It was her—Lorraine's mind could hardly think it—her father? Lorraine's stomach tightened as she thought back to conversations, how Mirabelle gave few details about Stuart, other than how cute he was with his puppy-dog eyes and the cowlick that never seemed to lay right. But whenever Lorraine asked questions about their relationship, how long they had been dating, what they had discussed about their wedding, Mirabelle changed the subject. And when it came to discussing her family, she avoided mentioning her father.

"Fine," Miss Mahoney said. "You can stay if you're gonna help me get her down the stairs to the car. But you"—she looked at Lorraine—"get along with yourself right now."

The revelation cemented Lorraine's feet to the ground. She didn't know if she had the strength to move. She wanted to lie down in her bed or curl up next to Mirabelle and comfort her. But she looked at Denise who nodded to her, giving her permission to leave. So, Lorraine gathered her clothes and walked to Mirabelle's side. She leaned down and whispered, "You'll be the best mama, I just know it."

She wanted to say more, to give her encouragement, tell her she loved her, but no more words would come out. She stroked Mirabelle's forehead, wiping away the sweat and hair, and kissed her before she left.

Lorraine walked into the last stall of the bathroom, closed the door behind her, and stood in stunned silence, so silent that the girls who came in after her didn't know she was there.

"That poor girl," one of them said. "Does that happen a lot? To everyone?" The girl must've been new, trying to get information, trying to anticipate what was to come.

"Nah. Not like that," the other one said.

"It sounds," the newer one began, "painful."

No one said anything. Lorraine could hear the girls brushing their hair, the sounds of bristles pulling through long tangles, but Mirabelle's voice rang above the quiet. "NO! Don't make me stand! Don't!" As hard as it was to hear her plead to remain in bed, the next word brought shivers down the spines of all who heard it, "DENISE!" The name echoed through the hallway and into the bathroom. The cry so intense it shook them all to stillness.

No one moved for a moment before the new girl asked, "Why doesn't she want to stand?"

"A while back," the other girl began, "before most of you all were here yet, there was this girl, Janet." Lorraine stood a bit taller. She held her breath, wanting to hear every word this girl had to say, this story she had been wanting to hear. "She was their roommate. We all came around the same time. She had a good three months still to go." The girl looked at herself in the mirror, fluffing her hair as she continued the story. "It was a typical day. We'd all been to town that morning, but otherwise typical…until that night."

"What happened?" The new girl stood on edge and Lorraine mimicked her, leaning in, holding her breath still.

"It was the middle of the night, and we all woke up to a scream, worse than Mirabelle's there." She stopped fixing her hair and looked back at her roommate. "It came from their room, so we all ran in to see what was happening. I was one of the first, and it was… I'll never forget… It was just all over the place."

"What was?"

"The blood."

Lorraine put a hand to her mouth to keep herself quiet as the new girl gasped, "Blood?"

"On the bed, the floor, their nightgowns."

"*Their* nightgowns?"

The storyteller nodded. "Story goes that Mirabelle was trying to help. She thought she'd get Janet cleaned up and things would be better. She told her to stand up, and that's when—" The girl telling the story paused. She'd whispered the details to other girls, but she never liked being reminded of what came next. "When she stood up, I mean it was innocent enough. Mirabelle didn't know. She couldn't have known, but when she stood, well, Janet couldn't hold on anymore and the baby just…the baby, it…it slipped out."

Lorraine's body involuntarily moved to protective mode, tightening and gripping onto the child that grew inside. Lorraine could feel from both the inside and outside that the baby stretched and pushed back against her.

"Slipped out?" the new girl asked.

"Yeah. It was so little. It never even cried or nothing."

A scream that could only belong to Mirabelle—even though it sounded nothing like any sound she had ever made before— pierced through the rooms of the second floor. The new girl dropped her hairbrush into the sink. It clattered against the porcelain. No one moved or made a sound as Mirabelle's voice grew louder, her sobs reverberating through the second-floor landing before descending the stairs.

Denise and Miss Mahoney held Mirabelle on each side, their arms vining through hers as they supported her down the stairs and into the waiting car in the front drive. The entire time, Denise whispered to Mirabelle, "It's almost over."

She kissed Mirabelle's forehead before she closed the car door and stepped back. Mirabelle looked at Denise through the window, her eyes large, filled with both tears and terror. Denise wanted to open the door and pull her out, save her friend, take her someplace safe, but Miss Mahoney put the car in drive.

Denise stood alone in front of the maternity home as the car disappeared down the drive. She didn't know if what she had said was true, if Mirabelle's labor would be short, easy. Of course, she hoped it was, but hope had long left her. If she took the time to reflect, she'd know that the threads of hope she'd had slipped away from her the moment Janet's baby lay still on their bedroom floor. But she dropped the final strand when she saw the fear in Mirabelle's eyes just then and when she thought of what was to come after the girl went home.

At the same time, Lorraine sat on the bathroom tile, still hidden behind the stall door. Until that morning, she had anticipated her release from that place. She couldn't wait to walk out those doors and never look back. But now, she realized that while she might soon leave the home, her time there might never leave her. It would always act as gravity, pulling at her. She couldn't yet understand it, but she could feel it as it held her to the bathroom floor, as she clung to her pregnant stomach, as her voice fought to whisper through tear-filled gasps, and she repeated Mirabelle's liturgy, "Please stop. Please stop. Please stop."

# CHAPTER TWENTY-FIVE

The chip on Alan Reynold's shoulder had been carved and sculpted over those last few months. Before Lorraine went away, Alan couldn't necessarily explain why he was mad at the world if someone asked. People did ask: neighborhood friends, classmates, adults tired of reprimanding the kid who didn't follow their rules. He never really understood why he was different. He simply knew he was, and on most days, he was okay with that. But sometimes, he wanted to be like the others, to not stand apart, not be the only one like him.

Maybe that was part of the reason he was the way he was, because just like everyone else, he knew he didn't belong. And if anyone wanted to point that out to him, then they could try to knock the chip off his shoulder. At their own peril, of course.

But as he waited for Lorraine to return, he began to carve out the shape of his discontent. He understood why they, the others, would push him out. Isolate him. Cast him aside. But Lorraine? Of all people, why would they desert her? What had she done? Well, of course he knew what she had done. He'd suspected something when she acted quieter, more distracted when summer ended, but the moment she stopped going to school, he knew. She cared too much to let anything else get in the way of being valedictorian.

But she hadn't done it alone. And, yet, just the other day, he saw Clint, home for the weekend, gallivanting around at the drive-in, no care in the world, laughing his ugly head off, going about his life as he felt entitled to.

He didn't know how that creep could go on with life like everything was fine. Alan, on the other hand, couldn't. He had done things over those months he had never thought he would. Things like homework. Passing tests with high grades. Holding down a job for more than a few weeks. He needed to get his act together, stop fooling around, and make sure he graduated so he could get a real job. He needed to make something of himself, be someone she could be proud of.

But one thing he couldn't do was drive by Lorraine's house without stopping. He never intended to stop, but he couldn't seem to help himself. It was as if his car operated on autopilot, pulling to the curb across the street from the Delfords', parking with the engine running until the clock ticked ever toward the start of school.

Each morning he waited for a few minutes. Sometimes he looked at the house. Other times he couldn't. But every morning he waited for that front door to open, for that brown-haired girl to run to the car, open the door, and slide in next to him. He wanted to see her smile again, her grin so full her upper lip couldn't hide her gums, her eyes squinting, nose scrunching. He wanted to feel her lips pressed against his. Damn if that girl's optimism hadn't rubbed off on him.

———————————

While Alan's optimism grew, Lorraine's shrank, as if she had handed it to him for safekeeping.

Since Mirabelle had left the home a week ago, the place had gotten quiet. Lorraine and Denise barely spoke. They wanted to ask Miss Mahoney about Mirabelle and the baby, to know if they were okay. But they knew no answers would come. They never did. Denise had learned that lesson after Janet and all of the other girls who had come and gone since. Miss Mahoney considered that information part of the nothing-personal rule, and she held firmly to it.

Lorraine spent more time at the library, lingering longer than her scheduled time, not because she was so absorbed in her studies. Actually, she was having a harder time concentrating. She lingered in the space that didn't give her reminders of what had happened to Mirabelle, of what would happen to Denise quite soon, of what was to come for her.

Of course she wanted to spend more time in the library, the only refuge she had.

"I don't mean to make you go, but I wanted to make sure you hadn't lost track of time," Ms. Whiler said. She had noticed that Lorraine had been adding a few more minutes each day to her time there. Ms. Whiler was surprised that she hadn't heard Miss Mahoney complain about it yet.

"Oh," Lorraine said, reaching for a book to cover a piece of paper she had been trying to write on. She didn't know precisely what time it was, but she knew she had stayed longer than she had been given permission to.

"Sorry if I scared you," Ms. Whiler apologized. "You looked deep in thought. Mind if I ask what you were thinking about?"

The librarian was afraid to ask that question, afraid to know if Lorraine had been thinking of the baby. But she could usually tell when Lorraine was doing that because she would have her hand on her stomach, a small smile on her face. That day, Lorraine didn't smile. She didn't touch her stomach either.

Lorraine felt she needed to say something, but she didn't want to tell Ms. Whiler what she had been thinking about. Since hearing Mirabelle sob her way out of the home, she had been wondering how Miss Mahoney was helping any of them. For Mirabelle, her time at the home may have been a reprieve from her father's house. Yet, where was she now? Of course, Lorraine didn't know. Couldn't know. But she guessed she was back in his house, under his roof, scared again to be alone with him. The bigger question was: Where was the thing she really wanted? Where was her baby?

She hoped Mirabelle had kept her. She hadn't signed the form, so surely they couldn't take her baby from her.

Over the last week, Lorraine had thought a lot about this, picturing the moment Mirabelle met Rose for the first time. She wondered if she ever allowed the nurse to take her to change her. She guessed Mirabelle would hold tightly to her daughter, delighted to be in her presence, grateful for the beauty that had come from tragedy, a nuance of life that made most people uncomfortable.

People like Mr. and Mrs. Delford.

Miss Mahoney had given Lorraine an assignment a couple of weeks ago, before Mirabelle left. Before her collection was destroyed. Lorraine had considered the list in her mind but hadn't been able to put her thoughts on paper, not until that day in the library.

"I was just working out a math equation," Lorraine finally responded. She felt bad about lying to Ms. Whiler. The woman had been so kind and accommodating.

"Here, let me take a look," Ms. Whiler stepped closer, reaching for the book that was covering Lorraine's secret assignment. Ms. Whiler grabbed the textbook and slid it toward her. The problem was the piece of paper on the table caught both of their attention.

"What's that?" Ms. Whiler asked, crossing her arms in front of her.

"Just something I've been working on." Lorraine grabbed the paper, folded it, and tucked it inside her skirt pocket, but Ms. Whiler had already seen it. Understood the implications.

The librarian knew this was possible, likely even. She had studied enough biology to understand that mechanisms exist to protect the young, ensure the survival of next generations, bond mothers to their babies so they would feed, train, and protect them. She knew this from a scientific perspective, but not a personal one.

She had seen written across the top: Better for the baby. Below were two columns, one labeled "me" and the other "them." Ms. Whiler hadn't read all that Lorraine had attributed to "them": mother and father, house, backyard, job, good cooking, friends. But she had read the one scrawled carefully beneath the "me" heading: *I'm her mom.*

Lorraine hadn't been able to think of anything else to put on the list, but she felt deep inside her soul that one single reason might be enough. She had seen it in Mirabelle, how she longed for nothing more, how she loved the child so completely before the baby had even fully developed. But she had also felt it for herself. At some point that abstract group of cells hiding within her had grabbed hold of her heart, and she didn't know if she could let go. She knew it wouldn't be easy, but nothing about this situation had been.

Over the last week, she had been considering an option her parents hadn't given her. Why couldn't she be the first in her neighborhood to mother a child without a husband? Besides, her parents were still young enough to help out. Surely her mother would enjoy having another baby in the house. Lorraine knew how much she delighted in holding the babies at church. Plus, what else was she going to do with her days once Lorraine left the house? In a way, Lorraine would be doing her a favor, giving her something to occupy her time. If Mrs. Delford would do that, then maybe Lorraine could attend secretarial school, or even junior college. Sure, that wasn't what she'd hoped for, but it was something.

Just like the speed of light through the universe, it can sometimes take years for us to see our history, to make sense of it, register what we are looking at. Since Ms. Whiler had started working with Lorraine, she had seen the girl's potential and intelligence. She wasn't just another girl. She could have a bright future ahead of her, be a rising star, filled with possibilities that most girls couldn't dream of. But only if she could walk away. If she chose to mother that child, her future would look too much like Charlene's, tied to shame, tempted to settle for a man who could provide but certainly not care. There was a lot that Ms. Whiler didn't know about birth and babies, but one thing she did know was that if Lorraine couldn't let go, her future would resemble a falling star.

She knew she couldn't push too hard. She couldn't bully the girl into what she believed was the right decision. But she would do what she could to guide her into not becoming Charlene.

"Lorraine." Ms. Whiler knelt on the floor, putting her just below Lorraine's sitting height. "Look at me." With eyes brimming with tears, Lorraine looked at her. "I know this is a lot. I can't understand what you're going through, what this must feel like. But as much as I can, I want to help you make a good decision, and sometimes the decisions we need to make aren't easy ones."

Lorraine couldn't look at her anymore. She put her elbows on the table, rested her head in her hands, and covered her eyes as the tears spilled.

Ms. Whiler had said she had a decision to make, but others had been telling her otherwise. Her parents, Miss Mahoney, the doctors, they all spoke as if there was only way through this: adoption. Up until just weeks ago, that had seemed right. But something had changed. She couldn't even meet the baby yet, but she now looked forward to it. She wondered what it would look like. How it would act. If it would like cats and hate brussels sprouts. If its favorite flower would also be the daisy. If she would be a strong swimmer, too.

At some point, she had begun to think like Mirabelle, to realize that the bump was actually a person. Someone who would, in some ways, be like her. The problem was, she wanted to still graduate, go on to college, to be like Ms. Whiler, so strong and independent, so smart and self-assured.

She wanted it all.

The clock ticked toward her future. And for the first time in her life, she had no idea what the right answer was. Her heart told her one thing. Her gut agreed. But the world and her circumstances and the people she trusted around her told her that she was wrong, that only one *right* answer existed and she'd be a fool to not choose it.

There was one thing she wanted that everyone told her she

could have. One thing anchoring all of this, that Lorraine could still find a way to vocalize.

"I just"—she stammered—"want to be normal again."

Ms. Whiler put her arm around Lorraine, her cheek against the girl's head, as she said, "Normal's a myth." She continued, "There's no going back. There's only what comes after this."

She let Lorraine cry alone in the study carrel as she phoned Miss Mahoney and apologized for keeping the girl longer than expected. "We're finishing up something and then she'll be on her way." She knew the housemother wasn't satisfied, but she didn't care.

She gave Lorraine time to gather herself, to catch her breath, wipe away her tears, but she didn't realize she had also given her the chance to complete the list. Lorraine waited for Ms. Whiler to step away and then she removed the paper from her pocket, scratched out all of her responses in the "them" column and drew a bold circle around "I'm her mom."

In all of her years of studying and making the grades and being a good girl, she finally understood the truth of things: sometimes the right answer makes no sense at all.

But that doesn't make it wrong.

# CHAPTER TWENTY-SIX

Some say Denise slipped. Lorraine herself echoed it. She didn't know what else to say when a few girls dared ask her what she thought. She had slept through it all. Didn't hear the thud. Didn't want to hear it. She must've been sleeping soundly that night, more soundly than most nights, seeing as how the larger her stomach grew, the more tossing and turning she did.

Most nights she'd wake a few times, reposition to try to resettle, but end up staring out the window until sleep finally returned. She longed to see the stars, find comfort in their persistent shining, but the leaves of the sweetgum trees continued to open, and in doing so, they blocked her view. They soon made it impossible for her to see much outside her window, her world growing ever smaller with each day her stomach grew bigger. As the stars faded from sight, their absence made her think of rockets and scientists and the effort to reach the faraway things. She began to realize that miscalculations could not be permitted when it came to going to the moon. Mistakes, even the unintended ones, had consequences.

The baby was extra active that night, moving and stirring, bumping against one side and then the other. Maybe it was trying to tell her something. Maybe it was saying, "Don't sleep tonight, Mama. Stay awake. Be alert." But, finally, she lost herself in sleep, a deep sleep that removed her from her world so she didn't hear the squeaking of Denise's bed when she got up before the sun had even risen. She didn't hear the door open before latching closed again. She didn't hear her roommate's body bounce down the stairs, banging against the wall and the railing before coming to rest on the landing, her head against the wall, her legs bent at degrees they shouldn't be, her bag of waters gushing from between her legs.

The thing about a multistory foyer is that the echoes of screams bounce through the cavernous opening, around the chandelier, and up the staircase. They ricochet and carry in all directions, including back to the one who released the scream, but she didn't have time to hear her own cries before she lost consciousness.

The few who heard it and went to see what the commotion was said that she was in labor, that the pains started before the ambulance took her from the foyer and down the front steps. But no one could say for sure if the pains and the release of her waters had started before, during, or after the fall. No one could say what or why any of it happened.

Lorraine blamed Denise's socks. With the wax polished to a sheen on the wooden steps, surely her socks slipped and in the darkness of predawn, she lost her way. That had to be what happened, Lorraine told herself, reminded herself.

When Lorraine finally woke in that moment, she did like the other girls and raced down the stairs, gasping when they caught sight of the twisted girl on the landing. Lorraine couldn't get through to her. She ran around to the other staircase, trying to approach from the opposite direction, but Miss Mahoney, who had sprinted from her closet-sized room and now peered over the banister, barked at her to get back.

Lorraine stood in the foyer, frozen in time. As the ambulance arrived and the medical personnel entered with the stretcher, she got pushed out of the foyer and into the dark hall. The rest of the girls watched from the stairs or hid in their rooms, trying to forget what they had just seen. Lorraine stood alone, arms crossed around her body, one hand to her mouth as if holding in the shock.

She thought back to a few hours ago, the last words Denise had said to her before they turned off the lights and went to bed. Denise had been so quiet since Mirabelle had left. She walked to Mirabelle's bed and grabbed Brown Bear, who was still wrapped in the pink blanket. Miss Mahoney had left it behind when she had packed up Mirabelle's box of things. Lorraine wished she knew where to send it, how to return it to its owner. Though Denise and Lorraine had both noticed it when they walked into their room that day, the air still thick with the smell of bleach so that it stung their nostrils, neither one of them ever mentioned it. Until that evening, neither had touched it. They left it on her bed, a tribute to the girl who had left.

Denise walked over, picked up Brown Bear, and unwrapped him. She turned the blanket in her hand, her thumb and fingers feeling the yarn. She tossed them both onto Lorraine's bed.

"Oh, no!" Lorraine said. "I can't."

"Take them," Denise said as she plopped down on her bed.

"Let's just leave them where they were." Lorraine went to stand, but stopped when Denise spoke.

"Take what you can."

Lorraine wasn't sure what she meant. She tried to ask, but Denise turned off the light, crawled under her blankets, and turned her back to her roommate.

As she stood in the hall, Lorraine thought of the night they had snuck into the clearing, and what Denise had said then.

*If that's what you really want, figure out a way.*

She had been talking about stealing the consent form, but under the stars that night, Lorraine wasn't sure if that was what she wanted. At that time, Lorraine didn't have things figured out like Mirabelle and Denise. She had so many questions and uncertainties.

But the night Denise fell, Lorraine did think she knew what she wanted. She had made the list like Miss Mahoney had asked. She had come to believe that Ms. Whiler was correct; normal is a myth.

So, if life is what you choose to make it, then why couldn't she choose to keep her baby?

Lorraine didn't mean to use Denise's tragedy as a distraction, the perfect moment to act, but she knew that her friend would probably tell her to anyway. While everyone else's attention was captured by the girl broken on the floor, Lorraine turned to her right, walked down the hall, opened the housemother's office door, and tiptoed inside.

She knew exactly what she was looking for. The woman's office may have looked like chaos, but Lorraine had sat in that room enough to get a sense for the filing system. Plus, she knew exactly what her folder looked like. She didn't need to read the names scrawled on each one. She needed to find the folder with the splash of coffee on the cover. She moved quickly, flipping through stacks until she found it.

"Got it!" She said those two words under her breath as she stood all alone in a room she had snuck into and needed to quickly exit before she was found. She didn't know why she said anything out loud. As chaotic as the scene in the foyer was, she still couldn't risk being discovered. Yet, there was something in that moment, a sense that someone was there with her, cheering her on, directing her, whispering to her to figure it out, and celebrating when she did.

She grabbed the folder and held it high, as proud of this as any trophy or award she'd ever received, wishing Denise was there beside her to see it.

Lorraine opened the folder and found the form that relinquished her parental rights. She snatched it out of her file as quickly as she could. She knew better than to dispose of it in the wastepaper basket in the office. She folded it before lifting her nightgown and tucking it into her underwear.

As she went to close the file and place it back where she had found it, she caught sight of a photo. It had been tucked behind the form, but now it stared at her. There was a man and a woman, him with brown hair, her a blond with perfectly straight teeth. His arms were wrapped around her, she leaning in to him, both of them smiling. They looked kind. Sweet. Happy. Seeing them made Lorraine's heart stop.

She stood anchored to the floor, immobile, incapable of fleeing. She kept looking at the couple, guessing they were about ten years older than her, staring until she heard Miss Mahoney's voice just outside the door, calling, "I'll be right there!"

Lorraine slammed the file closed and dropped to the floor, crawling into the alcove under the housemother's desk as Miss Mahoney entered the office.

Like a child playing hide-and-seek, Lorraine closed her eyes, as if not looking would prevent anyone from finding her. She could hear Miss Mahoney shuffling around, but thankfully she didn't come around her desk. Instead, she headed to the bedroom and flipped on the light. If Miss Mahoney had known she should be looking for someone, the light would've given away the hiding spot. But she was in too much of a hurry, gathering her coat and keys so she could follow the ambulance to the hospital.

Miss Mahoney left as quickly as she had entered, never knowing that she hadn't been alone. Lorraine waited a few minutes before crawling out. She took the time to put her file back exactly where she had found it, but she refused to open it one last time. She couldn't bear to see those faces again, the ones who wanted what belonged to her.

By the time she got back to the foyer, they had loaded Denise into the ambulance. Lorraine said a prayer for her as she went back to her room. She used the staircase to the right of the front door. Never again would she use the one with a stain that never fully faded regardless of how much cleaning and polishing they did.

# CHAPTER TWENTY-SEVEN

Lorraine thought she shouldn't have been pregnant anymore. She knew that most pregnancies lasted nine months, but she had thought she would be different, just as her mother had been. But now, she was thirty-nine weeks, full-term by the doctor's standards. As much as she had first hoped that the baby would come early and she could get on with life, she now thanked God that the baby had decided to wait. That time allowed her to rethink things, to realize what she really wanted.

She had only a couple of days before she would sit for the GED exam. Ms. Whiler said she was ready. Lorraine wasn't quite as sure. She felt tired, heavy, uncomfortable, her mind distracted. She wanted to pass the test, but what she now cared about more was going home with her baby, not just a diploma.

She had woken early that morning and begun pacing her room, moving back and forth from one spot to the next before repeating her path. Soon she fell into a rhythm of breathing and walking, swaying, and even moaning. Her stomach tightened and loosened, her back doing the same, while her mind tried to lift her from where she was, from the empty room in the maternity home through the atmosphere and into space where only the stars were visible.

Lorraine decided to do what she had been learning to over

the last nine months: ignore the unpleasant. So, she got dressed for the day, ate a bit of breakfast, and headed to the library. She walked into town that morning. Her steps had become more like waddles, her feet pointing outward and her balance tipping backward.

Ms. Whiler gave her a math assignment and walked away to help a patron. Lorraine could hardly complete a couple of the problems. Typically, math gave her something concrete to focus on, a clear and absolute solution. That morning, she couldn't concentrate. And her back ached.

She decided to change positions, so she stood up. While it gave her slight relief, the sensation moved beyond a dull ache in her back. It tightened and gripped her around her entire midsection. Pain stronger than she had ever felt before.

She bent over the study carrel and began to sway her hips, dancing alone in the corner of the library, too tucked away within the bookshelves for anyone to notice her.

She labored like that for about half an hour until Ms. Whiler came to check on her.

"Lorraine!" she said, as soon as she caught sight of the girl, bent and swaying. "Oh, Lorraine! Are you okay?"

The contraction ended, and Lorraine stood up straight.

"I'm fine."

She sat down, hoping that by looking casual, Ms. Whiler would think she was okay.

"Are you sure?" she asked. "Can I get you something? Water? Should I call—"

"No, no!" Lorraine insisted. The last person she wanted right then was Miss Mahoney. While she had thought that this

THE GIRLS WE SENT AWAY

moment would've come sooner, now that she was in the midst of it, she wished it was still some point in the future, a time that would never arrive.

"I'm fine," she continued. "My back does that sometimes. I'm fine. Really."

Ms. Whiler watched her, waiting for something else to happen. Then the front desk bell chimed.

"Shoot! Are you sure you're okay?" Lorraine nodded that she was. "Let me take care of that and I'll be right back." Before Ms. Whiler walked away, she asked again, "You're sure?"

Lorraine nodded "yes" seconds before the next contraction took hold of her. By the time Ms. Whiler returned, Lorraine was sitting down again, acting as though she had been working on her math problems the entire time. But she couldn't hide the next contraction. Nor the one that came minutes after it.

"That's it," Ms. Whiler said. "I have to call Miss Mahoney."

"Please, don't," Lorraine pleaded.

"You know I have to."

"What if—" Lorraine thought, "what if you take me to the hospital?" That sounded like a much better idea than getting Miss Mahoney involved in the situation.

"I can't." Ms. Whiler looked around, as if not fully believing what she had just said. "Miss Mahoney's the one in charge, plus I need to be here."

Lorraine knew that was true, but she asked again, the word squeaking out of her, "Please?"

Over their weeks together, Ms. Whiler had wondered if she had done enough for the girl. They were so close to test day, but now with this, she knew there was no way Lorraine would take the exam in two days. She would have to reschedule it for when she got home, wherever that was. She knew Lorraine was ready for it. She knew she would pass. But that wasn't the real concern.

As far as Ms. Whiler knew, Lorraine had signed the form. She imagined this would be hard, on many levels, but she knew and trusted that it was for the best. A girl so full of potential, Lorraine simply needed to get through this. To stay strong. To let go so she could have a future.

The bell rang again.

"I'll be right back."

As she struggled to get comfortable, Lorraine lost track of time. She hoped Ms. Whiler was closing up and pulling the car around. This woman had been the only adult she had come to fully trust over the last few months.

When she finally returned, Ms. Whiler said, "The car's waiting."

Lorraine's heart pounded with joy and possibility. She wanted to hug the librarian. She knew she had been right to trust her, the only person over these long months who could truly help her.

She let Ms. Whiler guide her through the library and out the double set of doors. She leaned into her when another contraction consumed her on the sidewalk.

So comforted by Ms. Whiler's presence and care, she wanted to tell her the truth. After all, the librarian had believed in Lorraine's dream of being an astronaut. Surely, she cared about Lorraine's desires, whatever they might be, and would be an ally, someone to help her figure out how to move forward. How to bring home the baby. How to forge a path as a mother.

"Can I tell you a secret?" Lorraine asked, once she caught her breath and could speak again. "I'm keeping the baby."

Ms. Whiler stopped. Her stomach dropped. "What? Lorraine, no. I thought you promised to give up—"

"I did," Lorraine stopped her from saying more. "But I can't. I want my baby."

As the girl smiled, proud of what she had decided, Ms. Whiler thought of Charlene. Lorraine was not her sister, but she feared that their futures would be too similar, one moment of passion forever impacting the trajectory of theirs lives. Changing who they were. Who they could be.

"I know this is hard," Ms. Whiler began. "But it's going to be even harder, near impossible, to keep it. You're not thinking of the future, your possibilities, all you can do."

Lorraine pulled against Ms. Whiler, loosening her arm and standing on her own. She couldn't believe what the librarian—the woman who had shown her that she could be different—had just said.

"Don't you want me to be happy?" Lorraine could feel her stomach tightening again. She placed both hands under the curvature of her belly, trying to lift and offer support for the heavy child within.

"Of course!" Ms. Whiler stepped toward her, trying to put her arm around Lorraine again, but the girl moved away from her. "That's exactly what I want. But that's not going to happen if you keep the baby."

"You think giving up my baby is going to make me happy?"

"No." Ms. Whiler's mind raced as she searched for the right explanation. "Let's face it, you don't have a good choice right now. But only one option will give you a chance."

"How can you say that?" Lorraine's voice rose. She stepped farther away, wishing she could sit down, but wanting to run instead, to find a hidden place where no one could find her or the baby. "Especially when you're the one who showed me that I can be different, not like the rest."

"Yes! You can be different. You can go to college. You can have a career. You can go to space if that's what you want, but you can't do any of that with a baby. Don't you see that? I'm trying to help you."

Lorraine wanted to fire back, but she struggled to keep her balance as her knees nearly buckled with the pain of another contraction. Ms. Whiler ran to her side. She held on to Lorraine and kept her standing when the girl couldn't do it on her own.

"I'm so sorry," she whispered as two passersby looked at them. "I wish it wasn't this way. But for right now, let's get you off the sidewalk. The car is right over here."

Arguing on the sidewalk would not bring resolution. And she had no escape at that moment. She had no way to run and hide. But as long as Ms. Whiler stayed with her, she still had a chance of going home with the baby. She didn't need the librarian's approval. While that woman had been a mentor of sorts, she had no say in matters relating to the baby. She simply needed Ms. Whiler to help her hide from Miss Mahoney, at least long enough for her to claim her child as her own.

Lorraine let the librarian lead her to the car parked along the curb. As long as Ms. Whiler could get her to the hospital without Miss Mahoney knowing, she didn't care if they agreed on what Lorraine's future should look like. Ms. Whiler opened the passenger door of the car parked at the curb and helped position Lorraine in the front seat. Then she closed the door and kept her hand on it until Lorraine heard the driver's side door close, as well.

She looked at Ms. Whiler, who mouthed, "I'm sorry."

She looked beside her to see Miss Mahoney, who put the car in drive and pulled away from the curb.

"No!" Lorraine yelled. This was not the woman she wanted taking her to the hospital. She twisted in her seat, wanting to open the door and leave, but the car was moving. "Not you. No! Let Ms. Whiler take me!"

Lorraine looked out the back window to see the librarian, still on the curb, her arms wrapped tightly around her body as the car sped past shops and pedestrians, all with things to do. Places to go. Autonomy to do what they needed and wanted to.

"Soon enough this will all be over," Miss Mahoney said, ignoring her pleas. "Then you can go home."

Lorraine couldn't speak. She couldn't get comfortable. She moved and shifted. Her mind raged. Her back hurt. Her body ached. Her heart broke.

She had thought she had an ally in Ms. Whiler, but she realized she had once again been a fool. It started with Clint, then her parents, followed by Miss Mahoney. Each of them had abandoned her when she most needed someone. In that moment, she realized the housemother and the librarian were more alike than different, both attempting to coax her into their perception of a good beginning. Their motives may have been different—one focused on the baby, the other on the woman—but both reached the same conclusion. And neither bothered to consider Lorraine and what she most wanted.

"It's all nearly over. But don't fight it. That makes it worse."

In Miss Mahoney's allowance of mercy, she waited until the contraction ended before she slid an envelope across the bench seat of the car.

"This came for you."

In the three months that she had been in the maternity home, Lorraine had not heard anything from her parents. No phone calls, no letters, and certainly no visits on Sunday afternoons like a few of the girls had. The first few weeks, she had waited, but then she gave that up. After all, the maternity home was a few hours from the Delfords. It would be a long drive for a short visit, she told herself.

As she looked at that letter, she saw her name written on it in care of the maternity home. She opened the envelope and began to read:

*Dearest Lorraine,*

*I trust this letter finds you well. I am writing you today to discuss an important matter that Miss Mahoney brought to my attention. She informed me that while your file had been in order, the relinquishment form is now missing. We sent you there so that they can help you. Please let them do that. It's what's best for the baby and for all of us.*

*Sign the paper.*

*Sincerely,*
*Your Mother*

*Missing? When did Miss Mahoney find out? Why hadn't she said anything?*

Lorraine turned the letter over in her hands, thirsting for more from her mother, but there wasn't anything else. There wasn't an update on neighborhood happenings, there wasn't even a mention of her father other than the single *we* in the letter. Her mother didn't say anything about hoping to see her again or how they had missed her. Had they missed her?

She paused for a contraction and then reread the letter, trying to hear her mother's voice as the words echoed in her mind. It had been so long since Lorraine had seen her mother's handwriting that she didn't even recognize it. Some aspects of the cursive were familiar, but the way she signed "mother" was different. Her mother typically wrote carefully and with long leading lines and fluid curls, nearly combining calligraphy with cursive. But the "M" in the signature here didn't show any of that flare. In fact, it was flat. Utilitarian. Boring. Much like the overall tone and content of the letter.

"Before I can take you to the hospital," Miss Mahoney said, "I need you to sign this."

She placed a pen and a piece of paper on the seat between them. Lorraine didn't have to look to know what it said.

If Miss Mahoney knew the paper was missing, Lorraine wondered, then why hadn't she talked to Lorraine about it at the home? Why hadn't she spoken with her sooner? If she had time to tell Mrs. Delford and receive a letter from her, then she had apparently known for days that the form was gone.

Lorraine pushed the paper back toward Miss Mahoney. Judging from the sadness, confusion, puzzlement on the girl's face, she believed that her mother had written the letter. Good. Miss Mahoney had written it quickly on the way out the door. Thankfully, she had opened the folder and looked inside to make sure all was in order. Not finding the form, she looked around, checked the floor, moved stacks of files and papers on her desk, at first believing she had misplaced it, but she never lost something so important. She didn't know when or how exactly the girl had stolen it, but that had to be the only explanation. In a flurry, she grabbed stationery and a pen. She tried to calm her racing heartbeat, the anger boiling within her, to steady her hand and quickly craft a note that would coax the girl to stick with the original plan.

It seemed to have worked so far. Now the housemother needed to proceed.

"The real problem of the matter is that you're a minor," Miss Mahoney said as she turned onto another street. She reminded herself to remain measured. Lorraine's labor pains added urgency. Miss Mahoney had seen this often enough to know that the girls couldn't hold on forever. She needed to check her own anger and let nature push the girl to the brink. "Your parents' consent is all I really need. This letter makes it clear I have that much. So, your name is nothing more than a formality." She sent up a silent prayer of forgiveness for that little white lie.

"No!" Lorraine could feel the buildup of another contraction. Before it took away her voice, she blurted out, "I want my baby!"

Miss Mahoney turned the car again as Lorraine breathed her way through the pain. She appreciated the compliant girls, the ones who stuck to their promises. They saved her the headache of circling the side streets, waiting for them to give in. She still had ways of coaxing the difficult ones to sign after the delivery. One housemother she knew fooled postpartum girls in the hospital by telling them they needed to sign the form for the baby to receive medical care. Miss Mahoney preferred not to have to take that measure. Plus, she liked to take care of this matter in a private location, free of listening ears and before the mothers could hold the babies in their arms.

"I know this isn't easy. None of this is. And I'm so sorry you're going through this. I've helped a lot of girls like you, some who thought they wanted the babies, but they don't know how hard it is. They don't consider what it would be like for the baby. The looks people would give him. The names he'd be called. They think they are making this decision out of love, but really, when you think about it, it's quite selfish."

Miss Mahoney took the next curve a bit quickly, forcing Lorraine to hold on to the handle so she wouldn't slide any closer to the housemother.

"I know you want what's best," the social worker continued. "Trust me, this is best. I've found the nicest couple. They are waiting to love this baby."

Lorraine thought of the couple in the picture. She didn't want to. They had continued to come to mind ever since she had come across it that morning she took the paper. She wondered what they were thinking. Were they waiting for her baby? Were they at home making up a nursery? Had Miss Mahoney phoned them to tell them that her child was on the way?

Thankfully, another contraction distracted her from such thoughts because she didn't want to go on considering things from their perspective. So many parts of this had always been considered with other people in mind. Clint had thought of himself. Her parents, their own lives. Miss Mahoney, the parents she had chosen.

"It might be helpful for you to know," Miss Mahoney started, "that you can sign this now and then later on, if y'all change your minds, then of course you can explore legal recourse."

*Legal recourse?*

As much as she wanted her baby now, she wondered what her parents would say when they came to pick her up and she had a baby in her arms. Would they take them home? Would they welcome them? Months ago, she thought her parents would always welcome her with open arms and unconditional love. She didn't know if she believed that any longer.

But apparently, she could change her mind. Perhaps that's what she needed to do: go home, prepare the place, get her GED, and then send for her baby. She could still get her, later, after she had talked her parents into it. After she worked on her new normal.

No one spoke as the pain and discomfort ebbed and flowed. Miss Mahoney recognized the quickening of the pace. She knew to wait it out, to give it time for the right moment so the pain of it all would make it even easier to get what she wanted. It took only a few more minutes for Lorraine's body to seize her in that way. Twisting in the front seat of the car wouldn't help. Neither did the moaning she unintentionally began to do. Nor the sobbing that happened after coming down from the labor pains. When her own liturgy of "Please don't. Please don't. Please don't," didn't help, Miss Mahoney finally spoke.

"I noticed the scar on your forehead the afternoon you arrived. Such a shame on an otherwise pretty face. Let's not let this become another blemish."

Lorraine had a decision to make. As much as she wanted to

choose to go against what others advised, it had taken her nine months to realize that she really had no choice. Loving meant letting go. But loving in this way would leave a deeper scar, far more hidden than the one on her forehead.

"Please," Lorraine pleaded, pointing at the hospital out her window as Miss Mahoney turned away from it. "Drop me off! Let me go!"

"I will when you do what you need to."

Lorraine put her hands on her stomach. She felt it tighten with the start of another contraction. In all of her life, she had always thought she had choices. She decided to play in the mud instead of having a tea party. She rode her bike to the pond that summer day instead of staying in her neighborhood. She chose to go steady with Clint instead of any other boy.

But what choice did she have now?

The best Lorraine could see it, she could either sign the document and try for legal recourse later, or she could have the baby in Miss Mahoney's car. But that wasn't really a choice. Did she think Miss Mahoney would let her birth the baby, scoop it up, and walk home?

She had to do what they wanted her to, but she couldn't speak. She couldn't put words together. When Miss Mahoney asked if she was finally ready, she simply nodded her head yes.

Though she had been raised to never tell a lie, she did with that nod. She wasn't ready, but she never would be. She wasn't ready for anything that had happened over those previous nine months. But no one had bothered asking her if she was ready at any point during that time.

If it was up to her, she'd build a time machine, not a rocket ship, and she'd go back to when all of this had started and she'd speak up instead of lying there looking up at the stars as they shined through the roof that night. She'd not have taken that walk with Clint, had that picnic, let him lead her into that farmhouse and onto the floor, listened to the false promises of things to come.

If she had stopped. If she had spoken up, she wouldn't be in this predicament now. If only she had said something, anything, stopped it from happening, she wouldn't be in the front seat of the car with that short little woman with the same ponytail each and every day. The woman who had already signed her name to the piece of paper. It had been dated, even stamped. All other parties had done their parts. She was the last to do what needed to be done.

And she did it. She signed her name: Lorraine Mae Delford.

She looked at the document for a moment, taking in the signatures, the shapes of the letters, the finality of the decision. She wanted to be in her room, alone, secluded from the rest of the world just like that mother cardinal sitting on her nest tucked inside a bush.

But instead her body had betrayed her in front of Ms. Whiler and Miss Mahoney—whose signature looked quite similar to the one on her mother's letter, who immediately pulled into the parking lot and carefully filed the paper away as Lorraine was taken into the hospital.

# CHAPTER TWENTY-EIGHT

Lorraine's body ached. It seized up. It felt as if she was ripping in two. The waves drowned her in pain for hour after unrelenting hour, giving her moments to recover before the next tidal wave swept over her, flooding her body with a persistent, piercing reminder of her mistake.

She paid her penance in solitude, alone in a sterile room, the overhead fluorescent lights humming their monotonous tone. She heard the voices and footsteps of nurses outside her door, but they carried on with their duties, unfazed by the girl who lay sweating and contracting in a room all her own.

As the hours ticked away, her body fought against itself, and just as she felt as though she was about to tear into two incomplete halves, a voice emerged from her that she could not control. It started low and deep and hurled out of her. At one point a nurse came into the room and told her that that was quite enough; there was no need for her to act like that. Lorraine looked at the woman, dressed in white with a nurse's bonnet on her head. Judging from her outfit, she had seen women like this before, so Lorraine was confused as to why she would tell her that this wasn't necessary. Wasn't this part of the process? Lorraine had never been through it before, never seen anyone go through it before. All she knew was what her body was doing on its own without her consent or her control.

When she wouldn't control her body as she had been instructed to, the nurse brought in straps. "I didn't want to have to do this," she said as an orderly grabbed ahold of Lorraine's arm, "but you leave me no choice."

Lorraine began twisting and turning her body, trying to pull herself free from the grip of the orderly, but she couldn't fight as another contraction took hold.

When he reached for her legs, she tried to kick. She tried to fight back this time, to tell this man no, but she was too far gone to save herself, and no one in that room was there to do it for her.

Once she was strapped to the bed, her arms and legs bound into place, the doctor administered a cocktail of drugs. He didn't ask for permission. He simply did what he knew was in the best interest of the patient, or at least the medical staff.

The last thing Lorraine heard before drifting into twilight sleep was the sound of something hitting the floor. She knew it came from herself. It sounded like a wave crashing against the linoleum. Her body felt different, as if it had let go of something.

She thought of Janet.

She tried to sit up. She tried to ask questions. But the drugs pulled her from that room and into herself.

Or at least that's the last she could recall. Truth be told, she was awake for the birth of her baby, her passage into motherhood, into the other side of pregnancy. She felt the pains. She writhed with the contractions. She begged the doctor to help her. Her body found a way to push even as it lay bound on that hospital bed, humiliated and alone.

But when the labor pains stopped, her body fell into sleep, and when she woke, she had no memory of what had happened, of the continued screams of pain and confusion and loss.

She slept through the baby being weighed and measured. She wasn't there for the first bath and bottle. She was lost in the depths of twilight sleep when the nurse placed the baby in a bassinet and rolled it down the hallway to be lined up in the nursery, crying for a mother to come, to comfort, to promise that all would be well.

Lorraine's waters had broken. Her milk ducts had begun production. Her body sweated with abandon. Alone in a hospital bed, her entire body cried and sobbed and leaked until it was depleted and dehydrated.

# Part Three

POSTGRAVIDA

# CHAPTER TWENTY-NINE

As the twilight sleep loosened its hold on Lorraine, she told herself she was still dreaming. She opened her eyes to a different room. An empty one. She looked around for someone, anyone, but found it empty. She searched her arms for the baby, but of course the newborn had been taken to the nursery.

Lorraine fought to pull herself from the drugged sleep, and even as her eyes opened and she looked out the window across the room, her mind was heavy, distant, covered with a fog that refused to lift. Her mouth was dry, her lips cracked from hours of being parched. She sat up in bed gingerly, looked to the nightstand and saw no cup of water waiting for her, so she hung her legs over the side of the bed, ready to stand.

As her toes touched the tile floor, a chill traveled through her feet and up her legs and caused her shoulders to shiver. She placed her feet flat on the floor and pushed herself off the bed. Then she felt a gush of something between her legs. She stopped and looked down. The hospital gown hung like a tent over her body, but she could still see a soft protrusion of her stomach. Her hands sprang to cradle her stomach, but they didn't meet the same firmness they had come to expect. They still felt a mound and a roundness, but it had more give, more squish and less structure than what they had felt over the last few months. She pushed her hands into her belly, searching for the firmness, waiting to feel the movement, the twitches, the shakes and shimmies of the little one growing inside, but all she felt was a soreness within her.

Through the fog of her mind, the realization of her situation became more clear, more urgent than the need for water. She dropped to the edge of the bed, feeling another gush followed by a trickle of something dripping down the inside of her leg. She pulled up her gown to see a stream of deep-burgundy fluid meandering down her leg and onto the floor.

"Oh! Mrs. Delford, you're awake." The voice was optimistic and unfamiliar. With her back to the door, Lorraine turned to see who had walked into her room. A woman who looked barely old enough to have completed nursing school hurried to her side and placed her hands on Lorraine's shoulders. "Please, don't try to stand quite yet. You need more rest."

Lorraine resisted the nurse's urgings to lie back and pointed to her feet. The nurse looked down. "Oh. Well, I can clean that up, Mrs. Delford. Stay right there for now." The nurse hurried to the door but turned back to ask one more question before leaving. "Is there something you need?"

She wanted to ask to see her baby, to know what had happened, where her baby was, what her baby was. She didn't even know if it was a boy or a girl. Instead, she decided to start with a small request.

"Water."

"Oh, certainly," the nurse said. Each sentence started with an "oh" as if it was a revelation, something she hadn't considered before. She left the room and returned a moment later with a full glass of ice water. Lorraine's lips began to purse in anticipation before she even had the cup in her hands. "Oh, my. Start slowly. Thatta girl," the nurse coached her.

After Lorraine finished drinking the cup of water, the nurse began a sponge bath. She lifted Lorraine's gown out of duty and without permission. Lorraine's hands blocked the gown from going above her waist.

"Oh, I'm sorry. Once we get you tidied up, you can have a good rest."

Lorraine looked at the woman who crouched in front of her. Her blond bangs curled high, nearly taller than her bonnet, with the rest of her hair tucked neatly within it. Shorter than Lorraine and with a frame as slight as her voice, she looked to be only slightly older than most of those in the maternity home, but her eyes held more hope and light.

Lorraine moved her hands out of the way and allowed the nurse to remove her underpants and blood-soaked pad.

"Steady," the nurse guided her. "One foot at a time. That's it."

With the soiled garments removed, the nurse reached beneath Lorraine's gown and used the warm sponge to remove any trace of the overflow. Lorraine leaned against the edge of the bed for support as the nurse knelt before her, wiping and cleaning her as no one had done since she had been potty trained.

Lorraine followed the nurse's instructions as she guided one foot and then the other into her clean replacements. With what felt like a wide, dense pillow between her legs, Lorraine eased back into bed.

"Oh, you must be tired," the nurse said as she crouched to the floor and wiped away the last traces of blood. "I'll leave you be, but is there anything else I can get for you?"

Lorraine licked her lips, the cracks rough against her tongue. She hesitated for a moment, her body hungering for the request, but her mind nervous that it would not be fulfilled.

"My baby," she finally said.

"Oh!" Her eyes and mouth both rounded before a smile lit up her rouged cheeks. "Certainly! Let me check the nursery. I'll be right back with her."

*Her.*

She'd had a girl.

Mirabelle would be so happy.

"Wait!" Lorraine called, both delighted and terrified to meet her baby, but first she had to know, "Is she okay?"

"Yes, quite." Lorraine felt a sense of pride, as if she had done something right, given her baby the best start. The nurse continued, "She's quite healthy and happy. All seven pounds, two ounces of her."

Seven pounds, two ounces? That was two ounces less than Lorraine had weighed. And Lorraine had been early.

"Seven pounds, two ounces? She must be small."

"Not at all. That's quite normal. A good size for a full-term baby."

"But I weighed seven pounds, four ounces."

"Yes, sometimes babies weigh close to what their parents did," the nurse informed her.

"But," she thought back to what she had always been told, that she had been born two months premature, "I was early. Two months early."

The nurse giggled. "Surely not at that size! Sounds as if someone's math was off. I'll be right back with her."

With that, the nurse left Lorraine alone to calculate. Her parents married in November. She was born in July. Seven months. She had been early. Lorraine's body shivered, not from the adjusting hormones or the coolness of the hospital room, but from the realization that her birth hadn't come early.

Her conception had.

Lorraine's mind began to reel. She wanted to ask so many questions. To demand answers. To yell. To know how they could make her feel so ashamed for making the same mistake they had. How could they send her away? How could they leave her alone these last few months?

Her heart raced as she thought of their hypocrisy, their lies and double standard. But then she heard the bassinet wheels squeaking through the hospital hallway. As the nurse walked through the threshold, the baby grunted. That little sound caught Lorraine's ear and attention. Only one thing could distract her from wanting answers from her parents: meeting her baby.

Lorraine sat up in anticipation, straightened her gown, and pulled up the blankets for modesty. She finger-combed her hair, licked her teeth to freshen them, and took a deep inhale as the bassinet rounded the corner of the doorframe and arrived in her room.

The nurse picked up the baby, one hand carefully supporting the baby's neck, while the other supported her back and legs. She walked to Lorraine and held the little one out to her. Lorraine moved her arms, not sure how to receive the bundle. The nurse simply pressed the child against Lorraine's stomach, on top of her bent arm.

"Oh, she's beautiful," the nurse cooed.

Lorraine had been so nervous about transferring the child from one set of arms to the next that she hadn't even looked at the baby yet. Was she really beautiful? Lorraine reflexively smiled at the nurse, but when she finally looked down at the little girl in her arms, she realized how true that statement was.

"I'll be back in a few minutes. Be sure to keep her head supported."

The nurse left, but Lorraine wasn't alone. Not anymore.

She and her baby sat in each other's presence for the first time, yet as they absorbed each other's scents, they didn't feel as though this was the first time. A deep knowing knit them together. Lorraine pressed the little one into her stomach, which no longer felt empty.

Lorraine traced the little girl's face, her round pink cheeks, her button nose like her mother's, her skin so smooth. The baby licked her lips and nuzzled her head into her mother's side before opening her eyes and looking directly at Lorraine. They were a deeper color of blue than Clint's but undeniably his.

"It's nice to meet you, Grace," Lorraine finally spoke. The name left her lips before she realized what she was saying. She had not considered naming the baby, had not thought about what the child would be called, but as the little one looked up at her, the name came out seemingly on its own.

Still bound by the swaddle, Grace began to squirm in her mother's arms. Lorraine loosened the blanket from her daughter, who gladly extended her arms upward once they were free from their restriction. She stretched and arched her back as if relieved. Lorraine laughed. Then she took the baby's hand in her own. She felt all of her fingers, her nails, her palms. She traced the length of her arms. Then she undid more of the blanket and removed Grace's little white socks, so that she could look over every inch of her child, count all of her fingers and toes, see all the tiny nails, and even the little hairs that had grown and developed inside of her. Each time she ran her fingers over the bottoms of the baby's feet, Grace would flex and then curl her toes and pull back her leg.

"You're ticklish like me," she told her daughter.

As Lorraine memorized the landscape of her child, every fold and wrinkle, as she attempted to cram a lifetime of love into a few moments, Grace became restless. Fearing that any sort of cry would bring the nurse running back, Lorraine quickly wrapped the blanket around the baby, trying to tuck all of her bare fingers and toes into the swaddle just as the nurse had done. But Grace pushed against the confines.

Lorraine could see the wail building, so she scooted to the edge of the bed and stood, hoping that the movement would help calm her daughter. She paused as she stood, not because of the cool tile this time, but because of another rush of blood. She brought her daughter close, smelled her head, and whispered a *shhhh* into her ear. She felt Grace begin to relax. So she began a slight bounce and sway, which helped calm the child even more.

In the still darkness of the predawn hours, the window acted as a mirror, reflecting back to Lorraine the image of a girl she didn't recognize. The matted and yet wild hair, the tent of a gown over a swollen body, the puffy eyes of emotion all painted a picture of someone else.

Still shushing and swaying, Lorraine walked closer to the window, but now she looked beyond the reflection. She looked through the glass and into the sky. The morning light would soon be peeking over the horizon, but for now the stars still shined. If only she could dim the overhead lights so they would stop glaring and hiding the view. She turned to find the light switch, but it was too far away, too close to the door. With one arm cradling Grace, she used her free hand to pull the curtains closed around them.

Shielded together, the stars lit up.

"Do you see that, Grace?" Lorraine pointed to the sky. And that's when she began to sing.

*Twinkle, twinkle little star.*

Her voice hovered just above a whisper.

*How I wonder what you are.*

She paused for a moment as she heard a commotion outside her door.

"What have you done?" A voice in the hallway rose.

*Up above the world so high.*

"Oh, I didn't know—" A quieter, yet still frantic voice said.

"Are you honestly telling me that no one has explained protocol to you?"

*Like a diamond in the sky.*

"I'm sorry. I'm new."

*Twinkle, twinkle little star.*

"New or not, this is not how we handle these situations."

Lorraine's voice cracked, emitting a broken whisper without a tune.

*How I'll find just where you are.*

The door of her room opened. Lorraine stopped singing, stopped swaying, stopped shushing. She remained motionless, wrapped within the curtains that hung halfway to the floor.

"Where is she?"

Lorraine closed her eyes. She stopped breathing and spoke to Grace in her mind, "Stay quiet, little one. Just stay quiet."

But the hopes and practices of a childhood game could not stop the nurses from finding her, especially as the length of the curtains exposed her legs.

As the footsteps on the tile floor grew louder, Lorraine held Grace a little tighter. She held the baby's little head to her nose and inhaled one long, deep breath, wanting that smell to flood every inch of her body and never leave her. As the curtains tore back, the nurse found a girl, holding her baby as tears and snot flowed down her face.

The nurse she hadn't met yet held out her arms. "I'll take her now."

Lorraine looked at the other nurse and said, "But I've only had her a few minutes."

"Yes, well, it's time for her to return to the nursery."

The nurse continued to reach for the child as Lorraine held her close to her body. "Just a bit longer. Please."

"I'm afraid it's her feeding time."

By now the loud nurse's hands were on Grace, attempting to pull her away from her mother.

"I can feed her!" Lorraine said, her voice rising.

"That's not going to be possible."

Lorraine turned her shoulders to the woman who was trying to take her baby. "Please! Just please let me feed Grace. I can do it. I know I can. Just let me try."

"Who's Grace?" The two women's eyes met as they both fought for possession of the baby. A lump in her throat stopped

Lorraine from saying anything. "The child's parents will choose her name."

"But I'm the—"

"Not anymore."

Again, Lorraine felt as though she was tearing in two, but this time she didn't have any drugs numbing her to what was happening. The nurse took the baby, her blanket hanging loosely from her. Holding the baby tightly in her arms, she pushed the bassinet, as if she didn't trust that Lorraine wouldn't run and grab her before they could leave the room. The wheels squeaked as she pushed the bassinet down the hall, but all Lorraine could hear were Grace's cries until they faded. Then all she could hear were her own sobs.

The young nurse stood at the door, tears streaming down her own cheeks. "I'm"—*hiccup*—"sorry"—*hiccup*. "I didn't know."

Lorraine took in a deep breath, and with all she had in her, she yelled, "Get out!"

A different nurse brought in her meals that day and removed the still-full trays. She helped Lorraine to the bathroom, changed the pad between her legs, and walked her back to bed. Thankfully, the nurse didn't happen to see the small white socks that had gotten tangled in the blankets and left behind when Lorraine had attempted to swaddle her child. As night came and darkness fell, Lorraine held the socks close to her nose, inhaling the last scents of her daughter. When she left the hospital the next day, she tucked them deep inside her bag, a secret stowed away that she hoped would give her strength to walk out of that place and back to life.

# CHAPTER THIRTY

As her father pulled his Buick to the entrance, Lorraine waited at the curb outside the hospital. The doors had already closed behind her. Dusk was approaching, the stars waiting to shine and the moon already lit up, but she kept gazing in front of her, looking through the silhouetted trees, ignoring the headlights growing ever brighter.

She took her first step toward reentrance. Her father didn't come take her arm or help her with her bag that had appeared in her hospital room sometime when she was asleep. He stood at the passenger door, holding it open, waiting for her to come to him. With each step, she waited for gravity to loosen its hold to let her soar away into nothingness. But by now she knew not to hope, or reason, or love.

She remained earthbound, homeward bound to a place that no longer felt like home. When she had dreamt of disappearing into the clouds and through the atmosphere to explore new worlds, she had never realized that unknown worlds could exist in the same place she had always been, on the same street, in the same room. Apparently, launching into the abyss didn't always require a rocket.

She and her father said few words to each other on that drive home. This time she sat in the passenger seat instead of hidden in back, yet when they arrived home, he still pulled into the garage and closed the door behind them before getting out.

Her mother met them at the side door. Lorraine moved toward her, expecting a hug, but before she reached for her, Mrs. Delford noticed something.

"Oh!" she exclaimed, her hands going to her face, trying to hide the terror mixed with repulsion. "Go upstairs and change."

Lorraine had felt some dampness developing over the drive, since they had stopped at the gas station an hour outside of town. While an attendant pumped the gas, Lorraine looked at the car that had pulled up to the pump alongside them. Inside were a man and a woman. On her lap was a baby. As they waited for their car to be serviced, the two looked at the child. The mother held the baby, repositioning the squirming child on her shoulder, bouncing him as she held him close and he arched his back in a display of discontent.

As the man rolled down his window to talk to the attendant, Lorraine could hear the cries of the unhappy child burst from the car. Her father drove away, and as Lorraine played the scene over and over in her head, replacing the face of that anonymous woman with hers, she began to feel a dampness across her chest. Her breasts had felt full and tender since the birth. The nurse told her to wear a tight-fitting bra and that over time, her breasts would return to normal, but Lorraine knew she was far from normal.

She said nothing to her father as she sat beside him and felt the milk that was meant to feed her child leak from inside her body and moisten the maternity shirt she still wore. What would she say to him anyway? What words could she use that he would find appropriate?

After changing into a fresh nightgown, she tossed the wet shirt and bra onto the bathroom floor and returned to her bedroom. The room hadn't changed in the three months since she had left. Her mother had turned on the light for her. Apparently lighting was once again acceptable. Her shape had changed since she had last worn the nightgown, her hips, stomach, and breasts all pressing against the fabric, pulling at it.

Instead of returning downstairs for a bite of supper or to retrieve her bag, she crawled under her sheets and comforter. They smelled as they always had before, so full of scent compared to the blandness of those in the maternity home, but Lorraine didn't want to smell that scent just then. The only thing she wanted to smell was the baby's socks. Where were they? Where had she left them? They were tucked into a pocket inside her bag that her father had carried into the house and left at the bottom of the stairs. She would get them tomorrow. For now, her body cried for escape, and sleep was the closest thing that could offer her that.

------

The rumbles of the garbage truck woke her the next morning. Once it pulled away from the curb outside their home and proceeded down the street, she began to hear the birds sing outside her window. She walked to the curtains and pulled them open. The sun shone through the tree branches, peeking through the spring's green canopy. The neighbor's rhododendron bushes burst with shades of pink, their blossoms consuming the bushes and creating hedges of color.

Lorraine walked down the steps, passing her bag at the bottom. Her mother was in the kitchen, cleaning up breakfast dishes.

"I trust you slept well?" she asked as she wiped another plate clean in the kitchen sink before rinsing, drying, and putting it away.

"Yes." Much to her own surprise, Lorraine had slept well, deeply in fact, so deeply that dreams of realities didn't creep through the recesses of her mind and come to haunt her in the hours of darkness.

Without asking, her mother placed a single piece of toast and half a grapefruit on the kitchen table in front of her daughter.

"Do we have any eggs?" Lorraine asked.

"We do, but let's save those for your father. This will help you get back to yourself," her mother said as she walked to the kitchen sink.

"How about some coffee?" Lorraine asked.

"You drink coffee now?"

"Every morning."

"Since when?" Mrs. Delford didn't mean to ask that question. It was a typical response to a revelation of that sort, but of course they both knew when it had happened. It had happened in the time between when she had been the good daughter they had been proud of and that very morning when she sat at the kitchen table, her no-longer-pregnant stomach still bulging beneath her nightgown. "Never mind. I'll pour you a cup."

Lorraine took a bite of her toast, as perfectly crisp as it always was. Mrs. Belmont would be proud of how her mother had mastered such an even toast. She looked around the house and into the living room and noticed something she had failed to see last night when she had climbed the stairs in the dark.

"Did you put up wallpaper?"

"Yes! The Montegues did that just after Thanksgiving, and

I loved it so much that your father and I decided to try it for ourselves. What do you think?"

Lorraine looked at the pattern that now covered the plain, beige walls of her childhood. The geometrical design of crisscrossing lines surprised Lorraine, in part because of the bold pattern itself and also because she had never seen her father as the type to hang wallpaper.

"It's nice." And then something else caught her eye. "Is that a new chair?"

"Once we got the wallpaper up, your father's chair didn't match the decor. Plus, it was getting so old. You remember how it creaked. So, we got him a new one."

"But what happened to the old one?" The one that Lorraine had spent evenings in, cuddling on her father's lap, leaning her head into his chest so that she could hear the rhythm of his heartbeat.

"We put it out for the garbage. That thing was so old. No one would've wanted it."

Apparently, life had gone on with changes and evolutions while Lorraine was tucked away inside the monotony of the maternity home. One thing hadn't changed: her mother's insistence on routines. As soon as Lorraine finished her breakfast, her mother told her to go upstairs and get herself ready for the day.

Lorraine took her bag and closed her bedroom door behind her before she unzipped it. She pulled out her clothes, her few toiletries. She piled them all on her bed as she searched for the most essential items she had brought home with her. With the bag emptied of all other contents, she unzipped the small, inside pouch, reached in, and found nothing. She felt again. Still nothing. She searched the bag for any other nooks, crannies, tears that perhaps she had mistaken for a pocket. Still nothing. She began to rifle through the pile on her bed, shaking out every article of clothing, checking every pocket. Still nothing.

She ran down the stairs and into the kitchen. Her mother was washing up her breakfast dishes.

"Did you go through my bag?"

At the sound of her daughter's breathless voice, Mrs. Delford turned around. "What?"

"My bag. Did you go through it?"

"No. I saw it there in the front hall, but I didn't—"

"Are you sure?" Lorraine's voice began to rise as her cheeks reddened.

"Yes, I'm sure."

"Then where are they?"

"Your bag? In the front hall."

"No! Where are they?"

Lorraine had assumed her father wasn't home that morning. He shouldn't have been home that morning. He should have been at work, but he hadn't gone in. He walked up behind his daughter, who was still in her nightgown, standing in the kitchen well after breakfast time, and he confessed, "I put them in the garbage this morning."

Lorraine turned to look her father in the eyes. "You what?"

"Just this morning. I put them and that shirt you wore home into the trash."

"How could you?"

"Everyone, calm down." Mrs. Delford tried to bring some peace to the rising tension, but no one would listen.

"Do you know how hard your mother and I have worked to

cover up your mistake?" Her father's voice didn't rise with anger. It growled low and deep, as if trying to prevent the neighbors from overhearing. "The whole neighborhood believes you were helping your aunt Lois. We don't need baby booties and pregnancy clothes telling them anything different."

Lorraine ran to the front door. She had heard the truck. It had gone by, what was it, thirty minutes ago? It had to meander through their neighborhood before it came down the other side of their street. How long did that take? Maybe an hour. Perhaps there was time. Perhaps she could catch them on their way back by. As she grasped for the door and began to turn the handle, her father grabbed her from behind. She reached for the door handle, trying to hang on, but her father was a strong man. He pulled her away from the door and pushed her onto the couch as she yelled, "They were all I had!"

"I'm doing you a favor!" The veins on his neck protruded as he yelled. "Don't you know what even one sock could do to the rest of your life? You say you want to go to college, have a career? And how would any of that happen if people knew the truth? Why would any man ever want to marry you if he knew what you had done?"

Lorraine sat frozen in the living room, her body sweating as it had been more prone to do since she had given birth. Her breasts ached, and she feared they would start leaking again. She needed a shower. She needed so much more than that. What she needed most was to know the truth. She hadn't bothered asking him on the way home, in the car alone. She wanted to ask the question, but she hadn't mustered the strength yet.

But before she could, her father said, "If your mother and

I can forgive you for what you've done, the least you can do is move on."

"Move on?" It had been two days since she had ripped in two, but already he was demanding she get over it. "The only way I want to move on is with legal—" What was the word Miss Mahoney had said in the car? Ah, yes. "Recourse. Legal recourse."

The Delfords looked at one another and then back at their daughter.

"Don't be ridiculous," her father said.

"I think what your father means to say," Mrs. Delford put her hand on his arm and continued, "is that I'm sure this is hard. You've been through a lot. Now's time to rest and get back to things."

"The only thing I want to get back to is the baby. Miss Mahoney said I could. She said that I could still get her back."

*Her.*

Mrs. Delford heard the pronoun. She winced. She had wanted to know as little as possible, but that word made the entire situation more real than she wanted it to be.

"I don't know what that woman said." Mr. Delford spoke when his wife couldn't. "But this is all over. There's no going back. Decisions have been made. You signed the paper, right?" He turned to his wife who held her hand to her mouth, tears wetting her eyes. "She signed, right?" Mrs. Delford nodded the affirmative. "Then it's settled. There's legal nothing now. The baby's better off. *You're* better off." *Why couldn't she understand that?* he thought.

Lorraine wanted to fall to her knees. She wanted to throw herself to the ground, to pound and stomp and demand that her parents give her her baby. But she couldn't do that. She couldn't throw a tantrum. She couldn't be a child when she had a child. She demanded herself to stand strong. To not move. Not flinch.

But she had seen her mother flinch. She had seen her mother react when she said the word *her.*

Lorraine looked away from the man she had always admired and directed her statement to her mother. "You haven't asked about the baby," she began. "The baby was born healthy. Happy. A nose like mine. Eyes like Clint's." Mrs. Delford squeezed her eyes shut. Mr. Delford tried to get Lorraine to stop, but she wouldn't. "She's the most beautiful baby girl I've ever seen."

A sob escaped from Mrs. Delford.

"And do you know what she weighed?"

"Lorraine, please," Mr. Delford said. "This isn't going to help any of us."

"Your granddaughter weighed seven pounds, two ounces," Lorraine continued. "Two ounces less than I did. Even though she was born two months later than me."

Mr. Delford looked puzzled, confused. Mrs. Delford's eyes grew wide as all color drained from her face.

"Two ounces less when I was two months premature? At least that's what I had always believed. Married in November. Baby in July."

Mr. and Mrs. Delford looked at each other. They hadn't realized how good of an observer their daughter had become over her months of separation from the rest of the world. The girl who had spent so much time as the center of attention, spending more time being noticed than noticing things on her own, now saw movements and motions she may have missed before. But she didn't miss the look they gave each other, the realization of what their daughter was implying.

"Lorraine, sweetheart, you must still be so tired from everything. Why don't you go rest?" Mrs. Delford encouraged her daughter to go upstairs, but Lorraine was no longer as easily persuaded as she had once been.

"I guess you're right." Lorraine looked into Betty's eyes, her vision blurred by anger, exhaustion, and tears. "We're not much alike. You got to keep your baby."

They all heard the garbage truck on the other side of the street, the rumble of the engine, the sound of the trash being tossed into the back end before it pulled forward to the next house. None of the Delfords moved until the rumble faded down the road and disappeared into the day. Then her father walked into his office and closed the door; her mother went back to the kitchen and finished the breakfast dishes. As they went on with their day, Lorraine thought she heard her mother crying, but instead of investigating, she went to her room, closed the curtains, and went back to sleep.

# CHAPTER THIRTY-ONE

Betty Delford tried not to shake. She took a deep breath, straightened her shoulders, and clasped her hands in front of her. She had left Lorraine alone for a few days, which was long enough. Now she needed to get the girl up and moving forward. But first she'd have to face her daughter after the girl had figured out the secret they had long since tried to bury. They shouldn't have been surprised that she had figured it out. It seemed inevitable. Did they really think she would never suspect she had been conceived out of wedlock? They had hoped that she trusted them enough to take the assumption at face value and not to dig deeper. Ask questions. Make calculations for herself.

But one other thing Betty had failed to accurately account for was how difficult surrendering the baby would be on her. Sending Lorraine away had been hard, but it had also given Betty a distance that she needed so she wouldn't attach to what was growing and developing inside of her daughter. She needed to keep that distance. She couldn't think of what that baby was to her, but Lorraine had spelled it out for her: her granddaughter.

The evening of their argument, Betty had asked her husband if they should reconsider things. Maybe Miss Mahoney had been correct and they should get the baby back. She had learned over their years of marriage how to ask her husband for what she really wanted. It took time and deliberation. She had to devise a plan. Drop hints. Make him believe that he had come to the conclusion for himself, like with the swing set she had talked him into, the trips to the beach, even the wallpaper. But her heart didn't give her time to think of a strategy. It ached too much for that baby that was part her. Part him. So much more of their daughter. She didn't take the time to think through it; she simply asked him if they could change their minds.

"Don't be ridiculous," he had responded. He didn't even put down his fork. He kept right on eating his supper, shaking his head at such a silly thought, as if she had asked him to buy her a bright-pink convertible to drive to the grocery store. "She signed the paper, the adoption's done, documents are sealed. It's over."

As she stood outside her daughter's bedroom, she reminded herself of that fact. What was done was done. It was over. She had to stop thinking about the baby, wondering what that little girl looked like. She had parents now, a loving home, she had to believe. This was for the best. But it still hurt like hell.

Betty took another breath, grabbed the doorknob, and forced a smile.

"Wakey, wakey, sleepyhead." It was the greeting Mrs. Delford had used when Lorraine was young, which made Lorraine think she was dreaming when she first heard it that morning. "Let's go. Time to get up," her mother said as she placed her hand on Lorraine's hip and shook her awake.

Lorraine winced. She wasn't sure which she wanted to do more: curl into a ball or smack her mother's hand away. How could she so flippantly walk into Lorraine's room, singing childhood greetings as if the last nine months had never happened, as if the act of Betty's own waywardness hadn't been revealed?

"Time to get up and get dressed."

Lorraine turned toward her mother, her face clenched in a scowl that spoke without words. But her mother didn't see her. Instead, she walked to the window and began opening the curtains.

"You're not spending another day in bed. The ladies will be here soon. Let's go."

The ladies. That was the reason Mrs. Delford wasn't going to let her daughter lie around another day. It was time she make her reappearance into public and continue the narrative that all was well and fine, just fine.

"Look nice today," her mother said. "And be sure to wear this." She tossed a girdle onto the bed and walked to the door.

Lorraine grabbed the girdle and looked at it, still not sitting up in bed. She closed her eyes and tried to temper the rage that wanted to blast out of her.

She shouldn't have been surprised that her mother had it all figured out, Lorraine thought to herself. Mrs. Delford had months to plan exactly how her daughter would get back to life without being an embarrassment. Seems like she'd thought of every detail. The one she'd forgotten to consider was if her daughter wanted to go along with it all. Or maybe she hadn't forgotten to consider that. Maybe she assumed that in all that had happened over the last nine months, every choice that had been made for Lorraine had whittled away at her ability and desire to make her own decisions. The girl who once dreamed of going to the moon and believed she had the fortitude to make it happen—not because it was easy, but precisely because it was hard—ached for something simple and easy.

"Mama—" Mrs. Delford smiled at her daughter, nodded her head, patiently waited to hear what she had to say. She had missed her voice, her presence around the house the past few months. She tried to tell herself that it was the way of things, that she needed to learn to get used to the differences. Soon enough they'd be empty nesters. She'd gotten used to the quiet, but having Lorraine back home, well, it just made things feel right again.

Then Lorraine continued. "Do you honestly think I'm up for this?" The words dripped out of her mouth, heavy with disbelief and irritation.

"Surely not," Betty said as she picked up some dirty laundry off the floor. "But go on and get up. We don't have time to piddle."

"Piddle? Is that what you think I've been doing?"

Betty sighed. "That's not what I meant."

"But that's what you said. What do you expect me to do right now?"

"I know you've been through a lot." Betty attempted a gentle smile despite her clenched jaw. "That's why it's time to get up. Get on with things."

"On with things? Honestly, Mother—"

"Yes!" Betty's voice rose above Lorraine's. "On with things is *honestly* what you need to do. I know it hurts now. It will. But what choice is there? I'm trying to help." Tears tried to moisten her eyes, but Betty paused, pursed her lips, and refused to let them fall.

"You know what I can't understand?" Lorraine asked. "The way you made me feel, the way you looked at me, when all I did is exactly what you had. You're nothing more than a hypocrite!"

"You're right." She was, Betty realized. Lorraine had learned too much over the past few months, but there was an even greater truth that she still didn't fully understand. "We're not perfect. We all have our secrets."

Lorraine had learned a lot about secrets over the last few months. She had lived in a home full of them. She thought about Mirabelle and what her father had done to her. The whispers about Janet and the story too frightening to speak out loud.

What Lorraine didn't know was the ones she had been surrounded by her entire life. There, of course, were her parents and their premarital trysts that led to a quick walk down the aisle that ended the final dance dreams Betty Delford had tucked away in her heart. Then there was Mr. Walters and the venereal disease that prevented Mrs. Walters from getting pregnant again. And, don't forget Jane Montegue and the way she looked at Eugene, lingered in handshakes, leaned in close whenever he was speaking, touched his arm whenever he was within reach, and the way he smelled some nights when he came home late. But don't forget Mrs. Claiborne and her little yellow pill that kept her happy and even. It was the same pill that Betty had gotten Dr. Harris to prescribe for her as Lorraine had gotten dressed at the end of her appointment.

Betty knew she shouldn't say more. She'd said enough already. But the words came out anyway. The sentiment she'd been trying to veil for a while now, decades even. The reality that she tried to brush aside with each smile, every bit of gossip, all the tidying up that she busied herself with. "We all do things we're not proud of. Sometimes we don't have a choice."

"But I do have a choice. Miss Mahoney said so. She told me when I signed the paper that I could change my mind. That I could get her back."

"No—" Betty started to say.

"Yes, she did! She told me so. How would you know? You weren't there!"

Lorraine was right; she hadn't been there. She hadn't been with her daughter when she needed her most. It would be the moment Betty would regret for the rest of her life. She had gotten so used to the girl being able to take care of herself, demanding her independence. This situation had been different. Betty should've known that. She should've insisted. But instead she listened to her husband, who told her that the best thing was to leave her daughter alone, to let that place take care of everything.

"You're right. I wasn't there." Betty didn't want to say more, but she knew that if she didn't tell Lorraine, then this chapter would never be fully closed. After Eugene left for work the other day, she had tried to fight for her daughter and granddaughter. She didn't tell him she was calling. She surprised herself when she dialed the number and asked to speak with the housemother, but she needed to know. "I called. Yesterday. I spoke to Miss Mahoney. I asked her what we needed to do."

Lorraine sat up. Her eyes brightened. Her heart began to beat again. *What was her mother about to tell her? Was Grace coming home?*

Betty saw the change in her daughter. That made the words she needed to say feel like daggers, cutting into her, wounding them both.

"There's nothing we can do. It's done."

Lorraine wanted to vomit.

"No!" A sound similar to what had emerged during labor came out of her again. "But, she said—"

Betty held up her hand, asking her daughter to stop, silently begging her to not make the sound again, the one that shook tears loose in Betty's eyes. "She may have." She paused to swallow. "I trust you when you say she did. But she lied to you." She could only whisper what she said next: "It's over."

"No!" Lorraine howled, reaching for her blankets, wanting to tear them into pieces.

"I'm so sorry."

"That's not enough. You know that, right? That word will never be enough. I've lost everything now, do you realize that?" Valedictorian. Her first boyfriend. College. And of course: Grace. But Lorraine couldn't allow herself to actually name all she'd lost or the depression would drown her. Then, in a low voice, she hissed, "You at least got a family."

Betty's body vibrated when those words struck her. It was just the reality she hadn't allowed herself to fully consider, to completely empathize with. Until her daughter had stood in their living room and said she'd had a baby girl.

"Yes," Betty said, "but you're not the only one who lost something here. She is my granddaughter, you know." Thick, full drops streaked down her cheeks—only a couple—before she wiped them away and commanded no more to fall.

With Mr. Delford away at work, Betty and Lorraine remained silent in front of one another except for a few sobs that involuntarily escaped over the next few minutes. Betty walked to the window and looked out, but couldn't focus on anything. After a few minutes, she checked the time. The women would be there soon enough. She needed to get herself together, which, thanks to Dr. Harris, had gotten a bit easier. But she knew she owed her daughter something first. As much as it pained her, she needed to ask.

"Can you tell me about her?"

Lorraine looked up. She had not expected to hear that question. She assumed her mother wanted to go on believing that out of sight meant out of mind. And, given this situation, Betty probably believed that to be the best solution. Lorraine watched her mother walk closer to her. She couldn't help but respond.

"She is so beautiful," Lorraine said. She closed her eyes, wanting to see her baby with full clarity. "She has the cutest button nose. Her hair is dark. So much darker than I expected."

"Yours was that way, too."

"Really?" Lorraine opened her eyes and looked at her mother. She saw the crow's-feet beside Mrs. Delford's eyes. She saw the gray hairs that hadn't been there last August.

"Yes, at first. Before it changed." Mrs. Delford sat down on the bed beside her daughter. "What else?"

"She's ticklish." Lorraine laughed. "And a bit fussy."

"Like her mother," Betty said, before telling Lorraine how much she cried those first few weeks. She told her mother all she could about Grace, but she didn't tell her about how little time she'd had with her, how her child had been taken from her arms. How she'd sung to her. How she'd lied to her.

Lorraine put her hands on her stomach, feeling weak and tired no matter how much sleep she got. She didn't realize the words she was saying until they escaped out of deep inside herself and floated into her bedroom.

"Did you know how much this would hurt?"

"No," Betty said. She knew what it was to be a mother, to love and fear and hurt for the sake of a tiny, helpless person. But seeing Lorraine walk back into the house, her breasts leaking, her body depleted, her eyes darkened, she couldn't deny the pain. "I just hoped maybe you'd be strong enough."

When most people thought of strength, they pictured someone like Mr. Delford, the man with the muscles, the guy who could open stubborn pickle jars, the one who could change a flat tire, the daddy who could give his daughter airplane rides around the living room. But Lorraine and Betty knew a different truth. Strength isn't in the loud and obvious. Strength is often camouflaged in the quiet, reserved places where most people wouldn't think to look. It's grown in the moments when we give up things along the way.

"I'm not strong," Lorraine said.

Betty couldn't help herself just then. She didn't care if her daughter rejected her. She wrapped her arms around Lorraine and embraced her. She buried her face in her daughter's hair and held on as if she never wanted to let go. To her surprise, Lorraine did the same.

They held on to each other for a moment before her mother whispered into her ear, "You're stronger than you know." Betty loosened her hug and looked at Lorraine. She swept away a lock of hair from her daughter's eyes, tucked it behind her ear, and said, "You're a survivor."

If surviving was what it took to be strong, Lorraine had no interest in it. After all, survival only came from enduring pressures and circumstances, especially the kind that could break or even drown someone.

"I wanted more than survival," Lorraine said.

"Me too."

As her mother walked out of the room and closed the door, Lorraine remained in bed, holding the girdle. If she'd asked herself what to do, she would've covered herself with her blankets and gone back to sleep, seeking hibernation and withdrawal over social gathering. But she decided to do what her mother had asked her to, not because of blind obedience, but because, like it or not, choosing to survive was the only way forward.

# CHAPTER THIRTY-TWO

Lorraine felt like a sausage link, slithering her way into the casing of the girdle. By the time she made her way downstairs, Mrs. Delford had placed toast, half a grapefruit, and a cup of coffee on the kitchen counter. The table was too full of tea, glasses, and napkins for her to be able to eat there. Lorraine stood near the sink and tried to eat her breakfast, not sure if the girdle left enough room for even that much food in her now-constricted stomach. She squirmed in her dress. She was only a few bites into her breakfast when the doorbell rang.

Mrs. Delford answered the door immediately, inviting in Jane Montegue. Betty greeted her as usual with the tone she reserved for only that friend, always different with Jane. The looks, the distance she kept from the woman, the way her jaw would clench, teeth would grind. Lorraine felt like she had gotten to know her mother more, but there was so much she didn't understand.

Mrs. Delford called Lorraine into the living room, gathering her daughter close to her, and said, "Look who's home!"

Lorraine didn't know how Mrs. Delford could do that, how she could go on with the story they had been telling, how she could be so relaxed after they had exploded at each other. She was just thankful her mother led the way, told about how valuable Lorraine's presence had been to her sister Lois, you know the one, the sister who never quite had her act together, and with a fourth baby now, things had simply gotten to be too much, too many demands. Of course, if they had disciplined the older children a bit better along the way, perhaps she wouldn't have needed her niece to come to her rescue. But they were glad to have Lorraine back home. What a few months it had been!

Standing in the living room, Lorraine noticed a smell that reminded her of someone she missed: Denise. For as long as Lorraine had known Mrs. Montegue, she had smelled ripe with cigarette smoke, but now her mind associated that smell with someone else. Someone she wanted to see. But she couldn't see Denise. She wouldn't see her probably ever again. Even if she wanted to, how would she ever go about finding her? She didn't know her last name. She wondered if she even knew her first name. And she didn't know what had happened to her since the fall.

Lorraine began to sweat. Her breath quickened. Her heart raced.

"Are you alright?" Mrs. Montegue asked as she began arranging the refreshments on the table.

"Of course she is!" Lorraine's mother put her arm around her daughter again. She pulled her in and spoke for her as her daughter fought the early stages of a panic attack.

Lorraine did her best to nod along and smile, but she knew her acting skills couldn't match those of her mother. Thankfully her breathing and heart rate slowed. She wished more than ever that she could put on the face and the front, but then the door opened and in walked Mrs. Claiborne.

Lorraine's heart sank as Clint's mother walked into the living room and joined the rest of the Sunnymede Sisters who had trickled into the house. If it hadn't been for her mother's arm wrapped around her, she would've collapsed onto the floor.

Lorraine whispered, "Mama, I can't—"

Through gritted teeth and smiling face, her mother whispered back, "Yes, you can. And you will."

Mrs. Delford kept holding on to her as Mrs. Claiborne approached. "It's good to see you're home! You've been missed."

Though Mrs. Claiborne smiled, Lorraine could see the strain, the tightness in her lips, the distance she stood from Lorraine, the hands that gripped each other and stayed pressed against her own body. Months ago, she would've hugged Lorraine, especially after such a long absence. After all, this girl was going to be her daughter-in-law. But for reasons that Mrs. Claiborne still didn't understand, Clint had broken up with her. She tried asking him why; she wanted the details. She needed to understand what had happened and why this girl was no longer going to be part of her family, her holidays, her future. But Clint had moved on and he'd told her to do likewise. He told her to not be like Lorraine, so wrecked that she needed time away to get over him.

Lorraine did her best to force a smile as she nodded and said, "It's good to be home." Her hand went to her stomach. She wanted to pull at her girdle and give herself some space, relieve some of the pain and pressure, but she couldn't do that just then.

That was the moment when her mother let go of her. Mrs. Delford walked to the front door to welcome more guests. Lorraine stood alone on her own two feet with no furniture around to hang on to, certain that her knees were about to give out and that she'd fall to the floor.

"We're going up to visit Clint this weekend," Mrs. Claiborne said. She didn't know what else to say. She didn't stop to consider if Lorraine cared about where he was or what he had been up to as she had been scrubbing toilets and begging her roommate to let the baby come. Lorraine's heart beat harder than she thought possible. "Gonna see the campus and meet his new someone."

Lorraine's eyes grew wide as her head began to spin.

"Oh, I'm sorry." Mrs. Claiborne stammered and squirmed, like her green gelatin dessert. Why had she mentioned this to the girl who couldn't get over her son? But the woman couldn't stop talking, digging a deeper, more hurtful hole. "Been seeing this girl named Susan for a bit now." She couldn't make the verbal fountain stop. "You know, after you left for your aunt's and all."

Lorraine needed to respond, to say something. She couldn't fall to the floor then and she couldn't remain silent. This was part of what it meant to survive. So, she smiled, willed her eyes to stop stinging with the start of tears, and said, "Ah, well, I hadn't heard that. You know, with all that was going on at Aunt Lois's."

"Of course. It really was so nice of you to help like that, especially during your last year of high school." Mrs. Claiborne put her hand on Lorraine's arm and squeezed it a bit. The poor girl had been so in love with her son, so heartbroken, that she had needed to get away. Mrs. Claiborne continued, "You're such a good girl to do that."

And that's when she heard a baby coo.

All the women heard it, and all but Lorraine responded in a chorus of "aw." Every head and body turned to the front door where Mrs. Walters stood with a baby in one arm and a diaper bag slung over the other. There was no denying how tired and yet ecstatic she looked.

Without taking her eyes off the child, Lorraine asked Mrs. Claiborne, "Who is that?"

"That's Mrs. Walters, of course!" Mrs. Claiborne began to laugh. She turned to look at Lorraine and, seeing her expression, realized the girl must not have been told. "Oh, I suppose you didn't know, happened when you were gone. The Walters finally welcomed baby number two after all these years." Then Mrs. Claiborne began to whisper, speaking out of the side of her mouth. "Of course it's not... The baby is... Well, they had to... They, you know, *got* one, but that's how it goes, I suppose. We're all just so tickled for them."

Mrs. Claiborne excused herself, making her way to Mrs. Walters and the child whose cheeks she wanted to pinch as she inhaled that baby scent she longed to smell again.

Lorraine couldn't stand any more. She looked for an exit. The stairs were too far away and surrounded by too many women looking to make small talk. The kitchen was her only hope. She slipped away while the baby held the women's attention.

As she walked out the back door, she heard her mother tell the guests, "I think we are all here now."

And then she heard the baby cry. She paused on the back patio. She had thought that a few minutes on the glider would give her the strength to return, but then that cry pierced through the walls and windows of the house.

Part of her wanted to rush back in and take a peek. Part of her wanted to see the baby's round cheeks and head full of hair. She wanted to know if she—he? She didn't even know—had ticklish feet. But her body responded to protect her when her heart and mind tried pulling her back into the baby's nearness.

The baby's cries came through the house and her milk again

began to leak. While her girdle hid the truth of her stomach, she had nothing to hide the biology of her breasts.

So instead of returning to join the women, she headed to the sidewalk and took it to where it ended at the forest. Then she began to walk along the wooded trail. Her shoes didn't offer the best traction and her feet slipped and slid through some portions of the trail. But she kept moving forward.

---

Lorraine walked over the place where the barbed-wire fence once stood and continued on through the clearing. She didn't stop to admire the place where they'd had a picnic. She didn't think about the surprise he'd had for her there. She kept walking to the house. She walked around the side and to the front and looked up at its weathered siding, shutters hanging crooked by one hinge, and broken steps leading up to the front porch.

There was a swing on that porch, but it no longer hung from the chain that was attached to the ceiling. It had long ago fallen, its wooden planks worn and weathered and crumbling from years of unkemptness. For a moment, she imagined what that house looked like when the farmer had lived there. She imagined it painted white, a weather vane resting at the peak of the roof. She thought of the sunsets that he and his wife must've witnessed from that front porch swing.

But then the imaginings fell away and the reality of what actually was stood in front of her. She picked up a rock. She didn't make a wish because what good did wishing ever really do? She was no longer a child, so it was time to put away notions of childhood. Wishing was the first one to go.

She didn't aim for a window. She heaved the rock with every ounce of might she had within her. It plunked against the siding, tumbled down the porch roof, and dropped to the ground. Then she picked up another one. She threw it, but she didn't wait for it to fall to the ground before she grabbed another.

She kept throwing rocks, whatever size she could find, moving to a new spot to find more when she'd exhausted the options at her feet. She kept going until her arm ached, her brow sweated, and her fingernails were caked with dirt.

And when she was too tired to throw anymore, she walked up the spongy, creaky, dilapidated steps and through the front entryway. She waited until she got into the house, into the front hall, before she screamed. She grabbed at fallen things and tossed them down the front hall and into the parlor. Tired of feeling bound, she pulled up her dress, tore off the girdle, and chucked it out the front door. Then she collapsed in tears and wept.

She didn't know how long she had been lying there when she heard the car coming down the long-hidden and overgrown drive. She knew the sound of that engine. She walked to the front door and stood in the threshold.

The driver recognized the silhouette. Alan saw her before he put the car in park. At first he thought she was a mirage. How many times had he been just as mistaken? How many times had he returned to that house, hoping to see her either real or imagined? But this time was different. This time he knew she wasn't a mirage because she looked just different enough, not the exact same as the Lorraine who had been missing. Her shape had changed. Her hair not as perfect. Her top damp with something.

But the differences didn't stop him from running to her.

They met each other on the broken front steps and Lorraine didn't hesitate to reach for him. She had expected her parents to hug her when she had returned, but neither had done that. At least not right away. Neither had said they had missed her. Neither had said they loved her. Both had continued as if three months and a lifetime hadn't passed between them.

"BB," Alan said as he held on to her on the creaking front porch. She couldn't yet speak, not until they parted and he said, "Gonna be honest, you've looked better."

Then she laughed and swatted at him. "I'd say the same of you, but I'm not sure I've ever seen you look good."

"Oh, really?" He laughed. "Already insulting me?"

While her parents had attempted to pull her into forced rhythms that had previously existed, there was nothing forced about returning to the familiar, comfortable presence of Alan.

"What're you doing here?" she asked.

"Came to listen to some music."

"Getting ready for prom?"

"You know me better than that." Alan looked around and saw the girdle lying in the corner. "Should I ask?"

Lorraine shook her head no and Alan shrugged.

"I should've known you'd come back for prom. Gotta get that crown," he said.

Lorraine's stomach didn't hurt anymore since she had pulled off that girdle. The front of her dress had begun to dry, or maybe she had gotten used to the dampness and didn't feel it anymore. She watched a hawk soar overhead as she shook her head no and said, "I'm not that kind of girl anymore."

Neither spoke for a few minutes. The songs of birds rose and fell through the otherwise silent air. Alan watched Lorraine twist and twirl the ring Clint had given her shortly before she was sent away. She pulled and tugged at it, so used to it not sliding off that she didn't even try to remove it.

"You don't have to tell me what happened," Alan said, "but at least tell me you're okay."

Lorraine looked at the ground, her fingers still fidgeting with the ring. Her hair fell along her face, clinging to the remnants of her salty sweat and tears. Alan reached for her chin. He lifted her head and began to part her hair away from her face. He cleared the clinging strands from her forehead and then he kissed the scar that refused to fade. She closed her eyes and leaned in to him ever so slightly until his lips parted from her forehead.

"I'll be right back," he said. He walked to his car and grabbed two things: his portable record player and his pomade. First, he set up the record player on the porch, and as the music began to crackle to life, he knelt in front of Lorraine, opened the pomade, and began massaging it onto her ring finger. Then he wiggled the opal ring back and forth, gently twisting and turning it until it slowly, but surely slipped right off her finger. He looked at it for a moment before he placed it in her palm.

Lorraine held her hand open. Out of conditioning, her finger still felt as though the ring pressed against it, but after months she had finally been set free. She closed her hand into a fist. Then she turned, pulled back her arm and threw the ring down the front hall of the house. She heard a faint clatter as it fell somewhere along the dusty floorboards in the distance, where she let it rest among the ghosts of the house.

Alan smoothed the residual pomade into his hair and onto his jeans before asking, "May I have this dance?" He waited for her to extend her hand before he took it. Then he placed his other arm tenderly around her waist as they stood and swayed to the sounds of The Stones that played through the record player.

Lorraine fell into Alan's arms, her empty stomach touching his, her cheek upon his shoulder, hoping he'd support her when the weight of the words of love and yearning and burning flames wouldn't let her stand on her own. The two danced together on the sagging front porch for song after song, holding on to each other without having to say a word. And when they finally separated, Alan didn't ask why his shoulder was damp. She didn't ask him why he had been shivering and holding on to her as much as she had been to him, as if alone they might fall, but together they could stand and dance and sway as the music played on.

# EPILOGUE

On July 16, 1969, when Apollo 11, positioned on the nose of a rocket booster, rose against the forces of gravity and left the earth's atmosphere, Lorraine watched like the rest of the world. But she didn't hold her breath. She observed the accomplishment through the lens of logic and reason, no longer dreaming of that moment with the same sense of wonder. After all, foolish optimism had been stripped from her in that old farmhouse nearly five years prior, the place where both glass and dreams shattered.

Four days later, when Neil Armstrong opened the hatch, stepped onto a ladder, and descended to the bottom, Lorraine sat at the corner diner, sipping coffee as she attempted to study for her mathematics exam—a subject that offered comfort in its certainty.

She didn't see the first moon steps. She saw them later as the news replayed the video and spoke of the significance of the moment. When it happened in real time, her eyes were not on the small step from ladder to new frontier. They weren't even on her books or out the window as she awaited his arrival. They were on the girl in the booth nearest the door of the diner, the little girl who looked different from the rest of the family she sat with. Lorraine guessed she was about four years of age.

While everyone else sat in silence, their attention on the small television hanging in the corner, Lorraine watched the girl with the brown hair who saw nothing but the science mixed with miracle that had landed on the surface of the moon. Lorraine should've been excited. She should've watched the screen like the rest of the world, but something else captured her attention.

The small girl held a tin rocket, a toy that her older brother apparently wanted for himself. As she bounced it across the table—her wavy hair springing off her shoulders before falling back down—her brother grabbed for the toy. But she wouldn't let him take it.

"Stop that!" Their mother scowled, shushing them so she could watch the history unfold in silence.

Proud of not letting go, the little girl looked up and saw Lorraine watching her. Caught in a stare, Lorraine glanced back at the television screen. The hatch had opened, the astronauts had descended. The world now existed in a time after a man had taken a giant leap for mankind.

For a moment, she allowed herself to watch Armstrong and Aldrin bounce along the surface, their toes touching moondust before their bodies floated upward and back down, bobbing in rhythmic slow motion as if swimming in a sea of darkness, a different atmosphere, one that did not bind them and hold them down, one that held them loosely.

Their motions on the moon's surface reminded her of little Barbara Ann Walters, the one who had gotten a tad too deep that day in the summer of 1964, in the time before Lorraine's atmosphere changed. She had been the one rescue Lorraine had made when she lifeguarded that one summer, that last summer of her innocence, moments before life launched her into a new orbit, one she had not calculated, couldn't have foreseen.

As silence and unity and awe fell over the world in those moments of watching men float along the moon, Lorraine couldn't help but think about astronaut Michael Collins, the loneliest man in the universe. While Armstrong and Aldrin walked across the satellite's surface, one man remained aboard Apollo 11, hurtling in orbit with no one else, a part of something and yet so far away. For over twenty hours, he would sit in the company of only his Creator as an infinite void expanded outside the windows of the spacecraft.

Lorraine's attention was brought back to the diner as she heard the boy say to his sister, "Give me the rocket."

"It's not a rocket. It's the Apollo command module!" The girl spoke sternly as she held the toy to her body. "And it's mine!"

"I don't care. I want it!" The brother reached through his sister's closed arms and grabbed the toy away from her, only to accidentally drop it onto the floor.

"Mama!" the girl cried, but the mother shushed her again.

Without a thought, Lorraine darted out of the booth. She reached for the toy and got it into her hands before the boy could. At first surprised by the stranger who had raced him to the floor, the boy then smiled and held out his hand, expecting to receive the reward.

"Is this yours?" Lorraine asked him. He shook his head no but still assumed that Lorraine would give him what he wanted. "We shouldn't take things that don't belong to us."

The boy's eyes grew wide as astonishment replaced the smirk that had covered his confident face. Lorraine looked at the little girl, handed her the toy, and said, "Don't ever let go of what's yours to keep."

She wanted to casually wink at the girl as she stepped away

from the table, but her eyes got that burning sensation that happens right before the tears build. So, Lorraine only offered a small smile before walking away.

Back in her seat, Lorraine reached for the coffee cup, the drink having long since cooled. As she brought it to her lips, she realized that she was shaking. She took only a sip before placing the cup on its saucer. Her heart raced, her cheeks flushed as the hurt and heartache that couldn't be dulled overwhelmed her. Years and months might have slipped away, scabbing over the wounds. But they remained. They festered. They morphed into permanent fixtures, constant reminders. Because, truth be told, no amount of time would ever fully fade that scar.

She closed her eyes. Took deep breaths. Tried to distract herself by running calculations, solving mathematical equations in her mind. With her focus deep within herself, she didn't hear him approach the table.

"How was class?" Alan asked as he slid into the booth beside her. Lorraine startled, her body jolted. Alan couldn't help but laugh. "That bad?" He put an arm around her as he kissed her cheek, lingering close to her, sensing a different mood than he had anticipated. "Are you okay?"

Lorraine looked again at the girl. *Didn't her nose look like Lorraine's? Wasn't the blue color of her eyes similar to Clint's?* Maybe. But she searched for those features in nearly every four-year-old girl she saw.

She couldn't let those thoughts continue—not there, in public, with others around. She needed to stop them before they consumed her. Trying to distract herself, she breathed out a short reply to Alan.

"I'm fine."

Of course, he knew better. He saw her hands shaking. He felt her shallow breathing. He had noticed her reddened cheeks. But he didn't ask more. He didn't need to. He kept his arm around her, pulling her deeper in to him, doing what he could to transfer his calm and comfort onto her.

With his other hand, he reached for her coffee and took a drink as he watched the television. "Someday," he began, nodding toward the astronauts, "that'll be you."

Lorraine shook her head in disagreement. She had given up on that dream at the same time she had been forced to give up other things.

"You know it could be. Still at the top of your class. Still proving what you're capable of. I've never doubted you, BB."

Lorraine whispered her response, her voice too shaken to speak fully. "I love you."

And he responded in his usual way, "I've *always* loved you."

As the world watched in stunned silence at the accomplishment of a nation built on freedoms, Lorraine longed for the girl who had disappeared. She tried to watch the moon walk, but her vision blurred, each tear a reminder that drowning doesn't look like you think it should. She melted into Alan's warmth, comfort, presence, his arm around her a persistent reminder that sometimes we need to hang on in order to let go. Sometimes surviving means finding the strength to pick up the remnants of shattered dreams and piece together a mosaic of new ones, a continual work in progress, a constant decision to put one foot in front of the other, to fight against gravity, and keep moving forward.

# AUTHOR'S NOTE

*Warning: This author's note contains spoilers. You're advised to finish the novel before reading this.*

Do we ever fully know where the idea for a story comes from? No. But sometimes we can identify individual sparks that unite to feed a flame. I can define three of those sparks that ignited *The Girls We Sent Away*.

## Spark 1:

Sometime in the late 1980s, my dad and I were in a video store picking out some weekend entertainment when he said hello to a woman I had never met before. Growing up in a small town, it wasn't too often that we ran into someone my parents knew whom I hadn't met yet.

As she walked away, I asked Dad how he knew her.

"She went to my high school," he said.

"So you graduated together?" I clarified.

"No." Seeing my confusion, he continued. "Back then, if a girl got pregnant in high school, she had to drop out."

Though I remember nothing else of that day, that snippet of

a conversation has remained with me. And then it latched on to another moment.

**Spark 2:**

In 2017, as the closing credits of the season one finale of *The Handmaid's Tale* rolled, I sat alone in my living room, attempting to process what I had just watched. I wanted to talk to someone, but my family was in bed and no one was around to talk to. So I opened IMDb and began scrolling reviews to see what other people thought.

One comment said something to the effect of "If you don't believe this could happen today, you need to look at the Baby Scoop Era."

Those three words, treated as a proper noun, were all I needed to lose myself in search results. Then that information attached to that moment in the video store and led me down a rabbit hole of research that created this book.

The Baby Scoop Era refers to the period of time from 1945 to 1973 when an estimated four million unwed pregnant women were sent to maternity homes, which could result in coerced or even forced surrender of their children. By the 1960s, more than two hundred homes for unmarried pregnant women existed within forty-four states, some operated by the Salvation Army, Florence Crittenton Homes, and religious denominations or organizations.

Through my research, I read and listened to women's stories. I heard the reports of how this moment in their lives forever impacted them. How this experience sometimes led to alcohol abuse, drug addiction, multiple marriages, and countless jobs because of the trauma and shame they carried with them for the rest of their lives. They couldn't talk about it but instead needed to hide, forget, and then get back to life.

A good summary of this practice appeared in the September 30, 2021, *Time* magazine article "What History Teaches Us about Women Forced to Carry Unwanted Pregnancies to Term." Writer Kelly O'Connor McNees explained the era of maternity homes this way:

> While philosophies and missions varied, most maternity homes tailored their services not to meet the emotional and psychological needs of frightened young pregnant women but to accommodate the social anxieties of their overwhelmingly white, middle-class and working-class parents: a strict commitment to privacy meant that no one— not the neighbors or the altar guild or the company boss— would find out about the pregnancy or the secretive closed adoption. Both the child and the birth mother would be better off in what the home framed as a win-win scenario: the baby would be saved from the stigma and shame of illegitimacy, and the birth mother could put the unpleasant chapter behind her and make a fresh start.
>
> There was just one problem: almost no one asked the young women themselves about their wishes. During the Baby Scoop Era, an unmarried pregnant woman sent away to a maternity home had no say in whether she would carry her pregnancy to term, no agency over the birth itself and, once the child arrived, no choice about whether she could raise the baby.

I'm a mother. I have birthed three children. My body has experienced the physical and emotional changes that are part of pregnancy, birth, and postpartum. I watched as my abdomen stretched and then deflated. I remember the feeling of breast engorgement and hormonal changes. There is a lot about motherhood, biology, emotions, and attachment that I don't understand on a scientific level. Like Lorraine, I want answers and explanations to satisfy my cerebral curiosity. But one thing is clear without the knowledge of facts: there is no returning to "normal" after an experience like that.

For the life of me, I cannot imagine what these women—some still girls by society's standards—experienced when they were told to forget the feelings, the hormones, the emotions, the physical changes, and go on with life. Get back to normal. Act like this never happened.

And some of them had to do that without their babies, even if they very much wanted that child.

Just like in my debut novel, *The Last Carolina Girl*, I wanted the reader to feel the depths of the main character, to laugh, hope, cry along with her. Which made the birth scene even more difficult to write. I've experienced birth three times for myself, but I have gotten to hold my babies, love them, take them home, and raise them. My heart broke for Lorraine's experience because I thought of all the women whose stories too similarly matched hers, whose arms remained empty, whose hearts still ache even decades later.

I'm going to be honest; for that reason, I struggled with how to end this book. I wrote and rewrote the closing chapter of Lorraine's life. I knew she was fierce. I knew that she had drive.

But in many ways, she had been left alone, abandoned by the society that had claimed to love her. How would she go on? Could she fully recover? Would she find hope?

Before this book even hit the shelves, women began sharing their stories with me of their aunts, cousins, friends, and sisters who had similar experiences. But never the men. Never the uncles, brothers, fathers. That is where the third spark comes into the picture.

**Spark 3:**

In 2019, we celebrated the fiftieth anniversary of the moon landing. I had already begun developing what would become this book. My youngest daughter, seven years old and an astronaut hopeful at the time, told me facts, showed me videos, read me stories of the accomplishment and the heroes who made Apollo 11 happen. As she celebrated that achievement, I looked at her. So hopeful. So much potential. Perhaps a trailblazer like Lorraine. And I couldn't help but think, as the Space Race took shape, as we blasted rockets out of our atmosphere, as a small step for man imprinted into moon dust hundreds of thousands of miles away from planet earth, how many women lay tucked away in a maternity home, lost, alone, ashamed, and uncertain?

The Space Race juxtaposed those who had the privilege of aiming for the stars against those who remained grounded by society's rules and chastised by its judgment.

When we take off the proverbial rose-colored glasses and look closely at our history, sometimes what we find shakes us. And it should. My hope is that this story, and others like it, can start a conversation to bring awareness to the women who spent months alone and ashamed inside one of these homes and then were told to get back to normal and move on with life as if nothing ever happened.

As a society, we have too often erred on the side of conditional love and acceptance. May we do better now and into the future. May we know and display grace, mercy, and love free of conditions.

# READING GROUP GUIDE

1. Lorraine hopes to become an astronaut in the Space Race, despite being a young woman in a time when those occupations were reserved for men. What was your biggest dream in life when you were young? Were you ever told that your dream would never be a reality? If so, how did that make you feel, and how did you overcome it?

2. There is a hierarchy in the Sunnymede neighborhood, and family image is worth everything. Where does Lorraine and her family land on that hierarchy, and how does that affect the way they react to her pregnancy?

3. Mr. Delford says that if Clint was man enough, he would have "dealt" with Lorraine's situation. What does he mean by this? What was your reaction to Clint's actions after finding out that Lorraine was pregnant?

4. What measures does Lorraine's mother take when she finds out her daughter is pregnant? If you were Lorraine, how would you have felt to be treated this way by your family?

5.  Lorraine's story is set during the Baby Scoop Era, a period of the 1960s where unwed mothers could be sent away to give birth. Were you familiar with this period in history before reading this novel, and if so, what did you know about it? If not, did you learn anything new about this time?

6.  The longer Lorraine lives in the maternity home, the more she realizes that it's not at all what she thought it would be. Describe what the home is like for those who live there. How would you feel if you were living in this situation?

7.  What are some of the rules each girl must follow at the maternity home? Why are these rules in place, and were there any instances where the girls broke them?

8.  Who is Janet, and why are the girls in the home keeping her story a secret from Lorraine? Were you surprised to learn the truth of what happened to her?

9.  When Lorraine strikes up a friendship with the librarian, Ms. Whiler, she begins to see the role of women differently. Discuss how Lorraine's values and ideas surrounding womanhood and motherhood change as the story progresses. How did watching this change make you feel?

10.  Lorraine was certain she didn't have a "motherly instinct." But when she feels like something is wrong with the baby, her immense worry proves that her attachment to her child has grown stronger than she previously thought. How does

this realization change everything for Lorraine? Were you surprised by the outcome of the story after this moment?

11. On the surface, Miss Mahoney and Ms. Whiler seemed quite different, but how did Lorraine come to see them as more alike than she first thought them to be?

12. A major theme of the novel is the freedom to have a choice. What parallels might be drawn between the ideas of the Baby Scoop Era and modern-day events surrounding women's rights?

13. What is Lorraine and her mother's relationship like after she returns from the maternity home, and how does it change after the secrets her mother kept are revealed? Did you look at Mrs. Delford differently after this? Why or why not?

14. Near the end, Mrs. Delford and Lorraine come to think of strength differently. The narrator says, "Strength isn't in the loud and obvious. Strength is often camouflaged in the quiet, reserved places where most people wouldn't think to look." How do you describe strength? Has your definition changed over time? Who are the strong people in your life?

15. Discuss Lorraine and Alan's relationship. How was he different from Clint? How did you feel when he found her at the farmer's house after she returned home and then at the diner in the epilogue?

16. At the end of the novel, the narrator states that survival is "a constant decision to put one foot in front of the other." How does Lorraine continue to survive even after her immense hardship? Then, think about your life. What does the word "survival" mean to you?

# A CONVERSATION
# WITH THE AUTHOR

**This novel is set during the Baby Scoop Era of the 1960s. What inspired you to write a story set in this time period, and what research did you do to bring this history to life?**

I have always loved this time period, in large part because it's when my parents grew up. I have long been fascinated with the pop culture and music of the 1960s, plus JFK and the space program. In some ways, my childhood was full of unintentional research thanks to my parents' reminiscences and the music that filled our house.

While I always loved the time period, believe it or not, the idea centering around maternity homes came from a random IMDb review of *The Handmaid's Tale*. The reviewer used the term "Baby Scoop Era," which was the first time I had ever heard it. I was so intrigued that I immediately searched the phrase and thus began the rabbit hole of research that consumed me.

As I dug deeper into the history of maternity homes, I couldn't help but see a disparity between the surface veneer of society and the reality that these women endured. While the Baby Scoop Era spanned from 1945 to 1973, I purposefully chose the mid-1960s because of the Space Race. I felt it was important to juxtapose the leaps society was making in some regards while limiting the autonomy of certain people.

For a greater understanding of these women's personal accounts, I read nonfiction books that delve deep into firsthand stories of maternity homes, most notably *The Girls Who Went Away* by Ann Fessler and *The Baby Scoop Era* by Karen Wilson-Buterbaugh. I also watched countless interviews, read magazine articles, blog posts, and the like. When I needed to know cultural context (like food, clothing, cars, etc.), I turned to firsthand experts: my parents.

**What's your writing process like? Is there anything you do to get creative inspiration?**

Once I have the historical context in mind, a character begins to form. I need to give her time to develop, which happens during the research. I read way more than is necessary about the time period, the historical aspect that is being explored, etc. Meanwhile, that main character is starting to find her voice. I typically write linearly, so once I hear the opening chapter, I know it's time to start writing. Of course, additional research will be necessary as the story evolves. During the writing of this book, my search history was full of random and strange searches, such as recipes for green goop salad, the Rolling Stones lyrics, Lysol douches, architectural renderings of 1960s cape cods, pomade, etc.

Music plays a role in this novel, including during the writing process itself. I created a *The Girls We Sent Away* playlist on Spotify and listened to it on repeat while working on the book. That helped put me in the time period. The playlist is available for anyone to listen to and would be great background music for book club discussions.

**This is an emotional read with difficult themes. What was it like for you to write such a story?**

Let's just say I shed a few tears along the way. My first draft is always the bare bones of getting the overall structure of the story down. With each additional pass (and there are several), I add depth and layers. So, with each edit, I had to delve deeper and deeper into Lorraine and unfortunately take her to places I didn't particularly want to. As I wrote, I would see the world through her eyes and imagine what it must've been like. From the scene where she prepares to tell her mother she's pregnant to the delivery room when she is alone and scared, then to the end when she's in the diner wondering if that little girl could be hers, I did my best to see through her eyes and feel everything she must've. Let's just say that it's a good thing I write alone in my loft with only my golden retrievers with me because some of those scenes broke my heart again and again.

**What do you hope readers take away from Lorraine's story?**

We have a way of looking at our past through rose-colored glasses. And that does us no favors. When we do that, we fail to see the nuances and multiple dimensions that existed. It is fun to look back on the '60s—the music, the silly Jell-O salads, and the plasticware parties—and reminisce about the surface experiences. It's great to celebrate the moon landing and the accomplishments made in the name of science and discovery. But what I hope the reader walks away with is the desire to look more closely, to ask what was beneath the shiny veneer of that era, to see who was on the margins. It's easy to love Lorraine, to root for her and against Mrs. Delford. But the truth of the matter is that many girls like Lorraine were shamed instead of loved. And even Mrs. Delford, as much as we love to hate her, was also drowning in her own existence within society. History and people are more complicated than those rose-colored glasses let us see. There is more nuance to us all, but instead of reacting with judgment, perhaps we could get better at extending empathy and practicing unconditional love.

**How did the novel evolve over the course of writing? Were there any major changes?**

The novel changed in multiple ways since the first draft. As I said, that first draft often has a bare-bones structure. I actually cut about 10,000 words from the beginning section. There were more scenes with Clint, but early readers told me they needed less of him. Everyone picks up on what kind of guy he is from the start, so we didn't need to spend so much time with him. I have to say, they were right. The beginning was truncated to get Lorraine to the maternity home faster.

Ms. Whiler very much evolved over time. An iteration of her existed at the beginning, but she was very different. As I worked through revisions, it became clear that Lorraine needed more of an ally during her time at the home. Though she doesn't turn out to be the ally Lorraine expects, she serves an important role in showing Lorraine that women can exist in ways different than how her mother and the Sunnymede sisters do. But she also shows Lorraine that each person's perspective can be complicated by their past.

The biggest change though was the ending. I wrote and rewrote the epilogue numerous times. It always ended at the diner with the moon landing occurring as Lorraine questions if the girl could be hers. But the first version was bleak. Lorraine ended up alone, sobbing in a dark alley. Next, I changed it so that Lorraine was working in the diner, but she was still alone. Then my wise editor, MJ, gently advised me to give Lorraine a more satisfying ending. You see, I had read and listened to the testimonies of women whose lives were forever impacted when they went home without their babies. Many of them never got over the hurt, heartbreak, and shame. Some struggled with relationships, unemployment, and addiction for the rest of their lives. The first attempts at the ending were in trying to stay true to those women and their experiences. MJ reminded me that Lorraine's story is her own. When I reexamined her as a character all her own, I reconsidered what her future could be. Sure, there would still be moments of heartache, but she could have the strength to persevere and pursue her goals. And that's when Alan found his way into the scene.

**What are some of the books you've read that have inspired your writing?**

Lately, I have spent a lot of time reading Elizabeth Strout, including her Lucy Barton series and *Olive Kitteridge*. I am in awe of how she tells such simple stories of everyday people but in such a deep and profound way. I read Thao Thai's novel, *Banyan Moon*, a few months ago, and I'm still thinking about the character dynamics of that beautiful debut. I am listening again to *Remarkably Bright Creatures* by Shelby Van Pelt. I love how she adds humor (especially through the octopus character of Marcellus) into a story that also has tragic moments. Perhaps the recent read that surprised me the most is *The Invisible Life of*

*Addie LaRue* by V. E. Schwab. While I don't typically read many books with magical realism (though I did love Van Pelt's narrating octopus), I was riveted by this story, impressed by the scale and scope of the timeline, and was on the edge of my seat for Addie. All of these beautiful novels have served as inspiration, whether for character depth, prose, pacing, humor, or even unlikely likable characters.

**What are you working on nowadays?**

I'm developing two more historical fiction novels. One is a mother-daughter story that spans the 1950s to the 1980s and explores their complicated relationship as they struggle with the consequences of having lived downwind of a nuclear test site. The second one is a coming-of-age story that takes place in the 1970s when a woman returns home from the adrenaline rush of volunteering in Vietnam to then attempt to reacclimate to everyday life in her quiet, rural hometown that no longer feels like home. While it's far too early to talk in depth about either one, both continue in a similar vein of *The Last Carolina Girl* and *The Girls We Sent Away*, giving voice to those whose lives have been irrevocably altered by the consequences of historical events.

# ACKNOWLEDGMENTS

As I write this, I have just wrapped up the book tour for *The Last Carolina Girl*. Being an author is an interesting dichotomy of tasks. You spend so much time writing alone, and then the book enters the world and you are asked to stand in front of people and discuss what you created during all that time spent alone. While I didn't know what to expect, I found so much joy in the travels, conversations, and discussions. What this tour showed me is that book people are so kind, generous, and encouraging.

Thank you to all the readers, booksellers, librarians, reviewers, podcasters, bloggers, and influencers who have read, shared, and reviewed my work. I often say that I'm a girl from an Indiana cornfield; no one knew me when my debut novel hit the shelves. But because of your support, my book has gotten into the hands of so many.

Thank you to Amy Allen Clark, creator and curator of MomAdvice.com and the *Book Gang* podcast, for championing me and my work. Laura Jones, I am still astonished by our shared family connection, and I'm so grateful for all your efforts in sharing my books with your patrons. And thanks go to Annissa Joy Armstrong and the Beyond the Pages book club for being so supportive of authors and for helping get the word out about our beloved books.

I am grateful to have found amazing and supportive authors to share this journey with. While we may not have a watercooler to gather around and chat, we certainly have coffee meetups and messaging. Thank you for your support, wisdom, and camaraderie, Joy Callaway, Heather Belle Adams, Lisa DeSelm, Terah Shelton Harris, Leslie Hooton, Erika Marks, and Kelly Mustian.

*The Girls We Sent Away* would not be what it is if it weren't for beta readers who read early drafts that still needed a lot of work. Your willingness to delve into problematic drafts and offer pointed feedback is essential and appreciated. So thank you, Dawn Beery, Kathy Casper, Jocelyn Chrisley, Lisa DeSelm, Heather Donahue, and Gary Pethe.

Rachel Cone-Gorham, you are so much more than an agent. Thank you for being a constant advocate, encourager, wise counselor, and trusted friend. You are the perfect blend of nurturer and challenger, always supporting me while also pushing me toward the potential you have a way of seeing. Thank you for helping me wrestle down the prologue. I'll see you at the movie premier. ;)

MJ Johnston, thank you for your keen editor's eye. Your gentle but persistent notes that pushed for more feeling, though frustrating at times, were so necessary! The text and characters have more depth and richness because of you. I am grateful for your expertise in storytelling. It has been an absolute pleasure working with you for these first two novels. And please thank Figgy for allowing me to use his name. My apologies if his feline ego gets too much of a boost from being chosen as the namesake.

To the amazing team at Sourcebooks, I cannot thank you enough for all you have done and for how you partner with and support your authors and get stories into the hands of so many. Books do indeed change lives, and I'm honored to change them alongside you. Thank you, Dominique Raccah, Diane Dannenfeldt, Ashlyn Keil, Caitlin Lawler, Molly Waxman, Anna Venckus, Jessica Thelander, Heather VenHuizen, Stephanie Rocha, BrocheAroe Fabian, and Mandy Chahal.

To my friends and family, who are constant cheerleaders, unofficial booksellers, and enthusiastic social media sharers. You know who you are, and my appreciation runs deep.

Mom and Dad, thank you for your constant and sincere support. Your stories and nostalgia over the years helped paint Lorraine's world. Thank you for answering questions about the time period and helping me make it as accurate as possible. And, Mom, thank you for your tireless and enthusiastic efforts to make sure everyone you meet knows about your daughter's books. You have earned the Top Salesperson Award multiple times over, and we may need to find you a bigger trophy.

To Jonas, Kenna, and Adelyn—the three whom I have the privilege of parenting—thank you for your encouragement and support. Adelyn, thank you for being the meal planner and chef extraordinaire during my book-related travels. Your love of space inspired Lorraine's dream, and your own research helped inform parts of this book. Kenna, thank you for always being willing to read and offer notes. You have a gift for storytelling, and I value your perspective and feedback. Though this book took us to the moon, I'm sorry that we haven't gotten to Mars quite yet. Jonas, thank you for your quiet but steady support and your questions, curiosity, and humor. Also, I appreciate you telling your classmates to buy your mom's book so that "we can eat." I love you all, and I cannot wait to see where your own dreams and determination take you.

Most importantly, thank you, Matt. Our last few years have been quite a journey of finding new passions and following new career paths. At. The. Same. Time. It has been a wild and winding road, and there's no one I'd rather navigate it along with. Thank you for showing me again and again, without falter, that love truly is unconditional.

And thank you, dear reader. None of this would be possible if you didn't take a chance on this book and decide to give it a read. May you always have the strength to piece together a mosaic of new dreams, even if your old ones have shattered. Like Lorraine, may you continually decide to put one foot in front of the other, fight against gravity when necessary, and keep moving forward.

# ABOUT THE AUTHOR

© Bethany Callaway

Meagan Church is the author of *The Last Carolina Girl* and *The Girls We Sent Away*. After receiving a BA in English from Indiana University, Meagan built a career as a storyteller and freelance writer. A midwesterner by birth, she now lives in North Carolina with her high school sweetheart, three children, and a plethora of pets. To follow her storytelling, visit meaganchurch.com.